THE LORD OF MISRULE

Castle Blackwood

M.A.Knights

White Harp Publising

Copyright © 2024 M.A.Knights

All rights reserved

The characters and events portrayed in this book are fictitious. Any similarity to real persons, living or dead, is coincidental and not intended by the author.

No part of this book may be reproduced, or stored in a retrieval system, or transmitted in any form or by any means, electronic, mechanical, photocopying, recording, or otherwise, without express written permission of the publisher.

ISBN-: 9798338702048

Cover design by: Art Painter
Library of Congress Control Number: 2018675309
Printed in the United States of America

To Hayley

CONTENTS

Title Page
Copyright
Dedication
PROLOUGE 1
CHAPTER ONE: The New star 4
1. 5
2. 10
3. 17
4. 20
CHAPTER TWO: KIPPERS, APPLES, AND KNIVES . . . 30
1. 31
2. 40
3. 48
CHAPTER THREE: LONGEST NIGHT 60
1. 61
2. 64
3. 66
4. 74
5. 76
6. 77
CHAPTER FOUR: AXE OR COIN 92

1.	93
2.	106
3.	113
CHAPTER FIVE: ATTACK IN THE NIGHT	**115**
1.	116
2.	122
3.	137
4.	142
CHAPTER SIX: AN ENSEMBLE FOR BREAKFAST	**144**
1.	145
2.	147
3.	159
4.	171
CHAPTER SEVEN: THE FACE OF A KILLER	**173**
1.	174
2.	182
3.	188
4.	198
CHAPTER EIGHT: CONCEQUENCES	**205**
1.	206
2.	216
3.	225
CHAPTER NINE: MONSTERS	**239**
1.	240
2.	247
3.	255
4.	260
CHAPTER TEN: BODIES IN THE RAIN	**272**

1.	273
2.	282
3.	285
4.	295
CHAPTER ELEVEN: GREEN FIRE	300
1.	301
2.	310
3.	322
CHAPTER TWELVE: LOSING CONTROL	334
1.	335
2.	340
3.	346
4.	353
5.	356
6.	359
CHAPTER THIRTEEN: THE GOLDEN BEAR	370
1.	371
2.	378
3.	384
4.	389
5.	398
CHAPTER FOURTEEN: LIGHTNING, FIRE, AND STONE	401
1.	402
2.	412
3.	416
4.	419
5.	424
6.	426

7.	430
8.	433
9.	438
10.	441
CHAPTER FIFTEEN: CLEAR SKIES	443
1.	444
2.	450
3.	454
EPILOGUE	460
Want more?	463
About The Author	467

PROLOUGE

If there is one thing you need to know before we begin our tale, it is this: Magic is a lot like sewage.
It might not be the most romantic notion, but that's the truth of it. Magic, like sewage, oozes through the world. It is all around, and yet, for the most part, is never noticed. Magic is thick, viscous, smelly and...

No, not smelly. It has a smell, a very unique smell, but humans are not equipped to smell it. Now if you were to ask, say, a tree spirit, or the like, what magic smelt like, then they would...

Actually, probably ignore you, to be honest. They're not the most sociable of creatures, tree spirits. It's what comes of having nothing but trees for neighbors. They never have much of interest to say.

Let's start again.

Magic is a lot like honey.

It is thick, viscous, and *sticky*. It coats the world in a fine film and, sometimes, if it is a particularly lumpy bit of magic, a bit of magic that hasn't quite filtered down to your everyday consistency, well, then it can cause a clog.

As the magic builds up, it grows in concentration, and if left undisturbed long enough, becomes potent to the point of self-combustion. Those who have seen a magical explosion and lived to tell about it are very few. Fewer still are those who live to tell about it *from the same face they had before*.

Magic is a force of nature, created from the essence, the energy, of every living thing that has died in the history of the world. Like any other force of nature, it can be incredibly hard to predict.

Not like honey. Honey is, generally speaking, quite a predictable substance. Comes from bees. Nice on toast. Yes, you're usually quite safe with honey. So really, magic isn't like honey at all.

It is probably best, on reflection, to think of magic like nothing else but magic itself.

Don't try to spread it on your toast.

Deep, deep in the Blackwood there was the kind of stillness that takes years to build up. It accumulates in layers over decades, one on top of the other like a rich loam. It was the kind of stillness that made the passage of a worm through the damp, leafy mulch feel like an earthquake. The trees pressed so closely together here that no light reached the ground, and therefore, apart from the trees, very little else grew. The trees themselves, mostly the black-oak from which the forest took its name, grew tall, thick and twisted, their leaves so dark a green as to look almost black.

But most of all, they grew slow.

The lack of birdsong only added to the oppressive atmosphere in this part of the Blackwood. Birds didn't come here. Whether it was instinct that kept them away, or simply a matter of natural selection, was hard to say. Curiosity was rarely a virtue in the Blackwood. It tended to kill the dog, pig, bird, and bear, as well as the cat. But away they stayed, and the absence of their song left a thick quality to the silence.

It was broken by a sound like a bag full of jelly being dropped from a height.

Leaves and branches rustled in an expanding circle from the source of the noise in a whispered hush, like the leaves were passing on a secret from tree to tree. The smell of rotting vegetation carried with the sound, with something altogether more repugnant underneath. It swept through the trees like a fart in a crowd.

Something opened its eyes.

It did it slowly because until a moment ago, it hadn't had any.

CHAPTER ONE: THE NEW STAR

1.

The town of Upton-Myzzle was, above all things, brown. It was its main defining feature. The streets, contrary to popular belief, were in fact cobbled. But it had been many a year since the cobblestone had shown through what was best described as a quagmire of mud, straw, and who knew what else that flowed down every avenue. Most of the buildings were wooden, but even those built in stone, or with plaster facades, were so weathered and mud-splattered that all they could do was offer a slightly different shade of brown. The recent weather hadn't helped. It had been one of the wettest autumns on record, and winter had so far not improved. Every beam and scrap of wood in the town seemed so thoroughly sodden that, even when it wasn't raining, water oozed from every pore.

In the streets of the old quarter, the denizens were out late, taking advantage of the first rain-free evening in a week. People waded their way through the waterlogged streets, intent on their own personal errands, stopping only to swear loudly at anyone who came too close, causing the muddy, smelly liquid that filled the streets to splash over their boots. The old quarter was so named, not for the age of its buildings, which were generally newer, sturdier and a good deal larger than those in the rest of the town, but because it was the site of the very beginnings of the town of Upton-Myzzle. It sat below the Castle Blackwood itself and boasted wide promenades and a central green that, in three or four months' time, would be awash with the colour of spring flowers.

Right now there was a duck swimming across it.

The duck appeared, as far as it is possible to tell with ducks, to be delighted at this watery turn of events, meaning it could now float all the way to the river Myzzle. Unfortunately for the duck, it never made it that far. It had barely crossed the green before something about four inches high and looking much like a radish with arms and legs burst up from below the water and knocked it out cold. The moglin, for that is what the radish-man was, wasted no time in hoisting the unconscious duck above its head and wading off, looking for all the world to the casual observer like a duck swimming upside down across the street.

Directly opposite the green stood a building most unlike the others. It was set back from the street by some twenty paces and was preceded by a pair of fine, golden-painted iron gates, supported by two wooden gateposts that were carved into the shape of gigantic trees. They towered over passers-by. Behind, the building itself was formed from similar, if even larger, carved trees which curved inward to create a latticework of branches that formed a domed ceiling. Each gap between the branches had been painstakingly glazed, and the glass glinted a moody orange in the last of the evening sun.

As this glow faded, and the sunset turned to purple twilight, the doors of the building opened and the congregation spilt out. They formed a microcosm of the town's social classes, ranging from workers wearing little more than rags to the lords in their garish finery, upstaged only by the ladies with their elaborate frocks. Even church—*especially* church—was a chance to show off one's wealth. Several of the women had tiny, fluttering figures hovering over their heads. Fairies, the ultimate status symbol, tethered by fine golden chains to their owners' clothing. A woman, dressed rather more soberly in dark green robes, struggled to keep ahead of the crowd. She only just reached and opened the gates before the congregation descended upon her once more. When a man wearing stark black breeches and coat shoved past her and headed out the gate, the woman in the green robes was barreled into the street and fell with, if not a splash, then a definite splat. She had been carrying a golden staff, split at the top into the many branches of an oak tree, complete with leaves depicted by dark green gems, or, more likely, coloured glass. As the woman fell, the staff fell from her grip and landed, half-submerged in the filth of the street. The man in black continued out of the gate, apparently oblivious to what he had done and to the oaths that followed him. He stalked off down the road like an angry cockerel, albeit an angry cockerel that is placing its feet very carefully to avoid the worst of the muck. It resulted in a strange, jilting gait that made the tricorne hat on his head bounce around like it had a life of its own.

The man was Sir Angston Krickwell, and he was angry. Not that this was an unusual disposition for Sir Krickwell, who spent most of his time passing from one hot-tempered episode to another, and then back again. This evening, however, he was in a mood so black it matched his breeches and coat very nicely. The cause of Sir Krickwell's considerable ire was the building he had just exited, or perhaps to be more accurate what the building represented. He had spent the last hour attending a sermon at the Church of the First Tree, and he had not liked what he had heard. No, he had not liked it one bit. To say so out loud, of course, would have been a risky business. It was the church of the state, after all. But, to Sir Krickwell, the ideals expressed under that many-branched ceiling strayed further and further from what he considered holy with every passing year.

'It's sacrilegious, that's what it is!' he grumbled to himself as he skipped awkwardly over a large patch of standing water. 'Shouldn't be allowed. Simply shouldn't be allowed at all!'

A boy carrying a tray of roasted chestnuts approached Sir Krickwell hopefully, but quickly changed his mind upon seeing the expression on the man's gaunt and wrinkled face, and beat a hasty retreat.

'Not a mention of Zigelder once!' Sir Krickwell barked to the street at large, earning a few wary looks. 'Waffled on for full sixty minutes and not a single mention of our lord Zigelder and all we owe him. It's a disgrace!'

Sir Krickwell mentally shook himself. He must hold his tongue. He knew the way the political winds were blowing, and to carelessly cause trouble for himself now would be unforgivable. There must be a way, he thought to himself, as he turned a corner and entered the slightly less well-to-do area of the old district known as The Thickets, to bring people back to the old ways. Back to Zigelder. The continual erosion of the proper ways was becoming more than he could bear. This modern, insipid doctrine that the Church of the First Tree was spouting was, to Sir Krickwell, an insult to both Zigelder and Melethin.

The Thickets comprised a small area of densely packed, moderately sized townhouses. These houses were home to many of Upton-Myzzle's wealthier citizens, who were, although indeed quite comfortable, not rich enough to live in one of the big houses in the old quarter proper. Nevertheless, The Thickets offered a certain respectability and prestige as an address, meaning that every lawyer, merchant, minor noble and entrepreneur with the funds to do so had squeezed themselves a home into what was ultimately a finite footprint. The result was something of a mess of mismatched buildings, squeezed together and separated in parts by the merest sliver of an alley. It was down one of these that Sir Krickwell strode now, defying anyone to get in his way with every inch of his body language. No one did. One man even flattened himself against a wall with water up to his ankles, rather than break the stride of the enraged apparition coming down the alley towards him. Sir Krickwell marched on, only stopping when he reached the mud-splattered door of a thin, wooden, four-story building. It had somehow been squeezed into roughly the same floor space as a horse and cart would have taken up, and leaned out over the street at an alarming angle. Sir

Krickwell fumbled with shaking hands, but eventually forced a key into the lock and pushed his way inside. He slammed the door behind him and stood in the gloomy hallway, clenching and unclenching his fists. He glared at a grandfather clock that dared to chime four o'clock. Still simmering with rage, he hung up his hat and went to the small kitchen. He fixed himself a simple supper of bread and cheese, then climbed the three creaking staircases to his bedroom on the third floor. He flung himself into a high-backed chair that was placed opposite the window and glowered out at the darkening street. Stars were starting to appear in the cloudless sky above the rooftops, the first to be seen in over a week. Sir Krickwell sat and stared at the house opposite, where a duck was somehow levitating up the wall. It reached the roof and bobbed along on its back, feet in the air, before disappearing behind a chimney stack. He noticed none of this.

'What should I do?' he asked the empty room. It didn't reply.

And then, in the twilight sky above the town, he saw the thing he had always feared most in the entire world, and at the same time, the answer to his question.

2.

The Castle Blackwood was not what could be called a pretty place. Sturdy perhaps. Striking even, in the same way that a desolate moorland on a misty day is striking. But never pretty. It sat on a small hill above the town of Upton-Myzzle and, surrounded by its moat, tended to give passersby the impression of a gigantic grey toad sat in a pond. Its walls were tall, thick, pockmarked after centuries of wear and host to at least a dozen most interesting species of lichen. They left splotches of green, yellow, and even blue on its otherwise sombre visage. The castle was not graceful. It had no interesting architecture. It had been built at a time when one's castle had to convey just a single message, and that message was 'Go away!'. The way Upton-Myzzle had grown up around the castle suggested this message had not been entirely successful. But Castle Blackwood had endured and indeed was endured in turn by the populace of a town that had in many ways surpassed it. It would be nice to say that the old fortress occupied a place of affection in the hearts of its people. Begrudging affection perhaps, for a once-beloved landmark that had fallen into disrepair, but affection nonetheless. It would be nice to say this, but it would be untrue. Many inhabitants of Upton-Myzzle regarded the castle as one might regard a giant boot, hovering forever overhead. It was the ancestral home of a long and torrid line of dukes and duchesses, and somewhat like a porous chest that absorbs a little of whatever is kept inside, so Castle Blackwood had absorbed the many sins of its keepers. It stank, it had to be said, just a little of repression. If it was redeemed in the eyes of any, then it was in those few dozen who still called it home.

One such man, Tanco Dribbets, was making his way up the hill towards the castle just as the grandfather clock was striking four in Sir Angston Krickwell's hallway. He was a large man, not in height, indeed not particularly in girth either, but he was a large man despite the limitations of his size. Something about his presence exceeded his fairly average physical frame, spilling over into the surrounding space. He had wispy grey hair atop an almost perfectly spherical head and was preceded up the hill by his belly. He drew the gaze of all those he passed, in no small part due to the fact that he rattled as he walked. This was caused by the many carved wooden tokens—good luck talismans—he wore on leather cords around his arms and neck, which swung and knocked together as he moved. It was also because he was singing. The tune to the song seemed to change whenever Tanco felt like changing it, and the words he appeared to be making up as he went along. He sang of tree spirits, great battles, green men, and forest ghosts. Tall tales he had been taught as a lad, many of which had fallen out of favor in recent years. He had a pleasant voice, though, and he sang with gusto.

A singing man in the street might not have always attracted such fascination, but on such a bleak winter's evening, Tanco's apparent frivolity made for a strange sight. The chill of the evening had led to the lighting of fires in large iron braziers that lined the path. They cast dancing amber light across the road and were a source of heat to several grateful citizens who clustered around each one. However, about halfway up the hill, Tanco was forced to stop and remove his brown coat. Sweat glistened on his chubby cheeks and showed in patches under his armpits where his white linen shirt was not covered by his waistcoat. He paused and looked down at the town below him, the smallest of frowns appearing on his otherwise cheerful face. Even from this distance, he could see the flooded streets. Absentmindedly, he began to sing about a devastating tsunami. Passersby regarded him in alarm. Unaware, he removed a small black notebook from his breeches pocket and, producing a stubby pencil from somewhere behind his ear, wrote something within its pages before pocketing it once more. As he turned to continue up the hill, he was intercepted by a group of four men coming the other way.

'Oi, Dribbets!' one shouted, cutting off the man's song. 'What's a posho lover like you got to be so happy about?'

'Traitor!' said another, spitting at Tanco's feet.

'Well, good evening, gentlemen,' replied Tanco, unfazed. 'I do hope this night finds you all well. Incidentally, if I were a traitor, legally speaking, I would have to stand *against* the leader of the state, not work as their steward. A minor point perhaps, but one that I feel is worth making.' This earned him blank looks from his assailants. He squinted through the gloom at the four men clustered around him.

'Is that you, Jack Plover? How's your mother's leg?'

The tallest of the group, a man with large cauliflower ears, shifted uncomfortably.

'S'alright,' he said. 'Bandages are coming off tomorrow.'

'Oh good! I am glad. Do give her my best, won't you? And let her know that if she should ever require these healing hands again,' he flourished his pudgy hands theatrically, wiggling sausage-like fingers, 'she need but ask.'

The man called Jack nodded silently, looking distinctly abashed. His comrades, however, were not so easily dissuaded from their sport.

'You're a class traitor is what you are, Dribbets,' said a short man with curly hair and a nose like a dropped dumpling. 'Pandering to those poshos instead of looking out for your fellow brothers. You ought to be ashamed!'

'Oh my,' said Tanco, with mock sincerity. 'I didn't realise the rules of the working class forbade gainful employment. I will, of course, resign from my position immediately. Unfortunately, my brother was eaten by a bear some forty years ago, so I will find it difficult to stand with *him*. However, I do have an elderly aunt, if that's any good?'

They stared at him blankly. Tanco could almost see the cogs working.

'The duke's a twat,' was dumpling nose's eventual reply.

'I'll be sure to let his grace know,' said Tanco, tiring of the exchange and starting up the hill again. 'A good evening to you, gentlemen.'

They let him pass, and it wasn't long before Tanco's song started up again. Those paying close attention, however, would have noticed that he sang with slightly less enthusiasm than before. In fact, by the time he reached the top of the hill and was crossing the moat's large drawbridge into the castle's barbican, his song had become little more than a sort of mumbled hum, and a frown had spread across his face. The barbican was a roughly semicircular courtyard with wooden battlements that controlled access to the castle's twin-towered gatehouse. The gate to the castle itself was open, the iron portcullis raised, but two men stood guard and Tanco knew that more would be inside, keeping watch from the gatehouse's small arrow slits. Strictly speaking, there should have been men upon the stone battlements of the castle wall too, but none could be seen and Tanco suspected he knew the reason.

He hailed the guards as he approached, and the two men snapped to attention. Here, at least, his position still demanded respect.

'Why is no one manning the battlements?' he asked. The two men shot each other a guilty look. They were dressed identically in the livery of the duke's private guard; green coats over brown waistcoats and breeches. The coats were heavily embroidered with gold thread and sported small golden buttons in the shape of acorns. Each carried a polished blunderbuss and wore a smallsword at their waist.

'*Is* there no one on the battlements?' asked one

man, looking up at the wall behind him with poorly feigned surprise.

'You know there is not.'

The men shuffled their feet, mouths gaping, each searching for a reply. Tanco took pity.

'Look, I know the weather is not the best, and I'm sure the men would much rather be inside by the fire. But a guard must be kept. You are both out here, are you not? Do not allow your fellows to shirk while you carry all the burden. Where is General Weltsmatter?'

Another guilty look.

'He's with the Watch commander, down at the watch-house in town.'

'Is he indeed? And what, pray tell, could have led him away from his duties here to visit the Watch?'

More tortured silence.

'Could it, perhaps, have anything to do with the watch-house being equipped with a large fireplace and comfy chairs?' Tanco prompted. 'Or maybe he has urgent enquiries to make about the bottle of gin that I happen to know Watch Commander Posternos keeps in his desk drawer at all times?'

'The general didn't say,' one of the men admitted.

Tanco sighed. 'No, I'm sure he did not. Boys, you both know me. I am not one to push my weight around. But we really must maintain a proper guard. There is more disquiet on the streets than ever, what with these floods threatening to ruin the festival's opening ceremony tomorrow. Continued vigilance is a necessity.'

'About the ceremony...' one man ventured.

'Look,' said Tanco, guessing the unsaid part of the sentence. 'I will personally see to it that a piece of pudding and a hot cup of spice find its way to both of you here tomorrow. But in return, do me a favor and one of you go and make sure your colleagues are at their posts. Tell them there will be pudding and spice all around. I won't have it said we don't look after our own at Castle Blackwood.'

The two men nodded eagerly and one disappeared inside. After a moment or two, figures appeared on the battlements.

Tanco proceeded through the gateway into the outer ward, pondering as he did so just how effective an army that had to be bribed with steamed pudding would be against an actual attack. He made another note in his notebook. The defence of the castle was not something that the duke's steward should have traditionally been concerned with. But these were not the golden days, and Tanco found that as the castle's staff shrunk, so his duties increased. This was just as Tanco liked it. As far as he was concerned, it was as much his castle as it was the dukes, and he took great pleasure in being indispensable to the great fortress's daily running. But the defence situation was becoming a worry. He felt the time had come to mention it to the duke. He didn't like to bother the man with such matters if it could be avoided, but he could put it off no longer. The sight of the dilapidated former armoury against the north wall only hardened his resolve. It had once held the weaponry and armour used for the protection of the entire town but had housed little but broken equipment and spiders for over a generation. The rise of the City Watch had seen to that. Taco clutched at one or two of the tokens around his neck and quickened his pace. His earlier good mood had now completely vanished, and he was eager to reach the keep. He passed through the inner gatehouse and entered the inner ward, circling the site of the ruined former great tower on his right. It stood atop its motte like a jagged broken tooth, yet another reminder that the castle's glory days were behind it. He headed, instead, for the tower that stood where the sweeping north and south castle walls met at a point. After the destruction of the original keep, this tower had been expanded and rebuilt to become the new keep, protected as it was by the moat to the west and cliffs that bordered the river Myzzle to the north. The inner ward was the busy part of the castle, with the kitchens, stores and servants' quarters lining the walls that surrounded the keep, all there to service the duke and his family who were housed within. However, with night having almost completely fallen, there were few people about and Tanco was able to reach the stairs that led to the first floor of the keep without further interruption. He climbed them with haste, entering the tower into a small antechamber that led to the great hall where the duke and his family dined and entertained. He paused briefly to wipe his wet boots on a mat positioned just for this purpose. It would hardly do to drag mud into the duke's rooms, especially as it would be he, Tanco, who would have to organise getting it cleaned up again. Satisfied he'd got the worst off, he entered the hall. A large banqueting table filled the room but currently lay empty. A fire was smouldering in the hearth, but there were no further signs of life. The duke must have retired to his chambers above. Tanco hurried across the room to the far side, where a recessed spiral staircase led to the next level. He ascended, but paused before entering at a small window set into the tower's thick walls. From this height, it offered a view across the castle grounds and out to the town below. Tanco looked out into the night, unsure at first what had made him pause. As he stood there, he fancied he could hear the faintest sounds of commotion in the town being carried up to him on the breeze. The pinprick stars mirrored above the lights of the town below, and it was then that Tanco saw properly what had caught his eye. In the night sky, above the lights of Upton-Myzzle, burned a star far brighter than all the rest. It blazed out with a hot, white intensity, like a small fire in the sky.

Tanco realised two things immediately. Firstly, he realised he could indeed hear shouts of alarm rising from the town. Secondly, he realised that the burning star had not been there several nights earlier when the sky was last clear. It shouldn't be there now. These realisations were chased by a third, and the third realisation drained the blood from Tanco Dribbets' face. His mouth opened in horror and, clutching at the tokens around his neck with trembling hands, he turned tail and ran to his master's chamber, wailing in alarm.

3.

Ged the night soil man looked up at the burning star in the sky above him.

'Huh,' he said, to no one in particular. 'Fancy that.'

Around him, the streets were erupting in panic. People came running out of their homes, pointing upwards and shouting excitedly. Others stood in the middle of the road, heedless of carts trying to pass, and gawped up at the sky. Some were crying. One man, already in his nightgown, came running past Ged, where he sat upon his wagon.

'It's the daemon!' the man screamed. 'It's the daemon Garselin, come to devour the world!' He pounded down the street, slippers slapping in the puddles, nightcap streaming behind him. 'Flee, you fools! Flee!'

Ged watched the man disappear and scratched his stubbly chin thoughtfully. Behind him, the load in his wagon steamed into the night sky. Ged was not normally a man prone to thinking about religion. His line of work kept a man grounded. But he wondered now, as more people around him broke into a run, just how effective trying to outrun the end of the world might be. He looked up at the star again, trying to decide if it looked like a daemon from space. It would help, he thought, if I knew what a daemon looked like. He had never really given it much thought before, and now that he did, he realised he had no clear picture in his mind at all. He tried to remember what he'd been taught about such things as a child, but it was no good. Truth be told, he had never paid much attention. When your work found you elbow-deep in human faeces on a daily basis, you developed a pretty pragmatic view of the world. Finding the quickest route to a washtub became a much more useful thought exercise than wasting time thinking about the exact nature of the apocalypse. What he needed, he decided, was an expert opinion. He climbed down from his seat and approached the animal between the shafts of his wagon.

'What do you think, Gladdis love?' he asked the beast, scratching the bridge of its snout affectionately. 'Is it a daemon?'

He was answered by a contented grunt and a tusk-filled mouth butted his shoulder in a companionable sort of way. Gladdis was a gwalmok, a large, furry, pig-like creature, famed more for their awful smell and immense strength than their philosophical, religious reasoning. In fact, they were mostly considered pretty stupid, on account of how they frequently knocked over trees by mistake. Ged, however, considered Gladdis a fairly accurate gauge of things worth worrying about. She had a tendency, he had noticed over the years, to keep her head when those around her were losing theirs. At that moment, she seemed supremely unconcerned by the surrounding ruckus.

'Nothing to worry about, huh?' Ged said, scratching under a bristly chin that was trying to rest itself on his shoulder. In answer, Gladdis defecated where she stood, a brown pile the size of a man's head plopping down onto the street.

'Fair enough,' said Ged.

Satisfied that the world was not about to end, Ged grabbed his shovel from where it was strapped to the side of his wagon and scooped up the fresh offering from the street. He paused, shovel in hand, as a woman came charging down the road towards him. She was wearing what looked, to Ged's admittedly inexperienced eye, like a rather expensive dress, which was now covered in mud. She looked terrified and, taking not a single bit of notice, she ran straight into Ged's outstretched shovel, splattering gwalmok dung across her front and raining it down across the rest of the street.

'*Oi*!' Ged squawked, outraged. 'That's a waste, that is!'

The woman did not seem to hear him, and she quickly disappeared, not even slowing down. Grumbling, Ged reattached his shovel to the wagon. He clambered back up to his seat, grabbed the reins, and began to encourage Gladdis to force her way through the street. As he did so, he found himself wondering if a space daemon produced shit just like everything else. If it did, he reasoned, then maybe it would keep him on, after the end of the world. After all, there was always a need for a man with a shovel.

4.

About the origin of the first acorn, there was no story. No ancient tale, no song passed from father to son, down the ages. No information whatsoever. It was, therefore, one of the most written about phenomenon in all the Blackwood. Great tomes by greater philosophers ran to hundreds of pages detailing all the knowledge that didn't exist. That's people for you. What came next was well documented, and therefore, of course, far less interesting.

> *The first acorn fell to earth several billion years ago. The exact date is debatable, but it is generally agreed that it was at about half-past two on a Tuesday afternoon. From it sprang the First Tree, the Grandfather Oak, Melethin. He grew tall and large for several hundred thousand years, his golden-green leaves fell each autumn to slowly cover the barren earth in a rich loam. Melethin produced just two acorns of his own in all his long life. The first was Bronien, and into him, Melethin poured all of his power and grace so that Bronien would grow just as large and just as splendid as did Melethin himself.*
>
> *However, so great was Bronien that Garselin, the devourer, smelt him from his home amongst the stars. He plucked Bronien from the branches of Melethin and swallowed him whole. Broken-hearted, Melethin mourned the loss of Bronien for a thousand years. Until, eventually, he bore a second son, Zigelder. Zigelder was lesser than had been Bronien before him, but still he reached the monstrous nostrils of that great beast Garselin. Once more, Garselin*

descended from the stars, and once more, he plucked Melethin's son from his branches.

However, this time, Melethin was prepared. Gathering all his remaining strength, he ripped his spirit from his body. With a deafening noise that would drown thunder, his gigantic trunk split and he emerged in the form of a great golden bear. Melethin and Garselin fought for many days and nights, but eventually, Melethin prevailed and drove the beast Garselin back into the stars. The price was great, however, and with his life force spent, Melethin fell to the earth, his tree form withered and dead.

Zigelder wept for his father. A noise said to have been heard all the way to the edges of existence, but there was nothing to be done. What's more, during the epic struggle, the acorn that was Zigelder had been stepped upon, and his shell cracked. Whose foot it was that caused the damage, Garselin or Melethin himself, it is not known. But, as a result, much of Zigelder's grace was lost. Nevertheless, he survived and eventually grew strong, though his trunk was twisted and his leaves blackened.

Alone and mourning, Zigelder's heart grew dark, but his life continued. The carcass of the great bear that had been Melethin lay where it had fallen and over time, new life sprang forth. It is said that all manner of beasts that roam the earth first emerged from that mighty form. Similarly, all plants came first from the broken trunk of that mighty oak. This new life was the saviour of Zigelder, who no longer felt alone. He himself bore many thousands of acorns that fell to the ground around him and grew into a mighty forest of his children. These were the first of the black oaks, twisted and dark-leafed like their father.

So the Blackwood was born.

Eventually, Zigelder grew aged and, feeling his powers wane, he gathered his strength and a mighty crack appeared in his twisted trunk. From it emerged the first humans to walk the earth.

But what of Garselin? The great beast, it is said, survived Melethin's attack, but was much weakened. Supposedly he resides still in his home amongst the stars, biding his time and gaining in strength, until such a time as he will return to earth and devour all life.
For now, he sleeps, Bronien's acorn still in his vile belly.

Madame Bitterwhack closed the book and looked up through the gap in the trees at the new star.

'Well now, there's a thing,' she said.

She was not, strictly speaking, a religious woman. She always thought of herself as more spiritual. Spiritual is what hedgewitches did. Yes, she believed in Melethin, but she didn't worship him. Not like the pompous priests at the Church of the First Tree did, anyway. Her love for the Grandfather Tree came from a place of appreciation for his works, rather than a blind reverence. She loved the Blackwood. She respected the creatures that called it home, and she understood the many herbs and plants that could be found there. The difference was that she didn't think it had all been put there for the use of humankind. That idea made no sense to her. She looked back at the book in her liver-spotted hands. It was bound in green leather and had "The Book of Oak" written on the cover in gold, sweeping letters.

'I think, Mr Nuggin, this'll be of more use to you than it will to me,' she said to the corpse on the pyre in front of her. 'And daemon or not, there's a job in front of us.'

She placed the book respectfully on the dead man's chest and stood back to admire her handiwork. As a hedgewitch, the Rite of Passage was traditionally her domain, and she always made sure she completed the ceremony to the letter. It's what her customers expected, and she wouldn't be able to face their families if she knew she had done anything but her best work.

'Oh, almost forgot,' she said, pulling an acorn from a pocket in her dress. It was one of many pockets. The dress was probably more pocket than it was dress. Each one bulged with useful bits and bobs and made the hedgewitch look like a sack of potatoes. She stepped forward, prised the man's mouth open with care and popped the acorn inside. She closed the mouth again and stepped back once more.

'That'll help the spirit trees find you,' she told the man.

She looked around the clearing, trying to think if she had missed anything else. She wasn't far into the Blackwood. Perhaps an hour's trek with the corpse of Mr Nuggin on her little hand-pulled cart. Even so, the trees crowded round thickly. There were a few black oaks, but here at the edges of the forest, many other species were present too. Their autumn leaves, orange, red and yellow, still covered the small circle in which Madame Bitterwhack had built the funeral pyre. The trees were still, but the hedgewitch knew better than to take that for granted. Black oaks had a tendency to sneak up on you if you weren't paying proper attention. But with the pyre so close, she was probably fine.

It was a work of art, each branch placed with the utmost care. The body of the former Mr Nuggin lay four feet off the ground, in the central pad of what looked like the wooden paw of a giant bear. She had lit the clearing with a series of lanterns, placed at intervals around the tree line. Their steady flames held back the gloom that pressed down from the trees. Madame Bitterwhack took some time to appreciate a job well done.

'You know,' she said to the dead man, 'less and less people choose this. It's been three months since I last performed the Rite of Passage. Old Lady Hilgeratten. She was the last. Died of a fever, which just goes to show.' Exactly what it went to show Madame Bitterwhack didn't elaborate. She stamped her feet a few times and rubbed her hands together to keep out the chill of the night.

'Nope, not much call for it these days,' she continued. 'Burial at sea. That's what they all want now. Bloody stupid idea if you ask me. Who wants to spend eternity with a bunch of fish?'

Mr Nuggin said nothing, which was only to be expected.

'Half of 'em wash back up on the beach, anyway. Strong tides in the bay, see, brings 'em right back home. Madame Reedswail buries 'em in the dunes. She's a better woman than I. I'd leave 'em for the gulls.'

She was silent for several minutes, lost in thought.

'People are scared of the Blackwood these days, I reckon,' she said eventually, eying the trees. 'scared and angry. Not that they shouldn't be, of course. There are things in these trees that'd swallow a man whole and not even spit out the bones. But time was people respected what's out there,' she waved a wrinkled hand at the tree line, 'now they just hate it. Or ignore it completely. Some folks would ignore it right up 'til the trees were growing through their floorboards. Then you've got the City Watch, hacking and slashing away every day. Convincing folks they're fighting the good fight. Trying to reclaim the parts of the town swallowed up. Did you know that even with all their stupid axe flailing, we actually lose something like twenty feet of the town every year?'

If Mr Nuggin knew, he didn't admit it.

'Twenty feet,' Madame Bitterwhack repeated, shaking her head. 'There are trees right up to Greensap Row now. You know my old granny, bless her soul, well she remembered a time before the Quickening. Before the trees grew so fast we couldn't keep 'em back.

Said she'd travelled to the capital on the king's road before it was lost. Said she met the king himself once, too. She was a terrible liar, mind you. Cheated at cards too.' Madame Bitterwhack gave a disapproving sniff, suggesting she certainly did not condone that sort of behaviour.

'All gone now, mind you. The capital, the king, his road, and the whole bloody kingdom all come to nought. And now,' she said, raising her eyes to the sky once again, 'they say old Garselin himself has come to finish the job. Blow'd if I know why he'd bother! Seems to me a daemon would have better things to do.

'But listen to me prattle on. Don't mind an old woman. I expect you'll want to be getting on your way.'

The hedgewitch seemed to take Mr Nuggin's silence as assent and shook herself out of her reverie. Taking the nearest lantern, she used it to light a small bundle of rushes she'd brought just for the purpose. Then, working quickly, she poked the flaming bundle as far into the centre of the bear's paw as she could reach. She waited a minute or two for the flames to take hold.

'Oh, great Melethin!' she intoned, in a special voice she saved for the occasion. 'Please take this man, Brian Dwindelsfelt Nuggin, and accept him as your faithful grandchild. Give him safe passage through the trees until he returns once more to the bosom of Zigelder.'

She left it there, having never seen the point in long, flowery speeches. She went and sat on the wheel of her cart and watched as the flames consumed the former Mr Nuggin. Fishing around in one of her pockets, she produced a toffee wrapped in a small scrap of waxed paper. She sucked on it in that noisy way that only elderly ladies can achieve, and smoothed out the square of paper, before poking it back into a pocket, in case it was useful for something. Then, from another pocket, she removed her battered diary and began to write. She liked to make a few notes on the day. It helped to order her thoughts. Today, she wrote about the star.

It was then she became aware she was not alone.

It wasn't totally a surprise. Madame Bitterwhack had spent enough time in the Blackwood over the years to know you were rarely completely alone. The trick was to know if you were being watched by a squirrel or something more dangerous. It was a source of great pride to the woman that she could feel the difference. It was a hard thing to describe to someone who couldn't do it themselves. She put it down to experience. If you were smart, or indeed lucky enough, to survive your first few predator encounters, then you started to feel their presence. A small prickling between the shoulder blades. She felt it now.

Casually replacing her diary, she slowly reached with one hand beneath the canvas cover of her cart, searching for the small, short-barreled blunderbuss she kept for emergencies. With the other hand, she removed a little canvas baggie from one of her many pockets. The bag contained a concoction of her own invention and was her first line of defence. The blunderbuss, although effective, made far too much noise to be used in anything other than the most dire of circumstances. There was little point in surviving an attack, just for the noise to bring down every bear, troll, wolf and who-knew-what-else for ten miles around. But it paid to be prepared, which is why she let out a tiny breath of relief when her groping hand found the smooth, cold barrel of the gun. It had a spring-loaded bayonet, just a few inches long, which she flicked out with a barely audible click. Because it also paid to have options. Standing slowly, she scanned the tree line for signs of life. The burning pyre had lit the clearing much further than the lanterns had managed. But the red light flickered and danced, making it hard to tell what was just shadow and what might be actual movement. She wasn't sure, but she felt that one patch of shadow was just a little darker than the rest.

She watched it intently.

After several minutes, and just as the hedgewitch was wondering if she was imagining things, something emerged into the light of the clearing. 'Emerged' was really the only way to describe it. It didn't walk, or trot, as to do so would have required legs, something that Madame Bitterwhack could not have said for certain it possessed. It wasn't a roll either. It didn't seem solid enough for that. Possibly it could be described as a slither, but that would have implied that it definitely *didn't* have legs. It was…something new.

It was rare these days that Madame Bitterwhack came across something that she didn't recognise in the Blackwood. But this was one of those times. Whatever it was, it was magical. She felt confident enough to say that. It had an aura in colours she had never seen before, and nothing purely biological could move in such an unsettling way. It was like someone had taken a pile of butchers offcuts, mixed them with a bucket of wet compost and then thrown them out from the trees. But instead of landing with a splat as you would expect, each bit seemed to have taken on a life of its own midair and was now independently trying to pull itself towards her. Somewhere in the centre of the roiling mess was a pair of eyes.

Madame Bitterwhack took a deep, steadying breath. It didn't do to panic. She could turn tail and run, but for all she knew, that would just attract the thing's attention. For right now, she wasn't certain it was even aware of her presence. Its eyes focussed, as much as it was possible to tell, on the pyre, on Mr Nuggin. It was approaching the flames, gaining speed with every inch. Madame Bitterwhack edged, slowly, around her cart, aiming to put it between her and the...what? Monster? It wasn't a term she used lightly, but it seemed to fit the bill. The monster did not react to her movements. It had now reached the edge of the flames and held for a moment, as if considering what to do next. Little tendrils reached out to flickering forks of fire like it was trying to catch ahold of them. Madame Bitterwhack reached the other side of the cart and readied the canvas bag in her good throwing arm.

Without warning, the monster launched itself at the pyre. It landed amongst the flames on Mr Nuggins' chest with a sizzling, splattering sound and sent burning wood spraying in all directions. Frozen, Madame Bitterwhack watched what happened next in horrified fascination. The creature was *eating* Mr Nuggin. At least, that's what it looked like. But it had no mouth that the hedgewitch could make out. It just attached itself to the unfortunate corpse, much like an enraged octopus, and chunks disappeared. There was soon a large hole where the man's chest had been. The monster kept going, apparently unconcerned whether it was consuming flesh, clothing, the pages of The Book of Oak, or indeed the burning wood beneath.

Transfixed, the first that Madame Bitterwhack knew that her cart had caught fire, was when one of her compounds exploded. It went up with a *whoomph* and a roaring purple flame that caught the side of her dress, setting it alight too. Lurching away from the ruined cart, she dropped her baggie. It hit the ground with a soft puff and a cloud of twinkling silver dust burst out of it, just to settle harmlessly on the leafy ground. Cursing, Madame Bitterwhack beat at her burning dress. Flaming nick-nacks fell to the ground as the pockets scorched and ripped. She flung her diary away, its pages alight. Flames smothered, the woman looked back at what remained of the funeral pyre with dread.

The monster had certainly noticed her now.

Its eyes fixed her to the spot, radiating with a hunger that terrified her. It moved out of the flaming wreckage, and this time, it was walking. She watched as it roiled and seethed, changing shape as fast as the surrounding flames. But there were legs now. Sometimes a man's, sometimes more like a bear's, but it strode towards her, regardless. With a shaking hand, Madame Bitterwhack raised the blunderbuss and fired. The noise echoed around the clearing as the shot sprayed into the creature at chest height. The monster didn't even falter. It leapt the remaining distance between them and landed in the scattered circle of her burning possessions with a thud that made the hedgewitch fall to the ground, letting out a strangled cry. It stood over her and she watched in horror as it grew, first arms, and then a head. The shape withered and changed and, for a moment, it was a bear looking at her, then something she couldn't name, full of teeth, and finally, the distorted face of Mr Nuggin. It was a horrible parody of the man, apparently put together by something that didn't entirely understand how the bits went together. The monster bore down on the woman and the stinking funk of earth, ash and decay filled her throat. Then, to her amazement, it began to eat the burning contents of her spilt pockets. It scooped them up in fists, paws and tentacles, shoving them into Mr Nuggin's face. Not the mouth, just the face, which opened to accept them greedily. She watched as her diary, still burning, was snatched up and disappeared with a spade-like handful of earth and leaves. To her credit, Madame Bitterwhack didn't scream. Instead, she flailed out with the blunderbuss; the bayonet sticking fast in what was, possibly, a thigh. The monster paused, turning its eyes on the gun, then carelessly knocked it loose with the back of what was, for a moment, a hand. It leapt at Madame Bitterwhack, landing on her as its form once again fell apart, covering her in a black gunge that slid and boiled all over her.

Then the hedgewitch screamed, watching helplessly the last thing she would ever see; the horrible head, reforming above her, piece by piece, into a terrifying mimic of her own.

Over time, the fires burnt themselves out. The lanterns too. Quiet returned to the clearing. Eventually, in the darkness, a darker form appeared. It looked a little like a woman, a little like a sack of potatoes, as it grasped the smouldering remains of a small handcart. It dragged the cart behind it, lurching off into the trees.

In the sky above, the new star burned.

CHAPTER TWO: KIPPERS, APPLES, AND KNIVES

1.

Wigbert Stonemorton III, His Grace, the twenty-ninth Duke of Blackwood, stared into his bedroom mirror and sighed. What was he doing with his life? Flecks of grey at his temples showed he was no longer a young man, but the beginnings of crows-feet showing around his hazel eyes spoke more to a legacy of anxiety than they did one of wisdom. It had been a long night and the coming day promised to be even longer. He touched a hand affectionately to the portrait of his dead wife that hung next to the mirror, then slumped back down behind his writing desk, more to put off going down to breakfast that with any actual intention of doing more work.

The writing had not gone well that morning. Usually it was a release. A chance to disappear into the lives of his characters and their problems. A chance to forget his own. His main character, a dashing hero by the name of Wolfe Starlingcloud, was deliberately everything that Wigbert was not. He'd probably have no problem being a duke. He certainly wouldn't have hidden behind make believe words when there was proper work to be done.

Because all was not well in the Duchy of Blackwood. Of course, he could not remember a time when it had been. But things seemed increasingly volatile in the last few weeks.

And now there was this new star…

Wigbert sighed again and began clearing his papers away into the desk drawer, which he then locked. The last thing he needed right now was his father finding out about his little writing hobby. The elder statesman would not approve, and it was an argument Wigbert could do without. He got to his feet and, with a rising sense of dread, collected his little pile of correspondence for the day and left his room. He descended the draughty spiral stairs but instead of going straight in, he paused and hid behind the anti-chamber's thick, wooden door, peeping through a crack into the great hall. Unfortunately, all he could see was a patch of tapestry-covered wall. He tried moving his head from side to side. He needn't have bothered, as he could hear his father's presence even if he couldn't see him.

'*Kippers*!' he heard the old man bark. 'Where are the bloody kippers? You people call this breakfast?'

The duke sighed. He was already getting one of his headaches. Again with the kippers. The old goat was obsessed. He considered forgoing breakfast entirely, but he knew he would never hear the end of it if he did. Still, perhaps, on this occasion, an argument about smelly, dried fish would be a welcome distraction. His head throbbed a warning, and he reached into his breast pocket, removing a small silver case which he opened with a click. A solitary brown pill lay inside. Wigbert sighed yet again. He would need to make another trip to the pharmacist. Popping the pill into his mouth, he swallowed it dry whilst straightening his shirtsleeves and coat, then stepped around the door and into the hall. He clutched the small packet of letters to his chest.

His father sat at the head of a long wooden table that ran the length of the room. It would have seated about thirty, but currently was set for just three. A shaft of weak sunlight from the sole window at the far end of the hall illuminated the man in the otherwise gloomy room. The threadbare tapestries that lined the walls did little to dampen the morning chill with the large fireplace laying dark.

'Good morning, father,' the duke said, uncomfortably aware of his faltering footsteps echoing around the room.

The erstwhile twenty-eighth Duke of Blackwood glowered at

him over the toast rack.

Wigbert found his father had begun to shrink with time. The man sitting at the table that morning was surely some puppet, a cruel caricature of the once robust statesman. His grey hair was lank, and his face painfully thin. A walking stick was hooked over the arm of his chair.

It was, of course, a somewhat unusual circumstance for one duke to be face to face with his living predecessor. The title usually got handed down upon the death of the former incumbent. However, there had been...difficulties a year before. The sort of difficulties that manifested in a pitchfork waving mob at the castle gates. His father had been forced to step aside. It was a sore subject and one that Wigbert did his best to avoid at all costs.

'They've forgotten the kippers again!' his father raged, a little spittle escaping his mouth.

'We've talked about this, father,' the duke said. 'You remember? I told the kitchen to stop bringing the kippers.'

The old man's leathery face crumpled into a scowl. '*Outrageous*! A Stonemorton breakfast table without kippers? *Sacrilegious*!'

'Father, you don't even eat them.'

'Course not horrible things. Like eating fish flavoured leather.'

Wigbert smothered another sigh. 'Well, as I've said before, Beatrice and I don't care for them either. So there is really no—'

'*Not the point*!' his father interrupted, banging his fist down into the spiced roll on the plate beside him. 'It's the look of the thing. Got to have kippers. The Wibberjacks will have kippers, and the Macewinds, you mark my words, boy!'

'Well, if they enjoy kippers, then they should certainly—'

'*Enjoy*? Who said anything about *enjoyment*? It's about the look of the thing!'

'We are talking about the same thing here, aren't we? When I say kippers I mean dried, salted fish, fried in butter. I fail to see how—'

'Acorns and roots, boy, you've got a lot to learn!'

Wigbert took a deep breath. 'I see. Well, the kippers aren't coming. Perhaps we could have some of this lovely-looking pound cake instead? There's jam too, I see.'

His father grunted by way of reply, but he accepted a large piece of pound cake when Wigbert seated himself to the man's right and cut them each a slice. He then poured them both a cup of spice from the large, tarnished silver pot that was sitting on the table.

'You should have a servant pour that. And clean the pot too!' his father grumbled through a mouthful of cake. He was eyeing the pile of letters Wigbert had placed on the table beside him.

'It's no bother—'

'It doesn't matter if it's a bother or not, you're the duke! What sort of message does it send? You pouring spice like a common tavern-boy?'

'Father, you know it makes me uncomfortable having people hovering over us at mealtimes. Besides, there's no one here but us, so...' This excuse was perfectly true, but not the real reason there was no one there to serve them. The simple truth was they no longer could afford to spare the few servants they had left for such a menial task. But Wigbert was not about to have *that* conversation.

'Uncomfortable,' his father repeated, making a face like the word physically hurt him. 'That's your problem, boy. Everything makes you uncomfortable.'

That wasn't entirely true, Wigbert felt. Books, for example. He was quite comfortable around those. Plants too. Sometimes, whole minutes could elapse without him feeling uncomfortable at all. This usually only happened, however, when there were no other people around to witness it. The trouble with people, as far as the duke was concerned, is that they were everywhere. His father was a prime example. He was always exactly where Wigbert didn't want him to be. They had never enjoyed the best relationship, but it had grown so much worse since his mother had died. Now that Wigbert was duke, it seemed not a day passed by without the two of them arguing over something.

'Anyway,' his father continued, apparently determined to keep complaining, even if it meant changing the subject repeatedly until he got a rise out of his son. 'It's only just past eight o'clock. Far too early for breakfast.'

The duke pinched the bridge of his long nose, eyes closed. 'We've been through this, father. Eight o'clock is a perfectly acceptable time to sit down to breakfast these days.'

'A gentleman never breakfasts before ten,' his father argued, slurping his cup of spice, the contradiction apparently lost on him.

'Father, by ten, most of the townsfolk are several hours into their working day. I feel that to govern effectively, I must be up and working with the rest of Upton-Myzzle. What sort of message would it send if I was yet to start the day proper when several hours' worth of correspondence was already awaiting my attention?'

'People should work to the duke's schedule, not the other way around,' his father declared. He picked up the letters from the table with his bony hand and waved them under his son's nose. 'And you know how I feel about this ridiculous habit of sending and receiving notes at all times of the day. There was none of that when I was duke. I made myself available at parliament between noon and four o'clock on Mondays and Wednesdays only. You have to have some boundaries, or they'll be hounding you day and night. Besides, it meant I was *seen* twice a week. That's important. You send all these letters, but when was the last time you actually went into town and showed your face?'

'I really can't remember, father,' the duke said, not meeting the man's eyes. 'I don't keep track of every public—'

'Three weeks ago!' his father interrupted sharply. 'You haven't even left this castle in *three weeks*. How can you possibly think to govern the duchy of Blackwood effectively if you never set foot in it?'

Wigbert busied himself with the jam to cover his discomfort. 'I'm sure that is not true, father,' he lied. 'Besides, I find the letters provide a very effective means of communication between myself and the court. The lords and ladies—'

'Have forgotten what you look like!' the old Duke cried, pounding his spiced roll flatter still with a clenched fist. 'This star business last night is a perfect example. You should have been down in the town, being seen *doing* something!'

Wigbert was saved from responding by the sound of someone politely clearing their throat out in the antechamber. Moments later, Tanco Dribbets strode into the hall, his tokens clattering as he came.

'Good morning, your graces,' he said, approaching the duke and his father where they sat, a stack of letters in one hand and a tray of kippers in the other. He deposited the latter onto the table, shooting the duke an apologetic look as he did so. The duke's father beamed triumphantly. Wigbert chose to ignore him.

'Good morning, Tanco. Are those for me?' he said instead, indicating the letters in his steward's hand.

'Indeed, your grace.' Tanco handed him the pile. 'And those, I assume, are for me?' He picked up the letters from the table. 'I shall have them delivered momentarily. Is his grace prepared for the Longest Night ceremony this evening?'

Wigbert resisted making a face. 'As I'll ever be. Assuming the blasted rain stays away a little longer. Is there any further news regarding the events of last night?'

'Not really, your grace. Most of the townsfolk have settled down now, seeing as the world has yet to end. But there is a lot of tension. The festival couldn't happen at a better time if you ask me. People need a bit of fun. A distraction. The new Wolfe Starlingcloud book would fit the bill, but it doesn't come out for another month.'

'Wolfe Starlingcloud? What on earth has he got to do with

anything?' said Wigbert's father, scowling.

Wigbert shot his steward a warning look. 'Nothing, father. I'm sure Tanco just meant the new book would be a welcome distraction from people's troubles.

'Bunch of poppycock,' the old man grumbled.

Wigbert was surprised. 'You've read the first book?' he asked despite his better judgement.

'Totally unrealistic,' his father said. 'Although, Sir Rumbould Theaksteak has a way with words, I'll admit. But I don't trust a man who hides in the shadows. Why doesn't he come forward, hmm?'

Wigbert knew only too well why the author hadn't chosen to reveal himself. Namely, because, even though his book sales had been keeping the castle afloat for months, he didn't actually exist. It was a point of contention between Wigbert and his steward, the only other man to know the truth. Tanco believed, especially after the wild success of the first book, that the duke should reveal himself as the true author. Wigbert believed that if his father didn't kill him for dishonoring the Stonemorton name, then the populace would. They might be willing to love a mysterious Sir Rumbould Theaksteak, but they may just change their minds if they knew he was really the very *un*mysterious Wigbert Stonemorton. He changed the subject.

'And the star?'

'Still there, as far as I can tell, your grace,' said Tanco. 'But faded from view now the sun is up.'

'And we're still no clearer on what it actually is? Assuming it's *not* a giant daemon coming to devour us all, of course.'

'I'm afraid not. I've reached out to the Institute of Propositional Logic as you suggested, but I haven't heard back yet.'

'Those quacks?' the old duke said with a sniff. 'What on earth do you want their opinion for?'

'Natural philosophy is a growing art father,' said the duke, stifling one more sigh. 'They may well be able to offer some explanations.'

'It's the Church of the First Tree you should ask for explanations,' his father retorted. 'If anyone knows the movements of the great beast, then it should be them!'

'Well, for the time being, father, I'm rather of the opinion that it is unlikely to be a monster of myth and legend. I'm sure the institute will be able to come up with a more satisfactory answer.'

His father narrowed his rheumy eyes. 'More satisfactory than the Book of Oak? Careful boy…'

'Whatever the answer may be,' Tanco interjected with delicacy. 'You will need to provide it soon, your grace, if we are to avoid public unrest. People are scared.'

'Of course, Tanco. Quite right. Contact the institute again and have them send a representative. I will meet with them this evening, after the festivities.

'Send someone from the church too,' he added, at a look from his father. 'Where is Beatrice, by the way?'

'I believe she is in your private garden, your grace.'

'Then I shall take these,' he brandished the letters Tanco had given him. 'And pay her a visit. Good morning, gentlemen.' With that, he rose from the table.

'Just a moment, boy,' his father said. 'We need to discuss this…' He produced a folded newssheet from his lap and threw it dramatically onto the table. Wigbert was greeted with a rather crude woodcut of himself, featuring his long nose and large teeth in a rather unflattering light. Above was the bold headline *'Longest Blight! Has the Stonemorton line finally led us to the end of the world?'* There was a smaller caption beneath the picture which read *'Wigbert Stone-moron? The new star that appeared in the sky last night has led to fresh concerns over the ability of the duke to lead.'*

Wigbert fell back into his seat. 'How bad is it?' he asked.

Tanco looked awkward. 'The Gazette has written worse,' he said. 'Although, I admit, rarely.'

'In my day I'd have had the entire staff rounded up and

thrown in the dungeon,' Wigberts' father said. 'We'd soon see how clever they all felt after a night on the rack!'

'And we know where that led, don't we, father?' Wigbert snapped, uncharacteristically sharp. He regretted it immediately.

His father's eyes grew wide with rage. 'How *dare* you!' the old man hissed.

Wigbert raised his hands in supplication before the old mans inevitable rant of indignant outrage could properly get going. 'I'm sorry, father,' he said. 'It's all this star business. It has me stressed out, is all.'

His father settled back in his chair, mollified for the time being.

In truth, it had not really been his father's penchant for throwing people who annoyed him in to the castle dungeon that had led to his eventual downfall. There had been a lot more politics involved. Politics that, if Wigbert were truthful with himself, he only half understood, even now. The Upton-Myzzle Gazette had certainly played its part, though. The publication had been printing unflattering articles about the Stonemorton's rule for years. But, short of banning the free press, a move that would see rioting in the streets for sure, there really wasn't much he could do about it.

Tanco cleared his throat. 'I assume the Castle Blackwood official response will be the same as usual, your grace?'

'Yes,' Wigbert said miserably. 'No comment.

'And now I really must go.'

2.

It had not taken long for Wigbert's parents to realise there was something not quite right with their son. He had been a quiet, secretive boy. Much more at home playing by himself in lonely corners of the castle than mixing with his peers. Of course, as heir to the duchy of the Blackwood, he didn't have any peers, which could have potentially been part of the problem. But, as his father pointed out to his worried mother, every duke and duchess that had come before grew up the same way. He'd spent *his* childhood in 'friendly' rivalries with the other sons and daughters of parliament. Not equals, not exactly, but the closest thing. It was expected. All part of training for the cutthroat world of politics that came with ruling the duchy. But Wigbert…well, Wigbert just didn't seem interested. Worse, he actively resisted his father's efforts to get him to engage. To the bafflement of his father, the boy seemed to prefer the castle's dusty book repository. What interest could there be in the pages of some old book? It was a mystery. As far as he, the duke, was concerned, a boy ought to be outside in the sunshine. Chasing things. Hitting them with sticks.

Eventually, he had a quite brilliant idea. At least he'd thought it brilliant, and seeing as he was duke, that's all that mattered, *thank-you-very-much*. Horticulture had always been a favoured pastime of the Stonemorton line, going back into antiquity. In fact, in more prosperous times, before the Quickening, it was said that the walled gardens at Castle Blackwood were the envy of the kingdom. They had fallen on somewhat harder times in the last hundred years or so. They had certainly held no interest for him, but perhaps they might be just the thing for little Wigbert. Gardening, he told his dubious wife, would teach their son some responsibility. His wife argued that if it was responsibility he was after, then it might be easier to just buy the boy a dog. But gardens, the duke insisted, would get the boy into the fresh air. And if it worked, he might even make some friends. There were plenty of big houses with gardens amongst the members of parliament. There were plenty of dogs, too, his wife pointed out. But no, it would be gardens, the duke decided. They were the thing. Very noble, horticulture, very aristocratic.

So the walled gardens of Castle Blackwood found themselves a new head gardener in the young duke-to-be and, in many ways, the old duke's plan had been a roaring success. Young Wigbert had taken to horticulture like a seed to soil. He was a natural. It wasn't long before he had tamed even the most wild corners of the neglected Castle Blackwood gardens. He seemed to thrive in creating order from the chaos. Tangled webs of weeds and brambles became straight cut beds with finely tilled bare soil and line upon line of perfectly cultivated plants, fruits and vegetables.

There were no friends, though. The social aspect of the experiment had been a spectacular disaster, and Wigbert, now the new duke and having seen his fortieth cycle, split the vast majority of his time between the empty garden and the empty book repository of his youth. He'd tried growing himself some friends, but it was very much still a work in progress.

He entered the garden now, letting the arched wooden door with its peeling white paint close behind him, cutting off the outside world. This was his domain. Here, he truly felt like a ruler, even if his subjects were cabbages and runner beans. Right then, of course, the growing season was coming to an end. Early frosts had seen to all but the hardiest of shrubs and perennials, and only the aforementioned cabbages, along with a few sprouts and some early planted leeks, were left of that year's crops. Many of the beds lay bare and a thick litter of leaves was on the ground. This made it a little easier for the duke to locate his daughter. He could see her by one of the apple trees, fiddling with something in its branches.

Beatrice was a tall girl of twelve harvests. She had that slightly unhealthy look of someone who has grown a lot in a brief space of time. She had her long brown hair in a pair of plaits, and, despite the early hour, had already stained her pastel blue dress with the powder-green of lichen. Her feet were clad in a pair of brown boots several sizes too large. Wigbert recognised them with a pang of sadness; they had once belonged to his one social success story, Beatrice's mother.

'Good morning, Beatrice,' the duke said.

The girl ignored him, continuing to fight with something in the branches of the large apple tree that rose above them. She was standing on a small wooden stepladder, but still had to go on tiptoes to reach, meaning she swayed alarmingly. A fairy buzzed through the air between them; a dash of pink and blue which rapidly disappeared over the garden wall. The duke cleared his throat.

Nothing.

Then he remembered. 'Good morning, Bea,' he tried again.

This time the girl turned her head, and treated him to a wide, gap-toothed smile. 'Good morning, father.'

Unfortunately, the movement shifted her weight just enough to unbalance her. The step ladder shot one way and she the other, ripping something from the tree branch as she fell to the ground. She landed on her backside with a bump, holding the object protectively above her head in both hands. 'Oh bother,' she said.

'Are you ok?' Wigbert asked, helping her back to her feet. She now had a wet, brown patch on her rump, as well as the green stain down her front.

'It's ok, I don't think I hurt him,' she said.

'Hurt who?'

She showed him the large, wizened apple she had pulled

from the tree. It was soft so, very carefully, she dug into the skin with her fingernails, prizing it open. Inside, the flesh was brown and pulpy and gave off an eye-watering fermented smell. In the very centre lay a moglin, curled up tight and apparently sound asleep. It had a big smile on its pinky-purple face and snored contentedly.

It wasn't hibernating. It was drunk.

'How do they do that?' Beatrice asked her father. 'Make the alcohol right inside the apple like that?'

'I'm not sure exactly, something to do with the natural yeast on their skin.'

'*Why* do they do it?'

'As far as I can tell, they do it for the same reason any person does it. They like getting drunk.'

'Is a moglin an animal or vegetable?'

It might sound like a silly question. You might imagine that the difference between the two would be fairly obvious. You might even worry about a girl of twelve harvests who couldn't tell the difference. But in the Blackwood things were not always so straightforward.

'The simple answer is both,' said the duke. 'It seems likely they started out as some sort of root vegetable, much like a radish. But from there they turned into something different.'

'They look like radishes,' Beatrice said. She gently stroked a finger through the moglin's tuft of green, leaf-like hair. 'So does that mean that any plant could become an animal?'

'Theoretically, yes, but it takes magic. It's not really a process we totally understand. Sometimes it seems to happen naturally, like with moglins, but if we want to replicate the process, it takes a lot of time and skill. Even then, it comes down to luck. The right concentration of magic in the right place.'

Beatrice looked at him with big eyes. 'But you've done it, haven't you, father?'

Wigbert smiled. 'Once. Sort of,' he admitted. 'With the dandelions.'

The duke's dandelions were something of a horticultural marvel in the town of Upton-Myzzle. The sort of thing that people talked about in hushed tones around smokey bonfires on wet autumn evenings. Evolution of plant to animal was a rare, wondrous thing, and many a gardener wished for the secret. Unfortunately for the duke, he had no real idea how it had happened.

Beatrice knelt down to examine a dandelion that was growing in the leaf-strewn grass at the base of the apple tree. It waved back at her.

'They're sentient, it would seem,' Wigbert said. 'But still very much plants at the moment.'

The moglin in his daughter's hands chose that moment to let out a belch, the volume of which was quite astonishing for a creature of its diminutive size.

'I don't know why anybody drinks. It's kind of gross,' said Beatrice, wrinkling her nose.

A new voice boomed across the garden towards them. 'Quite right, dear lady! You keep away from the stuff. Disgusting habit.'

A large, rotund man with a bushy brown beard bigger than his own head was picking his way through the flowerbeds towards them. Actually, 'picking' is rather a generous term. His significant bulk and booted feet were causing so much damage to the plants it made Wigbert wince.

'Anyway,' the man continued as he arrived at the apple tree, trailing an uprooted Begonia. 'That will leave more for your old uncle Punduckslew.' The man was wearing a long, burgundy coat that brushed the tops of his boots with its elaborate gold trim. The fabric of the coat itself was thick and embroidered with many complicated symbols and patterns, denoting his magical status.

'You're not my uncle,' Beatrice said, sticking her tongue out at the man. 'You're just my father's bodyguard.'

Punduckslew grabbed his chest theatrically. 'You wound me, my lady.'

Beatrice laughed, and Wigbert forced a smile.

His daughter's easy relationship with his bodyguard made him feel...what? Uncomfortable? Or just jealous? Really, he should be thankful that his daughter seemed capable of making friends. He just wasn't sure Punduckslew was the greatest influence.

'Do your trick!' Beatrice demanded of the wizard.

'I assume by my 'trick' you mean my sacred, Melethin-given Talent, which is only to be used in defence of the state, not for the amusement of spoilt little girls?' Punduckslew said, inspecting his fingernails with an innocent expression.

Beatrice put her hands on her hips and stared the wizard down. Punduckslew wore an expression of weary resignation, but then rather spoilt the effect by grinning widely and winking at the girl. He pointed at an apple still hanging from the tree, cocked his thumb like a gun and-

'Wait!' Beatrice said, before grabbing the stepladder and climbing to check the apple over. 'Ok, no moglins. Go ahead,' she said, scrambling back down.

Punduckslew 'fired' his finger, making a little '*pew*' noise for effect. The apple exploded, raining soggy bits of fruit over the duke.

'Lovely,' said Wigbert, wiping apple off his shoulder.

'Whoops, sorry, your grace'

'Now put it back together!' Beatrice cried delightedly.

'You know very well I cannot, my lady,' said Punduckslew, smiling indulgently. 'Every wizard has one Talent and one Talent only. Mine is making things go boom.'

'Which means you're pretty much useless at everything else,' said Beatrice, grinning.

'*Which means* if you're not careful I'll blow up your chair at dinner tonight, with you sat on it!'

Beatrice shot the wizard a shrewd look. 'It *also* means you can do anything you want, because all the other wizards and politicians are afraid of you.'

She wasn't wrong. It was one of the main reasons Wigbert

could never quite bring himself to trust the man. He could have bullied his way into any job in parliament he wanted, not to mention swipe the top position in the Wizards Charter while he was about it. Yet he had requested to be here. Bodyguard to a duke nobody liked.

Punduckslew gave a rather unconvincing gasp of astonishment. 'I'm sure I do not know what you mean,' he said. 'But, as fun as it is pandering to your every little whim, I'm afraid I'm going to have to steal your father for a while, my lady.'

'Let's take your moglin to the potting shed with the others first, shall we?' Wigbert said, by way of reply.

The potting shed was a small wooden building the duke used to store his tools and keep out of the rain. It had a musty smell, of earth and damp. On the walls hang rows of perfectly oiled and polished tools. On one bench was a complicated-looking contraption of glass tubes and demijohns. At the top, in little funnels padded with straw, sat a series of moglin-inhabited apples. Cloudy yellow liquid was seeping from the apples, down the tubes and into the waiting demijohns. Beatrice carefully placed her apple into an empty funnel before bending down to look closely at the gathering liquid.

'Can I try some?'

'I thought drinking was disgusting?' her father reminded her with a smile.

'Only if you do it so much you pass out,' Beatrice explained. 'And I only want to try a sip.'

'Moglin Mash is pretty powerful stuff, sweetheart. If you really want to try a drink, then maybe I'll let you have a sip or two of ale tonight at the celebrations.'

Beatrice made a face. 'Ale is gross!'

The duke raised an eyebrow.

'At least it smells gross,' Beatrice added quickly, looking guilty.

'Oh, let her have a drop, your grace,' Punduckslew said, ruffling the girl's hair indulgently.

'Perhaps tonight, at the celebrations,' Wigbert relented, massaging the spot between his brows with two fingers. His headache was getting worse.

'About the celebrations,' Beatrice said, turning upon her father. 'I was hoping to spend Longest Night with the troop. Oatey says there's going to be marshmallows and a bonfire and we're going to watch the unveiling of the giant pudding and...' she trailed off, watching Wigbert with big, hopeful eyes.

'The Forestry Brigade? Oh...well yes, I suppose that would be ok,' he stuttered.

He could hardly refuse. The Forestry Brigade had been his idea, after all. A little real-world education. He would worry about her, though.

'She'll be fine,' Punduckslew said, tucking his large thumbs into his belt. 'Master Lettuce will look after her. He might be a bit wet, but he's got his head screwed on right. But right now, we really do need to go, your grace. The high priest is waiting for you.'

Wigberts' heart sank. 'Oh no, really? That was fast. I was rather hoping to avoid her until the ceremony.'

'She took it upon herself to come to the castle, it seems. I believe she wants to discuss the star.'

'If she's come to tell me it really *is* Garselin, she had better have some very compelling evidence.'

'I don't like the high priest,' Beatrice announced. 'She smells funny.'

'Well, just give the word, my lady,' Punduckslew said, cocking back his thumb again. 'And ... boom!'

'I'm sure that won't be necessary,' the duke said with a sigh.

3.

The afternoon sun was just slipping lazily from the sky as the royal coach, moving almost as slowly, finally made its way down the hill towards the town. Its wheels cut two troughs through the muck of the busy street, but the carriage's progress was so slow the slurry collapsed back in through the spokes before they moved on. Two gwalmok pulled the ancient vehicle with an air of complete unconcern for the inexperienced coachman, who was jumping up and down in his seat, shaking the reins to no effect. They pottered along at a pace entirely of their own choosing, great hairy buttocks swaying back and forth.

The duke's party was running late. The High Priest of the Church of the First Tree—she of the Golden Branch, Melethin's own representative on the mortal plain, holder of the Holy Writs and the Sacred Chains of Office—leant her head out of the carriage window and swore loudly.

'I could piss us there faster than this, damn your eyes!'

The duke, who was sitting opposite in the cramped coach, looked at the woman, wondering exactly how that might work. The high priest had the thickset look of a person who has enjoyed a comfortable life. A little too comfortable, if the redness across her nose and cheeks was any indicator. She had thick, slug-like lips and a head where the only hair was the grey stuff coming out of her ears. She wore her ceremonial green robes and had insisted on bringing the golden branch into the coach with her. It lay across her lap and the branched end was digging into Tanco's side, who was unfortunate enough to be sitting next to her.

'My apologies, your holiness,' Tanco said, easing a jewelled leaf out of his crotch with as much dignity as he could muster. 'I'm afraid the coachman hasn't been able to practice much. Not a lot of call for the royal coach these days.'

'I can see that from the woodworm,' the woman replied. 'It's a disgrace. If you worked for me, young man, I'd have you flogged.'

'I'm sure there will be no need for that,' said the duke, after a moment's pause where he contemplated the use of the phrase 'young man' in regards to his steward. The high priest said nothing, but gave him a look suggesting she disagreed. In truth, the state of the royal coach could not be blamed on Mr Dribbets. It had been hard enough to justify the expenditure of the coachman himself. Woodworm treatment, or indeed a fresh coat of paint, were quite out of the question.

The coach trundled on. Outside in the streets, there was an air of slightly nervous celebration. People had not forgotten about the star, it seemed, especially as evening approached. But it was Longest Night, and people weren't about to pass up a state-approved excuse to party. Wigbert himself was not really feeling in the celebratory mood. Being out of the castle made him anxious, not to mention being shut up in a damp wooden box in close proximity to the high priest, who, if truth be told, he was ever so slightly terrified of. Today she was giving off a smell he couldn't quite identify; a mix of stale sweat and something thick and cloying that stuck in the throat. It was currently doing battle for his nostrils with the stench of pipe smoke emanating from the carriage's final occupant, Punduckslew, who seemed to be asleep. Far too many people, in far too small a space for Wigberts comfort. He was starting to sweat. He looked out the window to take his mind off it and saw people had placed various large wooden carvings along the edges of the street. Wigbert watched as they passed a bear, a fox, a poorly realised frog that looked more like a sick cat, and a giant moglin. The last was actually rather lifelike, and its oversized eyes bore into him as they passed. The high priest saw it too and made the sign of the First Tree with her hands, thumbs together, pointing at her chest, fingers interlaced and pointing to her chin.

'Disgusting,' she muttered.

'The carving and burning of totems is an ancient Longest Night tradition, your holiness,' said Tanco, a little more defensively that Wigbert thought was wise. His steward had always been of a superstitious mindset, hence the many good-luck tokens he wore.

'Ridiculous mumbo jumbo,' the high priest said, looking unimpressed. 'People should focus on the many holy traditions of the Church and leave these heathen practices where they belong; in the past.'

'I'm sure their popularity has more to do with them looking jolly and being a good use of the town's excess wood, rather than being a deliberate affront to Melethin,' the duke said. Wigbert suspected the Church's objections had more to do with the fact that their own ancient traditions were barely twenty harvests old. Of course, as the figurehead of the state-sponsored religion, the duke did not voice those particular thoughts aloud. The high priest had no such compunctions.

'If I had my way, the burning of Longest Night totems would be punishable by death,' she said conversationally. 'If they want a bonfire so much, let's see how they enjoy being burnt at the stake! And as for this stubborn clinging to the Lord of Misrule nonsense...well, I would do away with the lot of it!'

The pounding behind the duke's eyes was increasing. He really would have to send Tanco back to the apothecary soon. He took a moment to formulate his response in his head before speaking.

'We have, I believe, discussed this issue before, your holiness. As I'm sure you recall, it was decided that introducing that particular law might prove bad for the church's image.'

The high priest made a sort of phlegmy, gurgling sound in her throat which said exactly what she thought of that decision. 'Parading some fool around whose sole purpose is to play juvenile practical jokes is simply not the image we should be upholding. Longest Night is the holiest night of the Upton-Myzzle calendar. It is a time for prayer, giving thanks to Melethin and solemn contemplation.'

Just at that moment, as if to punctuate her words, the carriage rattled past a tavern that was doing a roaring trade. The sound of drunken profanity blared into the coach.

'Such language,' the high priest said, pursing her moist lips. 'The old, barbaric ways are no longer suitable in these enlightened times.'

'You swear all the time,' Punduckslew pointed out, eyes still closed. Apparently, he wasn't sleeping after all.

The high priest looked affronted. 'That is quite different! I am a holy woman, and therefore, any foul language I might use is wholly justified in the eyes of Melethin and used to further his glorious cause.' She actually said it with a perfectly straight face.

Punduckslew gave a great bark of laughter, making the high priest shoot him a look of pure hatred.

'I rather like the Lord of Misrule,' the wizard said, oblivious. 'My cousin was chosen once, you know?' he gave another sudden bark of laughter. 'He made parliament feed their Longest Night feast to the castle's gwalmok and had it replaced with the beast's swill!'

The high priest shot him a withering look. 'You must be so proud. Let us hope we are blessed with such hilarity tonight.'

Punduckslew did not respond, and a terse silence settled on the coach as it moved on through the gathering crowds, into the heart of Upton-Myzzle. Despite the oppressive atmosphere in the royal carriage, Wigbert was dreading the moment he would have to leave it. He was not a fan of crowds. Or perhaps, to be more accurate, he was not a fan of crowds that would inevitably be looking at him. He always forgot how to walk naturally when he thought he was being watched. It's hard to appear authoritative when you can't get your legs to move in conjunction with one another. He watched miserably as the coach entered the packed old quarter. The press of people was centered around a raised wooden platform which had been positioned in the centre of the waterlogged green. A valiant attempt had been made to jolly it up with swathes of greenery and red ribbons, but it did little to detract from the grey-brown mess that had once been a pretty patch of grass. *That's a lot of people*, the duke thought, his stomach beginning to churn. Braziers were just being lit against the gathering dusk. Surreptitiously the duke tried to look up at the sky, but he couldn't see much from inside the carriage.

'I shall make my announcement before we begin the crowning of the lord,' the high priest said, obviously catching his movement. 'The star will reappear soon. People must know that they will be safe so long as they remain faithful to Melethin.'

Wigbert nodded glumly. There was little point in arguing. He wished he had spoken to someone from the Institute of Propositional Logic before the high priest had cornered him with her version of events.

'It is indeed a comfort to know that if we have all prayed hard enough, we will be safe,' Punduckslew said, finally opening his eyes. 'Of course, if the star *does* turn out to be the daemon, well, I guess we can just say people weren't putting in enough effort.'

The high priest's glare would have melted Wigbert into his seat, but it bounced off the wizard like a ball of parchment. They pulled up at the side of the platform, the gwalmok apparently all too happy to respond to commands of 'stop', and the duke began his mental preparations for leaving the carriage. He could see a group of watchmen in their shiny breastplates and plumed helmets standing ready to meet them. Their presence did little to lift his fear. He could feel a sheen of cold sweat across his throbbing forehead.

All too soon, the coach door opened, and he was forced to step out into the hubbub of the crowd. He could feel the press of people, like a buzzing in the ears. A steam rose off the mass of bodies, like breeches left in front of the hearth. The duke could feel it on his face and in his throat as he tried to breathe.

There was a vague cheer and a smattering of applause, but there was no heart in it and it quickly petered out. Wigbert raised a sweaty hand and waved it a little while, doing his best not to catch anyone's eye. *Behold, your beloved duke*, he thought. For once, he was glad of Punduckslew's presence. It meant no one tried to get too close.

'Just remember your lines and you'll be fine, your grace,' said Tanco's voice in his ear. Wigbert nodded dumbly.

Tanco eyed him with concern. 'Have you taken your pills, your grace?'

'Yes, although I'm all out. I'll need you to pick up some more tomorrow, I'm afraid.'

His steward nodded. 'Of course.'

Someone booed. Trying to ignore it, the duke concentrated on getting his legs up the steps to the platform, sweat dripping uncomfortably down his back despite the evening chill. He reached the top and forced himself to look out at the crowd, waving again. The booing was getting louder but quickly faded away as Punduckslew followed the duke up onto the platform, glaring out at the audience. Wigbert, feeling his face burning with shame, hastened to take his seat, an elaborate wooden throne placed in the centre of the platform. It was cold, damp, and extremely uncomfortable, but Wigbert clutched at the arms like they were a shield. Punduckslew stood behind the throne like a hairy mountain, as the high priest ascended to the platform, golden branch in hand. She walked with an unhurried dignity, as if completely unconcerned with the crowd below her, who grew quiet with expectation. The tap, tap, tap of the golden staff hitting wood was all that could be heard as she made her way to the centre of the platform. Wigbert felt a stab of jealousy. He knew he did not cut such a commanding figure. He stopped trying to burrow into the throne with his shoulder blades and sat up straight, adopting what he hoped was a royal expression despite the waves of nausea washing through him.

The high priest threw her arms wide. 'Good people of Melethin!' she called in a clear voice that filled the square. 'I stand before you, on this, the holiest of nights, truly humbled by the Grandfather Oaks unending benevolence. *For he has blessed us once again*!'

The duke winced, thinking her rhetoric a little strong, but he looked out at the forest of pale, oval faces looking up in the gloom and realised she held them with every word. What he wouldn't give for that kind of natural showmanship.

'As many of you will know,' the high priest continued, her breath visible in the air as she stalked up and down the platform. Heads turned to follow as she moved. 'A new star has appeared in our sky. I am here to tell you, *do not be afraid*, for it is sent by the First Tree himself! His love for us is strong. He has sent the star to remind us we must be ever vigilant! We must remain true to the word within the Book of Oak. Yes, the great beast yet lives, and yes, one-day Garselin will return to devour this world. *But that day is not today*!' She threw her hands wide, the golden branch stabbing into the sky. 'Grandchildren of Melethin, *rejoice* this Longest Night! For you are loved and will remain so, just so long as you remain one of Melethin's *faithful* servants. So I say again, *rejoice*!'

This time, the cheers were genuine. Applause filled the square. The high priest gave Wigbert a self-satisfied smirk before turning back to the crowd and motioning for a little quiet. 'And with that, good people,' she said. 'I turn you over to your *fearless* leader, the Duke of Blackwood!'

There were more cheers, but some laughter too this time. Wigbert doubted anyone had missed the jibe. His face burned so much he was sure he must be glowing like a beacon. As the high priest strutted towards the steps, he stood. His head swam, so he took a couple of deep breaths before speaking as loudly and clearly as he could manage: 'Err…good people—'

The words were no sooner out of his mouth than an angry yell from the crowd cut him short. '*Melethin is dead*!'

There was a collective gasp. The high priest froze halfway down the steps, head whipping around, a scowl piercing the gathered citizens like a hail of crossbow bolts as she searched for the origin of the outburst. Wigbert stood uncertainly, uncomfortably aware of Punduckslew's heavy tread as he took a protective step forward behind him. The clanking of metal on metal told Wigbert that the watchmen at the base of the platform were suddenly alert. A hush had fallen over the gathering and, instinctively, Wigbert looked to the high priest for a reaction, instantly hating himself for doing so.

'It is true,' the high priest called out, slowly walking back up onto the platform. 'Melethin gave his mortal life in the protection of his son. But do not make the mistake of thinking that means he is gone! He is a *god*! Our god. And gods do not truly die.'

The voice came from the crowd came again, harsh but clear. 'You know nothing of what you speak!'

This time Wigbert watched as a movement in the centre of the crowd became a quickly widening circle around a solitary figure dressed in black. People pushed away from him, eager not to be associated. It was a man, perhaps of sixty harvests, with a thin, bony frame and a black tricorn hat, under which a sallow face glared up at the platform. He pointed a crooked finger at the high priest.

'You, with your *so-called* Book of Oak,' he spat. 'We have listened to you for far too long! Well, I say we will not stomach your vile lies anymore!'

Punduckslew stood protectively in front of the duke. 'Just give the word, your grace,' he whispered.

'No!' Wigbert hissed through gritted teeth. 'Acorns and roots, you can't blow a man up just for shouting.'

'Good people,' the man in black continued, now addressing the slowly widening circle of nervous citizens around him. 'Many of you know me. For those of you who do not, my name is Sir Krickwell. I come before you today because it is time for us to make a stand. It is time to remember who we are. *We are the children of Zigelder*! We have allowed these heretics to lead us astray, but it is time to renew the old ways. We must honour our father, the cracked acorn, for only he can save us now!'

The duke was aware of watchmen attempting to push through the crowd to reach the man, who had paused and was looking deep into the eyes of his audience. He spoke again and his voice was hot with passion.

'You are all in grave danger. They tell you to be faithful to them, to their book, a book written by *human hands*. They say that it will save you, but they deceive!' He threw an arm towards the sky and pointed, pausing again to make sure he had everyone's attention. '*The great beast approaches*!' he roared. In the crowd, someone screamed, and the square suddenly filled with a hundred whispered conversations. They cut off just as quickly when Sir Krickwell continued.

'Melethin is dead, and the daemon comes. Only Zigelder can save us now! I urge you, brothers and sisters, rise up, *rise up and be heard*!'

On the platform, the high priest was shaking with rage. 'For Melethin's sake, Punduckslew, will you do your job already?'

'No!' the duke insisted. 'The guards nearly have him. We must avoid bloodshed if we can!'

'This is no time to be *weak*!' the high priest spat, but Punduckslew made no move to obey her. Wigbert watched as the watchmen pressed on, shoving people roughly aside now as they got closer to their quarry. Sir Krickwell saw them too, it seemed, as he raised both hands above his head in surrender and stopped moving. The savage look on his face remained, however.

'See how they try to silence me?' he cried. 'Well, they cannot silence us all! Praise be to Zigelder! Pra—'

He got out no more because just then, a watchman finally broke through the crowd and bought his truncheon down on the man's head with a crack that could be heard all the way to the platform. Sir Krickwell crumpled to the ground, his hat rolling away in the mud, as more watchmen broke through into the circle and the first raised his truncheon again.

'*Stop!*'

The command rang out across the square and Wigbert was astonished to realise it had come from himself. Hundreds of faces swiveled to look in his direction and he felt the moisture evaporate from his throat.

The high priest stepped in smoothly. 'Take the poor creature away,' she commanded, and the watchmen hurried to obey, picking the prone man up from the ground and carrying him off. The crowd was obviously shocked, but angry murmurs were beginning to surface.

'Children of Melethin, do not be alarmed,' the high priest continued smoothly, raising her hands for calm. 'These were the ravings of an obviously very sick man. There is no reason to be afraid. Once again I say rejoice!'

There were no cheers this time. The atmosphere had changed. It was no longer one of celebration. Wigbert felt eyes watching, waiting to see what happened next. He realised with a start they were waiting on him.

'Well? *Get on with it!*' the high priest hissed at him, before turning and storming from the platform. Wigbert was aghast. They wanted him to continue? The crowd was silent, staring. He had to do something. *The script*, he thought, *just remember the script*. He cleared his throat and motioned for Punduckslew to step aside.

'Good people,' he said, stepping out from behind his bodyguard, in what he hoped was a confident sort of way. 'It is time to crown our Lord of Misrule.' He paused, but there was no reaction from the crowd. 'Um...yes...well, could you please welcome this year's selection, Mr...er...Mr Scroggan Peplow!'

A man was quickly ushered up onto the platform. He had the glazed, absent expression of someone who had no clear idea of what was going on but was quite used to it. There was a smudge of dirt across his chin and he had a haircut that might charitably be called a bowl-cut, if the bowl being used had been run over by a cart first. He wore the traditional dress of the

Lord of Misrule, a long cowl of green linen strips that fluttered and rustled like leaves as he moved. He waved out at the crowd with a wonky grin and there was some nervous laughter.

'Go on, Scroggy!' someone shouted. Mr Peplow's grin grew. Bolstered, the duke pressed on with the ceremony.

'Mr Peplow?' he asked the man.

'That's me, your grace!' Mr Peplow said, grinning wider still. There was more laughter. Wigbert relaxed, ever so slightly, letting the words of the ceremony rise to the top of his memory.

'Do you promise to do as you will, and let no man, be he low born or sitting upon a throne, deter you from your purpose?' he intoned.

Mr Peplow looked confused at this and it took Tanco running onto the platform, whispering urgently into his ear, and running back again, wooden tokens clattering all the while, before he said 'Yes, your grace.'

Yet more laughter. The crowd was relaxing again. *Thank Melethin for you, Scroggy Peplow*, the duke thought. 'Do you promise to uphold the sacred duty we, the citizens of Upton-Myzzle, place upon you this Longest Night?'

'Yes, your grace!' Peplow cried, warming to his role. People were cheering now.

'How will you do so?'

'*By letting chaos rule!*' Peplow howled. The crowd howled back.

'Then come and be crowned!' Wigbert cried, realising as he did so that he had forgotten to pick up the ceremonial crown. There were roars of laughter as Tanco was forced onto the platform again, red-faced and puffing with exertion, to deliver the crown to the duke. Wigbert received it gratefully.

The crown of the Lord of Misrule was not really a crown at all, but a wooden mask, carved into the face of a sneering man, wreathed with oak leaves that formed the only crown-like part of the ceremonial object. Wigbert, wasting no time, placed the mask over Mr Peplow's head and stepped back.

'I pronounce you, our Lord of Misrule!' he cried.

Thunderous applause filled the night as people stamped the ground and hollered. Wigbert felt a wave of relief wash over him.

It was cut abruptly short as he felt something in the air beside him suddenly shift. The noise from the crowd faltered.

A dark figure had appeared behind Mr Peplow, as if from the very air itself, and the sharp point of a long dagger was glinting in the centre of the newly crowned Lord of Misrules' chest.

A terrible silence descended over the square as Mr Peplow slumped to the wooden platform and the figure stepped forward, snatching the mask from the falling mans head in one fluid motion. He was dressed in a cowl of his own, only his was made of black and grey rags that whipped in a sudden breeze as the man placed the sneering mask upon his own hooded head.

'*I* am the Lord of Misrule,' he said, his voice nasal but loud, muffled only slightly by the mask over his face. '*Let the chaos commence!*'

And with that he was gone, winking out of existence as if he had never been there. Wigbert stared at the red stain spreading across the platform from the unmoving Mr Peplow. He felt the large hand of Punduckslew close around his arm.

'Time to go!' he heard the wizard bark.

Then the screams began.

CHAPTER THREE: LONGEST NIGHT

1.

The principal thoroughfare through Upton-Myzzle had been a surprisingly late addition to the ancient settlement. Surprising mostly because of the manner in which it had been constructed. It ran in an arrow-straight line—unusual in itself, in a settlement of twisting alleys and winding lanes—down the hill from Castle Blackwood, straight through the heart of the town, and ended abruptly at the bank of the Myzzle. It had been created, so the story went, when a monstrously enraged sea-bass, mutated by a magical eruption far out at sea, burst from the river waters and proceeded to plough a path through the terrified town. The fish headed directly for the castle, with which it apparently made a spirited attempt to copulate, before the magic wore off and it receded to its formative size, whereupon the castle cook brained it with a rolling pin.

The exact truth of this tale has been lost over the many scores of harvests since, and is, besides, somewhat irrelevant. What mattered is that 'Seabass Street', with its wide avenue, many shops, and ease of access (a feat that would have proved impossible for what passed for town planning in those days) became the natural hub of life in the busy settlement.

This was never truer than on Longest Night, and it was here, amongst the crowds of festival-goers, the haze of bonfire smoke, and the mingling smells of strong drink and roasting meats, that Master Lettuce and the Upton-Myzzle Forestry Brigade (Third division) could be found. Longest Night was traditionally a big night for the brigade, but that evening

Master Lettuce was uneasy.

It was a condition he had always been susceptible to, even from a young age. He supposed some people were just born that way. For him, it tended to manifest in what his mother had always called his 'dicky tum-tum', and he had found that over the last few weeks his poor tum-tum and been growing dickier by the day.

The cause of his gastrointestinal distress, which in the past could have been any number of everyday annoyances or little trifling problems, on this occasion could be narrowed to a singular cause, or rather, a single person. That person was about four feet high with plaited pigtails and heir to the Duchy of Blackwood.

It wasn't that he disliked the daughter of the duke. In fact, he found Beatrice to be a charming, if slightly unnerving, young lady. The Master had no problem with smart women. His mother was one, after all. The difficulty he was experiencing was that this smart young girl had suddenly become *his* responsibility. Again, that was usually not a problem. The Forestry Brigade (Third division) held about thirty boys and girls, all of whom he was responsible for. The difference with Beatrice was twofold; first, he had the distinct impression she was smarter than him. This, as already stated, would not usually have been significant, until coupled with difference number two. This was that if anything happened to her, he would find his neck horribly, if ever so briefly, associated with the razor-sharp Axe of the State.

When a man named Dribbets came to inform him that the duke's daughter would be joining the troop, he had thought it was some kind of practical joke. Not possessing a sense of humour himself, Lettuce had played along patiently, waiting for the inevitable, if unfathomable, punchline. When he eventually realised it would not be coming, he'd had a rather aggressive panic attack. His bowels had not been the same since.

Which brings us back to that particular evening amongst

the bonfires of Longest Night. Master Lettuce was beginning to suspect that all was not well. There was something in the air, a miasma of fear that he could feel spreading through the street from the direction of the old quarter. He saw it pass among the gathered people, moving from group to group as merry singing was replaced, one voice at a time, by urgent whispers and gasps of alarm. Most concerning of all, he suddenly realised, there was no longer a single watchman or castle guard in sight. With a twinge in his stomach, he stepped protectively towards the young duchess-to-be, trying not to imagine the bite of metal against his unprotected throat.

2.

About a quarter of a mile further up Seabass Street, Corporal Snekchesser of the Castle Blackwood Guard watched as his commander made the biggest mistake of his career.

'The Watch has called for all possible aid to be sent to the old quarter's main square, and I want every guard there helping to find this vicious murderer!' General Weltsmatter shouted at his assembled men. 'Commander Posternos has personally requested my help, and by Melethin I will not let him down!' The General's chest swelled, and he struck a noble pose, presumably intended to inspire the men.

Snekchesser was a good if unambitious soldier. He followed orders. He didn't ask questions. He had quietly made a career for himself over the past thirty harvests on those two terms and was proud to have no imagination whatsoever.

Until recently.

There comes a point in even the most fastidious soldier's life where they find themselves, if not questioning, then certainly closely examining the orders they receive. The corporal had been doing quite a bit of close examination in the past few months and had come to the reluctant conclusion that the Guard, *his* Guard, was being run by a fool.

'Now, intel suggests we may be dealing with some kind of rogue wizard, someone able to appear and disappear at will,' Weltsmatter continued, flaring the nostrils on his beaky, bloodshot nose and swaying slightly. 'Well, let me tell you men now, Talent or no, this fiend will not escape the clutches of the

Castle Guard and City Watch combined!'

A *drunken* fool, Snekchesser thought, as the general stumbled and had to grab the shoulder of a nearby soldier for support. The corporal was glad when another guard, a captain, raised his hand and said; 'Err, permission to speak, sir?'

General Weltsmatter squinted at the man through ever-so-slightly crossed eyes, but nodded his assent.

'Should some of us remain here to keep the peace, sir?'

'There will be no need for that,' the general said dismissively.

'It's just the duchess-to-be, sir—' the captain continued before Weltsmatter cut him off irritably.

'Her ladyship will be just fine in the protection of the noble men and women of the Forestry Brigade.'

'Um...aren't they mostly children, sir?'

'Nonsense, nonsense, fine body of men. But to more pressing matters! We must hurry, for who knows when the wicked killer may strike again! Follow me, men!'

General Weltsmatter, being the type of man he was, probably felt that he then strode away impressively. It was more of a totter. His men followed behind in various states of confusion, reluctance, and indifference. Corporal Snekchesser let them flow forward around him. Weltsmatter was done. That much was clear. The duke, for reasons Snekchesser could not understand personally, may have let the generals litany of mistakes and derelict of duty go unpunished till now, but when he learned of the danger placed upon his own heir by the incompetent man, he would have no choice but to finally act.

The question, Snekchesser found himself finally asking, was where did an old soldier such as himself want to fall in all this?

Once he had allowed himself to ask the question, he realised there was no real question at all. Ignoring his comrades, he turned his back and began trotting down the street in the opposite direction.

3.

'I want my pudding!' Beatrice moaned, knowing she sounded petulant even as she did so, but still struggling to quell the rising sob of disappointment in her chest.

'I really am very sorry, my lady, but it simply isn't safe enough for you to continue to be out on the streets,' Master Lettuce replied, taking her by the arm and leading her away from the largest bonfire, where the Forestry Brigade had been gathered. People were already dousing the flames. 'We must put your safety above all else.'

She stuck her tongue out at the man by way of response. Childish, perhaps, but it was just so *unfair*! Her trip to the Longest Night pudding ceremony that harvest had been the result of a great deal of planning and preparation, the likes of which her contemporaries may very well have been unequal, and her family completely unaware.

Beatrice was conscious of her father's shortcomings, more so perhaps than was Wigbert himself. As such, she had become sentient at quite a young age that, if she was to see something of the world, she would have to arrange matters herself. Do not mistake her, for she loved her father very much, but she was fundamentally not of the same makeup. In fact, had she been born in her father's place, then *his* father may very well have had the son he always dreamed of. But, alas, that is the way of the world. As things stood, she was forced to manipulate matters to achieve the outcome she desired.

Take the Forestry Brigade, for example. Now the duke was sure—and in his defence, most adults would be in his position

—that it had been entirely his idea for Beatrice to join the troop. Indeed, he was rather proud of himself for coming up with the plan. His daughter would gain a valuable education about the world outside Castle Blackwood, one he himself had never achieved, but in a safe and controlled environment. Now, Beatrice would never have dreamt of taking this notion away from the man, but the truth remained that she had worked extremely hard in order for the idea to be born. An innocent word here, a seemingly harmless anecdote there. The trick had been to come about the thing, not directly, but from the side, never quite mentioning the goal by name. The hard part had been acting surprised when he had finally taken the bait and suggested the venture.

The last hurdle had been her grandfather. But that had been less of an obstacle than she had feared. The old man had been so pleased that his granddaughter would be mixing with those outside the castle, he temporarily forgot that would include commoners, as well as nobility.

So, with all the work that led to her presence at the Longest Night celebrations that evening, it was rather too much for a young girl to bear when they seemed to be snatched away from her at the very last minute, like a sweetbread knocked from her open mouth.

'It wasn't even that big anyway,' she said sulkily. 'About four feet across, which I *guess* is large for a steamed pudding, but I wouldn't call that giant, would you?'

'I'm sure you're right, my lady.'

Master Lettuce was not looking at her. He was instead searching the dispersing crowds, wearing a worried expression that made him look like a frightened newt, which, as far as Beatrice was concerned, fit his character very well. She scowled at the lank blonde hair on the back of his head as he dragged her on.

'I wanted to see them set it alight! Oatey says that's the best bit. He says they use a whole barrel of brandy!'

'I think perhaps young Crabelbottom may have been

exaggerating,' Master Lettuce replied distractedly. 'Ah, *there*!' He turned and headed toward a figure dressed in the brown, green and gold of the Castle Guard, who was fighting his way through the crowds towards them.

And what a figure it was. The man was short and squat like a bulldog, with a mass of curly black and grey hair that doubled the size of his head. He wore a scowl so worn into his features that you might just believe the old wives' tale was true; the wind changed, and he really had got stuck like that.

'Acorns and roots, where have you been?' Master Lettuce said as they met the soldier in the busy street. He shielded Beatrice protectively as a dense crowd of people rushed by, faces grim. 'They've cancelled the pudding ceremony. There's been an… incident of some kind.'

'I know. We must get her ladyship back to the castle,' the man growled in a voice like a rusty saw. 'The streets are no longer safe.'

'If you know, then where have you been?' Master Lettuce whined. 'And where are the rest of the guard? I would, of course, protect her ladyship with my life,' he continued, looking horrified at the very thought, 'but I'm afraid I am not a particularly physical man.'

The guard's eyes flickered to meet Beatrice's ever so briefly. 'General Weltsmatter ordered them all away to help with the search for the…to help the Watch.'

Master Lettuce gaped at him. 'He deliberately left her ladyship unprotected?'

'An oversight, I'm sure,' the man said, and Beatrice could not tell if he believed it or not. 'But I'm here to help. My name is Corporal Snekchesser. Moving her won't be easy, I'm afraid. The streets are heaving for the festival. We have to get her away from the crowds because if things kick off, we don't want to be anywhere near.'

'I have a name, you know,' Beatrice said with a scowl.

'Of course, my lady,' Snekchesser said without looking at her.

'What's happened?' she asked, anyway. 'Lettuce won't tell

me.'

'Nothing to panic about,' the corporal said, with the closest thing to a blank expression his scowling visage would allow.

It is a quirk of human nature that, when told not to panic, the average person will immediately fear the worst. Had he understood more of the human psyche, then perhaps Corporal Snekchesser may have chosen his words more wisely, for no sooner had they left his mouth, than Beatrice became, for the first time, truly concerned for more than the loss of steamed pudding.

'Is...is my father alright?' she asked, a flutter in her chest.

'Like I said, my lady, nothing to worry about.'

'I'm sure the duke is quite safe,' Master Lettuce said kindly, giving her shoulder a small squeeze. 'He has that Punduckslew fellow with him, after all.'

Corporal Snekchesser grunted. 'We need to be moving. I suggest we make for Trunk Street, then swing round to Green Man Row. There will be fewer people there and then we can filter through, back towards the castle.'

Master Lettuce looked horrified. 'Are...are you sure, corporal? Green Man Row...well, it has a certain reputation.'

'Lesser of two evils. But we need to go right now before—'

'We can't leave without Oatey!' Beatrice cried.

The corporal blinked. 'What's an oatey?'

'He's my friend!'

'Your ladyship, I'm sure young Crabelbottom is halfway home by now. I sent the whole troop home with Master Cabernatoll.' The Master turned to the corporal. 'He's an old Forestry Brigade member, doesn't get out much these days, bless him, but I convinced him to join us for the festival.'

'Master Cabernatoll is like a hundred harvests old!' Beatrice cried.

The corporal raised his eyes towards the star-strewn sky and muttered something under his breath. Beatrice watched as the man seemed about to speak, but paused, his eyes caught on something in the heavens. She raised her own eyes to locate what he was looking at and saw that the new star was once again shining brightly above them. It felt like a giant eye, and Beatrice suddenly wanted to be back home, back at Castle Blackwood, safe in her quarters.

Luckily their dilemma was solved for them, for Beatrice spotted Oatey running through the moving crowds towards them. He was pushing a wheeled wicker chair in front of him, which contained what appeared to be a pile of dirty blankets, with an old cabbage resting on top.

'*There's* Oatey,' Beatrice said with relief, pointing at the boy who was fast approaching.

Master Lettuce frowned. 'He's still with Master Cabernatoll.'

And he was right. For as the wicker chair grew closer, it became clear that its contents were indeed Master Cabernatoll, his wrinkled head poking out from a tight weave of blankets. The confusion was forgivable. Especially given that, even as Oatey reached the group and the wicker chair pulled up beside them, from the blanket-clad form emanated a distinct aroma much like over-boiled greens.

Master Lettuce put his hands on his hips, his frown deepening. 'What have you been doing, boy? You were supposed to be going home.'

Oatey, wide-eyed and out of breath, stuttered his defence. 'I tried, but Master Cabernatoll needed some help and, well, he seems to have forgotten where he lives.'

'I haven't forgotten a thing! They've been messing with the streets again, is all,' Master Cabernatoll snapped. 'Always messing with things, you young-uns. Why can't you leave 'em be, huh? Streets was perfectly good as they were.'

The assembly was saved from responding to this accusation by Oatey, who announced with excitement; 'There's been a murder! Someone's killed the Lord of Misrule!'

Beatrice gasped. 'A murder!'

Corporal Snekchesser closed his eyes and massaged his temples with his thumbs. 'Yes, thank you,' he said, shortly. 'We are aware of the situation.'

'Oh my,' said Master Lettuce weakly.

'There's been a murder, and you didn't tell me!' Beatrice said accusingly. 'Father was at that ceremony!' She looked around with fresh eyes, suddenly understanding the change in the atmosphere. People were frightened. Whatever had happened, it couldn't have been any normal killing, not to cause this kind of mass hysteria. Beatrice may have been young, but she was far from stupid. She knew murders of one sort or another were not an uncommon thing in a large town like Upton-Myzzle.

'As I said before, your ladyship, your father is perfectly fine... as far as we know,' Corporal Snekchesser said.

'*As far as you know!*'

'I don't think it was the duke who was killed. Just the Lord of Misrule, poor Scroggy Peplow,' Oatey said.

'Are you sure? Did you know him then?' Beatrice asked.

'A little. Him and dad used to help with old farmer Tanners' harvests together. He was thick as gwalmok dung, to be honest.'

'Oatey! You shouldn't speak ill of the dead,' said Master Lettuce, aghast.

'Whose speaking ill of him? I ain't speaking ill of him. Just 'cos he was dumb don't make him a bad person. I liked him. He used to bring me sugared chestnuts. He didn't deserve...well, whatever happened.'

'And you're sure my father is ok?' Beatrice asked again.

'That's the word on the street. I think he was bundled off by that crazy wizard before things really kicked off.'

Beatrice looked at the boy closely, trying to ascertain if he was telling the truth. He had a dirty face, was wearing what might charitably have once been called clothes, and had hair that looked like someone had balanced a bird's nest on his head. She had no real reason to suspect he might be lying, as he was also her only real friend. A fact that would have troubled her grandfather greatly if he knew, for they were about as far apart on the social scale as it is possible for two people to be.

The truth was, they were thrown together by circumstance.

That circumstance being the rest of the troop hated both their guts. The reason they hated her was obvious; she was Beatrice Stonemorton, heir to the duchy. That wasn't a popular thing to be these days. Hence the guards, which hardly helped. The reason they hated Oatey she found rather harder to understand. But as far as she could figure out, it centered around the belief that extreme poverty might be contagious.

Corporal Snekchesser was looking impatient. 'Can we please get a move on?' he said. 'Unless, of course, there are any other pensioners or urchins we need to save? Someone's granny, perhaps?'

'I saved someone's granny once,' offered Master Cabernatoll, happily.

'Wonderful. Well done,' Snekchesser said, when it seemed the old man would not elaborate. 'But if you don't mind, I need to be getting her ladyship here to Green Man Row.'

'Can't. It's blocked. That's why we ended up back here,' said Oatey.

'Damn! Why?'

'Rabble rousers!' Master Cabernatoll cried, jerking irritably underneath his blankets. 'Young popinjays with their fancy haircuts!'

'Er...some pillock closed the Three Pigeons, sir,' Oatey explained.

Corporal Snekchesser's mouth fell open. '*On Longest Night*? Acorns and roots, there'll be a riot for sure!'

Oatey nodded agreement. 'Grannnock Bagstock's there. He don't like it when he can't get a drink. Only a matter of time before he hits something.'

'Might I suggest, corporal, that we retreat to the nearest safe haven and assess the situation from there?' offered Master Lettuce.

'Good idea. Where's your house?' said the corporal.

'The other side of the river, I'm afraid. However, Master Cabernatoll's place is not far.'

'I told you—' the old man began.

'Yes, yes,' said Master Lettuce soothingly. 'We quite understand, old chap. Luckily, I know the way.'

'Then for Melethin's sake, let's *move!*' Corporal Snekchesser barked.

4.

'For Melethin's sake, somebody find my daughter!' Wigbert shouted.

'Right away, your grace!' Punduckslew replied, before diving back into the throng.

The duke stood with his heart in his mouth, water in his boots, and someone's elbow in his ribs. Members of the Watch surrounded him so tightly he could hardly move. On the one hand, it was a stroke of tactical genius—no one could materialise behind a man and stab him in the back if there was already someone stood there—but on the other hand, Wigbert couldn't help but feel, if he had been an intended target he would have died up on the platform. As he hadn't, this invasion of his personal space, already pretty abhorrent to a man of the duke's disposition, was most likely a waste of time.

Also, he really needed a wee.

He attempted to peer out between the helmets, but couldn't see much of what was going on. He could still hear the roar of the crowd; hundreds of people all talking at once, trying to make themselves heard above the next person, their voices mixing together so the resultant sound boxed you in both ears like an angry drunk on…well, Longest Night.

And people were running. He caught glimpses of dashing figures, frightened faces. Punduckslew was not far away; he could pick out the wizard's booming voice, shouting orders, demanding answers. Wigbert toyed with the idea of trying to help. After all, he was technically in command. But what would he actually do? He realised he had no firm grasp of what might be required in this type of situation. What should a leader do in a crisis?

Lead, he supposed. But in which direction?

So he stood, feeling increasingly useless, and wondering if Mr Peplow had a family. Were they in the crowd? Did they see... He shuddered at the thought and was immensely glad Beatrice had not been there to witness the poor man's demise. But he worried about her now. He wanted her safe, back in the castle.

At length, Punduckslew reappeared, his face creased with worry.

'What's going on? Where is she?' Wigbert asked.

'There...there seems to be some confusion, your grace. She was in Seabass street with the brigade and the Guard, but... well the Guard now seems to all be here and she is not.'

Wigberts' heart chilled. 'Where is the general? He must surely know where she is?'

'I cannot seem to locate him at present. It is...odd. No! Your grace, you must stay protected!'

Wigbert had been trying to push his way out of the circle of watchmen around him.

'I must find Beatrice!' he cried. 'It was foolish to agree to her being out like this. I...I cannot lose her too!'

'Please, your grace, we must not panic. We have no reason to believe she is not perfectly fine. She may well already be back at the castle. I will send one of the Watch to find the general and return—'

'No. You go. Find her Punduckslew. If I cannot, then you must!'

'But, your grace, I should remain close—'

'*No*! Find her. Find Beatrice. That's...that's an order!'

'Yes, your grace!'

Punduckslew disappeared once more, and the duke groaned under his breath. He felt like screaming. Instead, he settled for running his hands through his hair. Around him, the watchmen said nothing.

5.

Corporal Snekchesser led the motley group through the dark streets, still slightly unsure how his protection duty had swollen from the young Stonemorton heir to include two masters of the Forestry Brigade and a young boy named after a cereal crop. He sincerely hoped that he hadn't made a huge mistake. The town was still alive with festival-goers, although the atmosphere had now firmly changed to one of fear and confusion. It felt unpredictable, and if there was one thing Snekchesser didn't like, it was unpredictability. People roamed the streets in packs, and although some were innocent enough, others certainly would not be. His Castle Guard uniform seemed to be effective at keeping most potential confrontation at bay, but he was concerned that if real trouble found them, it might serve instead to betray the duchess-to-be's identity. Luckily, she was clothed in the beige dress and yellow scarf worn by all female members of the Forestry Brigade. Unfortunately, her elbow length, fur-lined cape was not so unremarkable. Anyone looking too closely might still recognise her.

He was starting to wonder if this had been a good idea. Were something to happen to the young girl now, the blame would be placed firmly at his door. Then again, he thought, looking at the skinny figure of Master Lettuce, if he hadn't arrived, who knew what might have happened already? One thing was for sure; if he didn't play this right, heads would roll, and he'd grown rather attached to his.

6.

As for Beatrice herself, she was rather beginning to enjoy things.

Now she knew her father was most likely safe, this night-soaked adventure through unfamiliar streets had become quite thrilling. If only her father could see her now, she thought. He would consider this a rather fuller education of life in the town than he had bargained for. She proudly told herself she had seen more of the *real* Upton-Myzzle in the last few minutes than in all the rest of her life combined and thrilled at the new understanding of her home she would undoubtedly develop.

This was, of course, untrue. What the young duchess-to-be could not possibly have known in her inexperience was that all she saw that night was the real Upton-Myzzle of *that night*. Those more seasoned in the ways of the town, such as the good corporal, for example, could have told her that the ancient streets had many faces. The trick was predicting which one was coming next. Nevertheless, Beatrice was feeling very grown up. There had been drunkards, rats, stinking gutters, people of all types, and what she was fairly certain had been a Lady-of-the-Night. If there was one crimp in the situation, it was that her shoes were completely ruined. Beatrice cared little for the shoes themselves. She'd in fact argued to wear her mother's large boots, which were always her footwear of choice, but she had been overruled. She would have dearly liked to see them now, however, as her feet were soaking and becoming numb with the cold. It was for this reason that she had to admit, if only to herself, to being slightly relieved when they made it to the house of Master Cabernatoll, which turned out to be a small, squat cottage on the enigmatically named Secret Street. She was less impressed when they opened the door and found the dwelling submerged in two inches of dirty water.

'Walter, old chap, how long has it been like this?' Master Lettuce asked the old man with concern.

Master Cabernatoll shrugged his bony shoulders. 'Few days. Didn't want to make a fuss.'

Master Lettuce began fussing around the small living room, lifting what he could out of the water. 'You'll catch your death living in this lot. You'll have to come and stay with me!'

Truthfully, there was not much that could be done, at least not until the waters receded. An old oil lamp was lit, which cast a weak yellow light across the room. Thankfully, not all the man's store of wood was wet, so a fire was quickly kindled in the hearth's metal grate, which, luckily, hovered just above the waterline. It was smokey, but the room warmed a little. Beatrice and Oatey were settled in a moth-eaten, high-backed chair. The children stretched their soaking feet out towards the flames, resting them on a small wooden chest Corporal Snekchesser found in the bedroom. Master Cabernatoll's wicker chair was parked next to them and the old man all but disappeared under a pile of extra blankets that were pulled from the water-free cupboards.

'Shame about the pudding,' Oatey said, and Beatrice nodded agreement glumly. Now they had stopped, she realised how hollow her stomach was feeling.

'Oh, I almost forgot. I swiped this earlier. Was going to have it for my supper, but you kids go ahead,' Corporal Snekchesser said, handing Beatrice a misshapen chunk of dark fruit pudding he pulled from his coat pocket. 'It's a bit squashed, I'm afraid.'

It was extremely squashed, and rather sticky too, but Beatrice thanked the man gratefully all the same. She broke it in two and passed half to Oatey, who immediately shoved a handful in his mouth. Beatrice delicately broke off a small chunk and tasted it. It was better than it looked and rich spices filled her mouth.

"Ere, this puddin's got a fly in it,' Oatey said.

'It's probably a currant.'

'Oh. Bea?'

'Yes, Oatey?'

'It's got wings on it.'

'That's good luck, I expect.'

Oatey looked at the sticky lump in his hand forlornly. 'Oh good, I should hate to think I'd been unlucky. All the same, I think I'll leave the rest.'

'Check for the silver shilling first! You never know.'

'I shouldn't think I'd be lucky enough to get a currant with wings on it *and* the silver shilling,' Oatey said, but he pulled apart and searched the remainder of his pudding anyway. Beatrice did the same, but there were no coins to be found.

'Mum always says we don't get much luck, us Crabbelbottoms,' Oatey continued.

'Didn't you once say your grandfather was a wizard? That's quite lucky, a magical Talent in the family.'

'You'd think so, wouldn't you?'

'What was his Talent?'

'He could make teeth disappear.'

'What…just teeth?'

'Yup. He became a dentist in the end.'

'Well, there you go then, not a bad profession, being a dentist.'

'Yeah. Trouble was, he couldn't control it very well.'

'… what, it didn't always work?'

'Oh no, it always worked. Just sometimes it worked *too* well, if you know what I mean.'

'I'm pretty certain that I don't.'

'Oh, well, sometimes he'd accidentally take too many teeth. Or all of 'em. Actually, once, he took all of a man's teeth, all the teeth of everyone in the waiting room, and all the teeth of the people passing by in the street outside.'

'Oh dear.'

'They chased him out of town in the end.'

'Where did he go?'

'Where else? Into the Blackwood.'

'Gosh…did he…um…?'

'A bear attacked him.'

'Oh no!'

'It's ok, he made *its* teeth disappear too.'

'You mean he survived?'

'Well *then* he ran into a group of Green Men.'

'Don't tell me…'

'Yup. Somewhere out there is a family of Green Men who eat nothing but soup.'

'…Oatey?'

'Yes, Bea?'

'Are you making fun of me?'

'It's the truth! Brigades honour!'

Beatrice eyed him suspiciously, but decided he was probably not lying, however unlikely it might sound. She doubted he knew what the word 'fabrication' meant, let alone be capable of it. The boy may not have been her intellectual equal, but she liked the way he thought.

'I'm sorry about Mr Peplow,' she said eventually.

Oatey shrugged. 'Weren't your fault what happened.'

'But what exactly *did* happen, do you think? It's got everyone spooked, that's for sure.'

'Pete Sideways said it was—,' Oatey furrowed his brow in concentration, ' "*A clear and welcome display of anti-patriarchal aggression, and a call to arms for the oppressed brothers of the revolting masses*,' I think.'

'Did he? Gosh. And is Mr Sideways a reliable source, do you think?'

Oatey shrugged. 'Search me. All I know is he makes a living by nicking posh ladies hankies and selling 'em on at the rag shop.'

Beatrice looked at him in surprise. It really was an education talking to Oatey.

'Is there much to be made from old hankies, then?' she asked.

It was Oatey's turn to look surprised. 'You can eat for a week off a good silk hanky. So long as you scrape the lumpy bits off first, of course.'

Beatrice regarded the boy's tattered coat and breeches again and thought of the pack of hankies sitting in her drawer at the castle. 'I see,' she said, feeling slightly ashamed.

'I fought during the failed rebellion, you know,' Master Cabernatoll suddenly croaked, apparently out of nowhere. Beatrice had thought the old man was asleep.

'You never did,' said Oatey, leaning forward excitedly. 'I heard that was a hundred harvests ago!'

'Eighty-seven,' Beatrice corrected.

'I'd seen just twelve harvests myself. Didn't stop me sticking it to one of 'em dirty rebels and saving a general's life, though,' Master Cabernatoll said proudly.

'Gosh! Master Cabernatoll, I'm twelve now. You'd have been my age!' said Beatrice.

The old man nodded. 'I know, girl,' he said. 'You'll be duchess one day, of course. Just remember those of us what kept you there and you'll do fine.'

'Yes, sir,' Beatrice said meekly, unsure what else to add. That she would one day rule was something of an abstract concept for the girl. It was a bit like the idea of gravity the Institute of Propositional Logic had been championing recently. An invisible force responsible for keeping everything stuck to the ground made her head hurt if she thought about it too deeply, and so did the idea of being a duchess.

' 'Course, I fought in the great goblin siege too, as a young man. Took out twenty of the ugly buggers with nothing but a sharpened wooden spoon and a stale loaf of bread for a shield!'

'No way!' Oatey cried, clearly impressed.

'You callin' me liar, boy? Well, you can see for yourself, I kept their heads as trophies. What' you think was in that chest your resting your dirty trotters on?' the master said with a wicked grin. Oatey and Beatrice's feet shot from the top of the trunk like it had suddenly grown red hot and the old man wheezed a reedy laugh in obvious glee.

'Now, now, Wilfred,' said Master Lettuce, who had successfully made spice and was offering a cup to each of the children, who accepted gratefully. 'I'm sure these two don't want to hear about all that horribleness.'

'I do!' Oatey assured him, although he was still eyeing the chest uncomfortably, presumably trying to decide if it really did contain a score of goblin heads. Beatrice suspected it did not, but she kept her feet firmly on the edge of the chair, just in case.

'Come now, what would the duke say if he knew I had let his daughter, at just twelve harvests old, hear such gruesome tales?' Master Lettuce said, doing his impression of a frightened newt again.

'I should think that he would be most pleased,' Beatrice lied. 'After all, the whole reason I joined the Forestry Brigade in the first place was to add to my worldly education.' She sipped the spice, which tasted a little stale but spread a welcome warmth through her stomach.

'My dear lady, I hardly think he meant for you to be learning about such…such unpleasant topics.'

'No good just learning 'bout the pleasant ones,' Master Cabernatoll croaked. 'Not much of an education then, is it?'

'Exactly!' Beatrice said triumphantly.

Master Lettuce looked pained. 'Master Cabernatoll, really…' he began, but seemed unsure how to finish.

'All we ever learn is the pleasant stuff!' Oatey said, a little sulkily. 'I mean, I like knots as much as the next kid, but I can already do a sailor's knot, a timber hitch, a sheepshank and a fisherman's bend.'

'Eh? Fisherman's bend?' Master Cabernatoll said, mystified. 'Tosh! A good running knot's all I've ever needed. Bugger the rest.'

'Well, I can tie over twenty-five different types of knot,' Master Lettuce said, a little defensively.

'And I can wet me breeches and not even notice, boy. Don't make it something to brag about,' Master Cabernatoll said dismissively.

Master Lettuce flushed with colour, which made him look like a sunburnt newt. 'Well, I...I think they're fun,' he stammered.

Master Cabernatoll raised a bushy eyebrow. 'Oh yes? And what other fun things have you been teaching these kids, might I ask?'

'Well, there are the knots, of course, and we've done some rather entertaining bird calls. Oh, and how to build a proper fire!'

'Well, that's something, at least,' Master Cabernatoll conceded.

'Yeah, but you never let us actually light the fires,' Oatey complained.

'Well, fire can be extremely dangerous, young man. The point is to know *how* to build one, for emergencies,' Master Lettuce said, beginning to sound slightly desperate.

Master Cabernatoll regarded the man quietly for a moment, as if looking at him properly for the first time.

'Master Lettuce, have these children ever even been into the Blackwood?' he asked, eventually.

Master Lettuce blanched. 'Oh my goodness, most certainly not! I shudder to think of the things that might go wrong.'

'By the time I saw my twelfth cycle, Master Lettuce, the Forestry Brigade had taught me how to hunt, kill 'n' gut a wild deer. I knew not jus' how to light a fire, but how to keep it goin' till dawn. I could forage for wild berries. I could kill a squirrel with a slingshot from a hundred feet away 'n' fashion its fur into a serviceable pair of winter pants. I knew how to avoid the green men. How to check for dangling terrors. I could *survive*, Master Lettuce, or at least have a fightin' chance at it. With what you've taught these young uns, I'd be surprised if they lasted a day in the Blackwood.'

'Well then, let us all thank Melethin they will never have cause to enter!' cried Master Lettuce, who seemed thoroughly appalled by the whole notion.

'You're never going to take us into the Blackwood?' said Beatrice, deeply disappointed.

'I simply can't think why anybody could imagine I would! Seems a thoroughly irresponsible thing to do!'

'You run the Forestry Brigade, man! Proud men and women of the trees stretching back hundreds of harvests!' Master Cabernatoll cried, going a little red in the face. 'You've a responsibility!'

Master Lettuce quailed under his indignant stare. 'I'm afraid things have rather moved on since your day, Master Cabernatoll. The focus of the organisation is now to teach boys and girls how to be modern, forward-thinking members of society. Good grandchildren of Melethin.'

At this, Master Cabernatoll visibly bristled. 'Oh yes? And what of Zigelder, might I ask?'

Even in the poor light Beatrice saw the colour leave the younger mans face.

'Wilfred!' he gasped. 'You know it is no longer considered proper to—'

'Proper? Not proper to mention the name of our father? Nonsense! This ridiculous new church has turned your head, boy! The men and women of the Forestry Brigade have always been taught the old ways. He is the Blackwood, therefore so are *we*!' Master Cabernatoll raged.

'Wilfred, this talk is blasphemous!' Master Lettuce pleaded, and Beatrice was shocked to see tears in the man's eyes.

'Keep it down, the pair of you! The last thing we need is to attract attention from outside,' snapped Corporal Snekchesser, who was keeping watch at the window.

'I'm so sorry, corporal, I assure you there will be no more blasphemous talk—' Lettuce began.

'You can discuss the approaching daemon himself, for all I care,' Snekchesser hissed, pointing at the night sky through the window. 'Just do it in whispers.'

Master lettuce looked suitably chastised, but Master Cabernatoll simply smirked. 'Daemon my right eye! That stars no more the great beast than I am.'

'How do you know?' Beatrice asked the old man.

'Well, it's been seen before, ain't it? The world didn't end then, so I see no reason to expect it will now.'

'Seen before? When? I haven't heard anyone say that.'

Cabernatoll shrugged, as if to say what she may, or may not, have heard was of no consequence to him. 'People have short memories,' the man said, glaring at Master Lettuce. 'but yeah, the stars appeared before. My grandfather told me 'bout it when I was jus' a boy, so it was a good long while ago now.'

'What is it then?' Oatey asked, eyes round.

Master Cabernatoll shrugged again. 'No idea. Don't think anyone knew then neither. But it ain't no daemon.'

Beatrice's mind whirled. This was new information. Wait till she told her father!

She was about to ask further questions when Corporal Snekchesser straightened up sharply and hissed, '*Quiet!* There's someone moving around out there.'

Silence fell.

Beatrice watched as the corporal stared out the window into the street without moving a muscle. Eventually, she grew impatient and slipped from the old chair to join him. The street outside was lit silver, the sky above reflected in the standing water so that the buildings appeared sandwiched between two star-strewn voids. The new star and its copy blazed brighter than the rest, like fat diamonds, but Beatrice did her best to ignore them. She could see surprisingly well, but it took a minute for her to spot what Corporal Snekchesser had seen. Directly opposite Master Cabernatol's house stood an old warehouse, or something similar, now apparently abandoned. There was no sign of light in its empty windows and a pile of leaves in front of the door showed it had not been opened in some time. A black figure was moving around in front of them, barely discernible in the building's shadow. Beatrice might have missed him completely—and the figure did seem to be a man in the way it moved—if it wasn't for the tiny ripples his feet left in the shallow water, which set the lower stars dancing. The figure bent down and was fiddling with something on the ground.

'What's he doing?' Beatrice whispered.

The corporal put his finger to his lips in way of answer, so Beatrice peered once again out into the gloom, squinting her eyes to see better. It didn't work, but as luck would have it, the man shifted slightly away from the warehouse, onto a patch of the uneven street that rose above the waterline, and suddenly he was illuminated in the starlight. He was not a large man, although it was hard to tell under the dark cloak he was wearing. He had a wide-brimmed hat pulled low over his face, so it was impossible to get a good look, although Beatrice thought she had caught just the quickest glimpse of a pointy beard. The figure was placing a small cylindrical object onto the waterlogged street. It glinted like metal and Beatrice tried to think where she had seen one before. The answer came in a flash; it was a portable brazier, like the Castle Guard sometimes used to brew spice during long shifts on the battlements. She saw a spark of orange light and heard the chip, chip, chip of a flint and steel, then, sure enough, before long there was a small red glow coming from the brazier. What was he doing? It seemed like a funny place to boil a kettle.

She watched, bemused, as the man fed small sticks and grass into the fire and the flames grew. She'd hoped the light would illuminate his face, but whenever he bent over it, down came the hat brim, obscuring her view.

Once the fire was to his satisfaction, the man sat back on his haunches and withdrew a small leather-looking bag from his coat pocket. Then, peering up and down the street, he poured something out of the bag into his cupped hand and tipped it quickly into the flames. The reaction was immediate; the man raised his hand to shield his face as the brazier gave off a blinding flash of green light. Beatrice had not been prepared and flinched as the after-burn flared in her eyes, her night vision ruined. Apparently Corporal Snekchesser had been caught equally off guard, as she felt his hands come up to his eyes beside her and heard him curse under his breath. There was no choice but to wait for their eyes to reacclimatise. By the time Beatrice could pick out the figure again, he was standing back against the warehouse doors and the brazier was trailing a thin plume of green smoke into the air. It rose above the buildings and dissipated into small curls in the night sky. The man didn't let it burn for long before he knelt back down and snuffed out the flames. Then he returned to his standing position and appeared to wait.

Beatrice was baffled. What in the Blackwood had that been all about?

It wasn't long before she got her answer.

There was a faint sound, like wind blowing through trees, then abruptly cut off, and suddenly a second man was standing in the street, just inches from the first. He appeared out of nowhere, making even the man in the wide-brimmed hat jump, who Beatrice heard swear, then say; 'Acorns and roots man, do you have to appear quite so close?'

'My apologies,' the second man said in a smooth and high voice. He was dressed in quite a peculiar getup. He had on some sort of short cape or cowl that was made from hundreds of small strips of material, and covering his face was a sort of wooden mask. Beatrice's blood chilled when she realised what he looked like. The mask was carved into the face of a green man; the traditional costume of the Lord of Misrule. This man was the murderer. He had to be.

Beatrice was barely aware of her gasp, but she felt Corporal Snekchesser's hand on her shoulder and stale, warm breath in her ear.

'Easy, my lady.'

She nodded silently, unable to let out a breath.

'It is done' the man in the mask said, and he held out a hand expectantly.

'So I hear, well done,' replied the man in the wide-brimmed hat. He handed over a bag of something that clinked gently. 'The church will be pleased.'

'The next target?'

A tiny roll of parchment changed hands and the masked man unfurled it and read. 'I approve,' he said after a moment. 'This man has done much that must be…corrected.'

The man in the wide-brimmed hat nodded. 'That was the view of the church as well.

'It will create quite the statement,' said the masked man in his cold, treble voice.

The other man gave a dry chuckle. 'Indeed it will, friend. Indeed it will. And the other matter?'

'We can take care of it together.'

'Good. Very good. But for now, we should not linger.'

'Yes,' said the masked man, and disappeared. He did it so suddenly, the other man gave a start of alarm.

'Good evening to you too,' he muttered, a little testily.

The man in the wide-brimmed hat took somewhat more time to disappear, but that's not to say he hung around. He quickly slipped away, pausing only to scoop up the brazier he had left cooling in the street, before he, too, melted into the darkness.

Eventually Beatrice allowed herself to breathe.

'That…that was the killer! It must have been!' she hissed, still reluctant to speak loudly, even though the street was now empty.

'I believe you are correct,' the corporal said, and he passed a hand wearily across his face.

'The killer! *Here!*' Master Lettuce trilled in horror. He had backed up against the far wall and clung to it like it might offer protection.

'It's alright, I believe the danger has passed,' Corporal

Snekchesser said.

'Thank Melethin!' the Master said weakly, slipping down the wall until his bottom touched the water, at which point he squawked and sprang back to his feet. He stood looking embarrassed and said, 'We must get her ladyship out of here!'

'No,' the Corporal disagreed. 'I will go out alone and see what I can learn. I believe the safest place for her ladyship right now is here.'

'But the villains were right outside!' Master Lettuce spluttered, his face pale.

'And now they are not. I see no reason they would return here, so I believe her ladyship to be safe. The real question is, why were they here at all? Simple coincidence?'

'Did you hear them?' Beatrice said. 'The Lord of Misrule, it... it wasn't just a murder, it was assassination! And they've got more planned! We have to tell father!'

'I heard. Which is why I must go. We need information. Then I will take you to your father. But only once I'm sure it is safe for you to travel the streets.'

The corporal did not wait for her to agree, instead making directly for the door.

'But what if they *do* come back? What am I supposed to do if her ladyship is attacked?' Master Lettuce said, looking desperate.

'Give your life in her protection!' Snekchesser snapped gruffly. When the master looked like he might faint, he added, 'Look, I won't be gone long. Lock and bar this door once I leave. Keep quiet and I'm sure there will not be a problem. If I thought attack likely, I would not leave.'

With that, he cracked open the door, peered carefully, first right, then left, and stepped out into the street. Beatrice watched as he trotted across the road and bent to examine the spot where the two men had conversed.

Beatrice saw movement in the deepest part of the shadows far too late.

Before she could shout a warning, an enormous figure leapt

at the corporal with an ear-splitting cry and knocked him from his feet. Beatrice was out the door before she even realised she was moving. Only vaguely aware of Master Lettuce yelling at her to come back, she raced across the flooded street to where the corporal and a large man were struggling, splashing about on the ground. She hadn't really planned what she'd do once she reached them, but as luck would have it, her body decided for her. Her foot shot out and caught the large figure with a slightly soggy crack under its bearded chin. The figure grunted in a deep, guttural voice and fell backwards, away from Corporal Snekchesser, who scrambled quickly to his feet, drawing his smallsword in one well practiced and fluid motion. He advanced on his stricken opponent, raising his arm to strike.

'Stop!' Beatrice yelled. She had just got a look at the bearded face of the attacker. 'Uncle Ducky? Is that you?'

The corporal paused, momentarily taken aback. '*Uncle Ducky?*'

As the words left his mouth, the sword in his hand exploded into a hale of tiny shards and he dropped the remnants with a yelp. His attacker surged back to his feet, but before he could reach the corporal Beatrice was between them.

'Stop, Uncle Ducky! Stop, both of you!'

The large wizard skidded to a halt, and Beatrice saw clearly that it really was Punduckslew. His long burgundy dress coat was dripping and covered in mud, but there was no mistaking the man. He was looking at her out of the corner of his eye, but he glowered at Corporal Snekchesser murderously.

'What is the meaning of this?' he boomed. 'Are you alright, my lady? Who is this man?'

'I'm fine, Uncle Ducky. This is Corporal Snekchesser, of the Castle Guard. He's been looking out for us.'

'Us? Whose us?'

'Me, Master Lettuce, Oatey and Master Cabernatol. He escorted us to safety!'

'Safety? In dark streets where murderers meet? Why here,

why not the castle? Speak man or I swear to Melethin *and* Zigelder, I'll pop your head like a pumpkin!'

Catching up with the change in circumstances, Corporal Snekchesser snapped to attention. 'Corporal Snekchesser reporting, sir!' he barked. 'Routes to the castle were cut off, sir. Without backup, I withdrew to a defensible position until more information was available, sir. This property belongs to Master Cabernatoll. If I might ask, sir, how did you find us?'

Punduckslew regarded the man gravely. 'Tracking is part of my job.' Brown water was dripping down into his beard.

'I think,' he said at length. 'We had all better have a little chat.'

CHAPTER FOUR: AXE OR COIN

1.

Beatrice and Corporal Snekchesser emerged into the old quarter's main square just as dawn was breaking. In the cold, grey light they could see a lonely wooden platform standing in the churned mass of mud and brown water that had once been the green.

'That's where it happened, isn't it?' Beatrice asked.

'I believe so,' the corporal replied, eyes sweeping the square and its buildings. That was something she'd begun to notice about the man; his eyes were never still. Even when he was talking to you, they never rested on your face, but darted here, there, and everywhere. In another man, it might have appeared furtive, but Beatrice found it oddly comforting in the corporal. It was like having your very own guard dog.

'That poor man,' she said.

'Indeed, my lady. This way.'

He led her around the square, which was more or less deserted, and towards a grand looking building.

Punduckslew had left them in the middle of the night. The wizard agreed that the safest place for Beatrice was to stay put in the cottage with the corporal and the masters. He'd do some investigating, he told them, after he'd spoken to the duke, then send word where to meet.

The message had come an hour before the dawn in the form of a very confused private. As the killer had not been caught, she reported, an emergency session of parliament had been called for that very morning. They were to meet Punduckslew and the duke there.

'Are you sure this is where my father is? He usually does his best to avoid parliamentary sessions.'

'He's here,' the corporal said. 'They've called an emergency session. The duke's presence will have been demanded. This is the Lord's Chambers, where they do such things.' He indicated the building in front of them with a sweep of his hands. It was, of course, a wooden affair, with large windows on the upper floor and an unnecessarily massive arched doorway. It must have been twenty-foot tall and was carved with a pattern of overlapping oak leaves, so if you looked at it too hard, it gave the impression of a storm of falling foliage. A smaller, more normal-sized door had been cut out of the wood and Corporal Snekchesser rapped on it sharply with his knuckles, three times.

'I know what the Lord's Chambers are. I'm not a little kid,' Beatrice said irritably.

Snekchesser looked at her then, his eyes meeting hers with an unreadable expression. 'Of course, my lady,' was all he said before looking away.

The small door was opened by a castle guard with a pox-marked face and a single, black eyebrow that rose up his forehead in surprise as he took the two of them in.

'C…Corporal Snekchesser?' he stammered.

'Private Snelks, isn't it?'

'Yes, sir.'

'Well, private, how about letting us in? There's a good chap.'

'I…is that…?'

'If it is, you had better not leave her standing in the street, had you private?'

'Er…n…no, sir. Sorry, sir! Come in, sir, and…er…my lady.'

The private shuffled hurriedly back and Corporal Snekchesser motioned for Beatrice to go first, so she stepped over the threshold into some kind of lobby. Despite her claim of knowing all about the Lord's Chambers, she had never actually been inside before. The lobby was not particularly impressive, but it contained a roaring fire, which Beatrice approached gratefully. There was a large painting on one wall, which appeared to be a portrait of a past duke; she could tell by the enormous set of crossed axes moulded into the gilt frame. It was the Stonemorton family crest. He was quite a handsome man, with a strong chin and a long moustache, waxed into points. A plaque below the painting read; "His Grace, Cuthblington Stonemorton, the twenty-first Duke of Blackwood, and founder of these great chambers."

Beatrice tried to remember her family history. If she was right, the twenty-first Duke of Blackwood was something of a family embarrassment. Or hero, it really depended on who you asked. He was the duke responsible for giving up total power and forming the chamber of lords, which was the single most reprehensible, or revolutionary, act performed by a duke. Again, it depended on who you spoke to.

He certainly looked very pleased with himself in the picture.

Corporal Snekchesser followed her inside and pulled the door shut behind him, rubbing his hands together to warm them.

'Where's the duke?'

'He's on the Tongue, sir. The session is underway. Would you like to wait for his grace in—'

'No. Show us into the chambers.'

Private Snelk looked pained. 'B...but, sir, it's against protocol to—'

'That's an order, private!'

'Of course, sir. Follow me, sir...my lady.'

Beatrice left the fireplace reluctantly and followed the two men through an important-looking door. There were raised voices on the other side.

Directly down the centre of the Lord's Chambers ran a long, thin stone plinth. It rose about six feet off the wooden floor and dominated the room, not simply because of its size, but also because it was the sole object in the entire building not to be made from wood. It was known as the Toad's Tongue. That's not to say it looked like a toad, or indeed any part of one's mouth. It was named simply for its link to the castle. There were no fancy carvings, no amphibian motif. The tongue was perfectly plain, apart from on its uppermost surface where the smooth stone was marred by hundreds of irregular chips and gouges. Beatrice gazed in awe, for the Tongue had a bloody reputation. It was said that it fed on noble blood. High above the plinth ran an observation gallery, on the walls of which, Beatrice had been told, were kept the many, many leather-bound volumes of parliamentary proceedings. They numbered in their hundreds and contained transcripts of each parliamentary session, running back to the very first, as called by the twenty-first Duke of Blackwood himself. In their yellowed pages could be found, if one felt so inclined to look, the names of the three hundred and ninety-nine lords or ladies who had lost their lives to the Toad's Tongue.

An explanation is perhaps required.

The Duchy of Blackwood held a proud tradition amongst its lords and ladies of efficient conflict resolution, and for around the first five hundred years of parliament, the most efficient resolution to conflict was thought to be a sharp axe to the head. Hence the Tongue, whose primary purpose was to provide a place for political discourse, but whose pitted surface had been created by the many axe strikes to miss their mark over the generations.

It had always been axes. The Stonemorton weapon of choice. Times move on, of course, and eventually it was suggested that this method of solving political problems may no longer be appropriate for a modern, civilised society. This was suggested by a young, ideological count by the name of Sir Frince. The parliamentary transcript for that session lists Sir Frince as the three hundred and fifty-sixth life to be claimed by the Tongue. That very afternoon, in fact. But some ideas, once spoken aloud, prove impossible to eradicate, with even the sharpest of blades, and eventually the Frince Act was passed.

The Frince Act did not forbid the killing of one's political rivals on the Tongue, for to do so would have meant unravelling the whole constitution of law the duchy was built upon, in which the right to kill one's enemies featured heavily. It instead made it illegal to bring weapons into the Lord's Chamber. The number of deaths fell, but as was soon proved, the truly determined required nothing more than their own hands to end the life of a rival. However, as the harvests passed, the deaths dwindled. It had all become a rather energetic and undignified spectacle. It had been over sixty harvests now since any life had been ended in the Lords Chambers, with the unfortunate exception of old Sir Henry Houndslowe, whose stomach exploded one evening as he sat in his gallery chair. His death was eventually recorded as the result of a lifetime eating somewhat more than he should, rather than any form of foul play.

Bearing all this in mind, perhaps you can imagine why Beatrice Stonemorton felt less than happy to see her father perched upon a small stool at one end of the Toad's Tongue, with the lords and ladies of parliament glaring down upon him from the galleries like a cast of hawks. Standing opposite her father was a lady in a deep-purple gown. Her stomacher, the decorative fabric showing in the front gap of her gown, had a pattern of silver birds that were heavy on the beaks and talons. A chained fairy with violet wings tugged hopelessly at a chain from the woman's collar. The woman possessed a pair of exceedingly thin lips and a set of long, bony fingers that curled and uncurled, it seemed, unconsciously. They gave Beatrice the distinct impression they were eager to wrap around someone's neck. The woman spoke out of the side of her mouth, as if afraid that, were she to open it fully, her teeth might escape.

'What I should like to know is precisely what his grace proposes to do about it?' she was saying.

Beatrice's father sat hunched in on himself, arms folded across his chest, every inch of his body language telling Beatrice, and presumably the rest of the room, that he would rather be anywhere else than there.

'Catching a murderer is surely a job for the City Watch, Lady

Simper,' the duke said, and Beatrice knew immediately it had been the wrong thing to say when a small smile crept onto the woman in purple's face. Lady Simper raised her head to address the people in the galleries.

'The brave men and women of the Watch are indeed the people best placed to deal with this crisis. But the incompetence of the castle's rule manacles their hands. This killer would already be caught, indeed I expect the murder would never have taken place, if the Watch were not hampered with the responsibility of keeping the Blackwood from our doors! Every single day, precious resources and personnel are consumed because of the castle's failure to deal with the Quickening.'

Knowing her father as she did, Beatrice could tell from his expression that he thought it a ridiculous argument. Beatrice was inclined to agree. She'd read all she could find about the Quickening, because the idea of it fascinated her. Resources were indeed stretched thin, but the idea that her father was somehow personally responsible for an ongoing natural disaster that had plagued the entire kingdom for over a hundred harvests was ludicrous. It seemed not everyone saw it the same way, however, as Lady Simper received a chorus of approving sounds from many in the gallery above.

Corporal Snekchesser used the hubbub as an opportunity to quietly close the door, leaving the private on the other side, and motioned for Beatrice to follow him. They skirted around the edge of the room, keeping to the shadows as much as possible until they were standing just a few paces away from her father. The duke, however, appeared not to notice their approach. Indeed, from this distance Beatrice could clearly see the worry and the strain on her father's face. She knew he would be hating this.

'As I'm sure this chamber is aware, sanctions imposed by this very chamber have extremely weakened the castle's power to deal with the Quickening. With funding re-routed from the Castle Blackwood Guard to the City Watch, inevitably, much of the strain falls on them,' he said.

Lady Simper threw her arms wide and looked around the room as if the duke had made her point for her.

'You see how the castle tries to shift the blame for their failure to act on to the common people?' she said. There were jeers and stamping of feet.

Beatrice glanced up at the lords and ladies of the house. She didn't see any common people. People like Oatey, who would cheerfully admit to being as common as they came. What she did see, she thought bitterly, was a bunch of spoiled rich people.

There were no political parties in Upton-Myzzle. They were illegal. Many of Beatrice's ancestors had been to great and, somewhat bloody, lengths to make sure of this. Beatrice had read all about it.

She was herself unsure of how she felt on the subject. She certainly thought some things the previous duchesses and dukes had done were ghastly. Of course, the reality was that the parties were inevitable. Get enough people together in one room and they will soon split themselves into factions, almost unconsciously. Of the political parties that Upton-Myzzle did not have, the Golden Coins were one of the largest. Beatrice hated them. Whilst not an official organisation, and therefore breaking no law, the Golden Coins counted amongst its members a great many of the town's most important figures. Many of them were present in the Lord's Chambers that day, identifiable by pins in the shape of golden coins worn somewhere about their person. Lady Simper had hers proudly displayed on a sash across her chest. Such blatant rallying against the castle would have, in the past, resulted in a significant culling of the upper classes. But those days were gone.

'I feel we are getting off-topic,' the duke said, and Beatrice did her best not to notice the falter in his voice. 'This emergency session was called to discuss the troubling murder committed last night. My honourable friends, we must address the appearance of this apparent Talent user, and decide what actions we must take to bring him to justice for the killing of Mr Scroggan Pewplow.'

'Ask the wizards, he was obviously one of them!' someone shouted.

'How dare you!' cried another voice, and an elderly man with a neat grey beard shot to his feet in the gallery. He was wearing a long green dress-coat covered in copper patterns of moons and stars. 'I can assure you all, in my position as grand wizard, that the killer was most certainly not a member of the Wizards Charter. We have no registration for a wizard with the type of Talent he displayed.'

So that's the leader of the wizards, Beatrice thought. The man who's afraid of Uncle Ducky.

'Grand Wizard Pike,' Lady Simper addressed the man, getting in quick before the duke could reply. 'Are you saying that there are no recorded wizards with the ability to teleport themselves?'

The man named Pike still looked enraged at the accusation leveled at his organisation's door. 'That is what I just said, is it not?' he snapped. 'Naturally, I checked our records last night and there has only ever been one wizard who displayed the Talent described, and he died over one hundred and fifty harvests ago.'

'Necromancy!' someone screamed, and there was an outbreak of voices all speaking at once so that the grand wizard had to shout to make himself heard again.

'Do not be bloody absurd! I merely mentioned the fact to prove that this killer, whomever he may be, is not a registered wizard. Do not waste these chambers' time with talk of fantasy and horror stories.'

'So we are indeed dealing with a rogue,' Lady Simper continued. 'Tell me, your grace, how does the castle respond to the news that it has allowed rogue wizards to roam our streets, resulting in the death of an innocent citizen?'

Beatrice rolled her eyes. No wonder the lords never seemed

to get anything done. They spent their whole time trying to blame her father for everything. She just wished he was better at defending himself against them.

'The castle shall work closely with the Wizards Charter to discover how this could have happened—' the duke began, before the grand wizard abruptly cut him off.

'Will you indeed? Well, I can assure his grace that the Wizard's Charter is not at all inclined to allow the failings of the castle to tarnish its good name!'

Beatrice's heart sank as she picked out the golden disk on the wizard's lapel. If the Wizards Charter had joined the Coins, it would mean more trouble for her father.

Pike continued, 'As this chamber is aware, I have personally appealed to the castle several times previously for a strengthening of the laws regarding unregistered Talents. Perhaps if my words had been heeded, we would not be standing here now.'

The chambers erupted into another cacophony of raised voices. Pike was still standing, looking around importantly at the other lords and ladies, when, on the opposite side of the gallery, another man stood, calling for quiet. It was Punduckslew, whose presence created an almost immediate hush from the rest of the room.

'I should like to make it clear to this chamber that the views of Grand Wizard Pike do not reflect that of the whole Wizards Charter,' he exclaimed, his voice echoing around the room. 'A significant number of us, the majority in fact, feel that the current laws provide the best balance of freedom and control over the magical Talents in the Duchy's population.'

The grand wizard's face turned a deep crimson red, but he did not argue with his fellow wizard. He instead retook his seat in enraged silence. Punduckslew stared down at the rest of the chamber, daring anyone else to disagree with him. Beatrice saw him meet her father's eyes and give the duke a small nod. She felt a rush of affection for the burly wizard. At least her father had someone in his corner.

Corporal Snekchesser chose this moment of quiet to clear his throat loudly and a hundred heads turned in their direction. The chambers were suddenly full of the hiss of whispered conversations as the lords and ladies spotted the duchess-to-be standing in the shadows. Beatrice saw the relief on her father's face when he saw her.

'Ten-minute recess!' he shouted, not waiting for a response before climbing down from the Tongue and hurrying over to them.

'Beatrice!' he said, pulling her into a hug. 'Thank Melethin, I've been so worried!'

'It's ok, father. Really, I'm fine,' she said, trying to extract herself from his arms.

'It most certainly is *not* fine! This should never have happened to you! I was careless. I put you in harm's way and if something had befallen you, then…then I would never forgive myself!' her father continued, hugging all the harder.

'But nothing did happen to me, father, and what's more, we have important information about the killer!'

Her father nodded quickly. 'Yes, Punduckslew filled me in, but I should like to hear it from you as well.'

'We saw—' Beatrice began excitedly. But she never got to finish the sentence.

The door through which Beatrice and the corporal had entered the Lord's Chambers opened again, but this time it slammed back against the wall with a bang that damn near sent plaster floating down from the ceiling like snow. Through it strode a man who was clearly used to striding. He did so with an effortless grace and gusto that told anyone watching, yes, he was striding, and, yes, he would bloody well continue to do so until he felt compelled to stop. What anyone else thought about the matter was not his concern, and therefore irrelevant. He was a tall man, with immaculately styled blonde hair, chiseled features and piercing grey eyes. His frame was well-muscled, and his blue breeches and dress-coat cut a striking silhouette. He exuded a presence in to the room that made Beatrice feel pressed up against the wall, though he was nowhere near her.

'Who is that?' she asked.

'Sir Erasmus Sweetspire,' replied her father, who visibly crumpled at the sight of the man.

Beatrice had heard the name. The man wore no coin, but he didn't have to; coins were the Sweetspire family crest.

The Sweetspire line was said to be an offshoot from the Stonemorton family, going back generations. They were also responsible for the great rebellion and had been at open political warfare with her family ever since. She watched as the lord climbed up onto the Tongue. Lady Simper practically fell over herself in her haste to vacate the platform to make room for him.

'I'm sorry, Beatrice, we will have to finish this discussion later. Corporal, I want my daughter escorted back to the castle with all speed. Take whatever men you need,' her father said. He had gone slightly green.

'Of course, your grace,' Snekchesser replied.

'But father I—' Beatrice began. But Lord Sweetspire was already talking.

'Lords and Ladies of the Chambers. I stand before you on a dark day for the great Duchy of the Blackwood. A dark day indeed. For we are under attack!' The man spoke loudly and with confidence, striding up and down the tongue as if he belonged there. 'Precious blood of our citizenry has been spilt, and what's worse, one of our own did the act. Inside these very town walls. Fear! That is the goal of the dark forces that move against our great nation! They aim to terrorise us! To bend us to their will, and in so doing, destroy us!' Sweetspire paused to let his words sink in. He stood with his hands on his hips and stared up at the full galleries, where silence rained. He had their complete attention.

'How do I know this?' the man continued. 'Well, in the castle's failure to provide answers, I have been forced to employ my own resources in search of the truth. My men have learned much. Many of you will be aware of the seditious remarks made last night in public by a minor lord by the name of Sir Angston Krickwell. This man speaks out against the Church of the First Tree. Against Melethin. He stands in contrast to the values and beliefs upheld by the good citizenry of Upton-Myzzle and the noble men and women of these very chambers! He and his kind, and mark my words, this man does not operate alone, would see us return to an age of superstition and dark ritual. They would see us turn our back on the light of Melethin!'

The man paused again, and this time there were gasps of outrage and astonishment above him. Then there came the scraping sound of boots on stone and Beatrice's father appeared back on the tongue.

'Lord Sweetspire, just a moment, if you please! These are wild and dangerous accusations.'

'The Church of the Cracked Acorn!' Lord Sweetspire proclaimed, all but ignoring the duke, who faltered and lapsed into silence. 'That is the name my men were able to learn. That is the name of the organisation working against us, buried deep in this great town like a wriggling parasite! And this Sir Krickwell, this man who claims to speak of religious freedoms and truth, is the very man who set upon us the killer known as the Lord of Misrule!'

'That is a very serious accusation!' the duke cried, attempting to make himself heard over the din of outraged voices.

'It is very serious indeed!' agreed Lord Sweetspire, looking at his opponent for the first time.

'And what proof do you have of these things, which you speak of as if they were fact?'

'Proof?' Sweetspire turned his head to the galleries once more. 'The castle asks me for proof because it has none of its own to share. Tell me, lords and ladies, when did it become the responsibility of a humble lord, such as myself, to do the castle's work for it?'

There was a swell of agreement from the galleries.

'As it happens, I *do* have proof, but to whom should that proof be handed over? To the City Watch? No doubt Commander Posternos would do his due diligence, but at what cost? Every man it takes to bring this group of radicals to justice is a tree left un-felled, another house, another street lost to the Blackwood!'

A hundred voices were speaking at once now. It seemed everyone had an opinion and wanted their neighbours to know what it was. It was hard for Beatrice to make out what any single person was saying in the wall of sound that came from the galleries, but the odd word stood out, bouncing off the vaulted chamber's ceiling and spraying down to her position on the ground floor like shot;

Sacrilege!

Incompetence!

Outrage!

Disgrace!

Beatrice watched her father, standing small and alone before this great wave of discontent. She watched his face as he reached a decision.

'You can share your evidence with me!' he shouted. 'And I shall get to the bottom of this!'

The voices died away. People stared. And for the first time since she had arrived in the Chambers, Beatrice thought her father truly had the room's attention.

'You, your grace? Personally?' said Sweetspire, and his eyes were like a crossbow bolt at the duke.

'Er…yes. If no one else is able, or willing, to get to the bottom of all this…then I will!'

Her father's words echoed around the silent chambers, but Beatrice was watching Lord Sweetspire. It was hard to see, and no doubt most would have missed it, but he was smiling.

Which was when Beatrice realised her father had just given the man exactly what he wanted.

2.

'You're a bloody fool! *A bloody, bloody fool*! What were you thinking? Dukes don't solve crimes! Lead armies? Yes! Catch killers? No! Acorns and roots, boy, it's like you haven't learnt a damn thing from me in all these years!'

If Wigbert and been in any doubt about his father's reaction to the events of that morning, the old man was doing a fine job of putting him straight.

'With respect, father, you weren't there, I—'

'More's the pity! If I had been, I could have shut down this madness. You obviously let them walk all over you…again.'

The old duke was wearing his finest dress-coat; gold with white lace. He inexplicably had an egg stain on his neck-cloth and had obviously missed a spot when shaving. Wigbert was trying to decide whether he should point it out.

They were in the great hall for the Shortest Day feast, a tradition that stretched back almost as long as parliament itself. The usually cold room was glowing golden with lanterns and a roaring fire especially for the occasion, and someone, the duke suspected Tanco, had gone to the effort of draping greenery about the place in great swathes. It would have all seemed quite jolly, if not for the company.

For the second time that day, Wigbert found himself confined in a small space with all the lords and ladies of parliament. It was hardly his idea of a party. Actually, that is not true. It was exactly his idea of a party, which went a long way to explaining why he usually did his level best to avoid such affairs. Unfortunately, the Shortest Day feast was just another in a long line of duties that Wigbert, as duke, was forced to endure. He and his father had secreted themselves in a window bay, away from the throng of richly dressed nobles and the thunk of expensive perfume, which seemed to hang above the proceedings like a cloud. Wigbert was glad of the modicum of privacy, but he knew if truth be told that many of their guests would scarcely have noticed if they were there at all. Until the alcohol stopped flowing, that was. Such was the Stonemorton's current unpopularity. Even lords who were not Coins members did not go out of their way to foster ties with the ruling family.

'Yes...I should have been there,' Wigbert's father muttered. 'There'll be a coup before the primroses flower at this rate!'

Anger stirred in Wigberts breast. 'If you recall, father, the lords forced you to abdicate in my favour. I didn't ask for this! Perhaps if you had been as sharp a political operative as you seem to think you are, then we wouldn't be in this mess!'

He saw the words fall on his father like a physical blow and immediately regretted them. The old man turned and hobbled away without another word, leaving the duke alone in the bay. He watched his father go, his cane tap-tapping on the hard flagstones as he went. The lords and ladies all but ignored him. It was a harsh thing, old age, he thought. It slowly stripped a person of what they were, until eventually, there was nothing left at all. The truth was, even now, he would much rather see his father as duke than hold the position himself. He wasn't cut out for it. Deep down he knew this, which made it hard to disagree with the Coins when they called him out as inadequate. Because they were right.

And now he had agreed to find a killer. Something he had no idea how to do. He supposed he would have to talk to the Castle Guard. He was going to have to do that anyway, of course, he remembered with another surge of anger. General Weltsmatter had to be dealt with. He had let things slip too far; he knew that. Really, the current situation with the guard was as much his fault as anyone else's. This was the problem with being the duke; there were too many things to deal with at once. Concentrate on one thing and a dozen others fell apart behind your back.

Wigbert looked across the room at the men and women in their finery, clustered in groups, drinks in hands, talking... always talking. Right now there were probably around five conversations going on that were about things he ought to be thinking about, and at least two plots being forged against him.

A stab of pain pierced the base of his skull, and his ears filled with an insistent buzzing. He massaged a temple. He was getting one of his headaches again. Pills, he remembered. He needed to make sure Tanco had reordered his pills. Downing his drink, he left the empty glass on the windowsill and made for the door. He'd had quite enough company for one day.

Outside, the afternoon light was already taking on a distinct grey quality. It would be gone all too soon. The inner ward was a hive of activity, with servants trying to keep up with the demands of the feast. A few paused to bow to the duke as he passed, but most ignored him. Technically speaking, he should not have been wondering the castle unaccompanied, but the staff had grown accustomed to his ways.

Wigbert didn't make it far before his steward appeared at his side with a clatter of wooden tokens.

'A moment of your time, your grace?'

'Do I have a choice?' Wigbert asked, absently. He was still trying to block out the buzzing in his head.

Tanco pretended not to hear and continued smoothy, 'May I introduce Corporal Ambrosia Tritewine, from the Institute of Propositional Logic, your grace.'

There was a polite silence.

'You asked for a consult about the new star, your grace,' Tanco prodded.

'Ah. Yes...of course. Quite right. The star. Yes. How nice of you to come, Corporal...Tripewind, was it?'

A small female figure was pushed before him. 'Um... Tritewine, your grace. A pleasure to make your acquaintance.'

Wigbert stared. It was hard not to. The woman before him wore a scarlet gown over, not the usual skirts, but a pair of black breeches and matching stockings. On her feet were the most sturdy looking boots the duke had ever seen and wrapped about her shoulders was a weathered leather cape. Her hands were covered by fingerless woolen gloves and, perhaps most strangely of all, on her head rested a black felt hat, tied under her chin with lace and accommodating a number of empty glass vials tucked into the band.

'Um... nice boots,' the duke managed. 'My daughter would approve.'

Corporal Tritewine blushed. 'Sorry, I didn't have time to change them. It's the flooding you see...' she trailed off, looking mortified.

'Not at all Miss Tritewipe, er Titedine.'

'Tritewine, your grace. Corporal Tritewine.'

'Of course. Please excuse me...it's been a long day. I didn't know the Institute of Propositional Logic had corporals.'

'They don't, your grace,' Tanco cut in. 'Sorry, I should have explained. Ambrosia is also a member of the Castle Guard.'

Wigbert starred at her unusual clothes.

The woman looked embarrassed. 'Um...like I say, I—'

'Didn't have time to change. Quite alright. Would you perhaps like a drink of some kind? I think there may still be a little of something left somewhere...' Wigbert mumbled.

The corporal smiled weakly. 'Oh no, I'm fine, thank you, your grace. I don't drink.'

'Right. Right.'

There was an awkward silence whilst Wigbert cast around for something else to say.

'Did I say nice boots?' he managed desperately.

'The star, your grace,' Tanco provided tactfully.

'Ah. Yes, of course. The star. Yes. It is a star, is it?'

'Actually, the institute thinks not, your grace.'

'Good grief! You don't mean to say they think it's …'

'A space daemon? Um, no, your grace. Actually, we think it's a comet,' said Corporal Tritewine excitedly.

Wigbert tried for a smile. 'Well, I must say that's a bit of a relief. Well, well. A comet, aye? Well, er, as they say, well… Um…what, exactly, is a comet?'

The corporal's face lit up. 'Oh, it's very exciting, your grace! A comet, you see, is some sort of interstellar object moving through space. Or rather, a celestial body, completely unrelated to our own planet, traveling independently through the cosmos!'

'My word…is it, really?'

'The fascinating thing is, usually they disappear really quickly. In fact, most aren't even visible to the naked eye,' the corporal-cum-natural philosopher continued.

'Naked-eye?' Wigbert said desperately.

The woman did not appear to hear him. 'But this one, oh this one, is a different matter entirely. It's so much brighter! And its tail, well, it's so much bigger! We're calling it a Great-comet, your grace. It really is the most wonderful learning opportunity.'

'Um…it has a tail?'

'Oh yes, your grace.'

'But it's definitely *not* a daemon?'

'No.'

'Oh. Good. Good.'

'Not just good, your grace, revolutionary!'

'Really? That good, aye?' The duke was sweating. Revolutionary was not a word his family liked to hear at the best of times.

'Perhaps you would like to see it, your grace?'

'Oh, I've seen it, Corporal Typemine. I think the whole town has!'

'Tritewine, your grace. I mean with the proper equipment. Through our telescope.'

This the duke had heard of. There had been some kind of

memo. Someone, the duke forgot who, had suggested it might have useful military applications. Wigbert hadn't paid it much attention at the time, being rather of the opinion that a couple hundred more soldiers would have far more useful military applications, and since the castle couldn't afford those, he was not about to authorise the purchase of some doohickey that cost twice as much.

'Ah yes,' he said. 'the seeing-eye glass thingummy.'

'It's a concave eyepiece, aligned with another convex objective lens, allowing for magnification of an object up to five times, your grace,' Corporal Tritewine replied enthusiastically.

'Yes. Yes. Well, I must admit that sounds very interesting, however—' he began, but faltered into silence as a burst of braying laughter drifted down to the ward from the keep. The party was still in full swing, it seemed.

'How about now?' Wigbert said, gripped by a sudden and powerful urge to be elsewhere.

'I'm sorry, your grace?' Corporal Tritewine said, taken aback.

'I'd like to see it now. It will be dark soon, after all.'

'The lords and ladies, your grace, they will expect your presence—' Tanco began urgently.

'Well, let them expect away,' Wigbert said. 'Besides, I doubt they'll even notice I'm gone.'

'Never-the-less, your grace, I have several important matters awaiting your attention, and young Beatrice would like-'

'They can wait, Mr Dribbets. I shan't be long, and I'm sure you'll agree that a positive answer to the nature of this star...er, comet, will be of great comfort to the people of Upton-Myzzle.'

'The institute would, of course, welcome your visit, your grace,' Corporal Tritewine said hesitantly.

'Would they?' said Wigbert. 'How very unusual.'

Tanco gave in. 'As you say, your grace,' he said with a sigh. 'At least allow me to call for the royal carriage. We can't have you walking the streets unprotected.'

'Twice in one week? Are you sure the stables will cope with

the demand?'

'Very droll, your grace. If you will, please excuse me.'

The man hurried away and left the duke feeling slightly guilty. He was being difficult, he knew. But by the First Tree, he was *duke*. If he couldn't order people around occasionally, what was the point?

'Are you sure you don't mind missing the party, your grace?' said Corporal Tritewine nervously.

'Believe me Miss Tigervine,' Wigbert said. 'you'll be doing me a favour.'

'It's Tritewine, your grace.'

'Ah, yes. Quite. Quite. Sorry.'

3.

Sir Angston Krickwell was really quite angry indeed. In fact, he was bloody livid. Unfortunately, no matter how much he shouted, no one seemed to care. He lay in his cell, in the dark, somewhere deep beneath the watch-house building and was cold, wet, and had a painful lump on the side of his head the size of a pickled egg. Technically, it was the size of any egg, but Sir Krickwell was also very hungry and pickled eggs were his favourite snack. As such, they kept coming, unbidden, to the surface of his mind.

He was starting to think he had been abandoned.

Which is why he was relieved to suddenly find a short man with a pointy beard and a wide-brimmed hat peering in at him through the bars.

'It's about bloody time!' he said. 'I assume you're here to see to my release? I'm a lord, you know!'

'The sun sets on under-proven bread,' said the man.

This took Sir Krickwell by surprise. 'Do I know you?' he asked, squinting at the man in the darkness.

The man said nothing, but raised an eyebrow quizzically.

Sir Krickwell bristled. 'Yes, yes. The sun rises on plans of wood, alright? Do you know who I am?'

'The church can't be too careful,' said the man.

'I wrote the bloody passwords!' hissed Krickwell. 'I *am* the Church of the Cracked acorn!'

'Never-the-less.'

'I don't recognise you. Who recruited you?' asked Krickwell suspiciously.

'We can discuss that later, my lord, but right now, we must hurry. Arrangements have been made, but time is short.'

'I don't understand. Am I being released?'

'In a manner of speaking, my lord, yes.'

'Give it to me straight, man!'

'This is a breakout, my lord.'

'What? You mean...you mean they were planning on keeping me in here?'

'Oh no, my lord. They were planning on executing you.'

'But I'm a lord!'

'This was, apparently, taken into consideration, my lord.'

'Well, bugger this for a game of soldiers! Let's get out of here.'

'Quite so, my lord. If you would be so kind as to stand back?'

'What? Wh—'

The explosion left a hole in the ceiling wide enough to get a cart through. Debris was scattered everywhere, and a stray beam impaled one unlucky watchman. However, once the dust had settled, and the confusion cleared, there was a fresh problem. For, although the damage was extensive, it was limited to the internal parts of the watch-house only. In other words, any escape attempt would have had to be made right through the heart of the building, and perhaps more importantly, right through the heart of forty members of the evening shift. It would have been impossible for anyone to have got out unseen.

It was as if Sir Krickwell had simply vanished.

CHAPTER FIVE: ATTACK IN THE NIGHT

1.

For Ormus Stonemorton, there were precious few benefits to no longer being the duke. Therefore, he treasured those he could find all the more and at the top of that short list was The Green Man's Eyes.

It was not the most popular public house in town; being removed from the central hustle and bustle, down a small side street towards the farmlands to the west. However, it enjoyed the patronage of a select number of Upton-Myzzle's more well-to-do clientele. The landlord, a large, mustachioed man by the name of Aldergate, was the son of a second-rate blacksmith and had been more surprised than anyone at this fortunate turn of events. He eventually deduced the reason for the pub's sudden spike in sales was due to the nearby presence of one Miss Mille Scunthorpe. She was the buxom young daughter of a farmer who lived just two fields and a hedge hop away. Miss Mille was a girl of certain appetites, which various members of the town's gentry were only too happy to satisfy. The Green Man's Eyes was simply a convenient stopping off point, and somewhere to wait out the farmer's dogs.

To his credit, Mr Aldergate had capitalised on the situation splendidly, in the admirable tradition of the true entrepreneur. First, he hired a man to sit on the door and keep out undesirables. Then he'd got in a better class of alcohol, stuff you might actually drink for the taste, rather than simply suffer through for the result. He'd hired a new cook. One that made reductions, not gravy, and drizzled it, rather than dolloped. Finally, he'd cleaned. The accumulated filth of decades, along with families of spiders who could trace their ancestry to back before the Quickening, were ushered away. The small common room with its sturdy wooden tables and smooth tiled floor positively gleamed in the light of the fire and the lanterns (new, of course, with wicks so well trimmed the flames burnt with barely a flicker).

Miss Mille Scunthrope's youthful beauty had long ago faded, but The Green Man's Eyes had continued to flourish.

To Ormus, the public house had been a pleasure denied for far too many harvests. It had not been deemed *suitable* for him to visit as duke. Now it seemed no one cared what he got up to. When he'd first found himself a duke-no-more, he'd thought of paying Miss Scunthorpe a visit, but the hedge had defeated him. He'd hobbled back across the fields in defeat and sat in the common room with a glass of moglin mash, massaging his aching knees and reflecting on the passage of time. He'd bumped into Mille Scunthorpe some weeks later and realised he'd had a lucky escape. Time can be cruel.

'Hows young Wigbert these days?' asked one of the three aging gentlemen seated at Ormus's table, disturbing the duke-no-more's reverie. He eyed the man heavily.

'I assume you mean His Grace, the Duke of Blackwood, Gerald?' Ormus rebuked.

'That's the fellow, yes,' said Gerald, unapologetic.

'He's fine.'

'It's funny to think of little Wiggy as the duke, isn't it? Seems only yesterday he was suckling at his mother's teat,' said a second man, scratching his stubbly chin thoughtfully.

'Teat!' exploded the third and final member of Ormus's company, an ancient-looking man with a head like a boiled egg and a ragged grey beard.

'Yes, yes, very good, Terrence old chap,' said Gerald, patting the old man on the arm and wiping a little spittle from his mouth with a serviette. 'Honestly, Quinby! You can't go around saying things like that. You *know* what he's like, he gets all excited.'

'Sorry. Wasn't thinking.'

'Well, why start now, I suppose.'

'There's no need for—'

'Oh, do shut up!' barked Ormus irritably.

The two men fell silent. Terrence continued to gurgle happily, his white eyes staring at something only he could see.

'I'm worried if you want the truth,' Ormus said at length. 'Things at the castle have not been going well. Wigbert he…he tries. But our enemies, they move against us. The boy, he just… he's got no…why can't he…' he trailed off.

'Boys these days. They've got no balls. My son's the same. Lets that wife of his boss him around something fierce,' Gerald supplied, downing the last of his ale and smacking his lips enthusiastically. He had been a large, powerful man. But age had robbed him of most of his muscles. His face had turned red in recent harvests.

Ormus mused on the man's words. The trouble was, Wigbert was now far from being a boy. How old was he now? Must be nearly forty harvests.

'Well, my Wendel is doing very well,' said Quinby with pride.' He has a thriving set of businesses.'

Quinby had never been an attractive man, but age had not improved matters. His nose and ears seemed to have continued to grow, even as the rest of the man shrank, and they now took up far larger a proportion of his face than was strictly usual.

'Now there's proof the world's gone mad if ever there was any!' said Gerald.

Quinby looked affronted. 'My Wendel has always had a very sharp mind.'

Gerald scoffed. 'And as I recall, a very limp d—'

'How dare you, sir! That particular ailment is the result of an unfortunate hunting accident, as you very well know!'

'Teat!' repeated Terrence, in case anyone had not heard him the first time.

'If you two don't stop bickering,' said the old duke, 'I shall have you both thrown in the castle dungeon.'

'Do you have the authority to do that now? I ask purely out of academic interest, you understand,' said Gerald with a nasty grin.

'Carry on, if you truly want to find out,' Ormus warned.

'Look at us,' said Quinby glumly. 'Sat on the sidelines rotting, while the world goes on around us.' He was watching a large group of patrons who were sitting across the common room, singing and making merry. They made quite the bizarre sight. Some were dressed in cloaks of many-coloured rags, others of feathers. Some had painted faces. Others wore bells or pendants that clattered and clanked.

Gerald grimaced. 'If that's what the worlds come too, I want no part of it,' he said with a sniff.

'They've just been wassailing. Nought wrong with a wassail every now and then. Me and my Gran used to do it every year in the family orchard,' said Quinby wistfully. 'A good old sing-song and then we'd pour the last of the years' cider at the foot of the oldest apple tree and pray to its spirit for a good harvest to come.'

The old duke glowered at him.

"Course that was in the old days...' Quinby mumbled, looking down and burying his bulbous nose in his glass.

'Well, they look like buffoons,' Gerald said. 'And all this spirit worship is illegal now.'

'It's not illegal. Just discouraged,' sighed Ormus. It had been over twenty harvests, but still people seemed confused about the new church and its doctrines.

'You should have made it against the law. It's simple then. Believe in anything other than Melethin and suffer the consequences. After the first few executions, people would have soon cottoned on. You have to spell it out for these simpletons,' said Gerald.

Ormus sighed. 'Sometimes I fear you may be right. But the new church was supposed to simplify matters. Do you remember what it was like before? Every family worshipping a different spirit, with different worldviews and contrasting traditions. We'd be breaking up a religious row every other week! And then there were the Zigelder fanatics.'

'Still are,' Gerald pointed out. 'What are they calling themselves now? The Church of the Cracked Acorn, or something?'

'Some nonsense like that, yes. Melethin was supposed to bring people together! The Church of the First Tree was meant to be a rallying point for a new, civilised world. Now what's wrong with that, I ask you?'

'Oh nothing, nothing...' said Quinby awkwardly. 'It's just, well, people love their spirits is all. Our old apple tree, for instance—'

'Oh, blast your old apple tree, you ridiculous old coot!' Ormus barked, thumping the table in frustration. 'Anything can get a spirit. Did you know that? There's nothing special about them. We had a silver tea set once, been in the family for generations. Then one day at breakfast we find it's been inhabited by the spirit of a rat that died in the storeroom. Bloody thing kept eating all the kippers, and the tea tasted of piddle! We had to throw the whole damn thing in the moat. Now, what's holy about that, I ask you?'

'Well, there are levels of spirit, obviously,' Quinby complained. 'Now what about the spirit of the river, Myzzle, eh? You can't say *there's* not something worth giving thanks to. Many a farmer owes his very livelihood to the will of the Myzzle.'

'Do they? Do they really? Or, could it just be possible that the spirit of whatever drowned peasant or bloody duck that decided to hang around in the Myzzle's watery bosom has absolutely no influence on the flow of the water whatsoever?'

'You won't be saying that when it bursts its banks and washes your house away!'

'Quinby, I live in a bloody castle!'

'Yes, but the farmers don't do they. That's my point. They won't want to risk angering a water spirit no matter what the cost. A brief prayer here and there, maybe an offering or two. If that keeps their crops watered and their house standing, then no official decree is going to stop them.'

'I'll say it again; an axe to the neck would!' Gerald said.

'It would start a riot, I'm telling you,' Quinby said. 'I'm sorry, your grace, but the only reason people put up with this Church of the First Tree nonsense is because they can still quietly carry on worshipping the spirits like they've always done.'

Ormus regarded the man stonily. 'Not so long ago, I could have had your head cut off for that remark,' he said.

Quinby stuck his prodigious nose in the air. 'Well now you'd have to ask young Wiggy, and he's not the type to chop people's heads off for speaking sense.'

'That's true enough at least,' the old duke relented miserably. 'Seems I barely have the authority to take a piss without permission these days.'

'You can come have a drink whenever you like now, though. It's not all bad,' Quinby said, calming down a little.

'As nice as it is to enjoy a pint of fine cider in good company,' Ormus said. 'I used to command armies. I used to be respected! These days I'm not even allowed in the Lord's Chambers.'

'It's a crying shame,' said Gerald, shaking his head.

'Teats!' said Terrence.

'Teats indeed, old chap,' said Ormus, kindly. 'Teats indeed.'

2.

'Do you know, it's actually rather pretty up close,' said the duke, face pressed to the eyepiece of the long brass tube that was the Institute of Propositional Logic's prized telescope. It stood, supported by a tripod and poking out of an open window, which was letting damp, cold air and the sounds of the busy street below into the room. Through it, he could see the bright mass that was the so-called comet in the night sky. 'What causes the…um, sparkly long bit, do you suppose?'

'The tail, your grace?' asked Corporal Tritewine. 'Actually, we're not sure, but we have several exciting theories if you'd like to hear them?'

'Ah, that's the tail, is it? Of course, corporal, please theorise away, however, might I suggest that given the current circumstances, the institute might refrain from calling it that for the time being? We don't want any, ahem, misunderstandings.' He wiped a clammy hand across his face. He was starting to feel rather unwell. Was it stress? It was probably stress. The buzzing in his ears had become a constant hum.

'Oh, it's just a sort of nickname, really. It's actually called a coma, which we think might comprise some kind of dust particles, or possibly ice or gas. Although if you believe Sir Kindbody, one of our more, er, venerable members, it's most likely a trail of fairy dust. But I have to tell you, your grace, that, personally, I don't subscribe to that kind of old-fashioned thinking.'

'Quite right, Corporal Twiteswine.'

'Um, call me Ambrosia, your grace.'

'Capital. So, Corporal Ambrosia, where is this comet headed?'

'That is an excellent question, your grace. I've actually been attempting to answer that particular query myself,' said Corporal Tritewine, an enthusiastic gleam entering her brown eyes as she removed her felt hat and set it down on a cluttered desk. They were in a sort of converted loft space at the top of the institute's impressive headquarters on Seabass Street. The floor was littered with papers and books, and a large section of one wall had been recently whitewashed. It was now covered with incomprehensible scribblings and complicated looking equations, which the natural philosopher went over to now.

'As you can see, it's not been easy. But I think, given its current position, compared to its position when it first appeared, considering the apparent direction of travel and speed, and of course expected gravitational pull from both our planet and the sun, I can confidently say that it will not hit us,' she said proudly.

Wigbert paled. 'That...that was a possibility, was it?' he managed, fighting back a wave of nausea.

'Oh yes!' said the Corporal. 'In fact, it is my belief that many may have hit us before. Not for a very long time, of course.'

'I see. And, um, how large would you say the thing was?'

'Oh, about six miles across, I estimate.'

'Really? As big as that? My goodness.' The duke was feeling rather faint. He had enough to worry about without thinking of interstellar objects larger than Upton-Myzzle itself, falling from the heavens. 'Well, this really has been an education Corporal, I thank you kindly.'

'It's my pleasure, your grace.'

'I do hope I can count on your cooperation, and that of the institutes, of course, should I require proof of all this to provide the Lord's Chambers?'

'Anything we can do to help, your grace.'

'Splendid.' There was an awkward pause, and Wigbert fished

around for something to say. His eyes alighted on a familiar-looking book spine that was sticking out of a pile of papers. 'Ah! Are you a fan of Wolfe Starlingcloud, corporal?'

Her eyes lit up. 'Oh, yes! It's a brilliant book, isn't it, your grace? That Sir Rumbould Theaksteak is a genius!' A thought appeared to occur to her. 'You...you don't know who it is, do you, your grace?'

Wigbert smiled weakly. Perhaps that hadn't been such a good idea for a topic of conversation. 'I haven't had the pleasure,' he said, then changed the subject. 'On another note, what on earth is that?' He pointed to a strange, metallic object leaning up against the wall in one corner. It was a sort of metal box with a large, brass T-shaped handle sticking out of it. It was attached by some sort of long, flexible tubing to another cigar-shaped object that leant against the wall.

Corporal Tritewine blushed, looking a little embarrassed. 'Ah...that is...Well, my predecessor in the office left it here. He didn't leave any notes, but, well, I *think* it's an electrostatic generator.'

Wigbert looked at her blankly. 'A what?'

The natural philosopher's blush deepened. 'Actually, I haven't got a clue. No one's used this attic in years. In fact, the last person who did was actually Lord Nugent.'

'Should I know who that is?'

'Nugent is a name of legend in the institute. Rumour has it he was our founder, only he got pushed out in the very early days of the organisation.'

'Really? I've never heard the name mentioned. The institute's only been around a handful of years, hasn't it?'

Corporal Tritewine shook her head excitedly, warming to the topic now. 'That's wrong, actually. We've been around a good deal longer. But it's only in recent years that we've grown in size and been taken seriously. Anyway, Nugent was supposed to have been a genius.' She reached out a hand towards the long, cylindrical object, then hesitated, like she was afraid to touch it.

'What did he do to get kicked out, exactly?' Wigbert asked.

'No one's really sure. It might have been political. Or it might have been because he was crazy. Depends who you talk to. Whatever the reason, the institute at the time purged all mention of him from our records. He only survives as a sort of boogie man, a myth passed on from one member to another. It's said he had interests in all sorts of highly contentious areas of research. Which would make sense, given what little I *do* know about this...object. I was curious when I first found it, so I unpacked it to figure out what it was.'

'And?'

'I couldn't make heads nor tails of it, to be honest. I still have no idea what it's supposed to be for. But I almost killed myself trying to find out,' the corporal said, wincing at the memory. 'I call it the lightning machine.'

'Good grief! You're not saying—'

At that moment Punduckslew, who had insisted on accompanying the duke, entered the room looking scandalised, his magnificent beard quivering like an angry bee's nest.

'Finished star gazing, you grace? Good. Because I have just discovered that the body of Mr Scroggan Peplow is laying downstairs in the basement!'

'My word! Is it? Whatever for?'

'Oh, the institute often acquires the cadavers of the recently deceased,' Corporal Tritewine explained. 'It is surprisingly difficult to obtain fresh bodies, you know.'

The duke raised his eyebrows. 'I can assure you that I do not know, having not been in the habit of wanting to acquire one before.'

'It's a disgrace!' Punduckslew boomed. 'Dead bodies lying around like slabs of meat...unhygienic is what I call it!'

'Oh, but sir, I assure you the temperature in the basement is quite cool. It's why we use it. It means we have longer to work on the bodies before putrefaction sets in. Of course, at this time of year, we rarely have a problem.'

Punduckslew was shaking his head. 'A person should be sent on to the Otherworld as soon as possible after death. They shouldn't be left rotting in people's basements!'

'Surely you recognise the need for study of the human anatomy, though?'

'I most certainly do not!' said the wizard, bristling with indignation. 'The Wizards Charter has always been very clear on its position regarding necromancy—'

'Necromancy?' interrupted Corporal Tritewine in surprise, looking a little offended. 'I am not talking about some silly magic make-believe. Here we practice in hard facts, sir. What we can see and measure. We don't wave our hands around and see what comes out. We apply the scientific method in a methodical and—'

'You think magic is silly hand waving, do you?' said the wizard, drawing himself up to his full height and glowering at her through narrowed eyes. 'Well, let me tell you, young lady, the noble and mysterious art of the magical craft has been around for the span of history, unlike your ridiculous natural philosophy.'

Corporal Tritewine's eyes narrowed in turn. 'Natural philosophy is the future! Of course, I wouldn't expect a crusty old wizard to understand that. You people don't even seem to understand how your own Talents work.'

'How dare you! The Wizards Charter has a thousand-year history of magical expertise!'

'Oh really? Well, then you should be able to tell me how magic works then?'

'How it works?' Punduckslew spluttered.

'Yes. What are the exact physical or chemical reactions that take place when magic is used?'

'Young lady,' Punduckslew said severely. 'The gift of magic is not...is not some corpse for the likes of you to poke and prod and measure. It is divine! Given to us by the Grandfather Oak himself! Its use is something to be perfected, yes, like one would perfect any Melethin given skill, such as sword-craft or...or painting. It is an art! But it is not for us to mess with the nature of magic.'

'In other words, you have no idea,' the Corporal scoffed.

Punduckslew looked enraged. He was probably not used to being spoken to with such lack of respect, Wigbert mused. Even the wizard's enemies were loath to be so openly hostile in the face of the man's destructive Talent. It was surprisingly satisfying to see him openly challenged. Still, there were more important matters to attend to.

'If we could return to the matter at hand,' he said. 'I should like to see a report on Mr Peplow's body myself.'

Punduckslew gaped. 'Whatever for, you grace?'

'If I am to investigate the man's death, it might prove useful,' the duke said with a shrug.

'He was stabbed, your grace. We all saw it. What more could there be to learn?'

'We won't know until we look, will we?'

'I'm sure that can be arranged. Let us go see Sir Crumbwhistle. He's in charge of the dissections. He'll be able to tell you more about the late Mr Peplow than I will,' said Corporal Tritewine, directing them towards the door and shooting Punduckslew a smug look.

They followed her down creaking wooden stairs through the heart of the institute, the wizard muttering under his breath as they went. Wigbert looked around with interest, as he had done on their arrival. He had never been inside the institute before and was amazed to find it stuffed full of little offices and laboratories, all apparently dedicated to separate fields of interest. They passed a plaque announcing the office of the 'Chair of freshwater Palaemonidae studies', and another the intriguing 'Laboratory of experimental Maths'. This one had a second sign underneath which read 'Danger! Loose equations!' Wigbert couldn't quite decide if it was meant to be a joke or not. From the street, it had always seemed a rather under-inspiring building. It did not have the grandeur of some of the older organisations in town. But that was perhaps not surprising, given its unusual nature and relatively brief history.

When they reached the building's main atrium, they found a handful of people gathered around the windows, looking out into the dark street. From outside, raised voices could be heard.

'What's going on?' Corporal Tritewine called across to them.

'Some Zigelder nut-job is going to cause a riot,' a woman in a purple dress called back over her shoulder, before turning and spotting the duke with a start. 'Ahem, I mean there is some sort of commotion in the street, your grace.'

'We should look,' Wigbert said to Punduckslew, slightly taking himself by
surprise.

The wizard all but rolled his eyes. 'Yes please, let's head *towards* the riot.'

'If there is trouble afoot, it is my duty to intervene.'

'No, your grace, it is the Watch's duty to intervene.'

'Nevertheless, Punduckslew.'

The wizard met Wigberts' eyes for a moment, then sighed, seeing that he would not win. 'I think I preferred it when you didn't leave the castle,' he said.

'Relax, no one is going to attack the duke with you by my side.'

'With all due respect, your grace, with the way things have been going, I wouldn't bet on that.'

'Well, if anyone tries to assassinate me, you have my permission to make them go boom.'

'Oh, don't worry, I will. But there are limits to my power, you know? I can only make so many people 'go boom' at once.'

'A fascinating discussion for another time. Corporal Ambrosia, if you would be so kind as to flush out that report for me?'

The woman gave an awkward bow. 'Of course, your grace.'

Punduckslew insisted on checking the safety of the street before allowing Wigbert to exit the building. He stuck his head out of the door, looking left and right into the night, before giving Wigbert a nod and opening the door fully.

Well well, some action at last! I never thought I'd see the day!

Wigbert froze in the doorway, his gorge rising. Oh no, not now. *Please*, not now!

I'm proud of you, Wiggy. Really. Jumping into the fray like this. It's like something I *would do.*

Go away! Please, please go away, Wigbert thought, feeling a cold sweat break out on his forehead. When had he had his last pill? It hadn't been that long ago, surely?

'Changed your mind, your grace?' Punduckslew asked, looking at him quizzically.

Wigbert forced his legs to move. 'No, not at all. Lead the way,' he said, trying to remain calm.

Yes, don't chicken out on me now, Wiggy old boy! said the voice in his head.

Shut up, Wigbert thought desperately, shut up, shut up, shut up. He really didn't need this right now. Not again. By Melethin, his head hurt!

There was a small crowd gathered on the opposite side of the street, huddled around a lit brazier. A man dressed in black robes stood atop a crate in their centre and could be seen gesticulating wildly above the gathered heads. His words drifted clearly across the dark street.

'... now is the time to return to Zigelder. The burning fire in the sky above our very heads prophesies the coming doom of this land. The daemon returns! With him will come *death*. Our only chance is to pray to our father for forgiveness...pray for salvation. Only his love will save us!'

'These zealots get more brazen every day,' Punduckslew observed.

Wigbert said nothing. The voice in his head offered no opinion, either. He was shaking. He needed to get back to his chambers before...well, before *things* got worse.

But he wanted to watch the crowd's reaction. It looked like some people were nodding along to the man's words, but others were looking cross.

'Rubbish!' one man called out. 'The new star is nothing to worry about. The high priest herself said so.'

'And you'd trust that old crone, would you?' shouted another. 'What would she know with her puppet religion?'

'You dare to disrespect Melethin?' cried a third man with a red face.

'Ain't no one here got nothing against Melethin, you fool,' retorted the second man. 'It's the Church of the First Tree that we think is wood rot!'

'Only wood rot round here's in your head!' the red-faced man shouted back angrily.

'Come here and say that you pox faced little rat!'

A small scuffle broke out within the crowd. Even from across the street, Wigbert could see the smile that stole onto the robed man's face.

There'll be a riot, said the voice in the duke's head, *if you don't do something. Go on, go over there and punch him in the face. That'll shut him up by Jove!*

I'm a duke, thought Wigbert. I can't just rush over there and punch someone, so shut up.

Just a suggestion.

'We have to do something before this gets out of hand. I'd bet anything that man in the robes is Church of the Cracked Acorn. He might have answers we need,' the duke said out loud.

'Well, as much as I'd like to stride over there and arrest him, it's not really in my skill set. If you want his innards decorating the faces of the crowd, then just give the word. Otherwise, we really should call for the Watch,' Punduckslew said.

'He might be gone by then!' Wigbert protested.

'It's a risk we will have to take, your grace. If you go over there now, we have no idea how the crowd will react. The WatchHouse is just up the street. If we're quick, we may catch him yet.'

'Oh, very well,' Wigbert agreed reluctantly. 'But let's hurry!'

The WatchHouse was indeed just a short way further up Seabass Street. Wigbert and Punduckslew made their way there as quickly as was possible without attracting too much unwanted attention. This resulted in a sort of awkward power-walk that Wigbert felt was probably unbecoming in the ruler of a duchy. The royal coach might have been quicker, but hardly inconspicuous, so they left it outside the institute.

They arrived at the grand double-fronted WatchHouse feeling slightly ridiculous and vaguely out of breath. The doorway was tall, wide and filled almost entirely by the largest Watchman Wigbert had ever seen. He was holding a blunderbuss threateningly across his chest and glowered down at them as they approached. Wigbert watched as the man's expression became first quizzical and then slightly alarmed.

'Your grace,' he said, standing to attention. There was a dull thud as the top of his head hit the doorframe.

'We'd like to see Watch Commander Posternos,' Wigbert said.

This proclamation appeared to trouble the watchman considerably. A series of emotions chased their way across his face like the flicking pages of a picture book.

'Um...I'll see if he's in,' he said after an awkwardly long silence.

Punduckslew leaned towards the man. 'Do you know who I am, son?' he asked pleasantly.

'Yes, sir.'

'Well, if you don't let us in immediately,' he continued, pointing his finger at the man's chest. 'I will decorate this lovely doorway with the inside of your head, understand?'

'Yessir!' the watchman said, hurriedly stepping to the side and allowing them to enter.

The inside of the watch-house was not what Wigbert expected. Mainly because it was covered in rubble.

'What in the name of Melethin...' said Punduckslew, looking around with concern.

'Where's Posternos?' Wigbert called to a passing watchman.

'His office.' The man hurried past without even looking to

see who had spoken.

'There would appear to be a sizeable hole in this floor, your grace,' said Punduckslew, peering into the chasm.

'We must find out what has happened here. Where's the office, do you think?'

Punduckslew lead the way to the back of the building, where he believed the Watch commander's office could be found. It turned out to be a large room, lined with fine paintings and containing a rather grandly proportioned desk. Behind it sat the Watch commander himself, a man of middling years with a flush of course, grey hair and startlingly black eyebrows.

'If you don't have news of the fugitive, then you can bloody well turn right back around, or I swear by Melethin's craggy trunk I will demote you to privy attendant before you can blink,' growled the man, without looking up from his paperwork.

'I'm afraid you don't have the authority,' replied the duke. *Shoot him*, said the voice, *shoot the insolent cur right in the chest!* Shut up, Wigbert thought back, massaging his eyeballs until he saw spots.

Posternos looked up, and the light of recognition slid across his face. 'Your grace,' he said smoothly, getting to his feet. 'A thousand apologies, I didn't…I was not expecting this visit.'

'Clearly,' said Punduckslew. 'Why is there a hole in your floor?'

The Watch commander regarded Punduckslew for a moment with a carefully blank expression before turning his attention back to the duke without answering.

'Is there something I can do for you, your grace?' he said, coming out from behind his desk. 'It is highly unusual for you to visit me like this…in fact I would have suggested strongly against it, had you thought to consult me, the streets are still not safe at present.' He stood before them and looked so stern that Wigbert had to remind himself who the superior was here. It wasn't easy when Posternos cut such a commanding figure. He was dressed in the rich, red frock-coat of the Watch, but his had blue trim with gold braiding and what looked like pearl buttons. His waistcoat and breeches were also blue and reflected in the large, shiny brass buckles of his leather shoes. He was a tall man, at least a head taller than Wigbert, though still shorter than Punduckslew, who was glaring at the man with contempt. He doesn't like being ignored, Wigbert thought.

'I, er…' Wigbert began, before nerves stuck his tongue to the roof of his mouth. Now he was here, stood before this impressive man, he suddenly wondered what the hell he thought he was achieving. What was he, the Duke of Blackwood, doing, running around the streets of Upton-Myzzle like some…what? He wasn't sure he even knew what he was trying to be.

Posternos raised an immaculate black eyebrow questioningly in the lengthening silence.

Well, say something *Wiggy, old frui*t, said the voice in the duke's head. Wigbert did his best to pretend it hadn't. 'The streets are indeed not safe, sir,' he began in the best duke-like voice he could muster. 'In fact, at this very moment, not five hundred yards from this watch-house, a man is attempting to incite a riot. We believe him to be associated with the group calling themselves the Church of the Cracked Acorn and require you to intervene with all haste. If the man truly is of this new radical group, then he may have valuable information about the killer styling himself the Lord of Misrule.'

The Watch commander's placid face shifted subtly. Wigbert did his best to decode the man's guarded expression, but gave up.

'Well, that is interesting,' said Posternos slowly. 'A riot, you say? Well, thank you, your grace. I shall certainly send someone along to investigate, just as soon as I can spare them. Now, if that was all, I really am quite busy. Allow me to call a man to escort you home to the castle.'

Wigbert felt the stirrings of anger in his chest. He's trying to dismiss me, he thought. Me. The bloody duke!

'We brought the royal carriage,' he said coldly.

'Splendid, then please allow me to show you to the door. As I'm sure you saw on your way in, we are having a little work done—'

This is intolerable! Does this man presume himself above you? You should have him clapped in irons, said the voice with disgust. Wigbert found himself agreeing. He swallowed down the urge to allow himself to be led and forced himself to say, 'Commander Posternos, that simply will not do.'

The black eyebrows rose up the Watch commander's forehead. 'Oh?' was all he said.

'Firstly, if you think I will believe the gaping hole in your watch-house floor is due to building works, you insult me. Secondly, I, as your duke, have made an official request for your services. I will not be so easily ignored, sir!'

Commander Posternos said nothing. He was looking at the duke like he had never seen him before.

I've pushed it too far, Wigbert thought, taking a deep breath. What was I thinking? This isn't me. I'm not cut out for this sort of thing.

You're the duke, dammit! It's about time you demanded some respect around here, said the voice excitedly. *By Jove I'm proud of you Wiggy, it fair makes my blood boil with vim and vinegar, old boy!*

Oh please shut up, Wigbert thought desperately. Where was an apothecary when you needed one? He could feel the sweat in his armpits.

'Well?' Punduckslew prompted. 'What of it, man? Answer your duke!'

At this, the Watch commander's bland mask finally slipped, and he scowled angrily at the wizard.

'I am not accustomed to being spoken to this way in my own office,' he snapped.

'Well, get accustomed. The duke has ordered from you both answers and action. I strongly suggest you comply.'

'Do not threaten me, wizard!' Posternos snarled. 'His grace

will have to understand that, in this instance, he has no direct authority over me. The City Watch answers to the Lord's Chambers, not Castle Blackwood.' He did not look at Wigbert, instead speaking directly to Punduckslew, who was glaring back.

'This man is your duke!' he bellowed. 'Do not talk to me about the chain of command. Do as you are requested!'

Posternos sneered. 'I am afraid I must decline,' he said.

'Just give the word, your grace. I'll make his eyeballs pop in his head,' said Punduckslew.

Wigbert was saved from replying by the sudden bang of the office door opening with such speed it hit the wall behind.

It was General Weltsmatter, who spoke before he'd even entered the room. 'It's no good, commander. Krickwell's long gone damn his eyes.' The man froze as he took in the scene inside the office, his own eyes widening in surprise.

'General,' said the duke, a sudden surge of hatred rising inside him at the sight of the man who had put Beatrice in danger. 'Now, what might you be doing here? And what is this about Sir Krickwell?'

The man seemed stumped. His mouth flapped up and down silently.

'He's escaped!' Punduckslew said with sudden understanding. 'You've let the bloody man escape!'

Commander Posternos looked furious. 'It would appear so,' he said tightly. 'He had help of some kind. My men are searching for him now.'

A manhunt, said the voice. *Now we're talking! Oh Wiggy, we've not had this much fun in years!*

Wigbert tried to concentrate against the inner monologue and the pounding in his ears. He was still full of seething hatred, and events were moving faster than he could keep track of.

'I think,' he said at length. 'We had better start this conversation from the beginning. Oh, and general ...'

'Yes, your grace?'

'You're relieved of command, I've been meaning to say.'

3.

Ormus sat in his private garderobe, the picture of abject misery.

'A curse on this treacherous bladder,' he muttered, pulling the blanket tighter around his shivering shoulders. The night was bitter and his nightshirt thin. A quilted nightgown hung on his chamber door, forgotten, whilst his chamber's smouldering fire had long since suffocated under its own ash. This was the venerable Stonemorton's fourth trip to the icy privy that night, and he was beginning to suspect, as has many a man of a certain age before him, that the alcohol had not been worth this ordeal. Grumbling, he stood, dropped the bunched linen from his waist to once more cover his knock-kneed legs, and shuffled back into the candlelit chamber. He lowered his aching bones onto the edge of the bed and belched loudly. A stirring in his guts told him his hangover was arriving ahead of schedule.

His mood was melancholic, but it seemed he no longer possessed the words to articulate, even to himself, exactly why. Or rather, if he possessed them, he had temporarily mislaid them. He merely sighed, swore to the room at large, and massaged his aching knee.

Looking around, his eyes stuck to the closed wooden shutters of the room's only window and the sudden urge gripped him for fresh air, despite the chill. Reaching for his stick where it leant against a small table beside the bed, he rose with a grunt and hobbled over to the window. He fumbled with stiff fingers over the latch, but eventually pried it open, pushing back the shutters to reveal a star-strewn sky. He breathed deeply, enjoying the burning of cold air in his lungs.

The fog in his brain seemed to lift a little, and he looked out into the night. There was a good view across the castle towards the town from up here, near the top of the keep, and the stars provided just enough light for him to pick out the gatehouse in the distance and the rooftops of the old quarter beyond. Closer, he watched as a tiny orange glow, most likely a guard with a lantern, made its steady way along the battlements. Otherwise, the castle seemed deserted, the only sounds the croaking and scratching of crows on the tower's roof. Ormus was fairly certain the blasted birds had colonised the entire upper level of the keep. He hadn't been up to check; stairs were now the enemy. He found he could no longer recall what the top floor had been used for. Storage perhaps. Truthfully, it could have contained almost anything. The duke-no-more found increasingly that memories eluded his once agile mind. It was a poor reward, Ormus contemplated, to survive to old age only for your mind to desert you and your body to fail. His wife had it right; she'd got out years ago. Taken by a fever after forty harvests. They hadn't been close. Political marriages were the norm for the ruling class in the Blackwood.

Perhaps if he'd been more strict about that with Wigbert, things would have turned out differently, he mused. The old man tried to conjure up the face of his son's wife, but failed. She had been fair of hair, he seemed to recall, and quite pretty, but her features were lost to him. She, too, had died young, too young in her case; just twenty five or so harvests. She'd been a nice girl. Bought a womanly warmth to the old castle. She had never been a smart match for his son, however. Marrying for love was all very well, but there was a reason most Stonemortons didn't.

No money in her family. The Stonemortons badly needed money, and old money was the only type worth having. Real coins from the capital before the Quickening. The new stuff was basically useless, a promise built on a promise.

Upton-Myzzle had no mint, so once the kingdom fell apart, that meant no new coins. The economy had basically collapsed. They might have built one, of course, but materials were also scarce now. Everything was scarce. But people carried on. Crops still grew. The present system had evolved slowly over time. With no new coinage, people had regressed to an almost barter-like system, swapping scraps of paper stamped with an official seal that promised favours when time was short; A duke's favour. The old coins, those that were left, were only swapped for big favours; A king's favour. It worked, after a fashion. Want a hot meal? Well, chop me some wood or it'll cost you three duke's favours. Want my house? Well, work my fields for ten years or it's ten king's favours.

The trouble for the Stonemortons was that for a duke or duchess, a favour could be a dangerous thing. Coins were best, but the coins were dwindling. The bloody Sweetspires seemed to have plenty, of course, which really wasn't fair at all, Ormus thought bitterly.

As the old man stood, leaning against the sill of the window, staring out at the new star in the black sky and thinking how coin-like it looked, he heard the tiniest sound in the chamber behind him. It was barely a whisper, just the shadow of a noise, a change in the air pressure. He turned to find a blade plunging down towards him.

Ormus had been duke for a long time. He'd led armies once. Instinct moved his old bones for him and he lurched to the side; the knife that had been meant for his back grazing his shoulder instead. Someone cursed and Ormus stumbled, falling heavily against the wall with a cry, dropping his walking stick. Before him stood a man dressed in black. His torso was partly covered in a long cowl made of black and grey rags and his face was hidden behind a wooden mask, carved into the rictus grin of a man's face, fringed with leaves and flowers.

'The Lord...of Misrule,' Ormus growled between heavy breaths with his heart punching the inside of his ribs.

The man said nothing, but bowed theatrically before advancing again, knife in hand. There was a large part of the duke-no-more's brain that was quite ready to lie there and wait for the knife. But Ormus Stonemorton was nothing, if not stubborn. The part of his brain that had kept him duke for all those years woke back up. It looked, it saw, it assessed the situation. He had maybe one good move in him. He'd better make it count.

As the Lord of Misrule bore down upon him, Ormus's hand scrabbled for the walking stick, which had fallen to the floorboards beside him. In a smooth arc, the old man swept the stick through the air and was rewarded with a sharp *crack* as it met his attacker's wrist. There was another curse and a clatter as the man dropped his knife and it skidded away under the bed. Ormus used those precious seconds to scramble to his feet, bones screaming at him. He circled his attacker, stumbling as his knee tried to collapse, until he stood in the centre of the room with the man between him and the open window. The Lord of Misrule didn't move, just stood, massaging his wrist.

'Well, well, you've got some spirit left after all, you old codger.' His voice was high and cold. 'I might admire that in another man. But you know what you've done. You have to die.'

He said it matter-of-factly, almost like he regretted it. But he reached around behind his back with one hand and produced a small blunderbuss, cocking it with his thumb and aiming the wide barrel square at Ormus's chest.

'Don't be a fool! If you fire that in here, you'll wake the entire castle,' Ormus croaked, playing for time.

The man said nothing. What was there to say? They both knew his Talent would take him far away before help might arrive.

Time was up.

Ormus made a desperate rush for the man. It must have taken his attacker by surprise, because when he pulled the trigger, his arm had already been forced upwards by the duke-no-more. The blunderbuss exploded into the ceiling; the noise stabbing into Ormus's ear like a hot blade. Ignoring the pain, the old man continued his momentum, pushing hard until his attacker hit the windowsill and pivoted through the open shutters. The Lord of Misrule swore and fell backwards, striking Ormus across the face with his gun as he went. Ormus collapsed against the window frame and saw the man fall. He disappeared before he hit the ground. Ormus's pain overwhelmed him then, and he fell to the floor with a cry. As the darkness closed in, he felt the floorboards reverberate with the sound of running feet.

Then there was nothing.

4.

On the far side of the river Myzzle, the trees of the Blackwood loomed large. They bore down on the semi-abandoned slums like an army of forty-foot soldiers. The steady thud and buzz of axes and saws surrounded Babu Necket where he sat on a freshly cut log, his little circle illuminated by a small bonfire. The sounds meant little to the Watchman who, as a member of the deforestation crew, had long ago learnt to ignore the continuous noise of his vocation. It was heavy work, and Babu was covered in an uncomfortable layer of sticky sweat and sat in his shirtsleeves despite the chilly night. He looked up from the book in his hands at a shout that drifted across to him from a brightly lit area a couple of hundred paces away along the tree line.

Babu tutted. The captain making a fuss again, no doubt. It was why he had removed himself to this distance, away from the rest of his shift; it was impossible to read with that man around. Babu suspected it was because the captain was not particularly good at it himself. It was perhaps an unusual hobby amongst the watchmen, but Babu found it relaxing. Relaxing is important when you spend your days and nights with an axe in your hands. His palms were so calloused they could practically stop a blade. On the plus side, he had developed an upper body strength that seemed to quite please many a young woman in the public houses on the other side of the river. Right now, however, Babu had eyes only for the words on the page before him. It wasn't a book of any literary merit, but that suited Babu just fine. It was story he cared for.

Adventure. Something to take his mind off the monotony of his daily life.

Behind him, in the darkness of the trees, came the sound of a branch snapping.

Babu sighed, putting down his book reluctantly and picking up his axe, which lay ready nearby. The forest was probably stirring again. If it was, he would have to sound the alarm. So much for break time. He peered into the gloom, searching for movement. Eventually he saw it; something was coming towards him, out of the trees.

It wasn't what he'd expected.

Babu stared, openmouthed, axe all but forgotten in his hands as the…creature? stumbled out of the tree line. It looked like a woman pulling a small handcart. Sort of dumpy. A hedgewitch, maybe? But there was something wrong. It didn't move like a person. The arms and legs went up and down, sure, but they didn't correspond to the things actual movement. It slid forward continuously, whether its feet touched the ground or not. As it covered the ground between them with unnerving speed, the thing raised its arm and pointed at Babu with a long finger that bent and wriggled in unnatural ways.

'Miiiiine!' it hissed, in a voice like gravel sliding down a tin roof.

This was quite enough for Babu, who, suddenly remembering the axe, raised it above his head and brought it down on the beast with all his considerable might.

Later, when his captain came looking, there was no sign of Babu. All he found was the splintered end of an axe and a strange hand cart. There was some sort of trail leading through the grass toward the river, and the captain, being an unimaginative and impatient man, simply assumed Babu had finally deserted the service and gone home. He made a mental note to register the desertion when he was next at the watch-house and thought no more about the matter.

CHAPTER SIX: AN ENSEMBLE FOR BREAKFAST

1.

The next morning dawn broke unenthusiastically over Upton-Myzzle. A dank gloom lingering in the muddy streets. Thick clouds the colour of ditchwater had formed before daybreak and now hung over the sodden town, like the bulging underbelly of a wet dog. If these particular clouds had a silver lining, it was that they were insulating the town from the worst of the winter bite. That was little appreciated by the populace, however, who shivered in their damp houses and thought of the rain that was undoubtedly to come. The river Myzzle already lapped dangerously high against its banks.

The Lord of Misrule shivered himself, crouched as he was amongst a collection of chimney pots on a roof of chestnut shingles, not far from his lodgings. He had not yet been inside, deeming it too dangerous after such a disastrous night, and his limbs were stiff from the pre-dawn air. After fleeing Castle Blackwood, he had spent the remaining hours before the light came, taking a very complicated route home. He was a hard man to follow, but he could ill afford another mistake.

Ormus Stonemorton had survived.

His sponsors would not be happy about that, but their disappointment was nothing compared with the white-hot rage the Lord of Misrule felt with himself.

For that was how he saw himself now, since Longest Night. He had been reborn as the Lord of Misrule, his previous name now all but forgotten to him. He was the living embodiment of the old ways: Zigelder's representative.

And he had failed in his holy mission.

Truthfully, the duke-no-more had taken him by surprise. He'd expected to find a dribbling old fool, only too ready for the knife. He hadn't expected any fight from the bony old bastard.

Cocky.

Witless.

He would have to make up for this. Once it got out that his intended victim had survived, people would fear him less, and he couldn't have that. Not if the plan was to work. He needed to do something…big.

There was a thin plume of green smoke rising into the murky sky from the other side of town, but the Lord of Misrule ignored it. As the first of the rain fell, he stared at the peaked dome of the Church of the First Tree, just visible in the distance.

He'd had an idea.

2.

Dull light pressed through a single, high window, just enough to make dust motes sparkle in the wood-panelled room. Beatrice crept between the bookcases, treading lightly to avoid setting off the creaky floorboards. She clutched at the straps of a leather satchel she had slung over her shoulder, made heavy with books she'd deposited inside and so liable to swing her off balance. It was awkward, but her dress contained no pockets, so what was she to do? The Castle Blackwood book repository was technically off-limits to all but a select few, and even the duke's daughter should not have been wondering the aisle unaccompanied. It had never made sense to Beatrice, who held the opinion that if she wanted to look at a book, then no ridiculous rule was going to stop her.

The old bibliothecary seemed to hold a different view, and he would undoubtedly have her removed and punished if he ever caught her in the act. Beatrice thought it was sad; all those words locked up with no one to read them. The book repository, situated high in the east tower, was the finest in Upton-Myzzle…once. But, like with so much else in the beleaguered castle, time had not been kind. Books, and indeed reading, had not always been as high a priority to some of Beatrice's ancestors as perhaps they should have been. Things had not been looked after well. Many books had been sold to pay for whatever pressing business each consecutive ruler had deemed of most importance. Some had been stolen, due to lack of care or security. Yet more had simply been lost and were, to that day, languishing in forgotten corners of the castle, unloved and forgotten.

The result was a once impressive collection reduced to a few dozen tomes of varying quality, some dusty scrolls, and a lot of empty shelves. The current bibliothecary, installed by Beatrice's father, was at least competent and indeed took his responsibility seriously. But one man cannot undo decades of misuse, however vigorously he might wield a feather duster.

What he could do was start to grow the collection once more, and indeed, many more modern books were being added to the shelves. They were easy to pick out because they were undamaged, their crisp leather covers shining out from the shelves with titles depicted in gold print. There was one particular volume that Beatrice sneaked a look at every chance she got. It was entitled 'The Heroic Adventures of One Wolfe Starlingcloud and How He Single-Handedly Defeated the Moss Men of the Silver Fen', which was a bit of a mouthful, but the book had been an overnight sensation on its release a year previously. Young Beatrice marvelled at the antics of its protagonist, Wolfe. The novel's author, Sir Rumbould Theaksteak, was a bit of a mystery though. No one seemed to know who he was, although Beatrice found that hard to believe. *Someone* must know, surely? Books didn't just print themselves after all. She'd considered setting her mind to solving the mystery of the author's identity, however, that morning Beatrice passed the book by without a second glance. She had more pressing concerns than Wolfe Starlingcloud.

The shelves were indeed clean and gave off a pleasant smell of wood polish. It mixed with the aroma of musty pages to form a heady perfume that filled Beatrice's head and made her yawn as she tiptoed around the room. She couldn't find what she was looking for. She was sure there had been an impressive—if slightly foxed—red leather-bound tome here the last time she'd snuck in. It had a long, confusing title she couldn't remember, but she knew it had something to do with the history of Melethin. Theology had never really interested the girl before; she took a rather hands-off approach to religion. It was something that happened. She was aware of that much. But usually, it happened to other people. Right now, though, she wanted to understand more about what the Lord of Misrule actually wanted. If he really was a member of the Church of the Cracked Acorn, then presumably he shared their belief that Upton-Myzzle should return to the Old Ways. Beatrice had lived her entire life with the Church of the First Tree looming large over all public occasions and as such possessed only a vague understanding of exactly what the Old Ways were. She knew it had something to do with worshipping spirits, but seeing as she rarely got to leave the castle grounds —and there were no spirits inside that she was aware of— she had little experience of such things. Zigelder was involved somehow too, but the girl was unclear exactly how, or indeed why, that seemed to upset people so much.

Zigelder was supposed to be the son of Melethin after all, and the father of humankind. So why was he only ever mentioned in hushed tones, if at all? And then there was the most pressing question of all; why had they targeted her grandfather?

She knew he'd been attacked. The entire castle had been in an uproar since the early hours of the morning. She had seen Mr Dribbets marching around the grounds, shouting at people all morning. As far as Beatrice could gather, for she had gleaned little information from direct questioning, the man had taken it upon himself to organise the Castle Guard in the absence of General Weltsmatter, who it seemed was no longer in command.

The news that her father had fired the general was nearly as shocking as her grandfather being attacked in his own chambers. Beatrice tried to picture her mild-mannered father confronting the red-nosed general, but found that she simply couldn't do it. However, apparently it had happened, and now Mr Dribbets was berating captains, lieutenants, corporals and privates alike, all of whom seemed so bewildered by the sudden change in circumstances that they hadn't stopped to question the steward's authority. There seemed to be more guards on duty than Beatrice had seen for months. The battlements positively bristled with them. It had been more difficult than usual to slip into the book repository unnoticed. Undoubtedly, her absence would be noted soon, so where was that damn book?

'*Thief*!'

The word reverberated around the bookshelves like the crack of a cannon, and Beatrice's heart leapt into her mouth. She was discovered! The silhouette of the ancient bibliothecary had appeared at the end of the row and was pointing at her accusingly with a trembling arm.

'Thief!' he screeched again. 'Intruder! Marauder! Book defiler! Guards! *Guards*!'

Knowing the game was up, Beatrice hurried towards the man, trying to limit the damage before he had the whole Castle Guard descending on the repository.

'It's just me, Mr Bombroffe, it's Beatrice!' she called.

The man ceased his caterwauling long enough to peer at her suspiciously through a pair of round spectacles that balanced precariously on the bridge of his long nose. They were so thickly smeared with finger grease it was a wonder he could make out anything through them at all.

'Who?' he said distrustfully, holding a large book out between them. Beatrice was unsure if it was meant as a shield or weapon, but she recognised it immediately. It was the book she had been searching for.

'Beatrice Stonemorton, Mr Bombroffe, the duke's daughter,' she said.

The bibliothecary continued to stare at her, sucking his teeth absentmindedly as he apparently thought about this statement. For a man who kept his books so fastidiously clean, he appeared markedly rumpled and dusty himself. He wore what looked like a somewhat shabby grey nightgown over his waistcoat and breeches and hunched over himself so far that he had to raise his head to keep her in sight.

'You ought not be in here, my lady,' he said eventually. 'For the repository is not a playground. Come, I shall have to inform your father.' Letting go of his book with one hand, he reached out bony fingers to where he evidently believed her shoulder to be, staggering unsteadily when it was not.

'Are you well, Mr Bombroffe?' Beatrice asked, hurrying to his side to steady him. The man's fingers grasped her arm painfully tight and felt like cold bone against her skin.

He gave her a small smile, some of his harshness leaving him. 'Oh quite well, my lady, thank you. Quite well. Just not as agile as I once was.'

'Should I carry your book for you?' Beatrice asked innocently.

'Oh, thank you. Yes, most kind of you, my dear.'

The old man handed her the red book and Beatrice eyed the title excitedly. *The Grandfather Tree: Or the history of the first tree, his offspring, the great beast in his home amongst the stars, and the genesis of the human race.*

She hoped the prose inside would not be as long-winded as the title.

'A ponderous tome,' opined the bibliothecary, noting her interest. 'Are you particularly interested in theology, my lady?'

Beatrice decided to appeal to the man's better nature and chose to tell a morsel of the truth. 'Well, after the attack last night,' she said, doing her best impression of a scared little girl, 'I just wanted to understand a little more about what the Church of the Cracked Acorn wants. I thought the repository would be the best place to find out. I'm terribly sorry for coming in without permission, Mr Bombroffe. Everyone was just so...busy.'

The old man eyed her for some time, his eyes comically large through his spectacles, but Beatrice could not tell what he was thinking.

'Nice try,' he said eventually, a small grin appearing on his wrinkled face.

Beatrice radiated innocence. 'I'm not sure what you mean, Mr Bombroffe.'

The old man gave a dry chuckle. 'I'm sure that little-girl-lost act works on many people, my dear, but you'll find me a shrewder opponent. Did you think your many solo sojourns to my repository had escaped my attention? I applaud your enthusiasm, my lady, but we have rules for a reason.'

Beatrice tried to hide her scowl. 'If you knew then why haven't you told on me before now? And it's not your repository, it belongs to my family.'

It was a rude thing to say, but the ancient bibliothecary merely nodded good-naturedly. 'A fair question. In truth, I must admit to a certain amount of pleasure in seeing someone so young developing a love for books. It stayed my hand. And technically the Castle Blackwood book repository now belongs to the Duchy of Blackwood. Your father bequeathed it when he came to power.'

'Did he?' Beatrice said in surprise. 'I didn't know that.' She thought about what else the old man had said. She'd never really considered she might be developing a love of books. They just contained useful information. Or interesting things. 'Then why turn me in now?' she asked the old man. He was shuffling along beside her at a snail's pace, leaning heavily on her for support. It felt more like she was leading him than he was leading her.

'Well, I can hardly ignore it when I run directly into you, now can I?' Mr Bombroffe replied. 'That would be a dereliction of my duties. But…perhaps I can help with whatever information you were seeking in that book. Was there something in particular you wished to know?'

Beatrice was surprised. This was the longest conversation she had ever had with the bibliothecary, but she had never had the impression he would be so willing to dispense information. If she had known, it might have saved her a great deal of trouble.

'Well, I really *was* trying to understand the people who attacked my grandfather. What exactly is it they want?'

They reached the door to the repository, and the girl held it open while Mr Bombroffe limped through. They were well on their way down the spiral steps of the tower before the man spoke again.

'That's quite a complicated question. The first thing you must understand, my lady, is that the so-called *Church of the Cracked Acorn* is just the most recent incarnation of a very old idea. The second thing is that, as yet, there has actually been no official confirmation that this group is connected to the man who attacked your grandfather and killed that poor fellow on Longest Night. We, as researchers, must learn to pick the grains of truth out of the sandcastles of misinformation, rumour and idle gossip.'

'Are you saying that Erasmus Sweetspire was lying when he told the Lord's Chambers that there was a connection?' Beatrice asked quickly.

Mr Bombroffe shook his head. 'No. I'm saying that at present there is no tangible evidence available to us that back up Sir Sweetspire's claims. He may yet be proved right. But we must consider the alternative outcome as well. Take nothing on faith, my lady. Tell me, what do you know of Zigelder?'

'Not much,' Beatrice admitted. 'Just that he's the father of humanity and son of Melethin.'

'And how about the phrase *'cracked acorn'*? What does that mean to you?'

Beatrice thought carefully. 'There's something about that in the Book of Oak, isn't there? Wasn't Zigelder cracked as an acorn in the fight between his father and Garselin?'

'Good. Yes, you're quite correct. So from that, what can we surmise?'

'...that the Church of the Cracked Acorn is a church dedicated to Zigelder? But why? Or rather, why is Zigelder mentioned so little in the Book of Oak? If he's our father, then shouldn't we be worshipping him?'

Mr Bombroffe stopped on a step beside a small slit window and smiled at her. 'And there you have hit upon the very nub of an argument that is far older than either of us. Many scholars have written about the cracking of Zigelder's shell, but few, over the decades, have agreed on much. Some say once his shell cracked, he lost much of the grace bestowed upon him by his father, and as a result, he became a darker, twisted being. The very look of the Black Oaks, his offspring, and the dangerous nature of the Blackwood would appear to bear weight to that interpretation, would it not? But if true, have you spotted the consequences?'

Beatrice thought hard. Then it came to her. 'It's us! If we're his children, then that makes us dark and twisted too!'

The Bibliothecary beamed at her like she was his star pupil. 'Exactly!' he said, continuing his slow descent of the slippery steps. 'Now ask yourself, what would you rather believe? That we as humans are the divine descendants of the Grandfather tree, Melethin himself? Or that we are the twisted offspring of his damaged son, Zigelder? Most prefer the former view, of course, which is why we have the Church of the First Tree. But not everyone agrees, and with the formalisation of the church by your grandfather, those differences are beginning to boil over.'

'So...Zigelder is evil, then?'

'Oh no. Nothing so simplistic as that. He is still the son of Melethin, after all, and one thing pretty much all scholars of the subject agree on is that he did not lose *all* of his grace. I suppose you could say he was something of a mixture; neither all good nor all bad. Much like us, his children, of course.'

They exited the east tower and stepped out into the castle's inner ward, where an eerie, watchful silence had descended. Castle Guards patrolled the walls above and stood in little huddles at every doorway. The servants went about their morning chores like they always did, but people looked uncomfortable. There was just a hint of drizzle in the air. Beatrice considered what she had learnt so far.

'So, people like the Church of the Cracked Acorn think we should be worshipping Zigelder. But why? Just because he's our father? Or is there more to it than that?'

'It all comes down to a matter of philosophy,' Mr Bombroffe

said, pulling his nightgown closer around his waist against the chill. 'The city of Upton-Myzzle has been developed in line with a certain philosophical way of seeing the world. But there are alternative views. We tend to try to suppress what we see as the darker parts of our nature, but to others, those traits are important elements of what it means to be human. Zigelder represents embracing them.'

'Like what?' Beatrice asked.

'Well, take murder as an example. Murder is currently a crime, yes?'

'Of course!'

'Well, to certain people, murder is an entirely natural part of life. Those who survive, thrive.'

'That's awful!' Beatrice cried.

The Bibliothecary nodded solemnly. 'Yes,' he said. 'But also, no. You have to understand that to a certain point of view, it is not an evil thing. And certainly, all followers of Zigelder are not evil either, and many would not even consider committing such an act. It is an extreme example I've used to illustrate a point.'

Beatrice was silent for a moment, then said, 'I'm not sure I understand.'

'Think of a fox,' said Mr Bombroffe. 'Its winter, food is scarce and her babies are hungry. If she does not find them food soon, they will die. So, she breaks into a chicken coup and kills a hen to take back to her offspring. Is the fox evil? Or is she simply being a good mother?'

Beatrice thought about it. 'Good mother,' she decided.

'Ah,' said Mr Bombroffe. 'But the hen had babies too, and with her dead, the chicks will freeze. Is the fox evil now?'

'I...I don't know.'

'It is a complex question. Good fortune, for one, often means bad for another. The question we have to ask ourselves is how much responsibility we should take for how our actions affect others.'

The two fell silent as they made their steady way towards

the keep. The red book in Beatrice's hand had grown heavy, but she dared not slip it into her satchel in case the bibliothecary thought she was trying to steal it. She wondered if he'd noticed the books already in her bag. Eventually she said, 'What about the new star, then? What has that got to do with everything?'

'That, I'm afraid, I cannot answer,' said the bibliothecary. 'There are simply too many unknowns.'

'Do you think it's Garselin?'

'I have no proof one way or the other, my dear. And, in our particular case study, it is almost immaterial. What matters is whether the perpetrators of these crimes believe it to be the great daemon or not. Did it prompt their actions? Is it a simple coincidence? We have no way to substantiate either claim.'

'But you must have an opinion?'

The man raised his crooked neck to look at her with dry amusement. 'And who should care about the opinion of an old academic? I'm afraid you'll find that few do.'

'I care,' Beatrice said, somewhat surprising herself. The dusty old bibliothecary was growing on her. She wasn't sure she had ever had a conversation quite like this one before.

Mr Bombroffe beamed at her. He looked smaller out in the daylight, like a gust of wind might blow him clean away. 'Well, I thank you for that, my lady. And if you insist upon it, then no, in my opinion, the star is not Garselin.'

'What makes you think so?'

The old man chuckled. 'Ah, and now, by appealing to my vanity, you have me trapped. I must back up an unsubstantiated hypothesis without the data to do so.'

'What's a hypothesis?'

'It's sort of another word for theory.'

'Well, then you must have some kind of reason for your theory, unsustainable or not.'

'Unsubstantiated, my lady.'

'That's what I said.'

'Well, if you really must know, then I suppose it's just a feeling, really. Or rather, something half-remembered. There is a lot of knowledge out there and it is hard to keep it all in one's head. That's why we have books, I suppose.'

'You read something in a book that makes you think the star is not Garselin?' Beatrice pressed.

'Yes. Or I think I did. It was a very long time ago, but I do seem to recall mention of something similar before. I've been wracking my brains trying to remember the details, but to no avail. The frailties of age, I'm afraid.'

'I met a man on Longest Night who said the star had appeared before.'

'Then perhaps I am not losing my mind after all.'

'Can't you just find the book you think you read it in and re-read it?'

The man smiled. 'Alas, it would seem not. That book you're holding was my last attempt to do just that, but no luck. I suspect it was something I read years ago, perhaps from the old town records archive. I used to go there a lot as a young man.'

Beatrice's ears perked up even higher. 'Where's that? I didn't know there was a town archive!'

'Ah, lost, I'm afraid, my dear. The building disappeared into the Blackwood decades ago and many of the documents inside were never recovered.'

'Couldn't we go in and get them? Where was the archive? It must still be there!'

Mr Bombroffe gave her a stern look. 'The Blackwood is a very dangerous place. I dare say something of the building may have survived. It was large, after all, and one of the few made of stone. But reaching it would be quite impossible. No, we shall just have to accept the fact that some knowledge is lost to us. Now, let us go and see your father.'

They had reached the keep steps, and the bibliothecary began his slow ascent. Beatrice gulped. She had quite forgotten the purpose of their journey. She hesitated for a moment, wondering if she could just run off. But when the old man wobbled dangerously on the third step, she hurried back to his side. She didn't want him to hurt himself, and perhaps a telling off was worth everything she'd learnt.

'One more question, Mr Bombroffe.'

'Of course, my lady.'

'The way you talk about Melethin and Zigelder, it's like you're talking about a theory. A hypothesis. Does that mean you think their...' she faltered, unsure how to phrase what she wanted to say. 'That their significance is somehow debatable. Open to interpretation.'

The old Bibliothecary gave her a strange look that Beatrice couldn't quite identify. Then he took her arm once more and allowed her to lead him up the steps.

'I think,' he said. 'That is a conversation best left for another day.'

3.

There were more people sitting around the long table in the great hall of Castle Blackwood that morning than Wigbert could remember seeing since before his wife died. His father sat stiffly in his usual chair at the head of the table, looking grey and tired. It had been politely suggested that perhaps he would have been more comfortable staying in bed after his ordeal. But the old man had described in particularly colourful language exactly what he thought of that idea, so the matter had been dropped. There was, however, a large fire burning in the hearth, a compromise Mr Dribbets had managed to get the old man to agree to. It meant the hall was actually pleasantly warm, for once, and cosy orange light danced across the drab tapestries, though Wigbert worried about the expense. Beatrice was also in attendance, along with the castle's bibliothecary, for reasons the duke hadn't entirely ascertained. His father had snapped at them to sit down before they could properly explain. Punduckslew and Mr Dribbets had suffered a similar fate. The final guest was a corporal of the castle guard whose name temporarily escaped Wigbert, as did the reason he had asked him to join them. That made a party of seven in total, four of whom were what his father usually referred to as 'domestics'. He called anyone who worked in the castle that, which always made Wigbert rather uncomfortable. The fact his father had allowed any of them to sit down to breakfast with his family was a testament to his reduced health. Wigbert certainly couldn't remember it ever having happened before.

There was a cloud of awkwardness hanging over the table. Punduckslew—a man who had never struck the duke as feeling in servitude to anyone—was making the most of the situation. Wigbert watched in fascination as the wizard shoveled buttered kippers and bread into his mouth with an almost indecent amount of enjoyment. Grease ran down his beard in little rivulets. Mr Dribbets did not seem nearly so comfortable. He perched awkwardly on the edge of his seat and sipped a cup of spice that must surely have gone cold some time ago.

'Well, this is nice,' Wigbert said, regretting it instantly in the ringing silence that followed. The duke was doing his level best to remain calm. Events seemed to be running away with him and he had what might be politely referred to as an *unquiet mind*. It often happened in times of stress. Unfortunately for the duke, he was the sort of man who took on stress in much the same manner that Punduckslew was currently taking on kippers. He felt like several people were holding a conversation in the back of his mind and he hadn't been invited. The corporal, who was sitting next to Wigbert with a slightly waxen look of horror on his leathery face, shifted uncomfortably. He seemed to be doing his best attempt at standing to attention whilst sitting down.

'I'm terribly sorry, old fellow, but remind me who you are again?' Wigbert asked the man, trying to keep his eyes on the guard's face rather than the mass of curly black hair that sat above it.

'Corporal Snekchesser, your grace. Castle Guard, your grace,' the man croaked. Sweat was glistening on his forehead.

'Ah yes, of course. The hero of the hour! I really can't thank you enough for what you did for my daughter.'

'Nothing but my duty, your grace.'

'Of course, of course. Even so, I felt I must show my appreciation somehow. Tell me, have you ever considered becoming a sergeant? Or even captain, perhaps, given the circumstances. The Guard needs good officers, now more than ever.'

There was a moment of silence that went on for just slightly too long. 'I'm not worthy, your grace.'

The duke watched as the guard's waxen face turned a delicate shade of green. Gastric distress, perhaps? 'Now, I'm sure that's not true at all, my good fellow.'

'I assure you it is, your grace.'

'Nonsense, nonsense. Well, that settles it. Congratulations *Captain* Snekchsser!'

There was a strange strangled sort of noise which Wigbert took as a 'Thank you, your grace'. Poor man. Perhaps the food was a tad richer than he was used to. He should really see to improving the Guards' rations.

'Now, as the newest officer of the Castle Blackwood Guard, I have your first commission.'

'Yes, I thought you might, your grace.'

'These are dangerous times, captain, as I'm sure you are aware. The attack on my father last night proves that no one is safe. As such, I would like you to watch my daughter day and night. Do you understand?'

'Yes, your grace.'

'I would, of course, set my own bodyguard to the task, but apparently I can't.' Wigbert shot Punduckslew a sharp glance. The Wizard shrugged his hefty shoulders.

'Out of my hands,' he said. 'I'm on secondment from the Charter as bodyguard to the duke, and the duke only. Any changes to the contract would have to go through the committee. So, unless his grace would like to keep his daughter with him at all times, there is little I can do.'

Wigbert said nothing. He felt the wizard was being rather uncooperative. Instead, he said, 'Well, you have your orders, captain. I'll leave the details in your capable hands.'

'Do I get any say in this?' Beatrice burst out angrily. Wigbert gave her a look which said '*We'll talk about this later*' and the girl sat back in her chair with a sullen expression.

'Permission to ask a question, you grace,' said the freshly minted Captain Snekchesser.

'Go ahead.'

'Will his grace the, er…former duke require extra protection as well?'

'My father assures me he has made arrangements of his own,' Wigbert said flatly, avoiding looking at the old man. After a blazing row earlier that morning, the duke had agreed to leave his father's protection to his father. He didn't like it. He knew his father was up to something.

'The men have also been wondering, your grace, what with General Weltsmatter no longer being with us, um…who exactly is in charge, your grace?'

'Ah, yes. We should probably settle that, shouldn't we? Who is next in command after the general?'

There was an embarrassed silence.

'That would now be Captain Snekchesser here,' said Wigberts' father, at length, who had been uncharacteristically mute until that point.

'Oh, really?'

'It would seem, your grace, that on General Weltsmatter's departure, he took a number of officers with him. Including all his captains,' Mr Dribbets offered apologetically.

'Ah, I see.'

'Youcan'tmakemeaGeneral! Um…your grace,' gasped Captain Snekchesser.

'No?'

'No!'

'It would certainly be…inappropriate,' the duke-no-more said, darkly.

'I see. Well then, for now, consider *me* in charge. I will expect daily reports from yourself, captain.'

'I see. Permission to go and get on with it then, your grace.'

'Of course, captain! We shall not detain you from your duties any longer.'

'Thank you, your grace.'

There was a loud scraping sound as the captain practically leapt from his chair, followed by the sound of hurried footsteps as he all but ran from the room.

'Odd man,' Punduckslew said, wiping his greasy face with the tablecloth.

'You cannot make that...*man* an officer!' Wigberts' father cried, smashing his fist down on the table.

'I believe I just did,' said Wigbert.

'Who are his family? Where did he come from?'

'I'm sure I don't know, father. What I do know is that he went above and beyond to protect Beatrice. That is good enough for me.'

'You can't just raise anybody up!'

'Snekchesser isn't just anybody, he's my friend!' Beatrice said.

The duke-no-more ran a bony hand across his grey face. 'No, he's not. He's a member of the castle guard. Just a corporal. Not one of your playmates!'

Beatrice scowled. 'I don't have playmates! I'm not a little child! And besides, he's not a lowly corporal anymore, is he?'

'It's done!' Wigbert said, cutting across his father's reply. 'We need people we can trust in command and I've chosen this Snekchesser. I am the bloody duke, after all!'

The old man slouched back in his chair and glowered. The other occupants of the table all suddenly became very interested in the ceiling.

The buzzing of conversation in the duke's head surged, and a voice broke through above the hubbub. *You tell him, old boy! Jolly good show!*

Wigbert closed his eyes and tried to ignore it.

Silence stretched on until Wigbert cleared his throat and turned to his daughter with a forced smile. 'Now then, Beatrice, I believe you and Mr Bombroffe wished to speak to me about something?'

'Um...possibly,' Beatrice replied, looking uncertain and turning to the ancient bibliothecary sat next to her, who appeared to have fallen asleep with his chin resting on his chest.

'Is he dead?' asked Punduckslew, helping himself to a rather generous slice of pound cake and knocking over the sugar bowl in the process. This earned him a tut of disapproval from Mr Dribbets.

Wigbert cleared his throat as noisily as possible. 'Er...Mr Bombroffe?' he called.

The man gave a start, which dispersed small clouds of dust from his person. The ensemble watched in horrified fascination as it slowly drifted over the table, depositing itself onto what was left of breakfast. Mr Dribbets picked something out of the bone-china cup he had been holding like a talisman, but pulled a face and put it down.

The bibliothecary's magnified eyes blinked at the group in confusion. 'Did I miss something?' he said.

'Um, you wished to speak to me?' Wigbert replied, pretending to not see his father rolling his eyes.

'Ah yes, I should very much like to talk to you about young Beatrice here,' Mr Bombroffe said, as if he had just walked into the room.

'Oh?'

'Look, can I just say—' Beatrice cut in, but the old man waved her into silence.

'There is really no need, my lady. Now, your grace, I should like your permission to take charge of your daughter's education.'

Beatrice looked shocked. 'You would?'

'I understand she already has several tutors, your grace. However, I humbly suggest that she could do more. I believe there is much I could teach her, with your permission, of course. I would suggest perhaps two hours a day.'

Wigbert looked at his daughter, who appeared stunned.

'You feel there is currently something lacking in Beatrice's education?' He asked.

Mr Bombroffe nodded. 'No offense meant to her other tutors. But I believe your daughter to be capable of more advanced study than she is currently being tested with.'

'I see,' said the duke, a swell of pride rising in his chest.

You raised a clever one there, Wiggy!

Wigbert swallowed and tried to concentrate. 'And what about you, Beatr...Bea? Is this something you would like?'

His daughter seemed a little lost for words, but she looked at the ancient Bibliothecary appraisingly. 'Yes,' she said eventually. 'I would like that.'

'Well then, I think it's a splendid idea, Mr Bombroffe.'

The man nodded with satisfaction and began getting slowly to his feet. 'Excellent, your grace. In which case, I shall leave you in peace. Beatrice, I expect to see you in the repository at nine sharp tomorrow morning. You can bring those books back with you,' he added, indicating her satchel and a large red leather book with a sweep of his hand.

'Yes, Mr Bombroffe,' Beatrice replied, still looking rather surprised.

With that, the old man shuffled out of the room and disappeared.

'Can we move on to more pressing matters?' Wigberts' father grumbled. Wigbert ignored him.

'I'm proud of you, sweetheart,' he said to Beatrice, shooting her an encouraging smile.

'Excuse *me*, but has everyone forgotten that I was almost murdered in my bed-chamber mere hours ago?' his father cried.

Wigbert sighed. 'No one has forgotten, father.'

'Well, I should hope not! The duchy is practically falling apart around us and here we are chatting and drinking spice!'

'There are things we should discuss, your grace,' Tanco offered tentatively. Wigbert waved him on with another sigh. 'News of the attack has already reached the town, I'm afraid to say,' his steward continued. 'Coupled with the sudden dismissal of General Weltsmatter, and the further news of Sir Krickwells escape from Watch custody, it might be prudent to offer some kind of reassurance to the populace.'

'What did you have in mind?'

Mr Dribbets made the face of one who is delivering

news he knows will not be welcomely received. 'Given the circumstances, I think perhaps a public appearance might be in order.'

Wigbert groaned inwardly.

'Are you mad? He'd be a sitting duck!' Punduckslew protested.

'Actually, I don't believe so. You see, I've concluded that his grace may not, in fact, be a target at all.'

'May not? *May*? And that's good enough for you, is it?' Punduckslew retorted. 'Look, I know where you're going with this, but it's not worth the risk!'

'Well, would the two of you idiots care to enlighten the rest of us to what it is you're prattling on about?' the duke-no-more snapped angrily.

'They are alluding to the fact that the killer, whoever he is, has now had two opportunities to attack me and has failed to do so on both occasions,' Wigbert said levelly.

'Quite so, your grace,' said Mr Dribbets. 'Last night in this very tower, and on the platform on Longest Night. It would have been only too easy for the man to go after you both times, but he did not. The logical conclusion is that you are not his target.'

'Perhaps not yet—' Punduckslew said, but the duke silenced him with a raised hand. He turned to face his daughter with a smile.

'Beatr-...Bea, my love, I think it might be best if you were to leave us to it.'

'What? No, I want to hear!'

'Come now, this really isn't an appropriate conversation for a girl of your age. Why don't you go to your chambers and...'

'Play with my dollies?' his daughter said, eyes narrowing.

'Er, read or something?' Wigbert finished.

'But you still haven't heard my report of what I saw on Longest Night! *And* I've found out more information about—'

There was a loud bang and the clatter of crockery as Wigberts' father slammed his fist down on the table once again. *'Do as you are told!'* he roared at the girl, who jumped in surprise. She looked entreatingly at Wigbert, who said nothing. Scowling, and with tears welling in her eyes, Beatrice jumped to her feet and ran from the room. Wigbert felt a little more of his self-respect go with her.

Oh, very well done, said the voice in his head. *That man has all the tact of a rock.*

Punduckslew was smiling fondly after the girl. 'Older than her years, that one,' he said. 'Don't worry, your grace, she'll get over it.'

Wigbert pinched the bridge of his nose and took a deep breath. 'I think Mr Dribbets is right,' he said heavily.

'You do?' his steward said, somewhat surprised.

'Yes. I need to make a public appearance.'

'I'm glad you agree, your grace. I was thinking—'

'Just as soon as we have the Lord of Misrule in custody.'

'That's not quite what I meant.'

'I know. But I promised I would bring the man to justice, and it seems to me, the best way to restore confidence in the Castle is to do what I promised.'

'I really think the people would feel better if they could see you—'

'And they will, Tanco. They'll see me conducting my investigations. As for the matter of Sir Krickwell's escape, well, I think the people should know just where he escaped *from*, don't you?'

'From the Watch, as opposed to from the Castle Guard, you mean?'

'Quite. Make sure the Gazette has that point straight, will you?'

'And General Weltsmatter?'

'His services were no longer required due to my taking a more hands-on role as leader of Castle Blackwood's armed forces.'

Mr Dribbets took out his little notebook and scribbled down a few words. 'Anything else, your grace?'

'Yes. Let people know that my investigation is proceeding… promisingly.'

'Is it, your grace?'

'Exceedingly so.'

'Our only lead blew a hole in the watch-house floor and legged it,' Punduckslew pointed out.

'An unfortunate, but minor, setback,' Wigbert replied, on a role now. 'We have a new lead.'

'Do we?' asked the wizard.

'My father saw the killer's face last night, didn't you, father?'

His father grunted. 'Fat lot of good that will do any of us. It was only a glimpse as he fell over the balcony and his mask slipped. Didn't recognise the bastard.'

'Tanco, find someone who can draw and get them to draw a portrait of the face my father saw. Father, you can describe it to them. Then we can have copies made and get them pinned up all over town. You might not have recognised him, father, but someone will.'

'I'll see to it right away, your grace!' Mr Dribbets said, getting hurriedly to his feet and making for the door.

'Oh, and get the royal carriage ready to go out again!' Wigbert called after him. He could feel his father looking at him.

'Leave us, wizard,' the old man said after a moment of silence.

Punduckslew raised a bushy eyebrow, then looked at the duke, who nodded almost imperceptibly.

'I'll just go help get the carriage ready then,' he said, lumbering to his feet.

Once his heavy footsteps had faded away, the duke's father spoke again. 'That was almost…political,' he said. 'Well done.'

'Thank you.'

'However…'

Of course there was a '*however*', Wigbert thought.

'We need to talk about some of the decisions you've been making. All this running around playing thief-taker, it's not dignified.'

'I'm merely trying to stop a killer. How can that be wrong?'

'It's not your place.'

'Look, father, you know as well as I do what's riding on this. The Coins-'

'The Coins? Don't speak to me like you understand the first thing about the Coins, boy! If you did, you wouldn't have allowed them to put you in this position. Do you think Erasmus Sweetspire would have allowed himself to be manipulated so easily? Now *there's* a man with presence. He's going to eat you alive, boy, and we simply can't afford—'

'You weren't there, father!'

'No. Well, perhaps I should have been.'

There was a heavy silence.

'You know that's no longer possible, father,' Wigbert said carefully.

His father's face showed he'd heard him, but the man pretended he hadn't. 'Son, you need to commission a proper general for the Castle Guard. Don't get me wrong, Weltsmatter had to go, but we need to be showing strength right now and …'

'And you don't think my leadership shows strength.' It wasn't a question.

'It's not about what I think. The Castles popularity, *your* popularity, is at worryingly low levels right now. We need someone experienced at the helm. Someone that the people can have confidence in.'

'I'm not going to make you a general, father.'

'I'm not talking about me,' the duke-no-more said coldly. 'Sir Quinby Thistledown has a son, I believe, who—'

'I'm not employing one of your nobby friends' sons.'

'*We're* nobs.'

'My point is, I'm not handing the Castle Guard over to another posh born idiot, whose only qualification for the job is being born with the right name!'

'People expect—'

'No, father! You expect. You! I will find someone who I feel is right for the job. And if I can't, well, I shall just do it myself, rather than handing the reins over to one of your cronies.'

'Cronies? You make me sound like some kind of crook!'

'It's…it's nepotism!'

His father gaped at him furiously. '*Of course it's bloody nepotism*! That's how this works! The only reason you're duke is because you're my son!'

'No father, the only reason I'm duke is because you made such a mess of things you had to abdicate before you were deposed!'

The words hung in the air over the table like great fat hornets. Wigbert was panting. His father's face looked like it had turned to stone.

'Get out!' the old man said tightly.

Wigbert felt like a man who has jumped off a cliff. There was no climbing back up. All he could do now was fall till he hit the bottom. 'This is my castle,' he said. '*You* get out!'

The words landed like a slap to the old man's face. With very deliberate care, his father pushed back his chair and got to his feet. 'Well,' he said. Wigbert could hear the rage simmering in his voice. 'I'm glad we had this little chat. I see how things are now.'

'Father wait…' Wigbert said, but the old man had picked up his cane and was limping from the room.

The duke stood alone at the table. The detritus of breakfast were spread across the wood like the wreckage of a battlefield.

Well, that went well, said the voice.

'Oh, shut up!' Wigbert cried, burying his face in his hands.

4.

In her chambers, Beatrice lay on her bed and tried to sob. It wasn't working. She'd tried kicking her legs a bit. Nothing. She'd even tried pinching herself, but still nothing. It was really very frustrating. It's what a young lady was supposed to do, wasn't it, in situations like these? Ladies in Wolfe Starlingcloud's world were always sobbing. Or swooning. Beatrice had tried to swoon once, but all she'd got was a muddy back and a bruise on her forehead that lasted a week. And now the more she tried to cry, the angrier she got. In the end, she got up and stamped on her pillow for a while, which made her feel a little better.

After that, she paced a bit and thought again about how unfair the world was. They treated her like she was…was some kind of kid! But she was just as capable as any of them! More so, probably, on account of them being all old and achy and so on. Probably all got dementia, she thought bitterly. They should be thankful they had her around.

She looked down at the books from the repository that were lying on the floor next to her bed. Well, at least someone thinks I'm worth something, she thought. Mr Bombroffe had rather taken her by surprise, but she liked the idea of learning more from the man.

It was while she stood, staring at the books and thinking of the old bibliothecary and their earlier conversation, that the first seeds of an idea formed. If no one would listen to the information she had so cleverly gathered, well, then she would just have to act on it herself. She went to her window and looked out at the dark treetops of the Blackwood in the distance.

'And I know just where to go,' she whispered to herself with a smile. Mr Bombroffe would have to wait.

CHAPTER SEVEN: THE FACE OF A KILLER

1.

They hadn't even left the castle before they found the body.

Wigbert held his nose and tried to breathe as little as possible whilst staring glumly at the sad, crumpled form on the grass before him. It was a castle guard, he could tell that much despite the heavy soiling of the man's uniform.

They stood in a quiet corner of the outer ward, behind the gatehouse, where the hustle and bustle of the castle's principal thoroughfares were hidden from view.

'He was only just found, your grace,' the newly minted Captain Snekchesser was explaining. 'He wasn't even on duty last night, so no one…'

'What was his name?' the duke asked

'Willoby, I think, your grace. I didn't know him well.'

'Family?'

'I'll find out.'

'Good. What happened, captain?'

'It would seem he was…pushed, your grace. He was only found when Ged here turned up just now.'

The duke turned to look at the man Snekchesser indicated. He was familiar with Ged, who had been coming in and out of the castle daily since Wigbert had been a child. He still distinctly remembered the first time he had laid eyes on the night-soil man, mainly because he hadn't slept for a week afterwards. It is hard to properly convey the appearance of a man like Ged. If you were to imagine something akin to a walking compost heap, you might not be far from the mark.

That's not to say that he was dirty. Not exactly. In fact, due to his profession, Ged was the most frequently bathed man in Upton-Myzzle, by quite some considerable margin. So no, not dirty as such, but the ghost of dirt stuck to the man like a miasma.

'It was Gladdis what found the poor bugger, your grace,' Ged said, smiling apologetically. His face looked like weathered wood.

Gladdis, the man's gwalmok, was tethered nearby, happily munching on something unspeakable in a bucket. She was contributing enormously to the almost physical unpleasant smell that occupied this small part of the castle grounds, like a thug slouched in the corner of a pub. The aromas that did not emanate from the beast were coming from a large, lumpy brown pile that lay at the base of the gatehouse wall; the result of the guards garderobe above, and the reason Ged was there.

'She sniffed him out as soon as we arrived,' the night-soil man continued.

'In all this?' Punduckslew said, waving an arm around at the muck. The wizard was trying to breathe through his sleeve.

'Excellent nose, my Gladdis. Ain't nothing-nor-no-one who smells like her!'

'Of that, I have no doubt,' the duke replied, his eyes beginning to water. 'So I'm assuming this is the work of our visitor last night?'

'It would certainly appear so, your grace,' said Captain Snekchesser. 'There were no witnesses, obviously, but I don't believe in coincidences.'

'Which tells us something rather important,' Punduckslew said, thoughtfully.

'Does it?' Wigbert replied. All he could see was a dead man who he was responsible for.

'Yes. It tells us the Lord of Misrule's Talent has a maximum range. Otherwise, why stop in the guardhouse? Why not just transport himself right in and out of the castle grounds completely? Remember when I said there were limits to my power? Well, now we know one of his. He must have to be within a certain distance of a place before he can jump to it.'

'But why attack a man in the middle of... of his business?'

'Wrong place, wrong time, I expect. The killer probably thought the garderobe would be a quiet corner of the gatehouse. I expect he intended to slip in and be on his way to the keep without being noticed.'

'More likely, the attack happened on his way out of the castle,' Captain Snekcheser said. 'His attack on the duke-no-more failed. He would be panicking, less careful.'

Punduckslew nodded. 'Right. He zaps in, right on top of poor Willoby here and...'

'Pushes him down the loo,' Wigbert finished for him.

'Not a nice way to go,' Punduckslew acknowledged. 'A fifty-foot drop into a great steaming pile of sh—'

'Yes, thank you. I get the picture.'

Simply beastly, said the voice.

'No one asked you!' the duke snapped.

'Er...I'm sorry, your grace?' said the wizard, looking confused.

'Nothing,' Wigbert said, flushing. 'Captain, forgive my ignorance, but what is the procedure in circumstances like this? As I'm technically in charge of the Guard right now, is there something I ought to do?'

You ought to be saddling up the calvary, old boy, and riding this dog down!

'Shut-up!' Wigbert whispered, whilst trying to concentrate on the captain in front of him. Snekchesser was regarding him with some concern.

'Er...leave it all to me, your grace. I've been a guard long enough to know the drill. I'll make sure everything is taken care of.'

'Thank you, captain,' the duke said. He gazed at the body again, still lying in a heap at his feet. 'Poor man.'

They left the captain to deal with arrangements and joined

Mr Dribbets in the royal carriage, which set off for town at its usual slow rumble. Tanco had already procured a rough sketch of the face Wigbert's father had described to him.

The face of the killer was strangely unremarkable.

It was the sort of face you passed in the street every day, attached to butchers, carpenters, masons or any number of other people. It was thin, with short-cropped hair and a clean-shaven chin. The nose was not overly long, or particularly bulbous. Lips were neither thin nor swollen. The eyes, far from being the hard, icy portals into the soul of a madman the duke had expected, were in fact soft, oval and really rather plain.

'Are you sure this is accurate?' Wigbert asked.

Tanco shrugged, sending his wooden tokens clattering about his neck. 'Your father proclaimed it a fair likeness. I'll have some flyers made up to hand round. Are we offering a reward for information?'

Wigbert hadn't considered this. 'Should we, do you think?'

'It might loosen a few tongues. We will undoubtedly attract time wasters, but I think it worth the risk.'

'Very well. I'll leave the amount up to you.'

'Very good, your grace.'

Wigbert sat back, closed his eyes and listened to the thud, thud, thud of the coachman bouncing up and down in an attempt to encourage the two gwalmok to gather speed.

What's the plan then, Wiggy old fruit?

Wigbert's eyes flew back open to find Punduckslew regarding him quizzically. He avoided the wizard's eyes and looked, unseeing, out of the window.

The sodding plan is to get rid of you, with all speed, he thought.

Aww, no need to be like that. I'm just trying to help, you know?

Well, you're not helping! I'm talking to myself and no one wants to see that in their duke, Wigbert thought bitterly.

You're not talking to yourself, you're talking to me!

Same difference!

I hardly think so, old chap! I may be currently residing in your fine bonce, but you know very well I'm entirely my own man.

Well, that's the bloody problem isn't it, this...*situation*, it's not normal!

Oh, and why not, might I ask?

Because I made you! You can't go around thinking for yourself!

Well, I do hate to beg to differ, but I'm here, Wiggy, and I don't see why I should go anywhere, the voice said sulkily.

Wigbert was left with the distinct impression of retreating footsteps in his head, followed by the slamming of a metaphysical door. This was getting out of control. He had to do something, and fast. He hadn't been joking. If people found out their duke was talking to voices in his head, it was all over. He slid down the window and leant out to speak to the driver.

'I'd like to make a stop at the apothecary in Pingle Street, please.'

The driver nodded his assent and Wigbert withdrew his head into the carriage, where Punduckslew and Tanco were regarding him with concern.

'Is everything all right, your grace?' his manservant asked.

'Fine...fine. Just a headache. I'm out of my, er, my usual pills.'

Realization dawned on the other mans face. 'I'm so sorry, your grace. I didn't realize you were running that low! I completely forgot in all the commotion.'

'No harm done,' Wigbert said quickly. Tanco may have known about the pills, but he didn't know about the exact nature of Wigbert's ailment, and Wigbert had no intention of telling him now.

When they reached Pingle street, the coachman brought the carriage to a creaking halt, more or less directly outside a black-painted shopfront with the word 'Gruntnthunk's' depicted in silver over the door. Wigbert entered the apothecary alone, convincing his two companions that he was unlikely to be attacked by a mob in the time it took to purchase a cure. Defeated, Tanco continued on foot to the printers, to 'Get a start on things.'

Inside, the apothecary shop was dark, with little light filtering through the solitary street-facing window, which was thick with dirt. The walls were lined with hundreds of dusty glass bottles, and behind an elaborate wooden counter sat the expansive frame of the apothecary himself, Mr Albert Gruntnthunk. Gruntnthunk was easily twice as wide as any other man in Upton-Myzzle, and far more spherical. It was said he achieved his impressive frame through a strict diet of bread, ale and beef drippings, which he consumed in vast quantities and swore was the only cure to some mysterious ailment he was afflicted with, but refused to name. One of the many symptoms that Gruntnthunk attributed to this curious illness was excessive sweating, and indeed the man had pearls of the stuff running down his fleshy face, even as he staggered to his feet to greet the duke.

'Your grace, a pleasure to see you in my humble establishment once again,' the man wheezed, supporting himself on the counter with both arms.

Gruntnthunk had been the apothecary of choice for the Stonemorton family for at least a generation. His cures were generally thought not to be the most effective in town, but this was counteracted by his uncompromising patient confidentiality. He never uttered a word about a customer's complaints, something that had been invaluable to Wigbert in particular.

'Good morning, Mr Gruntnthunk,' the duke said. 'I hope I find you well?'

The man grimaced. 'It's my knees, your grace. It eats away at the bone, this affliction of mine. Agony just to stand.'

Wigbert thought it likely that any man's knees would give way under the tremendous load that Albert Gruntnthunks had to bear, but kept it to himself. 'Well, I certainly wouldn't have you suffer on my account,' he said instead.

The huge apothecary grunted with relief and collapsed back on to his stool. There was the momentary sound of tortured wood before the long-suffering appliance readjusted to its load.

'Much obliged to you, your grace,' Mr Gruntnthunk said. 'Now, how may I be of service?'

'You may remember I have approached you before about a... certain problem...' the duke mumbled.

Mr Gruntnthunk nodded sagely. 'Ah yes, the, *ahem*, headaches. Bothering you again, are they?'

'They are becoming something of a nuisance, yes.'

Rude! Wigbert ignored the voice, focussing on the ample face of the apothecary, who was scratching his wobbling chin with swollen fingers and looking thoughtful.

'And when did the symptoms begin?' he asked.

'Only yesterday, but they're...worse, this time.'

'I see. And have you been under an unusual amount of stress—. He began, then smiled ruefully. 'Actually, don't bother answering that, your grace. Nasty business. Well, I can, of course, prepare the usual concoction.'

'I was wondering,' the duke interrupted, 'if there might be anything stronger we could try this time?'

Mr Gruntnthunk mopped his sopping brow with his coat-sleeve, regarding Wigbert with a serious expression. 'The cure has not proved to be robust enough before?' he asked.

'It has provided some limited relief,' Wigbert admitted. 'But the...problem is rather more, shall we say, fully formed on this occasion.'

Folds of fat bunched together on the apothecary's forehead as he raised his eyebrows. 'Indeed? Well, there is perhaps another avenue we could pursue, although I would remind his grace of what I have mentioned on previous occasions. This type of ailment might benefit from a more invasive solution. I have the skull drill in the back. It would only take a few minutes—'

'I think I will stick to the oral solution, if it's all the same to you, Mr Gruntnthunk,' Wigbert said quickly.

The apothecary looked disappointed, but nodded his ascent. 'Very well, your grace. Then I shall have a concoction prepared and delivered to the castle this afternoon.'

'Ah. I was rather hoping you could give me something now.'

The fat man shook his head, looking apologetic. 'I'm terribly sorry, your grace, but that simply can't be done. The cure will take some time to prepare, you see, and I don't keep this sort of…specialist concoction in stock.'

'I see,' Wigbert replied with a surge of despair. 'Well, as quick as you can then, Mr Gruntnthunk. I will be much obliged to you.'

'Of course, your grace. I shall begin the preparations at once.'

'You have my thanks.' Wigbert gave the apothecary a nod and made for the door. Before he reached it, Gruntnthunk spoke again.

'Your grace, I hesitate to mention this…but if this cure proves ineffective, we will have to revisit the idea of more drastic measures. It is my experience that ailments of this nature rarely go away of their own accord, and we do not want your situation to worsen.'

The duke looked back at the man, and in that moment he fully appreciated just how much of his future might rest in the apothecaries rather bloated hands.

'Of course, Mr Gruntnthunk,' he said. 'Good day to you.'

2.

Tanco was waiting for them outside the printers in Seabass Street. He approached the royal carriage as it rumbled to a halt in front of the building, opening the door and climbing inside before Wigbert or Punduckslew had a chance to get out. He had a worried expression on his spherical face.

'The printers have promised five hundred fliers by this evening. I got them to sketch out a copy to work from so we could keep the original in the meantime,' he said, brandishing the sketch. 'However, I feel we may want to reconsider our plan. I'm not sure the streets are safe for you, your grace.'

The duke rolled his eyes. 'Last night, my father was attacked in his nightgown, Tanco. I rather think that *nowhere* is safe right now. Besides, didn't we just get done deciding I wasn't a target?'

'You may not be a target of the Lord of Misrule, but take a look out the window.'

Wigbert did as he was asked. A fine drizzle was still falling and leaden clouds were reflected in the many pools of standing water on the muddy road. The street was busy as usual, but not with shoppers. Instead, large groups had gathered at intervals, huddled together in shop awnings or around braziers, still lit against the damp chill. Wigbert realised with a shock why Tanco was so concerned. Many faces were turned to the royal carriage, and their expressions mirrored the dark sky above.

'Has something happened that we are not aware of?' he asked, feeling decidedly uncomfortable. He felt like the crowds could see his every thought, despite the intervening distance. He knew that morale was bad, but things seemed to have taken a decided turn for the worse since the previous day.

'It seems some people have been whipping up discontent, your grace.'

'The Church of the Cracked Acorn,' Punduckslew said, smashing a fist into his other palm. 'Like that bloody man yesterday. I knew the Watch wouldn't deal with him. Damn that Posternos!'

Tanco nodded. 'I think you are most likely correct. It was hard for me to gather much information myself. It would seem my own popularity has taken something of a nosedive because of my association with the Castle, but from what I could find out, a group of men and women, dressed much as you described the man you saw yesterday—'

'In black robes,' Wigbert said.

His steward nodded again. 'In black robes, yes, have been going around telling everyone that Garselin has awoken and is descending on Upton-Myzzle as we speak. What's more, they seem to blame you, your grace—and the Church of the First Tree—for his return.'

'Because the Church of the First tree preaches against the old ways, and my family started the church,' Wigbert said, pinching the bridge of his nose. 'We're the obvious choice to target. Look, it would be all too easy to turn this coach around and head back to the castle, and believe me I would like nothing better, but wouldn't that just confirm what everyone out there is already thinking? That I'm some distant aristocrat, completely divorced from the feelings and struggles of the everyman? Or worse, that I'm some coward hiding away in his riches? I think I need to get out there and speak to these people!'

There was a slightly embarrassed silence in the carriage. Punduckslew was fastidiously examining the tips of his fingernails, whilst Tanco was looking at the duke with an expression suggesting he was trying to find the right words to say something delicate.

'Public speaking has never been your...' he eventually managed, apparently unable to find an appropriate way to finish the sentence.

'Well then, I need to bloody learn, don't I!' Wigbert snapped, making to leave the carriage. 'Earlier at breakfast, you were telling me I had to speak to the people. Anyway, if anyone doesn't like what I have to say, then Punduckslew can threaten to blow their heads off or something.'

'I could do that, yes. But I wonder if that would really be—' the Wizard began.

Wigbert cut him off abruptly. 'What would you have me do? Run away? Acorns and roots, not a day goes by without someone telling me I need to interact more with my people, and now I actually want to suddenly everyone's changed their minds!'

'I'm not sure that tackling angry mobs is quite what we had in mind, your grace,' Tanco said, clearing his throat nervously.

'I applaud your conviction, your grace, I really do. But I think perhaps now is not the right time,' Punduckslew added.

The duke stared back out the window, unseeing. Were they right? Was he being stupid? He felt his conviction waiver.

Wiggy, you need to get out there right now!

No one asked you, Wigbert thought bitterly.

By Melethin's craggy trunk, use your eyes! Look!

The duke found himself doing as he was told. In the street, there were movements amongst the crowd. The people were drifting towards one spot, gathering in a large circle around...

Wigbert was out of the carriage door and striding towards the disturbance before either of the other men could stop him.

'*Your grace, no*!' he heard Tanco shriek behind him, but he didn't stop.

What the duke said next, in a loud and carrying voice, was quite remarkable, in the genuine sense of the word, by which it is meant that many people remarked upon it afterwards, often whilst sniggering.

'I say, *excuse me!*'

As the opening line to a confrontation, it was lacking a certain something. 'Reach for the sky!' might have had more punch. Even 'Oi, you!' would have carried a more inherent menace. As it was, the words did not quite evoke the reaction Wigbert had hoped for. They did evoke quite a few raised eyebrows. The duke plunged on regardless.

'What do you think you are doing? Step away from the young lady at once!'

There were some stares, and some muttering, and the general sense that people were not sure of what to do when they were being shouted at politely by a duke. Eventually, the tight knot of people drifted slowly outwards, and in the centre, the cause of the commotion came back into view.

'Hello, your grace,' Corporal Tritewine said, readjusting her hat and smoothing down her crumpled gown.

'Are you alright, corporal? What on earth is going on here?' Wigbert asked, glaring at some of the retreating crowd who were milling around uncertainly.

'Just a minor difference of opinion,' Corporal Tritewine said brightly. 'Some of these good people seem to be labouring under the misapprehension that there is a daemon descending on the town. I was merely trying to show them the evidence proving that the so-called daemon is a comet, as we have already discussed, your grace.' She opened a little folder full of paper that showed graphs and diagrams.

'Liar!' a woman somewhere in the crowd shouted. 'You're just trying to trick us!'

Wigbert looked around for the source of the voice, but it could have been any women present.

'My good woman, what possible motive could we have to lie to you?' he called out.

'That's what you government types do!' a man standing a few feet away said angrily. He was shabbily dressed, a few days' stubble standing out on his pointed chin.

'I can assure you—' Wigbert began.

'We don't believe you!' the man shouted.

'But I haven't said anything yet!'

'Doesn't matter. We don't believe a single thing you people say.'

'Look, I appreciate that things have not always—'

'Appreciate? Appreciate! Why should we care about what you appreciate? You people, with all your luxury and wealth, what do you know of the common man, huh?'

The crowd had closed in again. Wigbert was aware of an angry buzzing, like a hive of bees. Then the people faltered, and he felt the reassuring presence of Punduckslew at his side. The wizard said nothing; he didn't have to. He just folded his thick arms across his chest and glared.

'Perhaps we should go, your grace,' Corporal Tritewine suggested.

'Why won't they listen?' Wigbert asked.

She gave a little shrug. 'They're scared.'

The duke looked at the faces milling around uncertainly. The natural philosopher was right. There were angry faces there, but far more of them were simply worried.

'I am sorry, I truly am,' he called out. 'You are right to say that I know little of what your lives are like. Mine has been quite different. Perhaps that is something I need to work on. And you may not believe that I have your best interests at heart, but think about this; if I truly was lying to you about the star, would I really be hanging around here? If I thought Garselin was coming, why would I be bothering to convince you otherwise? The world would be over, right? What would be the point of trying to keep the peace?'

'Err, your grace, are you sure this is the right course of action?' Tanco appeared at the duke's side, looking concerned and clutching the sketch.

'Well, nobody's shot at me just yet,' Wigbert murmured.

'How very reassuring.'

Wigbert continued, raising his voice to the crowd. 'I am not here to lie to you! I am here because I need your help. There is a very real evil stalking our streets. A man who kills without mercy. This man!' He grabbed the sketch from Tanco's hands and held it aloft. 'And I need your help to stop him.'

He had their proper attention now. They weren't looking at him, but at the face on the piece of paper in his outstretched hand. 'So please, if anyone recognises this man—'

'That's him? That's the Lord of Misrule?' asked the shabby man, scratching the stubble on his chin.

'That's right. We have a witness who—'

'But that's just young Toflo Higginbottom!'

There was a murmur of assent from the crowd and a nodding of heads.

Wigbert's heart leaped. 'You know this man?'

The man stared at him like he was stupid. 'We all know him! Why, he's the baker's apprentice! The baker on Wood Smoke Lane!'

3.

South of the river Myzzle, towards what now served as the outskirts of town, just a street or two away from the encroaching Blackwood, stood what would probably have been assumed by passers-by to be a derelict building, were it not for one thing. A brightly painted purple sign hung above the door that proclaimed it, in slightly shaky letters, 'The Upton-Myzzle Forestry Brigade Third Chapter Headquarters!'. The exclamation mark had been added by someone who obviously felt this declaration deserved far more excitement than it generally achieved in those who happened to read it. 'Headquarters' was also rather a grand word for what was essentially a wooden hut, and a wooden hut that had begun the slow decline from wood to compost quite some time ago. It stayed upright mainly by stubborn force of habit. If one felt so inclined, it was quite possible to push one's finger through the softened wooden panelling and the kitchen, which normally backed onto the marshy bank of the Myzzle, was currently sitting in a foot of foul water. It wasn't so much that the roof leaked, it was more that it occasionally interrupted the rain. From inside there came the distinct smell of mushrooms and the noise of children enjoying themselves…or possibly killing each other. It is always so hard to tell. The door creaked open, the building shuddered ever so slightly, and two children crept out.

'You're mental!' Oatey was saying. 'Absolutely bonkers!'

'Ssssh! Keep your voice down,' Beatrice hissed back, closing the door on the game of Thump piggy thump that was currently causing the rest of the troop to thunder up and down the hall in a whooping, screaming mass of legs, arms and hair. Master Lettuce had again been chosen as 'Piggy'.

Oatey shook his head in disbelief. 'Ain't no one here gonna hear me over that racket. And besides, the crazy people worship you and you're their duchess, so I ain't gotta listen to anything you say.'

'I ain't...I mean, I'm *not* crazy.'

'You want to go into the Blackwood alone! You're the Queen of the crazy people!'

'Don't be so dramatic,' Beatrice said, with a little sniff. 'We'd be in and out in no time at all. All we'd be doing was visiting another part of the town. It can't be more than an hour into the trees.'

'We? *We?*'

'I thought you wanted to go into the Blackwood?'

The boy hesitated, the pain of indecision on his grubby face. 'Well, yeah, I do. In *theory*, like. But now?'

'Seems like as good a time as any.'

'What about your bodyguards?'

They were a bit of a problem. It had been bad enough before, but since Corporal Snekchesser had become Captain Snekchesser, she didn't seem to have had a single moment to herself. A succession of guardsmen had followed her about all day.

'That's why we have to get a move on!' she said, urging the boy away from the building. 'They're distracted right now, but they'll soon notice I'm not there and then we'll have lost our chance.'

She'd been waiting all afternoon for the right moment, and when it came, she hadn't hesitated. Thump piggy thump could be a rather...vigorous game. Master Lettuce had once tried to ban it, but the uproar it caused from the rest of the troop had been so bad he'd been forced to relent. All Beatrice had had to do was wait for the inevitable moment when the two guards were caught up in the thick of it and sneak out whilst their backs were turned. It wouldn't last long though, so they had to hurry.

She dragged the still protesting Oatey down the street and around the corner before stopping again to check over the contents of her satchel one last time.

'What you got in there, then?' Oatey asked, peering over her shoulder.

'Provisions and essentials for our trip! I've thought of everything,' Beatrice said, proudly.

'You got food?'

Beatrice rolled her eyes. 'Obviously.'

'A blanket?'

'Yup!'

'What about a bear trap?'

'Don't be ridiculous.'

'Powdered sludge root?'

'What on earth would I have that for?'

'I heard if you blow it in a green man's face, it scares him off.'

'That's absurd.'

'What do you know about it? You suddenly an expert on the green men, are you?'

'I don't need to be an expert to know that blowing a cure for constipation into someone's eyes is more likely to really piss them off than make them run away.'

'I ain't going in there if you ain't prepared.' Oatey crossed his arms and frowned. 'You got any ointment, at least?'

'What type of ointment?'

'I don't know do I! Just ointment. Me ma put it on me pa's toe when he got bitten by a gnome.'

'You're not going to get bitten by a gnome!'

'You don't know that! I might get bitten by a gnome. They're tricky buggers. Disguise themselves like mushrooms.'

'Well, just stay away from any mushrooms then!' Beatrice hissed, throwing her hands up in exasperation.

'But I like mushrooms,' Oatey said sulkily.

'Look, do you want to do this or not?'

'No! I bloody said I didn't back at the hut!'

'Fine! I'll go on my own then. I'll tell you all about it when I get back.'

'Well, you can't do that. That's not fair!'

'Well, you'll just have to come with me then, won't you?'

'This is blackmail!'

'Don't be such a baby. Come *on*!' Beatrice headed off up the street, unwilling to wait any longer. Behind her, she heard Oatey's footsteps as he reluctantly followed.

'Spirits help us when you become duchess,' he grumbled.

'I heard that!'

'You were meant to, *your grace*.'

'Oh, stop sulking.'

Beatrice had deliberately worn a woolen coat with a hood that morning and she now pulled the hood up, hiding her face. She didn't want to be recognised.

'Oh, very nice! And what am I supposed to wear? I didn't realise I was dressing for an exhibition this morning!' Oatey whined.

Beatrice retrieved the blanket and threw it at the boy's head. 'I think you mean an expedition,' she said.

He scowled. 'Forgive me, *your grace*. So, come on then, what's this master plan of yours?'

Beatrice set off confidently down the street, her mother's hob-nailed boots splashing through the puddles and clicking on the occasional hard surface hidden beneath the muck.

'Well, obviously we need to avoid the Watch teams that are working at the edge of the forest,' she said.

'And here was me, thinking you hadn't thought this through.'

Beatrice ignored the boy. 'So, I thought we could walk all the way to the end of Frogman's Row, then slip down Shadeswell Alley, which will bring us out behind the old abandoned Trumpton factory. Then, if we stay low, we should be able to sneak along the edge of the factory's yard wall and straight into the trees without being seen.'

Oatey gave a low whistle. 'I'm actually impressed. I didn't expect you to know the streets in this part of town that well.'

'There's a map of the whole town in the great hall,' Beatrice explained.

'Really? An up to date one? I didn't think anyone had one of those,' Oatey said in surprise.

'Well, technically it's more of a tapestry than a map. And it's about one hundred and fifty years old,' Beatrice admitted. 'But it still shows all the right streets. I just had to adapt it for the advance of the Blackwood.'

Oatey raised an eyebrow. 'Very nice. So you know exactly where this town archive we're looking for is supposed to be, then?'

Beatrice grimaced. 'Not exactly. None of the buildings on it are labeled. But it's given me a good idea where to go.'

'And you're *sure* that it's not that far into the Blackwood?'

'Well, it can't be that far, can it? It's still got to be somewhere inside the old town walls.'

'You know they say that up to half of the towns been lost?'

'Exactly. I can walk from the castle to the troop hut in just under an hour. So it shouldn't take much longer than that to reach the far town wall.'

'Well, maybe, if we knew where we were going. But we don't. We could end up searching for the right building all night!'

'Look, if it takes too long, we can always just retrace our steps and try again.'

'Good. Because there's no way I'm staying in the Blackwood after dark! There's worse things in there than gnomes and green men, you know?'

Beatrice was very well aware of this. She'd heard the stories, just like anyone else. She'd probably read a few more. There was a tiny part of her brain that was telling her this plan was a bad idea, but she had never been one to listen to negativity. Besides, it was exciting! Just think what they might see!

The streets were pretty quiet as they made their way along Frogman's Row and turned into Shadeswell Alley. Besides, in this part of town, two children walking alone raised little comment. They reached the abandoned factory without incident. Trumptons had been a marvel in its day. A four story square building of dressed stone, it stood out amongst the wood and plaster of the surrounding town like a grey monolith. When operational, it had belched smoke out into the sky at such a rate it became known as the Grey Chimney. Now its walls were cracked, its roof collapsed and its fires long since extinguished. At the end of its walled yard the furthest trees of the Blackwood clustered, tall, dark, and brooding. Even from this distance, Beatrice felt sure she could see them rustle, though there was little wind.

'What'd this place make, anyway?' Oatey asked, kicking one crumbling walls so that little bits of stone were dislodged and sprinkled into the mud.

'It was a brass mill, I think. They made pans, kettles, that kind of stuff,' Beatrice replied. She'd read about it somewhere. The operation had moved to a site on the other side of town years ago, its owner showing surprising foresight at how quickly this part of town would be at risk of falling to the trees. The two children stood for a moment, in the shadow of the broken building, looking out at the dark trees beyond. They could hear the buzz of saws and thwack of axes drifting up the tree line from out of sight.

'We really doin' this, Bea?' Oatey asked.

'I want to know about the star, Oatey. It might be important.'

'Ok. Well, let's get on with it, then. Ma's making stew and dumplings tonight and there ain't no way I'm missing that!'

The two of them started towards the trees, bent low to keep themselves hidden by the jagged wall of the factory's yard. They'd barely moved ten paces when a harsh voice cried out behind them.

'You two, stop right there!'

Beatrice's head whipped round. Captain Snekchesser had appeared around the corner of the factory, red faced and breathing hard. As she looked, Master Lettuce came barreling around the corner at full speed, knocking into the captain and bouncing off like a rag doll. He landed sprawled on his face in the mud.

'Children, please, what are you doing?' he spluttered, spitting out mud. 'You must return with us to the troop headquarters at once!'

'Run!' Beatrice hissed.

Oatey gaped at her. 'What?'

'I said run! We can lose them in the trees!'

'You've gone mad,' Oatey said in wonder, but he followed the girl's lead, the two of them breaking into a mad dash for the tree line, the sound of Captain Snekchesser howling like an asthmatic dog at their heels.

In a few short seconds, they were through the tree line. Beatrice nearly stumbled on a broken cobble-stone in her path, pushed above the muck by a huge tree root. Mud splattered up her legs, cold and wet. She was hit by a sudden overwhelming peaty smell, like a punch to the chest, but she couldn't tell if it had come from the disturbed mud beneath her feet, or was emanating from the forest itself. She felt a thrill of excitement.

This was it! She'd really done it. They were in the Blackwood!

Only just admittedly, but this was the furthest she had ever gone. She couldn't help but also feel a twinge of disappointment, however, as she raced on through the trees, jumping over a sapling that she could swear reached out for her legs as she sailed over it. This wasn't quite how she'd pictured her first steps into the famous trees. There was no time to take it in. To savour the moment. Out of the corner of her eye, she could see Oatey scampering through the undergrowth like a startled fox. Behind her, she could feel the captain gaining on them, his heavy footfall hitting the ground like a drumbeat, his ragged breath coming like a series of throat ripping wheezes. It was getting darker. Branches blocked patches of the sky and it was harder to see where to put her feet, as more and more roots disturbed and broke the path.

'Stop this madness!' Captain Snekchesser gasped behind her.

She re-doubled her efforts; she would not be beaten now!

'We'll lose them in the trees!' she cried to Oatey, who responded by matching her increased pace. A string of curse words trailed behind them, telling Beatrice that the captain was tiring. They raced on, jumping roots, dodging branches, as the surrounding trees grew steadily larger. The peat smell persisted. Then, just as she thought they were going to get away, Oatey gave out a squawk of alarm at her side.

'Mushroom, *mushroom!*' he cried, leaping sideways from his path and crashing heavily into Beatrice. There was a spinning flurry of arms, legs, and backsides before the pair of them came to a bouncing, crashing halt on the woodland floor.

Beatrice lay on her back, heart thumping in her ears, breath ragged in her chest. Damp seeped through her clothes from the waterlogged ground. She groaned, opening her eyes to see a thick, dark canopy of leaves high above her. Then the head of Captain Snekchesser hove into view. He was practically frothing at the mouth.

'Is your brain infected with wood rot!' he wheezed, before bending double, hands on his knees, sucking in great lungfuls of the forest air. He looked like he might be sick. Beatrice sat up, wondering if she might still escape while the captain got his breath back. But Master Lettuce soon came trotting into view, sweaty faced.

'Don't you even think about it, young lady!' he warned, looking sterner than she had ever seen him. She looked to Oatey, but the boy was still flat on his back, eyes closed and groaning.

She relented. There would be no escaping on foot. But that didn't mean she couldn't still talk her way out of this. She clambered to her feet, but before she could even open her mouth, Captain Snekchesser bore down on her, grabbing her roughly by the shoulder and not letting go.

'*You stupid, stupid little girl!*' he croaked before breaking into a vicious coughing attack. 'Do you have any idea how much danger you have put us all in?' he hissed at her once he'd sufficiently recovered.

Beatrice was slightly shocked by his level of vehemence. 'I...I just—' she began, but the captain cut her off with a shake of his curly haired head.

'I don't want to hear it,' he snapped.

'Er, captain...' Master Lettuce said.

Snekchesser ignored him. 'Of all the selfish, irresponsible, reckless things to do...'

'Acorn and roots! Alright, I'll go back! No need to give yourself an aneurysm!' Beatrice cut in, a surge of resentment rising inside her.

'Captain, I really think...'

Snekchesser actually growled, his wide nostrils flaring. He spun her around, then let go of her shoulder. '*Back*?' he spat. 'And which way would you say that was?'

Beatrice scoffed, but then she looked back the way she thought they had come and all the fight left her body at once.

The trees gathered thickly around them, their great trunks reaching high, high into the air and their long, arching branches drooped like long trailing fingers. The ground was covered with a squelching layer of moss, mud, and decomposing leaves. Of Upton-Myzzle there was no sign at all. She couldn't even tell which way they had been running.

'We...we can't have come that far in,' she stammered.

'This is the sodding *Blackwood*! You think that matters here?' Captain Snekchesser replied heavily, glaring at her.

'Captain Snekchesser!' Master Lettuce cried.

'WHAT!' the captain shouted, finally tearing his eyes off Beatrice and looking up.

'I...I really think you ought to see this, captain,' Lettuce quavered. 'Is it just me...or is that a pair of eyes in the shadows over there?'

They looked to where the man was pointing with a shaking finger, and immediately saw what appeared to be a pair of large, yellow eyes staring out at them from the shadowy foliage.

Even as they looked, a second pair appeared.

Then a third.

Finally, a single eye opened, all on its own. Which was the most terrifying of all.

4.

Tanco took his usual seat, several rows back from the altar, and rested his back against the wooden pew, deep in thought. Around him there was some pushing and shoving, as the rest of the congregation found their own places. A small altercation broke out between a blacksmith and a minor noble over an aisle seat, a clear sign of the palpable tension in the air. The congregation's hubbub was almost enough to drown out the patter of rain on the glass dome of the Church of the First Tree. The midday service was always the busiest of the day. However, in Tanco's experience, few of them would have their minds truly on the divine. But then he had other reasons for attending himself.

They hadn't found Toflo Higginbottom. They'd arrived at the bakery—an enraged mob in tow—only to find it locked up and deserted. The only thing that stopped the almost rabid citizens from breaking the door down and tearing the building apart was a little old lace-maker from the opposite shop. She'd hobbled outside to demand they kindly keep it down. She was trying to concentrate, you see, on a particularly tricky lazy-joint windmill stitch and their caterwauling made her prick herself in the elbow, not once, but *twice*. It really was quite unacceptable. Once the situation had been explained, at volume and by at least a dozen different people, she volunteered the information that she hadn't seen Mr Plum, the baker, for days, and, if they found him, they were to remind the cheeky so-and-so that he still had her best china spice-pot.

They found him inside the bakery. Tanco had entered

with the duke whilst Punduckslew held back the crowd. Unfortunately, they weren't able to remind him of spice pots or anything else because someone had cut his throat and dumped his body in a kneading trough. It had been really quite upsetting. Tanco wasn't sure he'd ever be able to properly enjoy a loaf of bread again.

They searched the house, but of course, there was nobody else there. More annoyingly still, no one seemed to know much about Toflo, apart from he'd worked at the bakery. The trail had gone cold.

Tanco left Punduckslew and the duke to carry on the search without him. He wanted to visit the church. To sit amongst the people and test the atmosphere. Mr Dribbets was not, strictly speaking, a religious man. He would have described himself more as spiritual. He had little time for the rules and scripture of organised religion, but had his own firm beliefs, many of which did not align with popular dogma. The power of fortune, an insubstantial entity, was never-the-less one he set great store by. This manifested in the many wooden tokens about his person, each a powerful (as far as he was concerned) charm to keep fortune in his favour. But he had made it his habit to attend services regularly, more for the people-watching opportunities they provided than for their moral guidance. He found it a reasonable gauge of what the town was thinking at any one time. Public opinion; it was a fickle beast, and the steward found it just as interesting to see who was absent as who was present.

The pews were looking particularly inauspicious that afternoon. The feeling of the common man (and by the spirits, if Upton-Myzzle didn't have a healthy supply of *those*) had been turning against the church for some time and, knowing his master as he did, Tanco had taken it upon himself to regularly measure the levels of discontent. That's not to say he didn't respect the duke. Wigbert Stonemorton was, in Tanco's humble opinion, a fine man. But he knew his master's limitations. And having his finger on the pulse of his people's thoughts and opinions was not the duke's speciality. It hurt the old steward to know the depths of his master's unpopularity, but he took solace in the fact it wasn't really Wigbert that people despised. It was The Duke, and that was something different entirely.

There was a gathering hush as the high priest appeared, golden branch in hand and striding into the chancel in such a way as to suggest solemn superiority. She faltered somewhat at the sudden quiet her appearance achieved. Rarely, if ever, had her mere presence elicited such an effect before. Tanco suspected it was not a sign of increased deference, and by the look on the high priest's ruddy face, she thought the same. She ran a hand over her bald head in an uncharacteristic sign of discomfort, before taking her place behind a golden lectern in the shape of a giant oak leaf. She placed the golden branch deferentially on a white-clothed table beside the lectern, then turned to face her audience.

'Welcome, children of Melethin,' her voice echoed around the domed chamber, before being sucked in by the expectant congregation. Faces peered at her with a ferocious intensity. Tanco had experienced little like it before. If expectancy could be weaponised, then the high priest would have been skewered to the far wall.

'In these difficult times,' the woman continued. 'I come before you now with a message of hope and—'

'Tell us about the star!' someone yelled from the back of the nave, cutting her off.

'Yeah, tell us! Are we really safe?' someone else called.

The high priest looked furious. Tanco knew her to be a woman unused to suffering interruptions. 'As I have already stated,' she said in a tight voice, 'the star is not something to be frightened about. It is not, I repeat *not,* the great beast. The Church—'

'Who is the Lord of Misrule?' someone shouted.

'What does he want?' cried another.

The high priest was turning puce. She gripped the lectern

with her swollen fingers and glowered out at the congregation. 'I have no idea who the Lord of Misrule is! As I understand it, the duke is responsible for discovering the man's identity. It is not the church's place to get involved with—'

'He already has! It's a man named Toflo Higginbottom!' shouted a woman from the back of the congregation. This caused an uproar of voices. People stood up in their seats, yelling at each other to be heard over their neighbours.

That was fast, Tanco thought, still sitting and stroking his round chin thoughtfully. He craned his head to catch a look at the woman who had spoken. He saw her in the back row, gesticulating wildly; blonde with a lined face and fierce eyebrows. She might have been one of the people in the Seabass Street crowd, but it was hard to be sure. Regardless, the moglin was out of the apple now, as they said. He tried to tune in to several of the many raised voices around him.

'He's found him already?'

'What, the duke? He can't of done, he's useless!'

'It's true, I saw the whole thing!'

'Absolute wood rot, I don't believe it!'

'So the killer is in custody? We're safe?'

'Nah, he got away. Scarpered before they even got there.'

'Ha! Figures. I knew the Castle was useless!'

A sudden cry of anger rose above the hubbub. Heads turned as one to see the high priest raising the oak-leaf lectern above her head, arm muscles bulging, thick veins standing out on her flushed neck. She brought the thing crashing back down to the floor with a boom that echoed around the room.

'*Silence!*' the woman screamed, unnecessarily, as the congregation had already fallen into a stunned hush. Breathing hard, the woman advanced on her spectators. The lectern was, amazingly, still in one piece, but Tanco swore he could see fingermarks in the gold plating.

'*I will not have these uncivilized outbursts in my church!*' the high priest roared, spittle flying from her slug lips. 'This is the house of *Melethin*! I demand you respect it!'

The woman looked almost deranged and Tanco, having once seen her practically throttle one of her vergers to death because he bought her a cold cup of spice, was frankly amazed when one of the congregation answered her back.

'We deserve answers! The people are scared in these uncertain times, and you, as high priest, are duty bound to offer us comfort,' the man said, folding his hands across his chest defiantly. He was a noble of some sort. Tanco recognised his face, but he couldn't place him precisely. The look on the high priest's own face suggested she was contemplating making the man eat her ceremonial golden branch, noble or not.

'Comfort?' she hissed through clenched teeth. 'Melethin offers you all the comfort you shall ever need! I suggest you return your attention to the Book of Oak, for only in its pages can you find the true word of—'

'Yes, yes,' the man cut her off curtly. 'That's all very well if you're talking about spiritual comfort. But I'm talking about the *real* world here. We need facts!'

The high priest narrowed her eyes dangerously. 'Are you suggesting, sir, that Melethin does not impact the real world?'

It seemed to occur to the man for the first time that he might be skating on thin ice. The blood drained from his face, and he looked distinctly uncomfortable.

'Er…well, um…that is to say…Of course I would not doubt the power of Melethin for a second…'

'I should hope not!'

'No. No, of course not. Very powerful…Very powerful…'

'Indeed.'

'It's just…'

The high priest actually cracked her beefy knuckles. 'Just…what?'

'What can he actually *do* to stop the Lord of Misrule? And this star, if it *is* the great beast, and-I'm-not-saying-it-is, but…*if*, then what can he do, if he's…you know, dead?'

'DEAD?' the high priest bellowed, as the entire congregation burst into spontaneous arguments yet again.

Tanco sighed and slumped further back into his seat, letting his eyes travel upwards to the wood and glass dome above their heads and the grey sky beyond.

To his utter amazement, a face stared back at him.

A wooden face.

A masked face.

A figure perched in the branches of one of the immense carved trees that formed the bones of the building. A figure dressed in black, with a wooden mask over its face. Even as Tanco looked, it pushed off and dropped, disappearing in midair. Tanco surged to his feet with a warning cry that was lost in the surrounding din. A dozen arguments still raging around him, Tanco searched the building frantically with his eyes. Where was he? Where had he gone? He found him again at the church's big wooden doors, just in time to see a golden key flash in the figure's hands, before disappearing into a pocket. Then the figure vanished again. This time Tanco did not have to search to find where the Lord of Misrule had reappeared. The screams told him all he needed to know. As the rest of the congregation fell into a terrified silence, Tanco turned back to face the chancel once more. The high priest had fallen quiet and still. She stood, with a shocked expression on her face, and a stream of red blossoming down one side of her green robes.

There was a knife sticking out of her neck.

Horrified, Tanco watched as a black clad arm appeared from behind the woman and slowly removed the blade. The high priest made a sort of gurgling sound and fell to her knees. She flailed uselessly at the wound, blood spurting from between her fat fingers, before pitching over onto her face with a crash.

Above her, the Lord of Misrule stood, delicately wiping the blood from his dagger with a piece of cloth, like he had all the time in the world. The congregation seemed frozen. Any number of people could have been on the man in a moment, but nobody moved. Finished with his wiping, the man in the mask, Toflo Higginbottom Tanco presumed, dropped the cloth carelessly onto the now still form of the high priest and looked up at the crowd.

'Zigelder encourages us to do what we must to survive. But to deceive others of the true nature of existence is a sin against his name. We all must pay for these sins. This woman's spirit was thick with them.' He spoke quietly, his high voice muffled by the wood of his mask, but Tanco doubted if a single person in the church hadn't caught every individual word.

'This place is built on such sins,' the man continued. 'It spews them forth into the world like a contagion, and so it must fall. Zigelder demands its obliteration! And you people, who sit here and listen to its lies. You, who allow yourselves to be corrupted, who then carry that corruption out into the world? You, too, are sinners, and must be destroyed with this unholy place. In the mighty Zigelder's name, I shall make it so!'

In one fluid movement, the man grabbed the white cloth covering the table that stood next to the golden leaf lectern and yanked it to the ground. Beneath was revealed a row of four wooden barrels.

Tanco's heart stopped.

He had seen barrels like those before. In the castle armoury.

'*Gunpowder!*' he yelled, breaking the spell in a moment. The congregation came alive all at once. Several people screamed. Some fought to reach the door. Others, to reach the Lord of Misrule.

But it was hopeless. There was no time.

With a laugh that chilled Tanco Dribbets to the very core of his being, the man pulled a blunderbuss from his person, took aim at the barrels, and fired, disappearing as he did so. All Tanco had time to do was throw himself between the pews before the explosion hit him.

CHAPTER EIGHT: CONCEQUENCES

1.

As explosions go, if you're into that sort of thing, it was a pretty good one. It lacked some theatrics a magical detonation might have enjoyed, such as sentient flames, rips in the fabric of space-time, or being followed by a rain of purple frogs, but never-the-less it put on a good show. The first thing people outside the church heard was a great rushing *whoomph*, like the noise a pair of bellows make when they suck in air, only loud enough to hurt the ears. This was immediately followed by what is traditionally referred to as a *bang*. However, this word seems somewhat insufficient. We aren't talking here about the noise made by a dropped crate, or even a crashing carriage. We need something bigger. Perhaps *boom*? *Boom* is more guttural. It better conveys the way the people of Upton-Myzzle felt the sound in the pit of their stomachs, in the soles of their feet, even from way across town. Yes, *boom* is the word, or rather, BOOM!

For those people unlucky enough to be in the old district at the time, these noises were accompanied by a searing wave of heat, enough to knock several from their feet. Unluckier still were those walking the street directly outside the entrance of the church. Their bodies were thrown into the heart of the square as debris rained down like missiles. The glass panels of the domed roof blossomed outwards into a glittering flower that then fell down on the flooded square as deadly hail.

For Wigbert, several streets away outside the abandoned bakery, the explosion was a flash of white light above Wood Smoke Alley's shop fronts, followed by a deep rumble that shook the mud below his feet.

'What ...' he began, his head turning to the source of the noise like many of those in the surrounding crowd.

'That was an explosion!' Punduckslew cried above the sudden outburst of screams from the people in the street. He had grabbed the duke by the arm and was pushing him towards the royal carriage within seconds. 'We must get off the street immediately. You too, corporal!' he continued, herding Corporal Tritewine in the same direction. The natural philosopher appeared too shocked to resist and less than a minute later Wigbert sat opposite her, Punduckslew by his side, as the carriage rattled and splashed away. Even the pair of gwalmok seemed to feel the urgency of the situation as the carriage moved with more speed than Wigbert had ever seen.

'What just happened?' he gasped. 'Where was that? It seemed like it came from—'

'The Old District,' Corporal Tritewine finished for him. 'I think...I think it was the Church of the First Tree!'

'You mean it just...it just exploded?' Wigbert gaped at her like an idiot. This was too much. Then his stomach lurched. 'Tanco!' he cried, turning to Punduckslew. The wizard looked back at him, appalled.

'We...we don't know what's happened yet. We mustn't jump to any conclusions. First, we must get you safely back inside the castle, then—'

But Wigbert had stopped listening. He stood up, smacking his head on the carriage roof in his haste, then began thumping on the curved ceiling with his fist. 'Take us to the old quarter at once!' he shouted at the top of his voice.

'Y...yes, your grace,' came the driver's muffled reply.

Punduckslew's brows furrowed further. 'No! Driver, we must get the duke to safety!'

'R...right-oh,' came the worried response from above.

Wigbert turned angrily on the wizard. 'Tanco said he was going to the midday service. If...if he was inside when... We have to go help him!'

Punduckslew shook his head defiantly. 'I am sorry, your grace, I really am. I want to help Mr Dribbets too...of course I do. But you are the *duke*. You can't just go running straight into danger. I *must* assure your safety above all else. We are going to the castle.'

Wigbert felt a sudden sensation, like someone had lit a fire in the very pit of his belly. Rage rose inside him like a ball of flames until he thought he might explode with the heat of it. He opened his mouth to let it escape, but instead he found himself shouting at the wizard, who started backwards in alarm. '*If you think for one bally minute that Wiggy is just going to run and hide when a friend is in mortal peril, then you can think again, old boy! To arms!*'

The wizard and the natural philosopher stared at him in a mixture of horror and surprise.

'Old boy?' Punduckslew said, his brow furrowed so deep now it looked like someone had ploughed it.

'Wiggy?' Corporal Tritewine added, equally bemused.

Wigbert sank back in to his seat, his legs practically buckling beneath him. He felt suddenly very weak. 'I am so sorry.' He ran both trembling hands over his face.

'What just happened there?' Punduckslew said, still frowning.

'I...I don't know what came over me.'

'Your voice...it sounded...*different*,' Corporal Tritewine said, white faced.

'That's because it wasn't *his* voice,' Punduckslew growled, getting to his feet so that he filled the carriage, hunched over almost double, pointing a stocky finger at the duke threateningly. 'What's going on?'

Wigbert eyed the fingertip warily. 'It was nothing... nothing...' he stammered.

'It wasn't nothing. The duke has never called anyone an *old boy* in his life, and definitely never referred to himself in the third person as *Wiggy*! Give me one good reason I shouldn't blow your impostor's head from your shoulders right now?'

Wigbert felt sick. 'I'm not an imposter...how would that even work? It's me! I just had a funny turn, is all.'

'Hilarious,' the wizard growled, his beard bristling, and Wigbert fully appreciated for the first time just how intimidating his bodyguard could be.

'Alright, alright!' he said, feeling a terrible weight settle on his shoulders. 'Calm down, I can explain. But...' and here he eyed both the wizard and corporal nervously. 'This cannot, under any circumstances, leave this carriage. Is that clear?'

Corporal Tritewine nodded dumbly. Punduckslew continued to scowl, but he sat back down and removed his finger from Wigbert's face. 'We will see.'

The duke shook his head. 'It must not. If it does...well, I shudder to think what might happen. Corporal Tritewine, I apologise,' he said, looking sheepishly at the woman. 'I know we have only just met, but having seen what you just saw...I must now take you into my confidence.'

'That's...that's ok, your grace,' the natural philosopher said with a small smile. 'Whatever it is, I promise I won't tell a soul.'

Wigbert smiled back gratefully. 'Ok, so here's the thing—'

There was a rapping on the carriage roof.

'I'm sorry to interrupt, your grace, but would someone mind telling me if we're going to the castle or the old quarter? It's just Ted and George here need a bit of time to get used to the idea of turning and...' the driver trailed off uncertainty.

Wigbert's' heart froze. Another witness. 'How much of that do you think he heard?' he whispered.

Punduckslew looked up to where the driver would be, sitting on top of the carriage. 'You up there!' he shouted. 'How much did you just hear?'

There was a moment's silence, then, 'I'm sorry, sir?'

'Knock three times and I'll pay you three times your weekly salary!' the Wizard called back.

There was another moment's silence before the faint reply. 'It's very kind of you, sir, but I bought some sandwiches. Cheese and pickle, sir.'

'I think we're alright,' Punduckslew said.

The duke let out a sigh of relief, then rolled down the window and shouted up. 'Take us to the old quarter please, and as quick as you can!' Punduckslew looked about to argue, but Wigbert shook his head at him as he rolled the window closed again. 'I'm sorry, Punduckslew, but we must. I *will not* abandon Tanco, and that's final. I can explain my situation on the way.'

His bodyguard was obviously still unhappy, but he did not object. He merely indicated with a gesture of his hand that Wigbert should get on with it.

Wigbert took a deep breath. But before he could say anything, the voice spoke out inside his head.

Are you sure about this, Wiggy old boy?

I don't really have a choice now, do I? Wigbert thought. Not after that stunt.

'I have a voice in my head!' he blurted out, then put his hands over his face, not daring to look at their reactions.

'Okay...' Punduckslew said, slowly. 'Um...what do you mean by that, exactly?'

'Look, you know the book 'The Heroic Adventures of One Wolfe Starlingcloud and How He Single-Handedly Defeated the Moss Men of the Silver Fen'?'

'Err... yeeees,' the wizard replied, looking even more confused.

'By Rumbould Tugendhat? I love that book!' Corporal Tritewine exclaimed.

'Well, yes, that's the one. Only Tugendhat didn't write it...I did.'

'But...it's Tugendhat's name on the cover,' the corporal said, uncertainly.'

'I made him up, I'm afraid. He doesn't exist. I suspected it would be deemed...*inappropriate* for a duke to be writing novels. However, the book's profits...let's just say the Castle finds itself in sufficient need of funds that I felt it was worth the risk. I needed a public face. Sir Tugendhat fit the bill.'

Corporal Tritewine gaped at him. 'You mean *you* invented

Wolfe Starlingcloud?' she asked incredulously.

Wigbert felt a slight irk of annoyance. 'Is that so hard to believe?'

The woman opposite him had the decency to look slightly embarrassed. 'It's just...you're so different. Not that that matters, of course! I just never would have thought you...'

She was saved from finishing her train of thought by Punduckslew, who said, 'As fascinating as this is, I cannot see its relevance.'

Wigbert sighed. He glanced out of the carriage window. They were travelling at a reasonable speed now and people were running in the opposite direction. They were getting closer to the old quarter, but it was taking too long. He was terrified of what they might find there, but...Tanco. He had to know. To help him if he could. If it wasn't already too late.

'I have a condition,' he said. 'I've had it since birth, as far as I know. However, it wasn't until adolescence that it manifested. It was weak at first. More of an occasional annoyance than anything else. When my wife died, it took a turn. It has been growing steadily worse for several years. I have managed, thus far, to keep it in check, to keep it hidden, with the help of medication from Mr Gruntnthunk.'

'That's why you wanted to see him this morning. Not for a headache,' Punduckslew concluded.'

'That's right. For several days now my symptoms have become...most distracting.'

'Your symptoms being a voice in your head?' the corporal asked. Her expression was unreadable.

Wigbert nodded. 'They were whispers at first. Almost like thoughts, except they didn't feel like *my* thoughts. But as time went by, they got...louder. More insistent. Then they took on a distinct personality. I fought against it. Tried to ignore it. Then, about a year ago, it became unbearable. I could hardly hear *myself* think. I was desperate to find a way of getting this...this *person* out of my head. And then I found one. I wrote him down.'

They stared at him. Then Corporal Tritewine's mouth fell open. 'You mean to say that it's Wolfe Starlingcloud in your head?' she gasped.

Wigbert nodded again. He could feel his face burning.

'But...but, he's made up! Tugendhat I mean, *you* created him,' Corporal Tritewine said, looking thoroughly confused.

'Well, I may have done. He's in my head, after all. But I didn't do it consciously. He just...appeared.'

The woman stared at him. 'That is...quite odd,' she said eventually.

The duke grimaced. 'You understand now why I've done my best to keep it a secret. I'm pretty unpopular as it is. If people found out about this, it would be a disaster!'

'I see your point,' the corporal replied, nodding slowly. 'Hang on though, isn't there a new Wolfe Starlingcloud book about to come out? Did you write that one, too?'

'That's right,' the duke continued heavily. 'I thought the first one had done the trick. My symptoms disappeared, and I was able to get back to something resembling a normal life. But it wasn't long before the whispers started again. Pretty soon I knew I'd have to write another. Only this time...this time it doesn't seem to have got rid of him. Wolfe, I mean. If anything, he's stronger than ever!'

Wigbert dared a glance at the wizard sitting next to him. Punduckslew had been silent for some time and was staring into the middle distance with a grim expression. Eventually he spoke, his voice a deep growl. 'You shouldn't have kept this from me.'

The duke ran another hand down his face. 'I'm sorry,' he said. 'I just didn't know if...'

'If you could trust me?' the wizard finished for him.

Wigbert hung his head. He spoke to the carriage floor. 'It wasn't personal. I didn't know if I could trust anyone. Not even my father knows.'

'That, at least, may have been a wise decision,' Punduckslew conceded. 'But I am supposed to be your most important line of protection. How can I do my job properly if I do not know all the facts?'

Wigbert said nothing. What could he say? In the back of his head, the voice, Wolfe's voice, spoke. *You don't have to explain anything to anybody, Wiggy old fruit.*

Wigbert ignored him.

'We're here,' said the corporal.

The duke looked up to see that she was right. The carriage rolled to a halt at the corner of the old quarter's square. Ted and George grunted and squealed in their harnesses, seemingly unwilling to go any further. With good reason, Wigbert thought.

What remained of the Church of the First Tree was a flaming, smoking mess of wood and glass. The rest of the building seemed to be strewn over the waterlogged ground of the square, as were at least a score of people. Some were moving, crying out in pain or fear. Others were not. The square was full of people too, staggering, running this way or that, trying to help the fallen, or just trying to get as far away as they could. Beneath their feet, the mud churned and a fine rain still fell from the dark sky above.

'All those people...' Corporal Tritewine whispered with her hand to her mouth.

'How?' It was all the duke could think to say as he starred out of the carriage's window in horror.

'Can you not think of how?' Punduckslew growled. He, too, was staring out the window, his face pale.

'You don't think it was him? The Lord of Misrule? This Toflo Higginbottom?'

'That's exactly who I think did this. Him or some of his friends in the Church of the Cracked Acorn.'

'Never mind who did it, we have to help these people!' Corporal Tritewine cried.

'You're right,' Wigbert agreed,' come on.' He opened the carriage door and made to step down, but was stopped by Punduckslew's heavy hand on his shoulder.

'Hold on, your grace.'

Melethin's craggy trunk! Blast that infernal wizard. We need to move, said Wolfe. Wigbert agreed and grunted with annoyance. 'Look *I'm me*, ok? We don't have time to argue about this. Tanco...the rest of these people they need out help!'

'That's not it. We'll discuss that later, and believe me, we *will*, but we can't just rush out there. We need a plan. We have to do this smart. The town will be watching,' Punduckslew warned. The wizard's face was grave; as serious as the duke had ever seen it.

Wigbert relented. Every fibre of his being was screaming at him to rush into the church, not to mention Wolfe, who was practically howling with frustration inside Wigberts' head. But he knew the wizard was right. 'What do we do?' he asked.

Punduckslew moved forward, scanning the scene before he spoke again. 'First things first. We've got to get a group of people together to help the wounded. We need to get anyone who can be safely moved as far from the wreckage as possible. It could be extremely unstable and we want to avoid further injuries if we can. We can send runners to the Guard and the Watch, but we need to move fast so we'll have to find anyone who hasn't completely lost their heads and get them organised. Then we need to get those flames out. It's raining, so that will help, but we need to set up a bucket chain to the river. We won't be able to get inside and search for survivors until we have. Your grace, if we are going to take charge of this situation, we cannot falter. *You* cannot.'

The duke nodded. 'Don't worry about us. *Me!* I mean, don't worry about *me!*'

The wizard looked sternly into Wigberts' eyes. 'That's my entire job,' he said. 'For this to work, you have to agree to one more thing.'

'Anything!' Wigbert said, desperate to get out there.

'You do not leave my side. You or this Wolfe,' Punduckslew said. 'Not even for a second.'

'Done.'

'Then let's get started!'

2.

Across the river, amongst the restless trees of the Blackwood, Beatrice felt the explosion as a distant rumble. It rose up through her legs till it shook the very pit of her stomach.

'What was that?' she whispered.

'I have absolutely no idea, but right now, I'm more concerned about what *those* are!' Oatey hissed back at her. The seven yellow eyes were still staring out at them from the gloom of the trees. They didn't seem to blink and Beatrice's eyes stung as she dared not do so herself.

'Stay close!' Captain Snekchesser ordered.

'Oh dear…oh dear…oh dear…' was all Master Lettuce seemed able to say, repeating it to himself like a mantra.

'Pull yourself together, man!' Snekchesser barked.

'O…of course, captain,' the master stammered. But he continued to wring his hands and tread up and down anxiously.

'I don't suppose,' the captain said carefully, giving Beatrice a slight nudge whilst not taking his eyes off the seven points of light in the darkness, 'that you have any kind of weapon in that satchel of yours?'

'Um, I think I have a small gardening knife of my fathers,' she replied.

'That'll have to do. Get it out. *Slowly.*'

Beatrice did as she was asked, fishing around blindly in the bag until her grasping fingers found the wooden handle. She carefully eased the blade out of the satchel and held it ready in her hand. It was tiny, rusted, and notched, mud still caking it in places. Her father used it for cutting string. She used to pretend it was a sword. It now felt totally inadequate.

Next to her, Captain Snekchesser was slowly easing his very real smallsword from its scabbard. He was simultaneously fumbling with the leather straps that held the blunderbuss in its holster on his opposite hip.

'W...what exactly are we dealing with here, captain?' Master Lettuce asked in a quavering murmur.

'I can only see what you see, man!' Snekchesser snapped back under his breath. He finally pulled the blunderbuss free and handed it to the trembling master. 'Take this, but only shoot if and when I tell you to.'

'Me!'

'Yes you! Or would you rather I gave the firearm to one of the *children*?'

'But I'm not very...I mean to say, wouldn't *you* rather...'

'I can't fight and shoot at the same time, and it's a last resort. And what I'd *rather* is that silly little girls hadn't run us all into the middle of something's blasted hunting ground!'

'Oh dear...' Lettuce repeated.

'No one asked you to run after us,' Beatrice retorted in a whisper, but her heart wasn't in it. Truth be told, she was wondering if her big plan had been a bit of a mistake. The little voice that had been telling her all day she had no business going into the Blackwood suddenly seemed to be making a lot more sense.

'We could shout for help?' she suggested. 'We really can't be that far from the edge of the wood.'

'Do you want to attract the attention of every other beast in these trees?' Snekchesser growled. 'No. What we need to do is very carefully edge in the opposite direction and hope to Melethin's craggy trunk that whatever they are, they aren't hungry. Boy, I need you to turn around and check if the woods behind us are clear.'

'Oh yes, I'd just *love* to turn my back on the vicious monsters!

No chance! You do it,' Oatey said.

'I'm the one with the *sword*! Just do it!'

Muttering to himself, using words that would usually have earned him a stern reprimand from Master Lettuce, Oatey began to slowly turn his back on whatever was looking out from the shadows.

There was a long silence.

'Well?' Captain Snekchesser hissed, eventually.

Beatrice heard Oatey gulp. 'I think,' the boy said. 'That you might need to use that gun after all.'

Beatrice risked a glance behind her. There were more eyes. She looked round to the sides and saw even more points of yellow light in the darkness. 'We're surrounded!' she said, trying to keep the tremor out of her voice.

Master Lettuce began chanting to himself again, and the captain swore under his breath.

'Right, new plan!' he hissed. 'When I say, *and not a moment before*, I want you all to yell as loud as you can and follow me, running as fast as you can. Lettuce, fire that gun at the first thing that gets close enough!'

'What happened to not attracting the attention of anything else?' Master Lettuce squeaked.

'Desperate measures,' the captain said. 'And the loud noise might just startle them enough to buy us precious seconds. Once we start moving, don't bloody stop. Our only chance is to hope we can outrun…whatever they are.'

That question was shortly answered, as one creature moved slowly further towards them. It was the one that owned the solitary eye, and the yellow orb drifted slowly out of the shadowy undergrowth until…

'Frogs?' Oatey said with a nervous laugh.

'Big frogs!' Master Lettuce said in a strained voice.

'Actually, I think you'll find their toads,' Beatrice said. 'You can tell by the—'

'*Not the time, Bea!*' Oatey hissed.

'Right. Sorry.'

The toad was indeed large. Roughly three feet in height, with knobbly, warty looking brown skin and feet the size of a man's face. Its bulbous eye regarded them with amphibian interest. The other was closed by a nasty-looking scar. As they watched, a large sack beneath the toad's chin swelled like a bubble and it let out a long, low croak. Beatrice had never considered there to be anything particularly threatening about a toad before. But that noise changed her mind in an instant.

'Is that a good sign, do you think?' Master Lettuce asked through clenched teeth.

'I doubt it,' Snekchesser growled. 'Lets not wait to find out. On the count of three, we run. One...two...th—'

But before he finished the word *three*, something else flittered out of the gloom, landing on the toads waiting back.

Master Lettuce screamed.

'Well, there goes the element of surprise,' Captain Snekchesser sighed.

Beatrice, however, could sympathise with the trembling master. The winged thing that had just appeared was truly repulsive. It looked something like a moth, but massively swollen in size, and with an almost humanoid, grey-haired body. Its eyes were large and black, no doubt invisible in the darkness of the trees. Its long, bony fingers caressed the toad's side, like it was a treasured pet, as it stared at them, buzzing like an angry hornet.

'Are they...working together?' Oatey ventured.

'Marvelous,' said Captain Snekchesser, as the buzzing was taken up by other hidden creatures all around them, until the air positively vibrated with the noise.

'Are we still running, captain?' Lettuce asked weakly.

'You want to stay here? Of course we're still bloody running! Go, *now*!'

Beatrice felt the guard give her a heavy shove from behind and she stumbled into a run, heading for the area of wood that seemed to contain the least eyes. No sooner had they moved than dozens of amphibian and winged forms erupted from the shadows towards them.

'*Move, move, move!*' Snekchesser roared.

Beatrice wasn't sure if they were still supposed to be making loud noises, but a scream ripped itself from her throat regardless as she flinched back from something fluttery that dived at her head from above. Running almost blindly, arms up around her face, she expected to feel the fluttering weight of a moth-man in her hair at any moment. She dodged away from any toads that came near, always heading for the emptiest looking patch of woodland she could see. She felt, rather than saw, the others at her heels. The captain's ragged breath, the masters stifled whimpers. A toad reared up beside her and she bounced off its flank, feeling its rough, moist skin against hers. Another of the moth creatures dived at her head and she instinctively lashed out with a fist, completely forgetting about the knife she was clasping. Her hand connected to something horribly furry with a crunch, and the beast fell away to the side. The buzzing was horrifying. It filled her senses as she dashed on desperately, her chest fit to burst, no clue where she was headed. Behind her came the echoing boom of the blunderbuss. Her foot landed on something squishy and she stumbled, grazing her knee on a tree root as she fell. Before she could regain her feet, a toad was upon her, and she fell onto her back in the damp mulch with a scream. She felt the toad's weight on her legs as it crawled over her, the buzzing beast on its back reaching out towards her face with its claw-like fingers. She lashed out wildly, but skinny fingers firmly gripped her wrist and the knife dropped uselessly from her grasp. The buzzing increased in pitch.

Then there was a blinding burst of white light. Beatrice closed her eyes against it, but it flooded through her eyelids. The grip on her arm released, and the weight on her legs was removed all at once. She prised open her eyes to see the toads scurrying away from her on all sides. The air was filled with retreating moth-men as the forest was illuminated with an unnatural white glow. Before long, the buzzing subsided, then disappeared altogether as the light faded back to black.

Blinking in shock, chest heaving, Beatrice looked around her. It was very hard to tell they had moved at all. This part of the Blackwood looked almost identical in her eyes to the one they had been standing in before. The other three were there, Oatey lying on the bent trunk of a tree, like he had been forced up against it, Lettuce and Snekchesser on the ground, like her. The captain was wheezing into the mud, the master crying to himself softly.

Then another figure emerged from the trees.

Beatrice scrambled backwards on her hands in shock, but the figure raised a palm placatingly and in a strangely accented voice said, 'Do not be alarmed. I mean you no harm.'

Beatrice got slowly to her feet, not taking her eyes off the stranger as he advanced towards them in the gloom. When he was a mere twelve or so feet away, she got her first proper look at him. For it was a man, a tall, thin man, with long dark hair that just touched the shoulders of his black cloak. Beneath this, he wore a charcoal dress-coat and matching breeches. On his feet were tough looking leather boots, designed for travel, which, if his disheveled appearance was any indication, he had been doing for some time.

He's handsome, Beatrice thought, which took her by surprise.

But there was something odd about the man, too. He had a pinched, unhealthy look, and his right arm hung limp to his side and didn't move. Then Beatrice realised it was in fact secured in place by three leather belts, one at his waist catching the wrist, another round his midriff, and the last pulled tight around his chest and securing the shoulder. Even more bizarrely still, his right hand was entirely encased in some sort of animal hide canteen that was strapped tight to his upper thigh. When Beatrice looked closer, she was sure she could make out smoke or steam coiling out from the flask and up the strange man's restrained arm.

'Who are you?' Beatrice demanded, sounding braver than

she felt.

Before the stranger could reply, Captain Snekchesser had heaved himself to his feet and sprung between them like a growling dog.

'I mean you no harm,' the man repeated, coming no closer. 'I merely heard the gwyf's attack and knew something must have riled them. I came to investigate, and lucky for you I did. Their territory, I fear, has spread with all this rain. It makes them uneasy. Had I arrived any later, I would have been too late to help.

'My name is Silas Gloamblight,' he added when no one spoke.

'The light...that was you?' Captain Snekchesser asked, still breathing hard.

Gloamblight nodded. 'Yes. I am a wizard. The gwyf, the moth-men, fear bright light.'

'Well then, how lucky for us that just so happens to be your Talent,' the captain replied, continuing to watch the newcomer closely. To this, the man said nothing. Instead, he looked into the darkness thoughtfully, then said, 'It is unfortunate you stumbled upon the gwyf and their amphibious steeds at this time. Normally they are a rather docile breed. But things are not right in the Blackwood at present.'

'Docile!' Oatey spat, picking himself up and joining Beatrice at her side. 'I'd like to see your idea of something vicious!'

On closer inspection, Beatrice realised the boy had a nasty gash down the side of his face, which was bleeding freely.

'You're hurt!' She cried, turning away from the wizard for the first time. A surge of guilt washed through her. This was her fault. They could have all died, and it was entirely her fault.

'Don't fuss,' Oatey said with a wince, batting her hands away as she tried to inspect his wound.

'That should be cleaned as soon as possible,' Gloamblight said. 'The gwyf are not the cleanest of creatures and it might get infected. I have some water and a purifying salve that—'

'We have our own water, thank you,' Snekchesser said bluntly, then whispered to Beatrice, 'You *do* have water in that bag of yours, right?'

Beatrice nodded and began searching for her canteen. She pulled it out and tried to pour some over the cut on Oatey's face. The boy grimaced at her and took the water out of her hands, then began to carefully wash the blood and muck from his face. 'That's what those moth creatures were? The gwyf?' he asked Gloamblight as he worked.

The strange wizard nodded. 'Yes. As I say, they rarely stray this far towards the edge of the Blackwood, but I have encountered them several times before. You do not have to worry, they will not come back. However, I suggest we do not linger here much longer. That gun-blast will have attracted a number of things I assume you would rather not meet.'

Captain Snekchesser nodded curtly. 'Very well, if you would be so good as to show us which direction Upton-Myzzle lies, we will be on our way.'

Gloamblight pulled at a silver chain protruding from his coat pocket and removed what Beatrice had assumed was a pocket-watch attached to it. In fact, it turned out to be a compass, which the wizard then consulted. 'I believe Upton-Myzzle lies to the north-east of here.'

'You believe?' Snekchesser said, sounding unconvinced.

'I'm afraid I have never actually been there,' Gloamblight explained. 'This is the furthest north I have ever travelled.'

'Wait...what?' Beatrice said in surprise. 'If you've never been to Upton-Myzzle, then where are you from?'

'I have been a traveler all my life. Originally, though, far to the south of here.'

'Are you saying there are still people out there? People outside Upton-Myzzle? Other settlements?'

Gloamblight looked at her curiously. 'Of course,' he said.

Snekchesser laughed humorlessly. 'Don't believe a word of it. Everyone knows the rest of the kingdom died out long ago.'

'Actually, that's not quite accurate, captain,' Master Lettuce said. 'It has certainly been believed that the other settlements around the Blackwood must have died out, simply because all communication with them ceased years ago. Upton-Myzzle has had no news from the outside since the Quickening began, but no one has ever been able to prove the kingdom's destruction one way or the other, given how treacherous travel through the Blackwood has become. There have been rumours for years that some people survived...perhaps this man is one of them?'

Gloamblight nodded. 'Well, I can tell you that scattered pockets of people indeed have survived. The big towns and cities fell, of course, after what happened to the capital.'

'What happened to the capital?' Beatrice asked with interest.

The wizard looked confused for a moment. 'I think perhaps I had better say no more about it at present. If Upton-Myzzle still has some kind of government, then perhaps I should speak with them. I was planning on traveling to the town after my mission was complete, anyhow. We, too, have heard rumours of survivors in the north,' he explained with a smile. 'I have long wanted to see if they were true. But Upton-Myzzle was remote, even before the kingdom fell.'

'Of course we have a government!' Beatrice cried. 'The duke is my—'

'Enough!' Captain Snekchesser cut over her.

'The duke?' Gloamblight said, his eyebrows rising. 'You mean to say the duchy is intact?'

Snekchesser glared at him. 'Never you mind. You'll see for yourself soon enough, when you guide us out of here.'

Gloamblight regarded the captain with an unreadable expression. 'Very well. I understand your reticence. You do not know me. However, I'm afraid I cannot do as you ask just yet. I have a mission I must accomplish first.'

Captain Snekchesser glowered. 'Oh, and what might that be?'

'Simple,' said the wizard. 'I aim to discover the origin of the new star.'

3.

Great billows of smoke rose above the old quarter, disappearing into the darkening evening sky. In return, the clouds provided a bounty of their own; a steady stream of raindrops that fell, arrow-straight, onto the heads of the Upton-Myzzle citizenry as they gathered in droves around the still smouldering remains of the Church of the First Tree. Occasionally, something in the debris would shift, sending a puff of cherry red sparks back up into the air, but these were quickly extinguished.

The duke stood and watched as the search and rescue team pulled another body from the wreckage. His heart was heavy in his chest, his face, hands and arms felt thick with soot. He wiped his face as the grime dripped into his stinging eyes. His muscles ached and his throat was raw from the smoke. It had taken several hours to subdue the flames, and Wigbert had been in the thick of it. Organising the bucket chains had been easier than he'd expected. The shocked people standing, mesmerised by the fire, seemed glad to have someone giving them orders. There had been an awkward few minutes when the Watch arrived on the scene and Watch Commander Posternos tried to take over the operation. However, as more and more curious people flocked to the square, it soon took all the force of the Watch to keep people back to a safe distance, which left Wigbert free to bolster the bucket chains with the arriving Castle Guard. It was with great relief, and even an impromptu cheer from the gathered crowd, that the flames had been prevented from catching a hold of the neighbouring buildings. Had they done so, only the river Myzzle would have stopped the fire's progress and a goodly portion of the town could have been lost.

But the good cheer had not lasted long. When the bodies started coming out, the atmosphere took a grim turn. Wigbert looked at them now, stretched out in rows along the muddy, waterlogged street. There were dozens of them, and many familiar faces. It was hardly a dignified end. Sheets, blankets, coats, and anything else that would suit had been employed to cover the dead in an attempt to offer some modicum of respect. When the body of the high priest was laid out, a great susurration swept through the assembled crowd. Or, more accurately, the body parts. They'd had to bring some of her out in a bucket. Wigbert had seen things he hoped never to see again. He doubted sleep would come that night.

None yet had been recovered from the church alive, but there were many horrific injuries from those unfortunate enough to have been close to the building when the explosion went off. Wigbert insisted they be sent to the castle's infirmary for treatment. It was only small, with just one or two healers, and usually reserved for treating the Castle Guard or servants. But the only other option was Upton-Myzzle's sole hospital, which sat in its own unkempt patch of ground far to the southeast of the town. It would take longer for the patients to reach it and, besides, the place had something of an evil reputation. Wigbert heard tell that of those unfortunate enough to enter its paint-peeling doors, most left only once they had ceased to breathe. Those still living were then faced with crippling debt. Charity had been a dirty word in the Blackwood, even before the Quickening, and these days the venerable medical institution was run on what little funds the castle could afford to send it. Wigbert knew very well how little that was, having argued with his father about it frequently. He could not bear the thought of anyone, having survived the explosion, dying needlessly because of less than exemplary care.

As the latest body was laid on the flooded street, Wigbert

released a breath of relief; it wasn't someone he recognised. It wasn't Tanco. He felt immediately guilty, just as he had with each of the other unfortunate souls he had been so callously relieved were not his steward. But his hope was dwindling. With no other survivors found so far, the likelihood of Tanco still being alive was becoming more remote with every passing minute. A lump rose in Wigbert's throat at the thought, and his eyes stung from more than just soot.

He was almost relieved at the distraction when Corporal Tritewine approached him with a worried expression. There had been no sign of Captain Snekchesser, but Wigbert was not overly concerned. He assumed the man was simply attending to the safety of Beatrice as he had been instructed. They were no doubt safely back at the castle by now, and Snekchesser would undoubtedly appear before long. In his absence, the duke himself had relayed orders directly to the men and women of the Guard. To their credit, and Wigbert's relief, they had accepted the new chain of command with little comment. Though it had not been said in so many words, Wigbert got the impression that many of them were only too pleased to see the back of their former commander. They may not yet have been totally convinced by the credentials of their new one, but he felt relationships between them had definitely thawed over the course of the afternoon.

'We have a situation developing, your grace,' Corporal Tritewine said as she reached the duke's side. She was still dressed in civvies. Was it really that same afternoon they had come across her in Seabass Street?

'I should think we have quite a few, but er, do go on, corporal,' Wigbert replied.

'It would seem a number of people are attempting to break the Watch's barrier and gain access to the square.'

'How high a number, corporal?'

'At least fifty, your grace. And they are armed.'

'Armed! Who on earth are they?'

'That does not seem entirely clear, you grace. However,

several of them are dressed in black robes and—'

'The Church of the Cracked Acorn. It must be!' someone hissed over the duke's shoulder. It was Punduckslew, who Wigbert had momentarily quite forgotten was there. True to his word, the wizard had not left Wigbert's side throughout the fire-fight, and the duke was almost beginning to get used to the man's constant presence.

Tritewine nodded. 'You may well be right, sir. They are apparently demanding the right to address the crowd.'

'We should demand that idiot Posternos arrest the ringleaders,' Punduckslew said, and there was steel in his voice. 'We cannot allow the perpetrators of this massacre to go unpunished. They have made our job easy for us!'

'More blood will be spilt if we try to take them on mass by force,' the duke mused. 'But you are right, they have been inciting unrest for days now and if they truly are responsible for this horrific act of violence, then they must be dealt with accordingly.'

'Just give the word, your grace,' the corporal said, a gleam in her eyes.

They won't come easy, old boy, Wolfe warned in the duke's head. *You'd have the numbers, but some would die in the skirmish. On both sides, I'd wager.*

Wigbert knew he was right. And for the battle hungry Wolfe to suggest caution meant the risks were high indeed. It might not be so bad were it not for the dozens already dead, he thought, then felt appalled with himself for doing so. Surely, losing even a single life was a tragedy at any time?

You're thinking like a leader, Wolfe said. *These are the tough decisions leaders make. Sometimes you must choose the lesser of two evils.*

That's all very well, Wigbert thought, but how do you tell which one is which?

'We must approach this with caution,' he said out loud. 'We must avoid further bloodshed if we can. Corporal, gather what men can be spared from the rescue effort and we will go and support the Watch.'

'Yes, your grace!' Tritewine said, throwing a smart salute and hurrying away.

'Look at you giving orders like a pro,' Punduckslew said with dark amusement.

'Unnerving, isn't it?' Wigbert said.

'That depends,' his bodyguard replied. 'If they were *your* orders, or if they came from someone else.'

Wigbert gave him a sharp look. 'Wolfe does not control me!' he whispered.

Punduckslew looked unconvinced. 'That is not what I saw earlier in the carriage.'

'We can talk about this later!' the duke said, scowling.

Punduckslew nodded. 'You're right. Now is not the time. But we do need to have a conversation about this. Possibly quite a long one. I am...concerned.'

Wigbert felt a stab of irritation with the man. 'Look, I am very much still in charge here, ok? I'm not about to start swinging from the chandeliers. You do not need to worry about my ability to lead.'

The wizard looked solemn. 'Your grace, you misunderstand me. I have never doubted for a second that you will become an outstanding leader. I still do not. My concerns are of a different nature. But here come the men. We will speak of this later.'

Shocked, Wigbert did not reply. He was not sure what was more surprising; that Punduckslew thought he would become a good duke, or that he had admitted it.

Corporal Tritewine had gathered about twenty guards together. Wigbert was not a military man. There were plenty of them in the Stonemorton family tree, but Wigbert's father had given up on the idea of interesting his son in the mechanics of military strategy at an early age. Therefore, as the rag-tag group of soldiers lined up in front of him, ready for orders, the duke was hit by a sudden bout of anxiety, made even more conspicuous by the apparent absence of it up till that point. No, not absence, Wigbert realised. It had been there all along, lurking in his chest, like a monster with its claws wrapped around his lungs. But perhaps the monster had been sleeping for a while. There hadn't been *time* to feel anxious, what with everything going on. Wigbert promised himself he would examine that discovery later, but right now, the anxiety was back with a vengeance, and he found himself suddenly unable to think of a single thing to say to the group of guards in front of him.

'Err…right then, lovely,' he stammered.

'Ready and awaiting your orders, your grace,' Corporal Tritewine announced, with a smart salute.

Wigbert pretended to inspect the group in front of him, while his brain raced desperately for something to say. He knew himself no expert, but it had to be said he'd seen more impressive groups of men. Excluding the corporal, there seemed to be an awful lot of doughy physiques among them. A couple looked unshaven, and the green and brown uniforms looked crumpled and faded. Some were even badly patched in places, and one man had what looked suspiciously like a custard stain down the front of his coat. Each held a blunderbuss across his chest and had a smallsword hanging from his waist. The weapons looked dirty and uncared for. Wigbert felt he might have to have a quiet word with Snekchesser once this was all over. But right now, he had to figure out how to appear duke-like. He felt himself sweat afresh, which he wouldn't have thought possible after the exertions of the afternoon. Why was this suddenly so hard? He'd been ordering people around all day with barely a second thought.

You're overthinking it. Just tell them what you need them to do, Wolfe suggested.

'We need to go help the Watch,' Wigbert blurted out, as normally as possible.

'You heard the duke!' Tritewine bellowed, making Wigbert jump. 'Move out, men!'

And with that, the men marched away, following the

corporal towards where Watch Commander Posternos could be seen barking orders at a group of citizens who were shouting back just as ferociously.

'See?' Punduckslew said, striding after them with a smirk. 'A natural born leader. Incidentally, you might want to think about promoting the corporal. She's a natural!'

Wigbert glowered at the wizard's back as he followed. He wasn't wrong, though. The chain of command was most definitely a mess, but Corporal Tritewine and been making his orders happen all day and even guards twice her age hadn't questioned her authority. He took one last anxious look back at the wreckage of the church, where several figures were still attempting to find survivors, before forcing it from his mind to focus on the current situation.

They arrived to find Posternos puce and trembling with rage. The group of civilians, the black-robed figures at their head, were still facing off against the line of armed watchmen that blocked their path into the square. They were likewise armed, with a collection of swords and firearms at their belts, but none were yet drawn.

'What is going on here?' Wigbert said with all the authority he could muster. The Watch Commander regarded him with extreme dislike, but he answered all the same.

'These filth are demanding entrance to the square. I've told them to piss off, but they refuse to leave. I was about to give the order to have the lot of them rounded up and arrested for breach of the peace!'

'We have a right to be heard!' shouted a robed woman, who stood at the front of the group of civilians. She was a sickly looking figure, with sallow, yellow skin and large grey bags under her blue eyes. Posternos whipped his head round to face her, his expression clearly stating he disagreed. Wigbert realised with a flash of fear that he would have to intervene before the man escalated things further. His mind raced as he opened his mouth, hoping something convincing would come out.

'No one here is trying to silence anyone, but, as you can plainly see, this is currently no arena for public speaking and debate. You are being kept out for your own safety, along with everybody else.'

'I disagree,' the woman spat, and Wigbert saw there was a strange fervor in her eyes. She turned and directed her next cry to the many curious bystanders who were drifting closer to the confrontation. 'I think this is the perfect time to discuss the many failings of this town's authorities to keep its populace safe! Brothers and sisters, do not let the truth be silenced! Do not allow yourselves to be sleepwalked into catastrophe!' There was an increased buzzing of conversation from the gathering crowd and Wigbert saw several people looking on and nodding in agreement with the woman's words. She eyed him down, a defiant grin on her skinny face.

Wigbert took a deep breath. 'There will, of course, be an investigation into what happened here today, and those responsible will be brought to justice. But now is not the time for such discussions. Right now, our focus must be on helping the injured, searching for survivors and making sure we save as many people as we can. All I ask is that you allow us to do that, by kindly dispersing.'

The sallow woman scoffed, actually laughing, like the duke had told an amusing anecdote. Several others joined in, in a forced, nervous sort of way.

'Words!' she spat at him, loud enough for all those gathered to hear. 'Empty words! The people are sick of your inaction, and we, the Church of the Cracked Acorn, will not sit idly by while the populace continues to suffer!'

There was a collected intake of breath from those gathered.

'So, they finally admit who they are,' Punduckslew murmured in Wigbert's ear.

'The Church of the Cracked Acorn, is it?' Posternos said with a humourless smile. 'Krickwell's lackeys. You blew a hole in the floor of my watch-house!'

'Sir Krickwell is indeed one of our number,' the sallow

woman replied. 'But I have no idea what might have happened to your floor, and we resent the groundless accusation that our peaceful church was in any way involved. We have been unable to contact him since he was savagely attacked by one of your men and unjustly imprisoned on Longest Night. Angston is a good, pious man. He tried to alert the people to a growing threat, a threat the duke here denies even exists, and he was silenced for his troubles. For all we know, it was the Castle that kidnapped him from his cell, so that they could disappear him!'

There were more murmurs from the crowd at this. Wigbert couldn't quite decide if the people were buying what the woman was selling, but he had a sinking feeling they were.

'The violence against Sir Krickwell on Longest Night was… regrettable,' Wigbert said loudly. 'However, he was lawfully arrested for causing a breach to the peace and inciting unnecessary panic—'

'The threat is real!' the sallow woman boomed, cutting over Wigberts words. 'Today's events are proof of that! The end is at hand! The Great Beast is upon us and already the nonbelievers have been struck down!' she raised her hands above her head and appealed to the still increasing crowd of onlookers. 'You think it coincidence that at the very time Garselin appears to us in the night sky above, the sinful Church of the First Tree is struck down? Their high priest obliterated? It is a sign! A message to those of you who have strayed from the true path! But all is not lost. We must beg for Zigelder's forgiveness! For only he of the cracked acorn, our own father, can save us from Garselin now. We, the church that carries our father's heart within our own bosoms, are here today to deliver that message to the good people of Upton-Myzzle. Do not be fooled by the empty words of those most covered in sin. Return to the old ways! Return to Zigelder! You must give him a sign that you accept his love in your hearts. If the deaths of those unfaithful, at the hands of the Lord of Misrule, Zigelder's holy envoy, did not convince you, then let this devastation before us open your blinkered eyes!'

'Enough!' Posternos roared. 'I will not allow you to stand here and spew your filth in the street. Everyone knows the Lord of Misrule is working for *you*, the Church of the Cracked Acorn. He is just a man, not some holy missionary. And both you and he will face justice at the hands of the law! It is *regrettable*,' he stressed the word with a bitter sidelong glance at Wigbert. 'that the Castle has failed in their attempt to apprehend the man, but he will be brought to justice. He would already have been so, if the Watch were in charge of his case. Now, for the last time, come quietly! Or you will receive a justice of your own,' he finished heavily, his hand resting on the hilt of his sword. Wigbert winced at the thinly veiled threat. He thought he saw the sallow woman smirk before she resumed her tirade of righteous indignation.

'These accusations thrown against us are simply the words of a scared, crumbling regime desperate to cling to its hold over the people, *at the expense of the people!*' she cried. 'There is no basis in them. No truth. They present you with no evidence to back up these claims because none exists!'

'She's showboating,' Pundukslew whispered in Wigbert's ear. 'We're giving them exactly what they want. We have to shut this down.'

'Yes, but how? They won't back down and if we attempt a show of force, it will be a disaster,' the duke murmured back, not turning his head. Then an idea struck him. 'We need to convince them they will get another chance to be heard. A better one. But one we know *we* can control.'

'Interesting idea,' the wizard whispered back. 'But where? And when?'

Wigbert thought for a moment, then called out for the crowd to hear. 'Perhaps these questions should be addressed in a more formal setting. They are clearly important, and both sides of the argument should be heard, so that the good people of Upton-Myzzle can make an informed decision for themselves about whom to believe.'

The sallow woman looked a little taken aback by this. She

clearly had not prepared a response to this kind of suggestion. She recovered quickly, however, shouting, 'We will not be silenced!'

'I am not trying to silence anybody. Quite the opposite,' Wigbert cried back, turning his attention to the gathered people watching the confrontation. 'Let me prove it to you! I invite you all, anyone who wishes to hear the facts laid out before them and reach their own conclusions, to join us, right here in the square, in two days' time. We will have a debate on the issue. I will speak, and I invite a member of the Church of the Cracked Acorn to do likewise.'

That got the crowd buzzing. He caught scraps of several excited conversations breaking out around them, before all the words were lost in one another as more and more people began to speak at once. The sallow woman looked even more unsure. She whispered urgently to the cloaked figures at her side.

'What do you all say?' the duke cried to the crowd, hoping desperately he hadn't misjudged their reaction to the idea. 'Will you come?' He was met with, perhaps not the roar of approval he had hoped for, but a definite swell of general acceptance. Wigbert let out a breath of relief. Emboldened, he continued 'And how about you, madame? Will you consent to take part? I'm terribly sorry, I don't believe you gave your name?'

'Clever,' Punduckslew whispered.

The sallow woman hesitated. Her companions were still trying to whisper into her ear surreptitiously. Eventually she answered, her self assured demeanour restored. 'We would be delighted. We will not pass up the opportunity to get Zigelder's message out to the people, and we would relish the opportunity to put to rest the sacrilegious accusations set against us. As for my name,' she smiled coldly. 'That is irrelevant. I am but a servant of our father.'

Punduckslew cursed under his breath. 'She's a snake, that one.'

'It was worth a try,' Wigbert murmured back, then spoke out

loud for all to hear. 'It is decided, then! We will meet here in two days' time to settle these issues. In light of this, I would please ask you all to disperse now and allow us to get back to helping the survivors of this horrible event. Thank you all for understanding!'

At first, nothing much happened. The crowd stared back at him. No one moved. Then, ever so slowly, and to the duke's utter delight and no small surprise, the crowd started to move away. They moved a little above a snail's pace, looking back over their shoulders in case they missed anything, gossiping with their neighbours, but move they did, and in the right direction. Wigbert beamed. He couldn't help it. He had done it. He had actually diffused the situation. Him!

Nicely done, old boy! Wolfe said. *Not that I wouldn't have minded seeing those villains get a good hiding!*

Thank you, Wigbert thought. He was too happy to even pretend he hadn't heard the voice.

Then it all fell apart.

'No!' Watch Commander Posternos shouted. 'I cannot allow you to let these common criminals simply walk away!' The man's face was scarlet, and he was glowering at Wigbert with a deep hatred.

The crowd hesitated. Faces turned back to the confrontation. The black-robed Church of the Cracked Acorn halted at once, faces furious.

'Watch Commander I—' the duke began, but Posternos cut him off immediately, shaking his head with rage.

'I won't stand for it!' he roared. '*I* am in charge of the criminal law enforcement in this town, not the Castle! And I will *not* allow criminals to walk free, let alone give them a public forum to spread their seditious ideas. Men! Take these people into custody at once!'

The man drew his sword and all hope of a peaceful resolution disappeared. Watchmen surged forward. The black-clad men and women drew their own weapons, advancing to meet them. There was the blast of a blunderbuss and Wigbert caught a spurt of blood from the corner of his eye as a civilian fell to the ground. More gunfire followed, and the crowd scattered in all directions.

'That bloody idiot!' Punduckslew roared above the sudden din as he tried to get between the duke and the skirmish that was quickly developing.

'Stop!' Wigbert yelled hopelessly. 'We can talk about this! There is no need for violence!' No one paid him the slightest bit of attention, except for Corporal Tritewine who, weapon drawn, cried 'Your orders, your grace?'

'What?' Wigbert shouted, horrified.

'What do you want us to do?'

'Protect the civilians!'

'Understood, your grace!' At a signal from the corporal, the Castle Guards waded into the fight, positioning themselves as best they could between the worst of the fighting and the running crowd. Punduckslew suddenly threw an arm forward and Wigbert saw the gun in a black-robed figure's hands explode into pieces. Seconds before, it had been pointed at him.

'There is no more we can do here. We must get you to safety immediately!' he cried, roughly shoving the duke back towards the square.

'I can't just run away!' Wigbert protested, watching in horror as a watchman skewered another black-robed man through the stomach.

'Don't be stupid! You're not even armed!'

The wizard continued to drag Wigbert away, and the duke let him, a deep sense of hopelessness enveloping him, as the clash of swords and booming of gunfire filled the square. He stumbled, which dragged his eyes away from the fighting and towards the ruined church where he could see the rest of the Castle Guard running towards them, weapons drawn. The square was in pandemonium as the people splashed in all directions. He saw several run blindly into the stretched out bodies and go sprawling into the street among the dead.

How many more? He thought. How many more were already

dead? This was his fault. If he had been *better*. If he could have found a way!

A man reared up in front of him and Punduckslew's arm shot out, hesitating only when he recognised the guard's uniform.

'We've found him, your grace!' the man sputtered.

Wigbert stared at him, uncomprehending.

'We've found him,' the man repeated. 'We've found Mr Dribbets. Your grace, he's alive!'

CHAPTER NINE: MONSTERS

1.

That evening, The Green Man's Eyes did a roaring trade. Food flowed from the kitchen in an almost constant stream. Servers, carrying plates of steaming meat to the jam-packed tables, swerved expertly around the groups of standing patrons who had arrived too late to claim a table of their own. Both dukes and kings favours changed hands almost as quickly as the gossip, which, if it had been a visible substance, would have filled the air like leaves in a gale, whipping around the punters' heads with a dizzying speed. The landlord, Mr Aldergate, was becoming a very wealthy man, and yet there was barely a genuine smile in the place. The common room was full, but, from the minor nobles to Ormus Stonemorton himself, people's faces were grave. A few regular ones were conspicuously missing, never to return.

Ormus particularly was wearing a frown that deepened the lines on his furrowed face to great shadowy creases in the light from the lanterns. Once again, he sat at a dark corner table with his companions, Gerald, Quimby and Terrance, although their seats had been hard won. It being already so busy when they arrived, they'd been forced to leave Terrence unattended by the table, until its former occupants were driven off by his unsolicited exclamations. That evening he seemed stuck on the word 'futtock', which Ormus was given to understand was a nautical term describing wooden timbers in the framework of a ship. However, there was something faintly obscene in the way Terrence pronounced the word, and it drove off their rivals in short order. Now the quartet of aging gentlemen sat slumped gloomily over their drinks, an uncomfortable silence presiding. When Quimby went to take a sip of his ale and found the glass empty, he cleared his throat awkwardly, and said, in a quiet voice, 'Sorry about your church, Ormus.'

Ormus grunted. 'Are you? I'd have thought you and your bloody apple tree would be only too pleased.'

'Now that's not fair. I may not have been entirely convinced by the Church of the First Tree's teachings, but I know how much work you put into founding it. I never would have wished for this.'

'It's a tragedy,' Gerald agreed, nodding his head sadly.

'Futtock!' Terrance said emphatically.

'The real tragedy is they're holding an emergency session of the Lords Chambers at this very moment, and where are we? Sat drowning our sorrows like the useless old men we've become,' Ormus said bitterly. 'Instead, my son is there. Pretending he knows what he's doing. You should have heard the way he spoke to me this morning. He wouldn't have dared, even just a single harvest ago. I never should have abdicated!'

Quimby gasped and Gerald shot the duke-no-more a sharp look. 'What do you mean by that?'

'Exactly what I said!'

'But you *had* to abdicate! Taking us with you, I might add. There was no other option.'

'Wasn't there?'

'You said as much yourself.'

'Well, maybe I was wrong. Maybe I should have hung on.'

'Futtock!'

'But there was talk of another rebellion! It was the only card left to play.'

'And what has it achieved? Do we seem any further away from rebellion now? There's fighting in the streets, man. *They blew up my church*!' Ormus struck the tiled floor with his walking stick for emphasis.

'As yet, we don't know who blew up your church,' Gerald pointed out, his heavy brow drawn together.

'Futtock!'

'Oh, come on, don't be an old fool!'

'Who are you calling fool, you old codger?'

'Codger is it? I'll have an axe embedded in your skull, you coot!'

'Not without Wigbert's say so, you won't. We've been through this!'

'Futtock!'

'Oh, shut *up,* Terrance!' Ormus shouted, rubbing both palms into his face. He took a steadying breath, then looked at the ancient man sitting next to him. Terrance was staring vacantly up into the rafters and wearing the only smile in the pub. Sometimes he envied the man, Ormus thought, as he watched his friend's beaming face. Terrance had once been a shrewd operator. The sort of political animal who could bring down an entire dynasty with a few well-chosen words. It was considered he had suffered a fate worse than death: to continue to live in a body that no longer remembered who he had been. Better the axe, many said. An honourable death. But on nights like this, Ormus wondered if it might not be nice to live in the childlike fog his friend enjoyed. He patted the man's papery hand, gently. 'Sorry, old chap,' he said. 'You carry on.'

'Futtock!' Terence replied obligingly, his eyes meeting the duke-no-more's for a brief second before returning to the rafters.

When the explosion at the Church of the First Tree took place, Ormus had been sitting, cold and miserable, at the long empty table in Castle Blackwood's great hall. It had taken him ten minutes to drag his aching bones up the stairs to a decent viewpoint, then only twenty seconds, as he looked out at the billowing smoke mixing with the clouds, to realise there was absolutely nothing he could do about it.

He could issue no orders.

Put no plans into action.

So he'd stood, shoulder aching where the knife had cut into him the night before, bones stiff from the fight, resting heavily on the stone window ledge and watching his life's work go up in flames. The Church of the First Tree had taken a full thirty years to realise, and just a few hours to destroy. The news had trickled in slowly at first, then came in a flood as the first patients arrived at the castle infirmary. This was his life now, he'd thought bitterly, as he watched events unfold around him. To sit on the sidelines and watch as life happened to other people. When news eventually reached him of the battle in the square, it was already over. It hadn't lasted long, apparently. Most people had scattered at the first gunshot. It didn't take much time for the Watch and Guard combined to round up the rest, though not before six more civilians had died. There had been no casualties on the side of the law-keepers, which Ormus considered a blessing and a curse. It wouldn't read well in the news sheets. When his son returned to the castle with his unconscious manservant—the only survivor found in the ruined church—Ormus had ordered the royal coach straight back out again. He doubted he'd be missed, and he found it unbearable to be around the hubbub when he could have no part in it himself.

But as he sat in the busy pub, listening to the roar of conversation surrounding him, being wholly ignored by people who would have fallen silent at his mere presence just two years before, he felt his anger growing, not abating.

'What are you thinking, old man?' Gerald asked, still watching Ormus closely. 'You think I don't recognise that look on your face? Melethin knows I've seen it often enough over the years! You're plotting something.'

'Ooh, I used to love a good plot,' Quimby said, with forced cheerfulness.

'Maybe I am,' Ormus said. 'You two can't be satisfied with this...this life we've been reduced to.'

'Maybe I am, maybe I'm not. Whatever the case, it hardly matters. We're not getting into the Lords Chambers, Ormus. Our seats belong to our sons now,' Gerald said.

'I do miss my seat,' Quimby admitted, waggling a finger in

one of his prodigious ears.

'You see!' Ormus pounced. 'Even Quimby misses the power!'

'Oh, well...I more meant the seat itself,' Quimby admitted nervously, now scratching his bulbous nose. 'It was next to the window, you know. And a small fireplace. Cool in summer, warm in the winter. Perfect!'

Ormus glowered at him, then said, 'Well, now your son sits in it, making the decisions you used to make. Wielding the power *you* used to hold.'

'True,' Quimby conceded.

'What's your point, exactly?' Gerald asked. 'Are you suggesting we attempt to overthrow our own sons? Where would be the point in that? You may not have noticed Ormus, but we're *old* now.'

Ormus scowled. 'You know we could do a better job.'

'That may be so. But *you* know the law better than anyone. Once you're out, you're out. We're not getting our seats back.'

'Laws can be changed,' Ormus growled.

Gerald said nothing, but he looked thoughtful.

Quimby looked worried. 'I'm not sure what you gentlemen are thinking, but I seriously doubt I could re-take my seat, even if I wanted to!'

'Oh?' Ormus replied, still watching Gerald. 'And why not?'

'You remember how long those sessions went on for. My bladder couldn't take it!'

Ormus finally broke eye contact with Gerald to glare at the other man. 'Are you seriously suggesting you're willing to let the Coins take over Upton-Myzzle because you're worried about pissing yourself?'

'It's a consideration, yes,' said Quimby defiantly, flaring his large nostrils. 'You think I want that sort of humiliation at my age?'

'Quimby, don't be a buffoon,' Gerald said, stroking his square, stubbly chin. 'We'd be back in charge. You think we couldn't work out adequate toilet brakes?' Ormus was pleased to see a shadow of the man's former power in his expression.

THE LORD OF MISRULE

'Don't you start! I thought you were against this?' Quimby wailed.

But Gerald's face had set. He leaned forward, resting a beefy elbow on the table and displaying his still powerful forearm. 'I just wanted to see if Ormus was serious, that's all.'

'So you *do* think it's a good idea?' Ormus said.

'That depends on exactly what it is you've been scheming in that balding head of yours?'

Ormus looked over his shoulder; awkwardly because of the wound. No one in the pub was paying them the slightest bit of attention. He lowered his voice anyway, looking at the two men seriously. 'Well, you're right, we can't just waltz in and take back our seats. This requires planning and numbers. We need information and we need to get more people on board to gather that information.'

'You mean...get the old crew back together?' Quimby asked, looking interested for the first time.

Ormus nodded. 'That's right. If we're going to take back power, we'll need the whole gang. I'm thinking Obadiah, Philo, Frank, Phineas—'

'Phineas is dead,' Quimby said.

'Acorns and roots, is he? When?'

'About a year now. Seizure.'

'Oh. Well, no great loss. I never liked the man.'

'He was at your wedding!'

'I was the duke. Everybody was at my wedding! Anyway, we can contact Obadiah, Philo and Frank—'

'Well, we could, but Obadiah's about as much use as Terrence here these days, and Frank hasn't left his bed in three months.'

'How do you know all this?'

Quimby pouted. '*Some* of us like to keep in touch.'

Ormus waved his words away irritably. 'Well Philo won't let us down. And we can think of others.'

'Very well, and what are we to do, this merry little band of ours?' Gerald asked.

'First, we gather information. Each of us has a son or

daughter in the Lords Chambers now. Let's use them. We need up-to-date dirt on everyone. Then, once we have it, we start applying pressure. We don't need to be in the chambers. We just have to know who to back into a corner to get what we want.'

Quinby folded his arms across his pigeon chest. 'And what exactly is it we want?' he asked. 'So we gather a little intel and needle a few pompous brats. What's the endgame here?'

Ormus grinned humorlessly. 'We're going to overthrow my son. I want to be duke again. Upton-Myzzle *needs* me to be duke again.'

2.

Captain Snekchesser was a stressed man. In forty-eight hours he had gone from a relatively carefree corporal to the Castle Blackwood Guard's only captain. His responsibilities had grown so fast he had whiplash. And where had it all got him? He was stuck in the Blackwood as the evening light faded, without backup, responsible for the welfare of the duchy's solitary heir—*for the second time in those forty-eight hours!*—and in the company of a wizard who was crazy, dangerous, or possibly both. To top things off, he had heartburn. And his legs ached from all the running. The cold was gathering and icy drops of rain dripped down from the bare branches which gathered thickly above, blocking out most of the remaining light despite their leafless state. He was not in a good mood and was emitting, unbeknownst to himself, a constant, low-pitched, rumbling growl. It had already scared off a trio of rabbits, two squirrels, and an aging badger. He was standing in a small huddle with Master Lettuce and the strange wizard, Gloamblight. He eyed the latter's right arm, bizarrely strapped to the man's side and definitely producing a thin stream of steam from the encased hand.

'I've got to ask,' he said, blowing on his own hands to warm them. 'What's with the arm?'

Gloamblight looked down at him. He was a full head and shoulders taller than the captain, something that only added to Snekchesser's dislike.

'That is a long and complicated story we do not have time for,' the wizard said, a little shortly. His breath made little puffs in the gloom.

'It kind of looks like it might explode,' Snekchesser persisted.

'It probably won't.'

'That's not really the answer was hoping for.'

'You need not concern yourself with it, captain, I promise.'

'Great, great. Remind me why I'm trusting you again?'

The wizard frowned. 'Not to put too fine a point on it, captain, but it seems very much like you have no other choice. I must admit I'm somewhat surprised to find an officer such as yourself in this situation with apparently none of the required equipment.'

Snekchesser glowered at the man. 'It was not exactly a planned excursion.'

Gloamblight nodded, then said, 'I suspected as much. I'll tell you what, I'll let you keep your secrets, and in return you let me keep mine.' He pulled his black cloak tighter around himself.

Snekchesser's eyes wandered unconsciously to where he'd left the duke's daughter and her friend, the boy Oatey, sitting against a tree, safely out of earshot. 'Whatever,' he said, trying to seem unconcerned. 'Just explain this all to me again, will you? Why can we not just make directly for Upton-Myzzle? It couldn't take more than an hour to walk out of here, especially with that light of yours.'

Gloamblight's dark eyebrows rose up his forehead. 'You think we are that close? I am admittedly not familiar with this part of the Blackwood, but I had thought it would be further. I can tell you from my compass where the old maps I studied said it would lie, but I have come across no signs of the town, no ruins. How much of Upton-Myzzle has been lost to the trees?'

Snekchesser shrugged, but Master Lettuce answered for him. 'About half, they say. Although no one knows for sure. Much documentation has been lost and people no longer enter the wood unless it is completely necessary. But the ruins must be quite extensive.' He was clearly still shaken, his face pale and his voice weak.

'And yet here you are. With two children in tow,' Gloamblight said.

'We entered the wood in something of a hurry,' Snekchesser added testily. 'Then when we were attacked by those bloody moth-men, we lost our way completely. We seem to have left the old town, but for all I know there could be ruins mere feet away. We can't have travelled that far. It's hard to see anything in this gloom. I can barely tell my arse from my elbow.'

'Well, if you feel we are truly that close, I suppose I could alter my plans a little and head straight for town with you,' Gloamblight said, seeming reluctant.

'If you were not heading for Upton-Myzzle, where were you headed? There are no other settlements around here,' Lettuce asked.

'That is...complicated,' Gloamblight said, looking increasingly irritated by the questioning. 'As I said before, I am searching for information about the new star. I assume you have seen it?' Snekchesser and Lettuce nodded, and the wizard continued. 'Well, my investigations have led me here. I had begun to fear they would take me to Upton-Myzzle itself. Although I am interested to see it, to be honest I had half hoped to avoid it. People can be...mistrustful.' He massaged the shoulder of his strapped down arm with the opposite hand, apparently without realising he was doing it. Snekchesser studied the man's face. He really did appear ill, and he had a faraway look in his dark eyes, like he was seeing something from a long time ago. It did little to improve the captain's impression of the man. Gloamblight's eyes refocused, and he continued. 'But I guess now that we have met, it is unavoidable. And I suppose there is something else I should tell you.'

'Oh?' said Snekchesser.

'Yes. There is a monster loose, somewhere in these trees.'

'A m...monster!' Master Lettuce squeaked, dropping the blunderbuss he had been clutching since the attack. He bent to pick it up, slipped in the mud and sprawled face first onto the woodland floor.

Ignoring him, Captain Snekchesser regarded the wizard carefully. 'I should think there are a great many monsters in these trees. We met a few just now.'

Gloamblight crooked an eyebrow. 'The Gwyf? They are not monsters. Just wary of outsiders. Besides, I mean a magical monster. Something that does not belong.'

'Oh dear, oh dear, oh dear…' Master Lettuce began, getting clumsily to his feet and attempting to wipe the soggy grime from his coat.

Snekchesser shushed him, then said 'Go on.'

Gloamblight looked at him intensely. 'This thing is dangerous. It is what I have been tracking, what led me here.'

'I thought you said you were investigating the star?'

'I am. They are connected somehow. I do not pretend to fully understand it, but I know the monster appeared at the same time as the star.'

'Do you…do you mean to say you think it is *Garselin*?' Master Lettuce asked in a weak voice.

'I thought the star was supposed to *be* Garselin,' Snekchesser said impatiently. 'It makes no sense that he would be running through the Blackwood if he was returning from… from wherever he comes from. Space, or whatever nonsense the book of Oak talks about. And besides, I've heard evidence that it's just a comet. Whatever *that* is.'

'I am not familiar with the Book of Oak or comets, but no, I do not think the thing I have been chasing is the great daemon. Nor the star, for that matter. Truthfully, I do not entirely understand what it is, which is partly why I'm following it,' Gloamblight said, a light appearing in his eyes. 'But I *felt* it appear. I have seen…Well, let's just say I want answers!'

'Wait, I don't understand. What do you mean you felt it appear? Is that a wizard thing? I thought your Talent was that light you used to scare off the Gwyf?' asked Snekchesser.

The wizard frowned. 'I should not have said that. I would rather not go into it. The important thing is that there is a dangerous monster on the loose and, if Upton-Myzzle is as close as you claim, it may already have reached it.'

'You're not making much sense, wizard,' Snekchesser growled.

'I am under no obligation to!' Gloamblight snapped. He was clearly getting more and more frustrated, and unless the captain was very much mistaken, the amount of steam escaping from his cloak had increased, too. The tendons on the right side of his neck looked strained, as if the restrained arm were fighting to get free. As the captain watched, they seemed to calm, and the wizard took a deep, steadying breath. 'I am sorry. I have become unaccustomed to traveling with company. Forgive me,' he continued, smiling weakly. 'I do not have time to explain everything to you right now, but the important point is this; Something potentially very dangerous is approaching, or may have already reached your town. You should warn your leaders. I assume you have wizards? They may well be needed. I may not understand exactly what the creature is, but I fear its intentions are not friendly.'

'I see. Well, if you don't mind, I should like a moment to confer with my companions,' Snekchesser said carefully.

Gloamblight did not look pleased, but he nodded. 'Very well, but please be quick. We must be on our way as soon as possible.'

Captain Snekchesser and Master Lettuce left the wizard and joined the two children under the tree.

'What's going on?' Beatrice asked immediately.

'That wizard is a wantwit,' Snekchesser said, his frown deepening.

Master Lettuce looked at him with surprise. 'Do you think so, captain? He's odd, I'll warrant you that, but something makes me think he is telling us the truth. Or at least some of it.'

The captain shrugged. 'Perhaps.'

'What did he tell you?' Beatrice asked impatiently. 'It's not fair, sending us away like that! We have a right—'

'To do as you're told!' Snekchesser hissed. 'Do not think I've forgotten whose fault it is we're in this situation. Perhaps it's you who's the wantwit.'

The girl gaped at him, then her cheeks flushed red, but with anger or embarrassment, he couldn't tell.

'You did act foolishly, ahem...my lady,' Master Lettuce said, giving the girl an admonishing look, slightly undercut by the leaf-mould smeared across his face. 'Whatever possessed you to run away like that? I expected better of you.'

The girl set her face defiantly, and captain Snekchesser was hit with a sudden surge of sympathy for the man who would one day become her husband.

'I was left with little choice,' the girl protested. 'No one would listen to me and I was being followed everywhere I went!'

'No one would listen to you about what?' Snekchesser asked.

'About what we saw on Longest Night! Or what I learnt about the star!'

The captain bit back his anger, instead saying in a level voice, 'I gave your father a complete report of the events of Longest Night. As for the star, the Institute of Propositional Logic is looking into that. Natural Philosophers. Grown men and women who specialise in that sort of thing. What was it exactly that you thought you, *a child*, could add to the subject that they could not?'

The girl grinned at him triumphantly, her blue eyes shining. 'That it's been seen before!'

'Is this about what Master Cabernatol said to you?' Master Lettuce asked, furrowing his brow. 'The Master is a fine man, but...well, he is no longer...um, what with his age...What I mean to say is that I would not put too much store in—'

'It wasn't just him. The bibliothecary said the same thing! *And* he thinks the answers may be in the old Upton-Myzzle archives. That's where we were headed, before you interfered.'

'Interfered?' Snekchesser barked, louder than he should have, with Gloamblight hovering a few feet away. He struggled once again to keep his temper in check, hissing at Beatrice furiously. 'If it wasn't for us, you'd most likely be in the belly of one of those ghastly frogs right now!'

'Toads,' the girl corrected him. 'And if we hadn't been

running from you, we would probably never have come across them in the first place. It is you two who mucked up our plan. Anyway, it was Gloamblight, the man you think of as a wantwit, who saved us from the attack. I'm not sure exactly what you've brought to the enterprise.' She folded her arms and gave him such a precocious look that his blood boiled anew. He got to his feet and turned his back on her, muttering obscenities under his breath that were probably a treasonous offence had he said them to her aloud. She is just a child, he reminded himself. You were one once. Try to remember what that was like. He did his best, but it seemed an awfully long time ago. Once he had regained his composure, he turned back to the group.

'You may not appreciate why I have been following you so closely,' he said. 'So let me explain it to you. I'm a soldier. The Duke of Blackwood gave me an order to keep his daughter safe. Do you know what happens to soldiers who fail to perform an order given directly from the Castle? They get executed for treason. So you may not care for your own life, but perhaps I can appeal to you to give a damn about mine. Not to mention the poor master here, and young Oatey who does not have the luxury of an important family to keep him safe. Do you know what I would have had to do if he became separated from us? I would have had to leave him to his fate. My duty would be clear; to return the only heir to the duchy home safely, *at all costs*. Oatey here would be on his own, and I would have to live with that decision for the rest of my life.'

Master Lettuce got to his feet also, laying a hand on the captain's shoulder. 'Steady on, she is just a child,' he said.

Snekchesser shrugged him off. 'She needs to see the consequences of her actions. Then perhaps she will not act so foolishly.' He stared hard at the girl, who did at least seem to have lost her smug expression. She glanced guiltily at Oatey, before lowering her eyes and saying no more. The captain felt a surge of guilt himself. Perhaps he had gone too far? Well, there was nothing he could do about it now.

'We must decide what to do next,' he said brusquely.

'Indeed,' Master Lettuce agreed, the fear returning to his thin face. 'Do you intend to travel with this Gloamblight? It would seem prudent, given the situation.'

Snekchesser saw Beatrice look up with renewed interest out of the corner of his eye. He ignored her, addressing the trembling master. 'The situation, according to him. As I've said, I do not know whether to trust the man. There is something about him that is…odd.'

'That's an understatement. The man *steams*! That ain't right.'

It was the boy Oatey who spoke. He had said little since the attack. The cut stood out as a dark slash on his white face in what remained of the evening light.

'It's not,' Snekchesser agreed. 'However, he saved us with that light Talent thingy of his, so separating may be the bigger risk. You may as well both know,' he added, looking at both children seriously. 'He says there is a monster loose. He thinks it is something to do with the star but refuses to say what. I'm not saying I believe him, but he may be of some protection to us, monster or not. As we have already found out, there is plenty to fear in these trees.'

Oatey paled a little at his words, but Beatrice looked at him with clear excitement.

'So you have decided to take him up on his offer then, captain?' Lettuce asked.

Snekchesser nodded. 'Yes. We will travel with him back to Upton-Myzzle. He can tell his tale to the duke.'

Beatrice looked set to argue, but she remained silent, simply looking back at the ground with a thoughtful expression on her youthful face.

'Come on,' Captain Snekchesser said wearily. 'We had better not keep him waiting any longer. He might literally explode.'

'Oh dear,' said Master Lettuce weakly. 'Oh dear, oh dear, oh dear…'

3.

The man in the wide-brimmed hat stood patiently, stroking his pointy beard, as the black-robed members of the Church of the Cracked Acorn filed in. They were unusually silent, a pleasant surprise for the man, who had grown tired of their inane chatter in recent weeks. However, it also showed they were anxious, which would need to be addressed. It was hardly surprising. Things had taken an unexpected, if not entirely unwelcome, turn with the destruction of the Church of the First Tree. Many would be nursing cold feet, cowards that they were. But then that was why he was here. Someone had to tell the idiots what to think.

The meeting was taking place in an unassuming wooden building, deep in the heart of the Thickets. The walls were bare plaster, dust covered the floor and not a stick of furniture could be found, unless you counted the broken crate that stood in the centre of the upper stories only room. He'd set a lit candle upon it, which served only to accentuate the cobwebs and decay. As a minor property his master could find little use for, the house had stood empty for some time. Until now.

He waited patiently as the last stragglers hurried up the creaking stairs and took their places. When he counted twelve heads in the ragged semi-circle in front of him, he cleared his throat and took a step forward, keeping the brim of his hat low over his face.

'Good evening, brothers and sisters of the Cracked Acorn. May your roots grow strong,' he said.

'And your leaves unfurl!' came the chanted response.

'As I'm sure you are all aware, we have much to discuss.'

A thin woman in the centre of the semi-circle made an irritated sound in the back of her throat. She possessed a large, pointed nose that stuck out of the shadows of her hood like a beak. For this reason, the man in the wide-brimmed hat called her The Bird. She paused, making sure she had everyone's attention, before speaking in a cold, imperious voice. 'Where is the Lord of Misrule?'

'I am afraid to say he has once again failed to make contact,' said the man. This caused a chorus of murmurs to break out among the rest of the robed figures.

'He has gone rogue!' The Bird cried, her voice all incredulous indignation. 'We did not authorise this…this level of *destruction*!'

'We do not know for sure he caused the explosion,' the man said reasonably. 'Though of course it is probably safe to assume he did.'

'Dozens of people are dead!' called out a corpulent man at the edge of the semi-circle. The man in the wide-brimmed hat called him The Pig. He was not the brightest of the bunch, and the man regarded him with contempt beneath the brim of his hat.

'Dozens of *sinners* are dead,' he corrected brightly.

The Pig shook his head. 'And what of our brothers and sisters killed or taken prisoner by the Watch? This isn't what I…what *we* wanted. So many dead. One of them was a cousin of mine. Don't get me wrong, I hated the dolt, but still…a cousin.'

'Forgive me,' said the man in the wide-brimmed hat. 'Perhaps I have misunderstood. I was under the impression your church was prepared to do whatever it took to ensure that the ways of Zigelder rose again? That is the oath you made to my master, was it not?'

There was a chorus of slightly embarrassed noises on the theme of 'Yes'.

'That is what I thought. You all know what is at stake. We cannot afford to waver in our resolve now, The plan—'

'The plan is a disaster!' The Bird cut over him. 'Not only does Ormus Stonemorton still live, now it seems that fool, the man *you* chose to become the Lord of Misrule, has completely eschewed our list of targets in favour of blowing up buildings!'

'I will admit that our man seems to have become a little... over zealous. But let us not forget our goal. We wanted the Church of the First Tree destroyed,' the man threw open his arms, 'and so it is.'

'I'm not sure we had something so literal in mind. And where is Sir Krickwell? You said you rescued him, but we have heard nothing!' said a new speaker. He was a short man with large feet. The Dwarf.

'And yet our goal is achieved! And in less time than we could have hoped. Do not worry about Sir Krickwell. He is safe and well with my master,' said the man in the wide-brimmed hat.

'I hope so!' said The Bird. 'He is the man who bought us all together. The only person to know our identities. Which is just as well, given the current circumstances.'

The man rolled his eyes beneath the brim of his hat. 'Look, I understand your hesitations. It is only normal to feel some trepidation when we are reaching to achieve such magnificent feats. I know this has all happened in a brief space of time. When the new star appeared and my master sent me to you, did I not say that there would be some challenges? As for those of our number who were sadly slain by the Watch, our Father will not forget their names. He will reward them with gifts we cannot even imagine. But remember what we are trying to do here. *Nothing less than saving the world!* Do you think people will quibble about methods when the great beast Garselin has descended upon us? Do you imagine people will bemoan the deaths of a few sinners when Zigelder appears to save us from destruction? No. We must remain strong. Resolute. It is up to us to lead the people to salvation!'

He saw a few heads nodding along. He was winning them around. The man always enjoyed this part of the job. Manipulating idiots into doing what you wanted never got old.

'Your master has always been good to our church,' The Bird admitted. 'His monetary contributions over the years have been instrumental. However, I think we would all be more reassured if he were here now.'

'Alas, that is not possible, my friends. As you know, my master has his own part to play.'

'Yes, but you never said what that was, exactly,' said The Dwarf.

'All will be revealed in time. For now, it is imperative that he remain hidden. But he wanted me to pass on his hearty congratulations for all that you have done so far, and he looks forward to the day of our glorious victory, when he will meet you all in person at last. And now we must move on. There is much to discuss for phase two.'

Some time later, when the last of the Church of the Cracked acorn had left, the man in the wide-brimmed hat blew out the solitary candle and made his way downstairs. He opened the front door carefully and stuck his head out, looking up and down the street for any signs of movement. All was dark and still. The only face was that of Toflo Higginbottom, staring blankly back at him from the new posters pasted every twenty feet along the opposite wall. The man sighed. It was unfortunate that the idiot had allowed himself to be unmasked so quickly. But he had played his part. No doubt the slippery devil would lead the Castle on a merry chase for a few days yet, and that was the time they needed. The man closed the door, then called out softly, 'It is safe to come out now, master.'

A tall figure emerged from the shadows at the back of the house.

'Well?' he said, his piercing grey eyes expectant.

The man in the wide-brimmed hat bowed respectfully. 'It went well, Sir Sweetspire. They are back on board and preparing for phase two.'

Erasmus Sweetspire smiled coldly. 'Excellent. You have done well. We cannot allow those idiots to ruin things now.'

'I will see that they do not, sir.'

'Be sure that you do. Now, we must go. There is much to prepare.'

The two men left the house, their footsteps slowly receding into the distance. For some time after, the street was quiet and empty. Then something dark detached itself from a patch of shadows and moved jerkily across the road towards one of the posters featuring the face of Toflo Higginbottom, the Lord of Misrule. It was human shaped. Almost. But it did not move in the right way. It had a torso, a head, two arms and two legs, but they did not always appear to be in their traditional positions. Whatever it was bent down over the poster, as if to read it. Instead, it reached out what was probably a hand. It hit the wall with a quiet squelch, and when it withdrew, the poster was gone, along with a good deal of the wall's plaster. The figure moved on, lurching in irregular steps to the next poster, some twenty feet away. It reached out its hand and, once more, the poster disappeared. The next poster was twice the distance away, but, in what can only be described as great excitement, the figure reached it in one step. It was as if it temporarily forgot how to move like a person, instead, stretching its foot to reach the distance in a single stride that would have made any real man wince. The third poster was consumed. The thing's head rose, pointing what may have been nostrils towards the sky. It sniffed like a dog tracking prey, and then jerked off down the street, soon disappearing once more into the shadows.

4.

'I should be eating stew right now,' Oatey whined, touching the wound on the side of his face tenderly and wincing.

'How can you be thinking about your stomach?' Beatrice replied excitedly.

'I'm not. I'm thinking about my mother's dumplings, that I should, at this very moment, be putting *inside* my stomach, like you promised!'

Beatrice stopped herself from rolling her eyes at the boy. 'Look, I said I was sorry, alright? I know things didn't exactly work out as planned, but look at where we are!'

'Yes. In the Blackwood. At night. Fabulous,' Oatey replied, staring sulkily at the dead leaves between his feet. Beatrice couldn't entirely blame him; it was very dark by this point and it was becoming increasingly difficult to see where to put her feet.

'And we may not have made it to the archives, but we *have* learnt something new about the star. There's a monster connected to it in some way!' she continued.

Oatey didn't look up, but said, 'Whoopee. Something else that wants to kill us.'

'We should question Gloamblight about it. I bet he knows far more than he told Snekchesser and Lettuce.'

This time Oatey didn't reply at all. Beatrice sighed. She felt bad, she really did. She never meant for him to get hurt, but what could she do about it now? Surely it was better to carry on and accomplish their mission than just give up? Otherwise, it would all have been for nothing. If she couldn't get the others to agree to let her find the archive, then, just maybe, she could get the information she needed from their strange new companion.

She had been watching the wizard Gloamblight. She found him both fascinating and slightly terrifying at the same time. He wasn't like the other wizards she had met. He was certainly *nothing* like her Uncle Ducky. Or the pompous Grand Wizard Pike. There was nothing pompous about Gloamblight. Mysterious, definitely. Even…alluring. She quickly buried that thought, but not before she felt a flush of warmth creep into her face. She risked a glance at Oatey, but the boy was still paying her no attention and did not appear to have noticed. Beatrice looked ahead to where she could just make out the figures of their companions. Three silhouettes in the grey-green light of the forest night. One was obviously shorter than the others, and a good deal stockier too. Beatrice could tell it was the captain from his halo of bouffant hair, even if it had not been obvious from his height. The next was skinny and stumbled seemingly every other step. Obviously Master Lettuce. The third was the tallest of the trio and made the blackest silhouette. Gloamblight in his dark cloak. He strode with purpose, his long legs taking him forward at a pace that had the other two trotting to keep up. A trail of white steam snaked out behind him and hung like mist in the still air between the trees. Beatrice increased her own pace, coming up closer behind the others and leaving Oatey trailing behind.

'Could we not have a little of that light of yours?' she heard Captain Snekchesser say to the wizard. 'I'm afraid the master here will break his neck.'

'That is out of the question, captain. It would most certainly shine out our location as good as any beacon, and besides, I do not use my magic for such trivial matters. The good master will just have to watch where he places his feet.'

'Excuse me for asking, I'm sure,' Snekchesser grumbled under his breath just as Beatrice drew level with him. If

Gloamblight heard, he gave no indication of it.

'Oh, I'll be fine,' Master Lettuce said in a bright but thin voice. Beatrice saw his head bow down, inspecting the ground before him intently. He almost immediately walked into a low-hanging branch and gave a cry of alarm.

'We should try to keep noise to a minimum,' Gloamblight added, without looking round.

'O...of course, so sorry,' the master stuttered, rubbing his forehead.

Beatrice put on another burst of speed until she was walking alongside the wizard. She had to do a sort of skipping dance to keep up with him and avoid the tree roots, rocks, and other detritus that littered the woodland floor. Gloamblight did not react to her presence, but she suddenly felt her throat go dry and the question she had been about to ask died in her throat. What was it about this man? He seemed to make everybody nervous in his presence, without so much as uttering a word. He radiated an atmosphere of...what, exactly? She found it hard to put into words. It felt like a summer storm. It gave her the same sense of tingling anxiety she felt as a small child, having seen a flash of lightning and awaiting the rumble of thunder. She felt heat on her face again and attempted to watch him out of the corner of her eye, whilst simultaneously keeping her footing. She could see little in the deep shade of night, but she made out his athletic frame and long, slightly wavy hair. It was a strain to pick out his face, and she could only discern the barest glimmer of his grey eyes.

'Is there something you wanted, girl?'

The man spoke without moving his head and Beatrice gave a guilty start, glancing away, but not before stumbling over a tree root.

'I...I was just going to ask how much further you thought it would be to Upton-Myzzle?' she gabbled. She'd been going to ask nothing of the sort, but he'd flustered her and that was the first question she could think of.

'As I have said before, I do not rightly know,' Gloamblight

replied, speaking quietly and still not turning his head to look in her direction. 'But I would expect us to reach signs of the abandoned part of the town soon.'

Beatrice took a deep breath, then asked the real question she wanted him to answer. 'What do you know about this monster? And how is it connected to the new star?'

The man was silent for a moment, walking on through the darkness at his brisk pace. Eventually, he said, 'That does not seem like a suitable subject to be discussing with a little girl.'

Beatrice felt her face burn for an entirely different reason.

'I'm not a little girl!' she protested.

'Really? Because you look just like one.'

'I'm twelve harvests old!'

'And you feel this disproves my hypothesis?'

'Yes!'

'I see. Never-the-less, I see no reason to discuss my business with you.'

Beatrice was fuming. 'But it's not just *your* business! It's all of our business! It's the whole reason I came to the Blackwood in the first place!'

'Oh, is that so?'

'It is so, yes! I came to find proof the star has been seen before.'

This got the wizard's attention. He turned his face towards her for the first time, although she could not make out his expression in the darkness. 'And where exactly were you expecting to find this proof?'

'There's an old archive,' she said, a little smugly. 'If I can find it, then I might find the records that prove the star was here before.'

'I see. And what makes you think it *has* been seen before?'

'I talk to people. I've had more than one person tell me they half remember something about it. That's how I learnt about the archive, too.'

'I see. That's very interesting, thank you.'

'You're welcome. So, will you tell me about the monster

now?'

'No.'

'What! Why not? I told you my thing!'

'And I thanked you for it.'

'That's not fair!'

'Then I have taught you something important, after all.'

Gloamblight turned his head forward again, as if dismissing her, and Beatrice dropped back, silently raging against the wizard. She'd changed her mind. He *was* pompous, after all! And arrogant!

She found herself walking next to Captain Snekchesser, who was chuckling to himself quietly.

'What's so funny?' she demanded.

'Oh, it's just nice to see someone get the better of you, that's all.'

'That's not what just happened!'

'Oh, no, of course not. You totally won that conversation.'

'Shut up!'

'I'm afraid I take my orders from your father, not you,' the guard said, laughter still in his voice. 'Look, why are you so obsessed with this stuff, anyway? The Lord of Misrule. The star. They're strange interests for…someone of your age.'

'Don't you care?' Beatrice hissed. 'Are you not interested at all in what's going on?'

She saw the captain's silhouette shrug. 'Either the world's ending, or it's not. Don't see there's much I could do about it either way. So I'll give Garselin a good fight if he appears, but otherwise, I try not to worry about it.'

'And the Lord of Misrule?'

'He's just a common murderer, if you ask me. Ain't nothing special about that.'

'So you're just content to let him run riot then, are you? He tried to kill my grandfather!'

'Oh, don't mistake me. I'll take him down if I get the chance. But I'm a soldier. I follow orders. Right now, that lunatic is not my concern. Keeping you alive is, and I'd appreciate a little cooperation on your part in that regard.'

'I promise not to die,' Beatrice said coldly.

'That's all I ask.'

They moved on in silence. As the minutes ticked by, Beatrice felt the first pricks of tiredness behind her eyes. She wondered what time it was. She'd lost track of how long they'd spent in the forest. In the darkness, the trees all looked the same and they could have been traveling for twenty minutes or two hours. She found her mind turning to, of all things, Oatey's mother's stew. She had never actually met any of Oatey's family, but she had a picture in her mind, and that picture made wonderful stew. How long had it been since she'd eaten? She was wrenched out of her beef and onion reveries by the sudden halt of the wizard in front of her. She just managed to stop before she walked into his back.

'What's—' she began, but Gloamblight turned sharply and put a finger to his lips.

'There is something in our path up ahead,' he whispered.

Snekchesser cupped his eyes with his hands and peered ahead into the darkness. 'Are you sure? I can't see anything.'

'I am sure. I can feel its presence.'

She couldn't actually see, but Beatrice felt sure Snekchesser raised an eyebrow at the wizard. 'What exactly does that mean?' he said.

'It means exactly what I said. I feel the presence of something ahead.'

'You are a very odd wizard,' Captain Snekchesser said.

'And you're a very short guard!' Gloamblight hissed. 'But you do not hear me go on about it!'

'What I *meant*,' Snekchesser said, 'is that I have never met another wizard with your apparent abilities.'

'Well, now you have. Congratulations!'

'I thought the light thing was your Talent, so what's all this about sensing things?' the captain persisted.

'I do not have the time to explain to you the complexities of my relationship to magic, captain! Either you believe me when I tell you there is potential danger ahead, or you do not.' A small cloud of steam was now surrounding the agitated Gloamblight, and Beatrice took an involuntary step backwards.

'Alright, alright, keep your hair on,' Snekchesser grumbled. 'So what exactly is the nature of this potential danger?'

Gloamblight appeared to get a hold of himself and the steam dissipated once more. 'That, I am afraid, I cannot tell,' he said. 'However, I think there may be some number of them.'

'It's not the gwyf again, is it?' Oatey asked anxiously.

The wizard shook his head. 'I do not believe so. I am reasonably certain they were traveling in a different direction from us. But whatever they are, I recommend we proceed with extreme caution.'

'P...perhaps I should stay here with the children, whilst you go check it out?' Master Lettuce suggested in a shaking voice.

'No, we should stick together. We do not want to become separated. We should go forward quietly, survey the situation and then decide what to do,' Snekchesser said decisively.

Gloamblight nodded agreement. 'Very well. Follow me.'

They moved on again, picking their way through the trees at a much slower pace this time. It wasn't long before Gloamblight stopped again, crouching low. The others gathered around him and he said, in the barest of whispers, 'Just up ahead.'

Before them was a gap in the trees. A small clearing through which Beatrice could make out the clouded night sky. Despite the clouds, the lack of canopy meant the clearing appeared slightly brighter than the surrounding woodland and Beatrice squinted her eyes and stared at it intensely. Just when she was beginning to think that the wizard had been mistaken, she caught a movement through the trees on the far side of the clearing. It had been something large. She could make out no more than that, but she heard Gloamblight draw in his breath sharply. The wizard turned to face the others. Beatrice could just see him mouth two words.

'*Green men.*'

No one replied, but a shiver went through the group. Beatrice's eyes met Oatey's for the first time since the gwyf attack. He looked stunned, his mouth hanging open. 'No way!' he mouthed at her. Beatrice grinned. She couldn't help it. This was beyond anything she had ever hoped for. She turned her attention back to the clearing. If she could catch a proper look at a real live green man…

'You must be joking,' she heard Captain Snekchesser murmur, so quiet she almost didn't catch it, despite being crouched next to the man. 'Surely you don't expect us to believe—'

Gloamblight shook his head vigorously, cutting the man off. 'Quiet!' was all he would say.

In the clearing, all seemed to be still once again. Beatrice held her breath, not daring to move a single muscle. Eventually, she caught another movement. At first she thought it was the silhouette of another person emerging from the trees, but then her eyes adjusted and she realised it was far too large. The figure must have been eight feet tall if it was an inch, with impossibly broad shoulders and powerful arms that hung down too far for a human, past its knees. It was also covered in shaggy fur. Or was it? Could those be…leaves? It was difficult to tell in the poor light. She couldn't really make out a face from this distance, but the head was large and wide, with tufted, pointed ears and a powerful jaw. The thing moved slowly, more like an animal than a person, lumbering into the centre of the clearing on its two legs, occasionally using its large knuckled hands to swing itself forward. It stood for a moment, looking around, then it leant back its head and let out a sound like nothing Beatrice had ever heard before. It was part howl, like a wolf or dog, but in the howl there was a croaking chatter, more like a raven.

The noise filled the night air, echoing around the trees and making the hairs stand up on the back of Beatrice's neck. It was beautiful, in a slightly terrifying way. The sound faded away and silence returned to the woodland. In it, Beatrice could hear the breath of the thing, slow and deep. The creature sat down in a surprisingly human-like movement, crossed its legs, and appeared to wait. Sure enough, its call was soon answered, by first one, then two, three, and then a whole chorus of chattering howls from the nearby trees. More of the creatures appeared, lumbering into the clearing in ones and twos, greeting each other with strange croaking sounds. Beatrice watched, entranced, as an even larger specimen greeted the first, who rose back to its feet and touched its enormous hand to the other's cheek, guiding its head down until their foreheads touched, gently. It was alien, other, and yet obviously the meeting of old friends, as sure as a handshake. These were not mere beasts, Beatrice thought. There was intelligence there. By now there were perhaps twenty of the creatures gathered together, milling around slowly, gently, greeting each other one by one, then eventually forming a loose circle, with the original creature at the centre. This was more than a random gathering. This was a meeting, Beatrice realised with a thrill of excitement. A conference. Before her unbelieving eyes, the creatures settled down, cross-legged, on the ground and waited. The original looked around the circle, as if acknowledging each of th m, then it spoke. The sounds were animal; grunts, croaks and whistles, but it was still clearly language. Beatrice listened, understanding nothing, captivated all the same. She felt like she was witnessing something secret, something sacred.

   The first she realised the others were slowly creeping away was the feel of Gloamblight's hand on her shoulder. He looked into her wide eyes with a smile, and in that moment she felt an understanding pass between them, even approval. Never-the-less he indicated with his head for her to follow, and with a deep reluctance she took one last look at the conference of creatures before turning her back and quietly moving away after the others. They travelled silently through the dark trees, back the way they had come, for perhaps ten minutes before coming to a stop beneath the bare branches of an enormous hazel tree. Beatrice rested her back against the smooth grey-brown bark and looked up at the nuts scattered through its branches in little leafy husks. She let out a long breath.

'That,' she said, 'was incredible.'

'It was certainly unexpected,' Gloamblight replied. 'Sightings of green men are rare enough, but to see a whole passage like that, and so close to a human settlement. Quite remarkable.'

'A passage?' Oatey asked. The boy's eyes were round in his face and he looked excited for the first time since the gwyf attack.

Gloamblight nodded. 'A passage is the name for a group of Green men.'

'It suits them. It's...gentle, like they are,' Beatrice said.

'Were they...were they really green men? Like from the stories?' said Captain Snekchesser. There was an odd, almost puzzled expression on the soldier's grizzled face. 'They were not what I'd pictured. Not quite. In the old tales, they're always so...so powerful. Vicious, even. But those creatures, well, they seemed so peaceful.'

Gloamblight smiled. 'Oh, do not be mistaken. They are far more peaceful than popular opinion would have you believe, but those stories evolved from grains of truth. Gentle they may be, but when raised to anger, they can be a terrifying force.'

'You speak as if you have seen them before,' Master Lettuce said, his voice full of wonder.

'Oh, I have been fortunate enough to run into them once or twice. But never in such numbers. This changes things.'

'Why?' Snekchesser demanded, an edge of suspicion creeping back into his voice.

Gloamblight looked thoughtful. 'I never expected...If the green men are meeting in large numbers, then things in the Blackwood are worse than I thought. I'm afraid we cannot return to Upton-Myzzle tonight.'

'*What*! Why not?' the captain was angry now, a deep crease

appearing between his eyes.

'Well, for a start, we would have to travel around the passage. It would simply not do to disturb them, and could be dangerous. This would take time. Time, I fear we no longer have. I must find answers.'

'What are you suggesting?' Lettuce asked.

'Something young Beatrice here has already proposed,' the wizard said, meeting her eyes with a serious expression. 'She got me thinking after our brief discussion earlier, but after seeing this, my mind is made up. We must find the Upton-Myzzle archive and learn everything we can about the new star. Many lives may depend on it.'

'*Are you mad?*' Snekchesser hissed. 'I need to get her ladyship...Beatrice back to her father as soon as possible! We do *not* have time to go wondering about the forest on some wild goose chase.'

'I recommend we stick together, captain. I am more convinced than ever that the Blackwood is not safe at present.'

'Then get us out of it!' Snekchesser insisted. 'Then go do whatever you like.'

Gloamblight shook his head firmly. 'I am sorry, captain but I fear there is no longer the time to spare. And if I am right, you will be no safer amongst the houses of Upton-Myzzle than the trees of the Blackwood. Powerful forces are moving.'

'I'm supposed to take your word for that, am I? We don't even know where this archive *is*. If it even survived!' Snekchesser scoffed.

'*Oh, it's not that far away. I could guide you, if that would be helpful?*'

It was a strange whisper of a voice. Like someone was talking from both very far away and right into your ear at the same time.

'W...who said that?' Captain Snekchesser said carefully.

'I think it came from above us,' Beatrice said, peering into the branches of the hazel whilst groping blindly for the knife in her satchel.

'It...it's not one of *them,* is it? A Green man?' Lettuce whimpered.

'Green men do not speak our tongue,' Gloamblight said, also peering up into the gloom.

'What in the Blackwood *does*?' Snekchesser asked, surreptitiously drawing his small-sword.

'*I do,*' whispered the voice.

Master Lettuce screamed.

Beatrice followed the petrified man's gaze to where, just above her head, two enormous eyes had appeared in the trunk of the tree. Two eyes, and a large, grinning set of teeth.

CHAPTER TEN: BODIES IN THE RAIN

1.

The eyes and teeth were soon followed by a face, then an entire head. It stuck out of the tree's trunk, about a foot above their own heads, and smiled down at them like it was the most ordinary thing in the world. It seemed a female type of face, and human, so far as it was possible to tell. All the important parts were there; a pointed, tapered chin, small button nose, feminine lips. The problem was they didn't seem to want to stay in strictly the right place, instead, drifting about in the general idea of a face, as if painted by a small child who has yet to learn the importance of proportions and perspective. They were also somewhat translucent, and glowing a bright greeny-blue in blackness.

Master Lettuce fainted, crumpling to the woodland floor with a little sigh.

'Oh dear! Was that my fault? I do apologise,' said the face. 'I don't get many visitors these days. Not human ones, anyway. Hang on!' A look of concentration appeared on several of the floating features; the eyes narrowed, the mouth set, the nose even wrinkled a little. Gradually, slowly, the face drifted into the correct assemblage.

'There we go, much better!' it said in its strange, half-whisper.

It was indeed a woman's face, although the age was hard to guess at. Beatrice felt she could have been a little over twenty harvests, but would not have been surprised to learn she was a hundred, or even more. It was something about the eyes. They looked through you like they'd seen a thousand harvests come and go.

'A spirit tree!' she exclaimed.

The face smiled at her. 'Actually, no, a common misconception. You might call me a tree spirit. I am a spirit and I live in this tree, but I am the spirit of a woman, not of the tree itself, as a spirit tree would be. Do you see?'

'Oh, sorry.'

'Not at all, dear. An easy mistake to make.'

'Well, it's very nice to meet you. I've never actually met a tree spirit before. I'm Beatrice, what's your name?'

The face looked thoughtful. 'Now that is a tricky question! It's been so long. Do you know, I've quite forgotten. But you may as well call me Hazel. That seems as good a name as any. Is he alright down there, do you think?'

Master Lettuce had regained consciousness but was still lying on the ground, making little whimpering sounds.

Oatey, who was staring at the spirit with a huge grin on his face, said, 'Oh don't worry about him, he'll be fine in a minute. I'm Oatey!'

A look of concern filled Hazel's face. 'Are you, dear boy? I'm so sorry. Is it painful?'

'What? No, I mean I'm *called* Oatey. It's my name!'

Hazel peered at the boy, then her green-blue eyes sparkled and she grinned once more. 'Ah, but of course it is! I see it clearly now. Oatey Crabblebottom, son of Juniper and Tonkin Crabblebottom. You have two brothers and three sisters. Oh, and a wee little cat called Cabbage, how sweet!'

Oatey gaped at her. 'How do you know all that?'

'If you get to be as old as I am, my dear, you'll find that information just wants to burst out of people. All you have to do is look. For example, I believe the short gentleman with the large hair to your left has something he wishes to say.'

All eyes turned to Captain Snekchesser, who looked back, nonplussed.

'Oh, not to any of you,' Hazel explained. 'To someone else. It will come out when he's ready.'

THE LORD OF MISRULE

Gloamblight took a step forward. 'Spirit, forgive me, but you mentioned something about the archive?'

Hazel turned her penetrating gaze upon him, her eyes soon widening in surprise. 'My, my, aren't you an odd little duck?' she said.

'I'm sorry?' Gloamblight said, his face expressionless.

'Oh, don't be dear. I don't mind. Besides, it's not really your fault, is it? No, you do quite well, given the circumstances.'

'Thank you,' said the wizard, with just a trace of irritation. 'But about the archive?'

'Oh, yes! The Upton-Myzzle archive. I can take you to it, if you should desire?'

'You know where it is?' Beatrice asked excitedly.

'Of course! It's not far. I used to go there all the time. Not much lately, of course.'

'Do you mean before you died, or after?' Oatey asked. 'Sorry, was that rude?'

Hazel chuckled, a strange rushing, echoing sound like the wind through leaves. 'Both!'

'So you can leave this tree then, if you want to?' Beatrice asked.

In answer, a pair of ghostly shoulders appeared from the tree trunk behind the spirit's head, followed by a torso, and finally arms and legs, as Hazel stepped daintily from the tree. She stood—if that is the right word to use—a few inches off the ground, in a gown that sparkled and swirled around her.

'For a time,' she said.

'Let's not get carried away here,' Captain Snekchesser said, frowning.

Hazel stared at him, then the light of understanding came into her eyes. 'Ah, but of course, captain, you fear for the safety of your charge and want to return her to Castle Blackwood. Her father will be worried. You need not be concerned. Gloamblight here has a way of contacting the duke, don't you, dear?'

Gloamblight looked a little disconcerted. 'Er...yes. I can send a message to anyone if required.'

Snekchesser looked furious, but before he could respond, Hazel spoke again. 'Fear not, good captain. The wizard does not wish to harm the child.'

Snekchesser glowered at her. 'And I'm just supposed to take your word for that, am I?' he growled.

'Oh, it's entirely up to you, dear. But it seems a shame not to avail oneself of the help of those around us, don't you think?'

The captain looked unconvinced.

'I can assure you I have neither the time nor the inclination to pose any kind of threat,' Gloamblight said irritably. 'I have no interest in the girl.'

Beatrice felt a little drop of disappointment in her chest at his words, but could not have explained why. Captain Snekchesser, meanwhile, wore an expression of pained indecision.

'You could really send a message to Castle Blackwood?' he asked Gloamblight. In response, the wizard reached into his cloak and carefully removed something from within. He opened his hand for them to see. Sitting in the centre of his palm was a small, ruffled looking robin. It blinked at them sleepily, its shiny black eyes taking them in with un-bird-like curiosity.

'This is Rupert, my familiar. He can carry any message we should want to send.'

'Your familiar what?' Snekchesser asked, bemused.

'He's like my partner, I suppose. A friend. We are connected on an intellectual level.'

'Well, that proves it then. You are bird-brained,' the captain grumbled.

Gloamblight scowled. 'He's far more intelligent than you might imagine.'

'He's adorable!' Beatrice squealed. 'Can I stroke him?'

The wizard rolled his eyes. 'Very well,' he said with a sigh.

Beatrice reached out a tentative hand and lightly stroked the robin's head with her index finger. Its feathers were soft and tickly against her skin. Rupert closed his little eyes and chirped appreciatively.

Gloamblight made an irritated noise in the back of his throat. As if in response, the robin opened one beady eye, fixed it on the wizard, and chirped again. Something about the noise held a note of ill-temper this time and Gloamblight sighed again.

'Rupert wishes me to convey how very nice it is to meet you all,' he said with exasperation.

There was another sharp tweet.

'And would like to say how pretty the young lady with the delicate finger is,' Gloamblight continued with a tight expression, eyes cast heavenward.

'You speak bird now?' Snekchesser said, eyebrow raised.

The wizard glowered at him. 'No, I can only communicate with Rupert. Like I said, we are connected.'

But Snekchesser wouldn't let it go. 'But...how? This isn't how magic is supposed to work!'

'Oh, you're a magic expert now?' Gloamblight shot back. 'Look, perhaps one day I will explain it to you, but not here and not now, ok?'

'Fine, fine. Whatever. So how do we send a message then?' the captain grumbled.

'It's really very simple, captain. We write a message. I give it to Rupert and he carries it to the recipient. He then carries back any reply.'

'How does he know where to go?' Oatey asked, bending over to examine the robin more closely. Rupert looked down his beak at the boy, achieving an expression of superiority Beatrice would not have thought possible in a bird.

'Birds have their ways,' Gloamblight said mysteriously. 'Do not worry. Rupert never fails.'

It took them several minutes to compose a suitable message for Beatrice's father. Master Lettuce was roused, caught up on the situation with only a minimum amount of whimpering, and then acted as umpire between Gloamblight and

Snekchesser as they hashed out the exact wording. Rupert sat on the wizard's shoulder, bobbing up and down with apparent excitement and puffing out his red chest with pride. Oatey and Beatrice meanwhile stared with open curiosity at Hazel, who continued to float a few inches off the ground and smiled back at them benevolently.

'Is it lonely, being a tree spirit?' Oatey asked at length.

'Oh, maybe a little at the beginning,' Hazel said. 'But you soon learn to appreciate the ways of the wood. The other trees, the birds, the animals and insects, they all make agreeable companions once you understand them. Don't talk to me about woodpeckers, though!' she finished with a small frown.

'But you were human once?' Beatrice asked.

'Yes, although to be perfectly honest, it was so long ago I remember little about it.'

'Don't people worship spirits?' Oatey asked.

'They do, for many hundreds of harvests,' Hazel replied, her eyes twinkling.

'Don't take this the wrong way,' the boy continued. 'But you don't exactly seem all that holy.'

'Hmm, tell that to the woodpeckers,' Hazel said. 'But no, you're quite right. I'm young, you see, for a spirit. Just a couple of hundred harvests old. Maybe in time I'll become something worth worshipping. Although there's few people around here to worship me!' she added with a laugh.

'How did you end up all the way out here?' Beatrice asked.

'Oh, it's not as interesting as you might think. When I was growing up, this area was part of my family's farm. It was just a little outcrop of trees at the edge of our land where I used to play as a girl. My father and brothers would coppice the hazel, including the tree I eventually joined with. The Blackwood has changed much since then, of course. Now I find myself in the thick of it!'

'Did you choose this tree? Or did it choose you?' Beatrice asked, looking at the venerable hazel the spirit had come from. 'I don't really know how it works.'

Hazel gave a ghostly shrug. 'Me either, I'm afraid. I just sort of woke up here. After I died, of course.'

'How...' Oatey began to ask, then trailed off, apparently unsure if he should finish the question.

Hazel laughed. 'How did I die? It's ok, I don't mind, dear. It's only natural you should be curious. But I'm afraid it's not a particularly exciting story. I was ill, you see. I forget what with. But it got the better of me and now here I am!'

The children could have asked the spirit questions for hours, but once the letter was written, and Rupert dispatched to the sky with one last excited chirp, the others were keen to get moving.

'The sooner we do this nonsense, the sooner I can finally get you home,' Captain Snekchesser barked at Beatrice as they set off.

'It's not nonsense!' Beatrice countered. 'We could discover crucial information. You might even get another promotion, captain.'

'Very funny!' the man grumbled, scowling unhappily. They traipsed through the dark trees after Hazel, who shone out in the blackness like a beacon for them to follow. It only became difficult when she floated straight through large trees, which the others were then obliged to scramble around to catch her up. After they had been walking for a while, Oatey caught Beatrice up and, grinning, said, 'Ok, I forgive you! This has been pretty cool so far, moth-men aside. We've met a tree spirit and seen green men in one night! The others in the Brigade will be so jealous! Or at least they would be, if they ever spoke to us.'

Beatrice grinned back. 'It's incredible!' she gushed. 'I never thought we'd see so much on our very first trip!'

Oatey's grin widened, and Beatrice glimpsed white teeth in the gloom. 'First, huh? I knew you'd be hooked!'

'Aren't you?' she replied.

'Perhaps,' the boy conceded. 'But I'm not keen to meet the gwyf again, and there's far worse than them in these trees.'

Beatrice strode forward with confidence. 'We'll just have to be more prepared next time.'

It wasn't long before signs of the old town ruins appeared in the surrounding trees. Just the odd lump of stone at first, covered in many harvests' worth of moss and lichen. But then, larger structures appeared. Beatrice ran her hands along the ivy-covered surface of a wall that still stood to about four feet, where it hadn't been tumbled by encroaching roots and trunks. It was odd to see so much stonework here when the modern Upton-Myzzle contained so little.

After they had been travelling for perhaps forty-five minutes, Hazel drifted to a halt in front of what appeared to be the remains of a once impressive building. The roof was gone, and trees had grown up inside the thick stone walls to form a sort of new canopy roof. On either side of what was obviously the original entrance must have stood two giant pillars, however one had long since toppled over, blocking much of the doorway with its shattered remains. Beatrice's heart fell.

'That's not the archive?' she asked.

Captain Snekchesser threw up his hands. 'Surely nothing useful will have survived in there. I said this was a waste of time!'

Hazel beamed at them. 'Fear not. Most of the books and documents were kept in the lower levels. The atrium and upper floor may have been destroyed, but the rats tell me much of the cellar levels survive intact.'

Snekchesser threw his hands in the air a second time. 'Oh well, if the rats say so...' he said, trailing off and shaking his head in disbelief.

Ignoring him, Gloamblight strode towards the building. 'Come, we must investigate with all speed.'

'I'm afraid this is where I must leave you,' Hazel said.

'You're not coming inside?' Beatrice replied, disappointed.

'I'm afraid not, child. I have been away from my tree long enough. But I wish you good fortune. Perhaps we will meet again one day.'

'Before you leave us, I have one question,' Gloamblight said, his face as serious as Beatrice had seen it.

Hazel looked at him—through him—with her sparkling, ancient eyes. 'The answer is yes,' she said, and Beatrice thought she saw a hint of sadness on the spirit's face for the first time.

'There is no other way?' Gloamblight asked, his face set.

'If there is, it is beyond my knowledge. But I wish you luck, strange wizard. Now, I must go.'

'It was very nice to have met you,' Beatrice replied.

The spirit simply smiled, took one last look at each of them, then turned her back and drifted away into the trees. Beatrice followed her green-blue glow for as long as it was visible, but it soon shrank to just a hint of light in the trees, then disappeared altogether.

There was silence among the group for several moments, then Captain Snekchesser said, 'This is turning into a very strange day.'

'There may be stranger yet to come,' Gloamblight replied. 'There is much work to be done and not much time to do it. This way.'

They followed the wizard, a trickle of steam still trailing after him, as he skirted the building, searching for a way in that would not involve climbing over the toppled pillar. As luck would have it on the far wall, an entire section about the width of a gwalmok had fallen away. Without another word, Gloamblight waved them onwards and led them into the darkness inside.

2

The Lord of Misrule was worried.

Despite his success at the Church of the First Tree, things were not going to plan. The night was bitter and damp. The rain that had begun the previous day seemed to be done with the dress rehearsal and was now ready for its big performance. It had started coming down in sheets about an hour ago, forcing him from the rooftops to take cover in an alley in the Thickets, where the walls leaned towards each other at an alarming angle and the jutting out roofs offered some small respite.

It was a dank hovel that smelt of mould and urine, hardly fit for the great Zigelder's holy messenger.

He had been unable to return to his rooms, just as he'd feared. It seemed the secret of his former identity had somehow got out and the town was full of the Castle Guard. The talk on the street was that the duke himself had made the discovery. He had not anticipated that. Wigbert Stonemorton was supposed to be a fool. Little threat, shut up in his castle like a razor clam; a wriggling, spineless creature with its head in the sand.

But it hardly mattered now. He had shed his old life like a skin, and he had no intention of returning to it. The finding of his pathetic former employer's body was nothing but a minor annoyance. But there were other worries. He needed to stay one step ahead of the watch and the guard. This was easy enough. He had already been doing so for days. His Talent made getting around the town a cinch and it had so far been only too easy to lose anyone on his trail. Until now, that was.

Something was hunting him.

He felt it in his bones, like someone staring at the back of his head. Only, whenever he turned around, there was nobody there. He'd had to jump several times already that night to keep ahead of whoever, or whatever, it was. For there was something about the presence he felt, something...inhuman. He couldn't entirely explain it, but whenever he felt it closing in, the hairs on the back of his neck would stand out like pins and a feeling of dread would creep over him. It was unsettling. He was not used to being unsettled. For as long as he could remember, he'd had a certainty of purpose. A holy fire that burned within him, telling him what to do next. For the first time, he was unsure of his next move. He'd been watching some of his brothers and sisters in the Church of the Cracked Acorn, and their behaviour disturbed him.

He'd learned their identities long ago, of course. His Talent made him well suited to spy work. After the explosion, he'd visited some of their homes, listened to their conversations. He had expected to hear praise and admiration for his holy work. Instead, he'd heard doubt. Weakness. Fear. Had they lost faith in their holy mission? That was the only explanation he could think of, for if they remained true to their cause, as he did, then none of the means used in its pursuit went too far. No amount of blood spilt could be too much. He felt lonely at their betrayal and unsure of his next move. He could not follow up on his strike on the Church of the First Tree, what with dodging his pursuers all night, and now he wavered on what his next course of action should be.

As he crouched in the fetid mud of the dark alley, shivering in his damp clothes, feeling the moisture of his own breath beneath the wooden mask, he tried to formulate a plan. But soon the nagging uneasiness returned. There was something out there, something in the rain and the dark that wanted him. He could feel it getting closer.

Lost in his thoughts, he didn't notice his legs cramping

underneath him until one spasmed, sending him sprawling in the muck. He felt the stinking liquid seep into his clothes like ice-water and staggered to a standing position.

Enough! He, Zigelder's chosen one, would not be made to cower in fear, trapped like a rat in its hole. He unsheathed his blade and peered into the murky street ahead. Whatever was out there was going to regret finding him!

3.

'What do you mean, you don't know where she is?' Wigbert buried his head in his hands and tried to concentrate. He wasn't sure he could take this, not on top of everything else. He sat behind a makeshift desk in the centre of the gatehouse infirmary, surrounded by piles of hastily scrawled correspondence. Corporal Tritewine stood in front of him and shifted uncomfortably.

'Her bed's not been slept in, your grace. And we've still had no word from Captain Snekchesser.' Wigbert groaned and the corporal continued, almost apologetically. 'She somehow slipped out of her Forestry Brigade meeting during a fracas—'

Wigbert looked up in alarm. 'Fracas? What fracas?'

'Nothing like that, your grace,' Tritewine said quickly. 'Just a rather spirited game of Thump Piggy Thump, I understand. Only minor injuries. Anyway, during the game she disappeared with that young friend of hers. Captain Snekchesser and Master Lettuce apparently went after her, but...well none of them have been seen since.'

'And why am I only hearing about this now?'

'Well...event's rather ran away with everyone, your grace. Messages were delayed. But we've got search parties out already. They probably just holed up somewhere to avoid the trouble. We won't rest till we find them!'

Wigbert nodded numbly, his thoughts in turmoil. Wolfe was ranting and raving in his head about incompetence, dereliction of duty and how, if he was in charge, he'd soon whip a few lazy behinds into shape. Around them, the hubbub of the overcrowded infirmary continued. The gatehouse hadn't seen this much activity in years, and a general atmosphere of shock and confusion reigned. No one had slept, and Wigbert felt like he had been putting out one fire after another for hours. Several of the injured had been lost overnight, but the survivors were now mostly stable. Wigbert found his eyes wandering to a bed against the far wall where Tanco lay, pale and unmoving. He had yet to regain consciousness. And now Beatrice. How could he not have noticed she was missing? Was he really so useless that he'd allowed his own daughter to…

Wigbert felt panic rising, but swallowed it down with an effort. 'What's happening in town?' he asked, to distract himself.

Tritewine grimaced. 'The situation is barely controlled. People are scared and angry. As soon as we break up one mob, another one forms. We're sending people home, but I doubt they're staying there and it's taking most of our forces just to keep the public and the Watch separate. I don't know what Watch Commander Posternos is thinking, but he's going to cause a riot for sure if he keeps goading the people like this. The watchmen are patrolling with their weapons drawn, your grace! It's like they're looking for a fight and our numbers are simply not large enough to stop them.'

'Posternos,' Punduckslew growled, appearing out of the throng and coming to stand by the duke's side. 'I'd like to make that man's liver explode!'

The corporal regarded the wizard warily. 'Can you do that?'

Punduckslew shrugged. 'It's technically possible, yes.'

Wigbert sighed. 'Well, let's call that Plan B for now, shall we? Murdering the commander of the Watch is hardly likely to calm the situation, however tempting it might be. Anyone got any other suggestions?'

'We could start arresting people for breach of the peace?' Tritewine suggested.

'How many could we hold?' Wigbert asked.

'Securely? Maybe twenty men in the gatehouse brig? The old

castle dungeons are vast, but they've not been used in years and I can't say what condition they're in. I could send some men to investigate?'

The duke shook his head. 'No, we can't afford to waste the personnel. For now, only use arrest as an absolute last resort. We don't want to make matters worse and something tells me twenty people won't make much difference. We need to find a way of calming the tension before a full-scale riot breaks out! What is the Church of the Cracked Acorn up to?'

'Conspicuously absent so far,' Tritewine said with a frown. 'Obviously some were taken to the watch-house after the skirmish last night, but they're not talking, at least if you believe what Posternos is telling us, and the others haven't been seen on the streets for hours.'

'They'll be plotting something,' Punduckslew warned. 'They didn't expend so much energy egging the town on to the brink of rebellion to suddenly stop now.'

'I agree,' said Tritewine, nodding. 'The only question is, what have they got planned?'

'Seeing as we don't have the resources to find out, I guess we'll just have to make ourselves as ready for whatever it is as we can be,' Wigbert said with a sigh of frustration. 'We need to coordinate our labour force to target the most likely hotspots for unrest.'

Tritewine nodded, then said, 'I'm afraid there's more, your grace.'

'Go on.'

'Two more bodies have been found. The wounds are...nasty.'

The duke massaged his temples. 'The Lord of Misrule?'

'It's probably safe to assume so. Although if it is, he's changed his methods. His other victims were not mutilated. We shouldn't ignore the possibility they're linked to the unrest, though.'

'Where were they found?' Wigbert asked, getting suddenly to his feet.

Both in the Thickets, your grace, but I'd seriously advise

against going into town right now!' Tritewine replied, reading the duke's intentions.

'I appreciate your concern, corporal, but the only way I can see to bring an end to this unrest is to capture the Lord of Misrule, and I can't do that from here.'

'The Castle Guard can—' Tritewine began with concern, but Wigbert overrode her.

'You said yourself you don't have the numbers and I need you to keep the peace. I'm going.'

Punduckslew cleared his throat awkwardly. 'Actually, you can't,' he said. 'That's what I was coming to tell you. I'm afraid Lord Sweetspire is on his way here to talk to you.'

Wigbert swore. 'Acorns and roots! What does he want now?' The Lords Chambers session the previous evening had mainly consisted of Sweetspire whipping the other lords and ladies up into an hour-long tirade against the duke. He couldn't possibly see what else the man had to say after just a few hours. The nobility were scared, of course. A lot of people had died and people needed someone to blame. Their primary concern right now seemed to be making sure it was Wigbert and not one of them.

'I do not know, I'm afraid. But I doubt it'll be good. Here he comes now, look,' said the wizard, pointing to the doorway and making Tritewine flinch as his finger waved vaguely in the corporal's direction. Lord Sweetspire had indeed appeared in the infirmary doorway, dressed in a pale salmon coat and his usual condescending smirk. The leader of the Coins looked about the busy room with distaste before he spotted them.

'There you are!' he said, striding towards them and glaring daggers at a servant carrying bloodied bandages unfortunate enough to cross his path. 'Get those disgusting things away from me!' he snapped at the man before turning his unfriendly smile back to the duke. 'When they told me at the gate I could find you in here, I could scarcely believe it, your grace. This hardly seems an appropriate place for our fearless leader to be doing business. But then you've never worried about appearances, have you?' The man smiled wider as he came to a stop in front of the duke's desk. But Wigbert felt the ice-cold hatred of his eyes burn into him.

'What can I do for you, Lord Sweetspire?' Wigbert asked, refusing to rise to the bait.

'Well, that is the question, isn't it?' the man said. 'What can the great Wigbert Stonemorton do for me? Or indeed any of us? I'm afraid, your grace, that the answer is absolutely nothing.'

'Don't talk in riddles, man!' Punduckslew snapped. 'The duke is very busy and does not have time to listen to you prattle. Get to the point.'

Sweetspire shot the wizard a furious look, his right hand twitching towards the empty scabbard that hung at his waist. Thankfully, even lords were disarmed before entering the castle, although Wigbert doubted Sweetspire would actually have been so suicidal as to attack Punduckslew.

'Very well,' Sweetspire said, all pretense at mirth now gone. 'The point is this; I have here a signed declaration of the Lords Chambers intent to conduct an official review into the duke's handling of the current crisis.' He reached into his jacket and produced a thick white envelope sealed with green wax, which he threw on top of the paper already strewn across Wigberts desk. 'You'll find all the relevant signatures there. We've had enough of your family's incompetence and I will personally be campaigning for a long-overdue change in leadership.'

There was a moment of silence between the four men. The noise of the infirmary seemed to rise around them as all eyes fell on the sealed envelope. It was Punduckslew who spoke first.

'Another rebellion, Sweetspire? I'd have thought your family would have learnt their lesson from last time.'

The corner of Lord Sweetspire's mouth curled up in a smirk. 'No need for rebellions when his grace is doing a fine job of losing the public trust all by himself.' He turned his gaze back to Wigbert. 'Some men are just not cut out for leadership.

In times past, perhaps the Stonemorton family would have got away with this level of incompetence, but we've rather moved on from all that, haven't we? This is a modern society, gentleman! It calls for strong leadership. I'm afraid the other lords and I rather feel Castle Blackwood no longer represents the future of Upton-Myzzle.'

Wigbert stared at the wax seal. Inside his head, Wolfe was howling in fury on his behalf, but the duke felt oddly calm. So it had finally come to this? It was a relief, in a strange way. No more wondering. No more worrying. Ok, still lots of worrying, but at least now he knew where he stood. It felt...freeing. He looked up at Sir Sweetspire.

'Was there anything else?' he asked.

The man's smirk faltered. 'Is that all you have to say?'

'You've made the Lords Chambers position quite clear. I shall peruse this correspondence when I have a moment and provide you with my reply in due course. But unless you have anything else of importance to discuss right now, I'm really very busy.'

Sweetspire gaped at him. Then, looking enraged, he spun on his heel and marched from the room without another word.

'Well,' said Punduckslew. 'That was interestingly handled.'

'You think I should have done it differently?'

'Oh, I didn't say I disapproved. It's about time you stood up to that man. But this is a problem.'

'One in a long line. Right now we have more pressing concerns. We can worry about the Lords Chambers if and when we've stopped the town from ripping itself apart.'

'Sweetspire will be out for blood now. And what he wants the Coin's want. It could make life very difficult.'

'Agreed. Which is all the more reason for us to act quickly. It will be easier to deal with the Coins once the Lord of Misrule is behind bars. Is there a problem, corporal?'

Tritewine had been staring at him with a quizzical expression for some time. 'Sorry, your grace. It's just, I think that robin is trying to get your attention.'

Wigbert blinked at her, then turned to see a small bird frantically fluttering behind his head. It swooped around him and landed on the desk, skidding a little on a loose piece of paper and causing a small avalanche. It was indeed a robin, and it appeared to have a rolled-up bit of paper in its beak. Wigbert stared at it and...it stared back. It didn't just look at him the way birds might occasionally do, it met his eye with a fierce intelligence and Wigbert got the distinct impression it was annoyed. It hopped towards him, pushing out the scroll of paper as if he wanted the duke to take it. Tentatively, Wigbert reached out his hand and plucked it from the bird's mouth with his forefinger and thumb. The robin chirped at him impatiently.

'Careful, your grace,' Punduckslew warned. 'I'd warrant there's magic at play here.'

'I think it's a note,' Wigbert said, unfurling the tiny piece of paper.

'A carrier robin? Seems an odd choice,' said Tritewine, staring at the bird wonderingly. The robin turned and glared at the guard, giving an unmistakably angry tweet that made Tritewine's eyebrows rise up her forehead in a mixture of surprise and amusement.

Wigbert scanned the note, which was written in an unfamiliar scrawl, and his heart lurched. 'It's from Captain Snekchesser!' He read the note aloud.

Your grace,

Your daughter is safe. She and her friend Oatey are with Master Lettuce and I. However, I regret to inform you we find ourselves waylaid within the Blackwood. How we got here I will explain once we have made it back to the Castle, which unfortunately may take longer than I had hoped. Circumstances have required that we team up with a wizard from the east, named Gloamblight, who we met not long after entering the wood. It is his bird, Rupert, who should be delivering this note and—Gloamblight assures me—can bring your response back to us. We are prevented from taking the quickest route back to the safety of the town by a passage of green men. We are therefore taking a more indirect route, via the old Upton-Myzzle archive (Again, I will explain once we are safely back.) and barring complications, I hope to reach the castle by the end of the day. Please respond to let me know you have received this message. I will protect your daughter with my life.

Yours faithfully,
  Captain Snekchesser

'Well,' said Punduckslew when the duke finished reading. 'I can't say I expected that.'

'Why would he take Beatrice into the Blackwood?' Wigbert asked. The letter had done little to quell his fears. It really only posed more questions.

'I obviously can't say for sure, your grace, but it didn't sound to me like the trip was intentional,' said Tritewine, scratching her chin. 'Let's think about what we already know. Snekchesser and Lettuce followed young Beatrice after she fled the Forestry Brigade meeting. So if entering the Blackwood was at all intentional, it would seem likely Beatrice herself led there them. Who's this Gloamblight chap?' This last she directed at Punduckslew, whose brow wrinkled in concern.

'That's the bit that worries me the most. Your grace, the Wizards Charter has no Gloamblight that I've ever come across. And what does Snekchesser mean by 'from the east'? The east of Upton-Myzzle? Seems an odd way to put it.'

'Surely you're not suggesting he means a wizard from outside Upton-Myzzle? Are there any?' said Tritewine.

'Until last week, I'd have sworn there hadn't been a rogue wizard for fifty harvests,' the wizard replied. 'Obviously, recent events have proved me wrong. But a wizard from outside Upton-Myzzle...I don't know. I've heard rumours of people surviving outside the town, but...'

Wigbert nodded. 'There have been scattered reports of people outside Upton-Myzzle for years. Travellers, vagrants, that sort of thing. Most are living rough on the outskirts of the forest and only stay long enough to trade a little before disappearing. I've never heard of any wizards before, though. Do you think we have another Lord of Misrule on our hands?'

'Snekchesser obviously trusts him enough to team up,' Punduckslew pointed out. 'Assuming this note has really come from him, of course.'

Tritewine leant over and inspected the scrap of paper. 'That's definitely the captain's writing. Of course, it's possible he wrote this under duress. We could send guards into the Blackwood to look for them, but it's an enormous area to search and...'

'And we can't afford the personnel,' the duke finished for her. 'What's a passage of green men?'

'A gathering of sorts, I believe,' Punduckslew replied.

Wigbert rubbed his eyes with finger and thumb until he saw stars. There was just too much to think about.

One thing at a time, Wiggy old boy, Wolfe said. *What needs doing first?*

Wigbert tried to think. 'Ok!' he said, eventually. 'I need to write back to the captain. Corporal, please prepare the royal carriage...no, on second thoughts, don't. Find a plain one. Best not to draw attention to ourselves, but I want you to show me these bodies. Oh, and see if there has been any more information from the bomb site. I want to know what caused the explosion.'

Tritewine looked set to argue for a moment, but then she nodded, threw a quick salute and hurried away. Wigbert sat down at the desk, unearthed a quill and inkpot from the piles of paper, and started scratching out a quick response to the note. The robin stood next to his hand, hopping up and down excitedly. Absentmindedly, the duke reached into his coat and produced a rather squashed lump of pound cake someone had handed him earlier. The bird chirped appreciatively and began pecking at the cake with considerable enthusiasm.

'What are you going to say?' Punduckslew asked. 'I suggest caution. We don't know if we can trust this 'wizard from the east'.'

'Perhaps not. But I'm pretty sure we can trust Captain Snekchesser. Right now he's all the help Beatrice has got, and he needs to know the town may not be safe once they get back.' He finished the note, ripped it from the larger piece of paper and then rolled it into as tight a scroll as he could manage, handing it to the robin, who clamped it between its small beak eagerly. It gave a muffled chirp, then rose into the air with a flutter of its wings, flew around the duke's head twice, and disappeared out the nearest window. The two men watched it go.

'This week just keeps getting weirder,' Punduckslew said, still staring out the window. Wigbert didn't reply. He had been fiddling with the note from Captain Snekchesser and a second piece of paper had just peeled away from the first. It was another note, in different writing.

> Your grace,
>
> I believe your town to be in grave danger. The new star may be more than it seems. I am still searching for the answers, but if I'm right, a monster may already stalk the streets of Upton-Myzzle. I have seen visions of its victims. A hedgewitch, writing in her diary in the depths of the Blackwood. A Watchman, reading by the edge of the forest. I will send more word once I have it. In the meantime, be on the lookout for anything odd.
>
> Yours,
> Silas Gloamblight

4.

The rain was now coming down in sheets. The skies were so dark a premature dusk had come to Upton-Myzzle, even though it was still early in the afternoon. In the Thickets, the muddy streets flowed with fetid water. It moved around the duke's boots, then swirled around the sad, wet little bundle on the ground in front of him, before running in streaks of red down the hill. Wigbert stared at the body, equally repulsed and unable to look away.

'Surely no person did this?' he managed to say. 'It looks...it looks more like an animal attack.'

'I'd be inclined to agree,' Tritewine replied, a grimace on her face. 'However, if you look closely at...at the wounds, you'll see there are no teeth marks, no tearing. The clothes too, they've not been ripped but large parts are missing. It's like...' she trailed off.

'Go on,' Wigbert urged.

'I've met alchemists. Worked with one or two. There was one man in particular who always had burns in his clothes, just like these. Some chemical or acid had eaten right through them.'

'Are you saying this is an alchemist?' Punduckslew asked. The wizard was holding a large hand over his mouth and nose.

'Er, no. The body has been identified as one Mr Crump, a scribe who lived not far away.'

'How in Melethin's name did you identify...*that*,' Wigbert asked with a shudder.

'We got lucky,' the corporal explained with a grimace. 'He had an engraved pocket watch which seemed to survive whatever happened to the poor man, although part of the chain has eroded away. We didn't get so lucky with the second victim. There's so little left I can't even be confident of their sex.'

Wigbert swallowed down his rising nausea. *That doesn't look like any normal murder I've ever seen*, Wolfe said.

'Are we sure this is the work of the Lord of Misrule?' the duke asked.

Tritewine shook her head. 'No,' she admitted. 'But it seems something of a coincidence if it's not. I've never seen anything like this before, and I can't even begin to guess how it was done. But if it's not the work of the Lord of Misrule, then that would mean we have a second killer on the loose…'

Wigbert ran a hand across his face with a sigh. Was that possible? He found his thoughts returning to the second note delivered by the robin, the one from the wizard Gloamblight. He'd talked of a monster in Upton-Myzzle. Surely it couldn't…

He hadn't mentioned the note to the others yet. He wasn't sure what to make of it himself.

'Any thoughts?' he asked Punduckslew, who was staring down at the body with a grim expression.

'Several,' the wizard replied. 'Each one more disturbing than the last.'

'Could magic have done this?'

'It's possible, I suppose. Although I've certainly seen nothing like it before. And if it was magic, it couldn't have been Toflo Higginbottom. We already know his Talent.'

'An accomplice?' Tritewine asked.

Punduckslew shrugged his broad shoulders, then appeared to reconsider and shook his head instead. 'No. I simply can't believe there are *two* rogue wizards that have escaped the notice of the Charter.'

'Great. So it's not our killer, but it can't be someone else either,' Wigbert said.

'You're assuming magic did this,' Punduckslew said. 'What about chemicals? You said this reminded you of an alchemist.

Could one of them have done this?' he continued, turning to the corporal, who shook her head uncertainly.

'I can count the number of alchemists operating in Upton-Myzzle on one hand, and I can't see any of them doing this. Besides, look at it. I can't think of any chemical that could do this much damage.'

'Do you know, I'd rather hoped we'd gain evidence here, not just more questions,' Wigbert said glumly.

'With your permission, your grace, I'd like to have the body removed as soon as possible,' Tritewine said. 'Things are tense enough as it is without more people seeing this.'

'Has anyone seen it already?'

She nodded. 'I'm afraid so. The news will be out by now, but it's still a good idea to clear up as soon as possible.'

'Very well. But let me know immediately if you learn anything new.'

Wigbert and Punduckslew stepped aside, sheltering the best they could under a nearby porch whilst Tritewine directed some men in the cleanup operation. They were silent for some time. The duke was deep in thought and therefore it made him jump slightly when the Wizard said, 'You need to promote that woman.'

He nodded. 'You're right. Just as soon as we have a moment. Although it would seem she has more or less promoted herself already.'

They both fell silent again.

'We need to have a conversation,' Punduckslew said eventually.

'If this is about Wolfe, it can wait,' Wigberts said firmly.

'It's not. Not solely, anyway.' Punduckslew looked out at the pouring rain speculatively. 'But that...*he* is part of it. There are a lot of odd things going on. Too many to be a coincidence. Something is happening, something...different.'

The duke looked at him with a raised eyebrow. 'What do you mean by that, exactly?'

The wizard turned to him. His face was troubled. 'I don't

know. I don't understand it all yet. But...Look, I've never been a particularly religious person. It's mostly superstitious nonsense, in my opinion. Mostly. But I'm a wizard. I've been around magic all my life. Seen things.'

The wizard lapsed into silence and eventually Wigbert said, 'Punduckslew, what exactly are you trying to say?'

But at that moment, a smatter of raised voices made them both look out into the rain-soaked street. There was a guard hurrying through the downpour towards where Corporal Tritewine was still organising the cleanup. They met, exchanged a few urgent words, then Tritewine hurried over to where the duke and the wizard were sheltering.

'They've found another body, your grace.'

Wigberts' heart fell yet further into the depths of his stomach. 'Where?' he asked.

'Just a few streets away.'

'Show me.'

They hurried through the driving rain, arriving in a thin, dark, pungent alley, already sitting in a good few inches of black water. It ended in the plaster wall of a house, sodden and turned greyish-brown by years of bad weather and neglect. A shape lay in front of it. Soaked through to his skin and beginning to shiver uncontrollably, Wigbert approached the bloody heap. It was indeed another body, more intact than the last, its head in one piece but face down in the muck. As the duke got nearer, his foot knocked against something floating in the water. He reached down into the freezing swill and retrieved it.

It was a wooden mask.

'Is that...' Punduckslew started to say behind him.

Silently, Wigbert knelt down next to the body, cold water soaking up from his knees and making him shiver even more. The body was in a bad way, with similar wounds to the poor scribe. Gently, Wigbert reached out and took ahold of what remained of the shoulders and turned the whole thing over. The head rolled out of the water and mud with a sickening sucking sound and the face was revealed, staring sightlessly up into the pouring rain.

It was Toflo Higginbottom.

The Lord of Misrule was dead.

CHAPTER ELEVEN: GREEN FIRE

1.

Master Lettuce had always considered himself a brave man. The way he saw it, if you were as terrified of everything as he was, it took considerable courage to even get out of bed in the mornings. That he went around in public, walking, talking and eating, sometimes all at the same time, was frankly nothing short of heroic. Not that he would share this opinion, of course. He doubted anyone else would see it the same way. But he couldn't help mentally patting himself on the back as he followed the others into the dark, ruinous remains of the Upton-Myzzle archive. It would have been all too easy for him to turn tail and run.

It was the smell.

It invaded every other sense so that he could taste the dampness, feel the cloying mould in the back of his throat and practically see the mushroom spores in the greeny-grey light. He found it overwhelmingly oppressive, and he wished desperately—not for the first time in the past twenty-four hours—that he was back in the cosy parlour of the little cottage he shared with his mother. He really, really wanted a piece of toast. With lots of butter. And honey. And by Melethin what he wouldn't give right now for a piping hot cup of spice.

Some might consider it strange for a man with the position of master in the Forestry Brigade to hold such an aversion to the Blackwood. Lettuce just considered it common sense. He hadn't always felt the same. When he was himself a young boy, the place fascinated him. He'd found a book of his mother's, tucked away in a dusty trunk. The Flora of the Blackwood.

It had captivated him. Each entry had the most beautiful watercolour illustrations, and he spent hours reading about the health benefits of the Yellow Sap Skunk Cabbage, or the defense mechanisms of the Black Veined False Beetle mushroom. How he'd longed to see the ancient Black Oaks themselves.

His mother would have none of it. No child of hers would skulk about in the undergrowth like a wild man. The book had been a poorly chosen gift from some distant relative, banished to the forgotten trunk mere hours after his mother received it. She would not allow him to join the Forestry Brigade. Denied access to that which fascinated him most, Lettuce's obsession only grew. Years later, when he announced his intention to train for a master's position, he let his mother believe it would be in the study of sacred texts. She found out the truth far too late. Too late for both of them, as it turned out. It was the evening of Lettuce's very first Blackwood trip. He returned home pale and shaken after what his instructor described as an 'unfortunate incident' with a creature known colloquially as a Dangling Horror. He'd admitted the truth to his mother straight away. She'd said she wasn't angry, just disappointed, which of course was far worse. She then chose that moment to reveal the book that had started the whole mess was, in fact, one of a set of two. His mother presented him with the second, a look of vicious satisfaction on her face. It was entitled The Fauna of the Blackwood. Oh, how Lettuce wished he'd had access before to the terrifying information contained within those pages. But it was too late. Lettuce's were not quitters, or so his mother informed him. He completed his training. Once qualified, he set about limiting his actual contact with the forest as much as possible. When he swiftly rose to a management position (Brigade Masters met with a disturbing number of 'unfortunate incidents') he stopped trips into the Blackwood altogether. There had been little resistance. Most of the kids were happy so long as they had something to kick or hit with sticks. Given the circumstances, Master Lettuce was perfectly prepared to let that something be him. Better that than Dangling Horrors. Some of the old guard had posed more resistance. The Master Cabernatol's of the world, who viewed things like a case of slight decapitation as character-building. But their numbers dwindled and soon Master Lettuce had orchestrated events so that in between all the lessons on knot tying, paper-mache sculpture classes, sausage cookout evenings and, of course, flora identification training, there was never quite any time to fit in a trip to the Blackwood at all.

But now here he was. And, after so much time away from the place, he had to admit...he'd been completely justified in staying away for so long! Humans were not supposed to be here. He felt that in his gut. This was no place for a species that had invented the water closet.

'I can't see a thing!' he heard the young duchess-to-be complain.

Then there came the sharp knocking of flint on steel and Master Lettuce saw the wizard Gloamblight's face, momentarily illuminated by red sparks, before a small glow developed in the tinderbox he held in his hands. After a few moments fussing, a miniature storm lantern was produced and a steady yellow light fought back the heavy murk. If there was one thing worse than the stinking darkness, it was being able to see what was producing the smell. Shiny black fungus covered much of the floor and broken masonry. It was like being surrounded by evil jelly. Lettuce was sure he'd had a dream about that once. That he could correctly identify the growths as the, actually rather rare, Black Stink Mushroom, gave him little comfort.

In the pale light provided by the lantern, the group spread out. There really wasn't much to explore, however. Any semblance that this had once been a grand room had long ago been erased by the Blackwood, leaving little in the way of defining features. Much of the ceiling was gone, open to the lightening sky above. As the others began looking around with apparent interest, Lettuce nudged a soggy pile of leaves with his foot and sighed.

'I know what the spirit said, but I highly doubt we'll find much intact in this place,' he grumbled.

'We have to find a way down to the lower levels,' Gloamblight replied. 'Everyone search for signs of stairs.'

Master Lettuce did as he was told, with roughly the same enthusiasm as a man searching for someone else's gold ring in a latrine pit. Why couldn't they just go home? He kept asking himself that same question. He was personally less than convinced by all this cryptic nonsense about monsters and falling stars. In his opinion, there was plenty enough to worry about in everyday life without going and looking for more. He shuffled about aimlessly, avoiding the Black Stink Mushrooms and dragging his feet through the mush and leaves. He gave a sudden cry and jumped back in alarm when, after he gave one pile of leaves a particularly vicious kick, a whole section of the floor seemed to disappear downwards in a cascade of mulch and detritus, splattering onto something solid below like wet sand. On closer inspection, he realised he had merely disturbed the top of a sloping pile of grime that led downwards through a rectangular hole in the floor. He'd found the stairs.

Bugger.

He thought about keeping the discovery to himself, but his startled cry had already brought the others running to his location. The boy Oatey reached him first.

'You've found it!' he exclaimed, getting down on his hands and knees amongst the slush and peering over the edge of the hole.

Lettuce shuddered at the sight of the boy's unprotected hands in amongst the filth. 'Oh yippee,' he said with as much sarcasm as he could muster. No one paid him any heed.

'We'll need to clear away all this rubbish to make sure the stairs are still intact,' Gloamblight said, edging Lettuce aside and looking down into the hole eagerly. 'Go slowly. We don't want anyone falling.'

He and the two children began removing as much of the

debris as they could, scraping it to the sides with their hands and feet. Captain Snekchesser came and stood next to the master, catching his eye and shrugging without expression. Gradually, the first in a set of descending stone steps were revealed.

'They look sturdy enough,' Gloamblight announced. 'I'll go first.'

He descended, clearing further as he went. The others followed, Lettuce taking up the rear, unsure of what he feared most; whatever horrors lay beneath them in the lower levels, or the exposed feeling he felt at being last in the line, therefore vulnerable to attack from behind. He tried not to imagine the feeling of claws ripping into the flesh of his back as they made their torturously slow descent. The leaves only seemed to get thicker as they went until the only way forward was to heap the stuff in piles against the walls at the edge of the steps. Pretty soon the piles rose to almost head height, and it became like walking into the very earth itself. Or a grave, Master Lettuce thought miserably.

Still they continued down until eventually the left wall opened out and the leaves, basically compost at this point, fell away in great heaps across the floor of what appeared to be another room. It was smaller than the first, colder, damper, and generally more miserable in every way. The remains of wooden structures lined the walls. They may have once been bookshelves, in much the same way as a cowpat was once grass.

'This does not look promising,' Captain Snekchesser observed.

'Hazel said most stuff had survived down here. We just have to keep looking!' Beatrice protested.

'In point of fact, I think what she actually said was that some rats *told* her some stuff had survived. I suppose we have to ask ourselves how much time we're willing to waste on the word of a rat,' the captain replied. Master Lettuce felt he raised a good point.

'You got somfin against rats?' said a voice.

The company froze. Master Lettuce, who had suddenly become uncomfortably aware of the contents of his bladder, said, 'Please tell me that was one of you who said that?'

No one replied. Gloamblight shoved the storm lantern into the hands of Captain Snekchesser, who swore loudly and fumbled with the hot metal. Shadows danced around the room, and Master Lettuce watched in horrified fascination as the wizard began to unbuckle one of the belts that held his right arm to his side. The room suddenly seemed full of steam and Lettuce became aware of a rapid bubbling sound. He soon realised it was coming from the flask that encased Gloamblight's hand, as was the steam, which issued out around the man's wrist with an angry hiss. Before he'd loosened the belt, however, there was a flare of much brighter orange light and the room was illuminated. A group of figures were standing in a doorway in the far wall.

Short figures.

Hairy figures.

With tails.

They were...rats. Rats the size of small dogs, standing upright on their hind legs and each holding aloft a blazing torch, beady eyes gleaming in the light, pink noses twitching. One of them stepped forward.

'I *said*, you got some kind o' problem wi' rats?' it squeaked at them. Around its waist, it wore a tiny belt, from which hung the smallest sword Master Lettuce had ever seen. Little more than a letter opener, really. In fact, it *was* a letter opener, Lettuce knew because he had one just like it, only his didn't look so wickedly sharp.

When the rat that had spoken was met only with stunned silence, it took another step forward, frowning angrily. An expression Mater Lettuce could honestly say he had never seen on a rat before.

'Any of you cloud-grazers got a tongue?' the rat asked.

It was Beatrice who replied. 'You're rats!' she said.

The rat gave her such a withering look that Master Lettuce felt a terrified bubble of laughter rise in his throat. He swallowed it back down with an effort.

'How very astute,' the rat said, unimpressed. 'The witch said you humans was smart but I'm dazzled, I really am.'

There was another stretch of silence as the human occupants of the room mentally recalculated their world to include sarcastic talking rats. Lettuce rather felt someone ought to defend the species, but he'd be damned if it was going to be him. He felt sure death by rat would be something his mother disapproved of.

Eventually it was Captain Snekchesser who took charge, stepping forward to meet the rat, knee-to-face. 'We come in peace!' he said.

The rat raised a furry eyebrow. Did rats usually have eyebrows? Lettuce found he couldn't quite remember.

'Oh yeah? What's 'is story. Ole steam pockets over there,' the rat said, indicating Gloamblight with a jerk of its clawed hand (Or was it a paw?). The wizard was still fiddling with his belts and issuing a goodly amount of white steam into the enclosed space. It was starting to hang around the ceiling in clouds. 'It ain't right that. Very suspicious.'

Gloamblight raised his free hand placatingly. 'It's an involuntary reaction, I assure you,' he said. 'You took me by surprise. It'll subside in a few moments. I mean you no harm.'

'Involuntary steaming, huh?' the rat replied, regarding the wizard appraisingly. 'Tha's a new one. I knew a badger once what had involuntary gas, but that was quite a different thing, if you know what I mean.'

And then the rat laughed, which prompted the rest of the rats to do the same. It was a funny chittering sound, but Master Lettuce was more impressed by the many flashes of long, yellow-white teeth. He swallowed and tried not to imagine them sinking into his flesh.

The laughter stopped as suddenly as it had begun and the head rat spoke again.

'What you doin' in our 'ome?'

'If we are intruding, we apologise. We did not know the structure was inhabited,' Captain Snekchesser said. 'But we have business here and were shown the way by a tree spirit. She neglected to mention that...well...'

'Oh, Hazel let you guys in? You should o' said,' the rat said, appearing to relax a little.

'What's your name, friend?' Snekchesser tried.

'Mostly I get called Boss.'

'Ok, but what should we call you?' Snekchesser persisted.

The rat just stared at him.

'Right, Boss it is then,' the captain said. 'I'm Captain Snekchesser. It's a pleasure to make your acquaintance. Excuse my curiosity, but what was that you said before about a witch?'

'Hedgewitch, she is. Arrived a couple o' days back. Crazy, if you ask me, even for one of you cloud-grazers.'

'C...crazy?' Master Lettuce squeaked, finding his voice again at the idea of a crazy witch haunting the bowels of the building.'

Boss sniffed. 'Yeah, right nut-job, I reckon. Keeps wittering on about stars and monsters. Unhinged, I'd say. Probably dangerous. You wanna meet 'er?' he finished brightly.

'No!' Lettuce cried at the exact same time Gloamblight said, 'Yes!'

The wizard stepped forward eagerly. The steam from his hand was lessening, and he seemed to have stopped fiddling with the belts. 'You say this woman has been talking about stars and monsters?' he asked the head rat.

Boss nodded sagely. 'Wackadoodle,' he confirmed.

'In that case, we would very much like to meet her!'

Boss grinned. An unnerving expression with far too much emphasis on teeth for Lettuce's liking. 'Tha's handy,' the rat said cheerfully. 'Cos' she's standin right behind you'

The intruders turned as one. Behind them, cloaked in darkness, was a woman's face, peering at them out of the corner of the room. She looked gaunt, with deep hollows in her cheeks and cracked, pale lips. Her eyes burned with a green intensity.

'*Doooooooooom!*' the witch moaned, at which point Master Lettuce's nerves failed him completely and he fainted once again.

2.

The populace of Upton-Myzzle was revolting.

They were rioting too, Ormus Stonemorton thought to himself with a humorless bark of laughter. The old man stood in the window of The Green Man's Eyes and glared out at the rain-drenched street. He watched through the distorted panes of glass as people prowled past the pub, taking advantage of the shelter offered by the overhanging rooftops. Prowled was the best word for it. It's like walking but when you're looking for trouble. Admittedly, this was all the duke-no-more had actually seen anyone do so far and, as much as he hated to admit it, walking was not actually an arrestable offence. Maybe he'd change that when he took back power. The people were rioting *in their minds,* and as far as Ormus was concerned, that was bad enough. It was only a matter of time before someone acted on it.

Behind him, the pub lay empty. It wasn't technically open at this time in the morning, but Ormus and the landlord had come to an arrangement. That arrangement being that Mr Aldergate would do as Ormus said, and Ormus wouldn't have the place closed down. The landlord was fairly certain the old statesman didn't actually have the power to do as he threatened, but why make waves?

The door to the pub was pushed open and Terrance's chair appeared in the opening, complete with Terrance himself, who beamed happily at the coat stand.

'About bloody time!' Ormus called over gruffly. 'We've got important things to discuss.'

THE LORD OF MISRULE

Terrance turned his head and fixed the duke-no-more with at least one of his milky eyes. 'Balderdash!' he cried.

Ormus glared at the man suspiciously. 'What?'

'Don't take it personally, he's been saying that all morning,' came a voice from the street outside. Terrance was pushed further into the room and Quimby appeared behind him, followed swiftly by Gerald, both wrapped up thickly against the cold. Ormus continued to glare, but let the matter drop.

'What news?' he asked instead.

'The populace is revolting!' Gerald announced, stamping his feet and blowing out his cheeks. 'They're rioting too,' he addend with a smug grin.

Ormus glowered at the man. 'That jokes as old as you are!' he snapped.

'Then it's still in its prime,' Gerald replied, nose in the air.

Ormus lent heavily on his stick and sighed. 'Do either of you have anything useful to report or are we just going to stand here all day and make puns?'

'Alright, alright. Let a man get a drink first,' Gerald snapped back, ambling over to the table where Ormus stood and easing into a seat. 'Barkeep!'

'The bars closed,' Ormus said levelly.

Gerald's red face fell. 'Then what in the name of Melethin' are we doing here at this hour?'

'It's eleven. Perfectly respectable time to start business,' Ormus sniffed.

'I usually have a nice nap at about eleven,' Quimby offered, parking Terence at the table and taking a seat himself. Ormus pinched the bridge of his nose and sank down beside them.

'For the sake of my sanity, can we just get on with it?' he sighed. 'Give me the list of supporters you've secured so far.'

There was an uncomfortable silence. Gerald scratched his veiny nose and coughed while Quinby seemed suddenly thoroughly fascinated by the view out of the window.

'Well?' Ormus demanded, thumping the wooden table. 'Do you have a list of names or not?'

'I'm not sure *list* is quite the word I'd use...' Quinby said wretchedly, not meeting the duke-no-more's eye.

'How many?' Ormus asked with a sinking heart.

'Five,' Quinby muttered.

'And not including us?'

'Err...one.'

'Who?'

'Obadiah.'

'I thought you said he was bed bound!'

'He assured me he's with us in spirit. Well...his wife did.'

'What about Philo? He's with us, surely?'

'I'm afraid not. He still seems rather upset about that business with his niece.'

'But was years ago!'

'Nevertheless.'

Ormus put his head in his hands. 'What went wrong?' he asked.

'Well, of those who would see us, the prevailing opinion seemed to be that...' Quinby began delicately, trailing off.

'You're too old to rule,' Gerald finished plainly.

'Outrageous!' Ormus spluttered, raising his head again.

Gerald shrugged. 'That's how it is.'

Ormus frowned at him. 'Are you saying you agree?'

Gerald made a noncommittal expression. 'Hardly matters, does it?' he said. 'Look, I'll admit I got excited about the idea of reliving the glory days, but—'

'But what?' Ormus snapped.

'But then I got home and needed a piss and a lie down!' Gerald shot back, staring the duke-no-more down defiantly. Eventually, Ormus ripped his eyes away and glowered at the grain of the tabletop instead. The men fell into silence.

Eventually Gerald spoke again, his voice thick. 'I don't like it any more than you do, old man. But we can't fight time. We're done.'

Ormus gripped the table until his fingers turned white. Then he burst to his feet, grabbing his stick and stumbled towards the door with purpose. 'Done, am I?' he cried. 'I'll show you who's done!' He ripped open the door and stalked out into the streaming rain, scanning back and forth until his eyes alighted on a group of apprentices making their way down the hill.

'You there!' he barked at them, striding across the street with righteous indignation, carrying his stick and ignoring the water pouring onto his head and the pain in his legs. The apprentices, little more than boys really, turned at his shout. At first they looked amused at the sight of this little old man moving stiffly towards them. But at least one grin faded as he moved closer and one of their number recognised the former duke. By the time Ormus reached them, he was practically vibrating with rage. Had he been thinking clearer, he might have noticed how the huddled group towered over his own shrunken frame. The shortest of the six, for six there were, was a full head and shoulders taller than himself.

'Well?' the duke-no-more demanded, glaring at an array of chests.

There was an embarrassed shuffling of feet and an exchange of baffled looks. Eventually one of them said 'Well what...your grace?'

Ormus squinted up at his face. 'Don't give me backchat, boy! I want an explanation!'

More looks. A snigger. Ormus became dimly aware of the smell of alcohol. 'Are you drunk?' he asked, scandalised.

A particularly large member of the group elbowed his way forward and leant over Ormus, looking down at him with unfocused eyes and flushed cheeks. 'You bet we're drunk!' he slurred, oblivious to the water running down his face. 'It's the end of the world, grandad, or didn't anyone tell you?'

'Disgusting! It's the middle of the morning. Have you no shame, boy?' Ormus demanded.

The large man swayed back and forth. 'Din't you just leave The Green Man's Eyes?' he said ponderously.

Ormus flared his nostrils in outrage, but before he could reply, a slightly more cautious member of the group came forward with a nervous smile.

'My apologies, your grace. We would, of course, be delighted to help you, if we can. If you would be so good as to explain what it is you require an explanation to?' He gently but firmly elbowed the larger man aside.

Ormus paused, unsure for a minute, then pulled himself up to his full height, mustering all the dignity he could. 'I want an explanation for all this...this ruckus!'

The man looked around with uncertainty. At present, there was just one other person in the street; a woman of middling years, hurrying along through the deluge with a nervous look over her shoulder.

'Um...ruckus, your grace?'

'Don't be smart with me, boy!' Ormus said, jabbing the man sharply with his stick. 'I know when there's trouble afoot in my town. What's the word?'

The apprentice was looking increasingly uncomfortable and his larger friend took his pause as an opportunity to rejoin the conversation. 'End. Of. The. World,' he bawled into the duke-no-more's face, still swaying slightly. 'Gotta have some fun while we can! Gonna burn me some books!' There was a chorus of tittering laughter from the rest of the group.

'What is this buffoon jabbering on about?' Ormus asked the other man.

The relatively sober member of the group was looking rather pale and refused to meet the former duke's eye. 'Oh nothing. Nothing. He's just had too much mash, your grace. He mumbled.

'Don't lie to me, boy,' Ormus growled.

The man started to sweat. 'Well...you see, thing is...and you must understand I only overheard this...just a passing remark, really...probably nothing to it...'

'Out with it!' Ormus spat, jabbing the man again with his stick.

The man took a deep breath, then spoke all in a rush, apparently hoping if he said the words quickly enough, the consequences would be less severe. 'The-Church-of-the-Cracked-Acorn-are-holding-a-book-burning-your-grace.'

The duke-no-more's eyebrows shot up his forehead. 'In this weather? What the devil for?' he demanded.

The apprentice looked utterly miserable now, but it was his larger friend who once again swayed back into the conversation. 'Burning all the Books of Oak, ain't they,' he said with a grin. 'They're an affront to Zigelder and must be destroyed if he's to come and save us from the daemon. 'Ere, what you doin'?' The smaller man had begun flapping his hands at his friend desperately and making little shushing sounds. Ormus's mouth was hanging open.

'What?' he spluttered. 'WHAT?!'

The sober man at this point obviously decided to cut his losses and began shepherding the large man and the rest of his friends away. 'So glad we could help, your grace!' he said with strained cheer, breaking into a trot.

'I'm not done with you yet!' Ormus shouted after them. He was met with another outbreak of sniggering laughs.

'Bye now!' the sober man called over his shoulder desperately.

'Get back here!' Ormus screamed, jumping up and down twice in rage before his legs gave out on him and he collapsed into the muck of the street.

'Well, that was dignified.'

Gerald had followed him out of the pub and was now standing over him, arms folded.

Ormus glowered up at him, the sound of laughter ringing in his ears. 'Shut up and help me.'

His thoughts were a whirl as the beefy Gerald helped pull him from the floor with a grunt and the sucking sound of mud. He was sodden. 'Did you hear them?' he hissed. 'They want to burn them. All the Books of Oak. It's not enough they've blown up my life's work, now they want to erase it completely!' he staggered against Gerald as he rose, pushing himself off the man's chest angrily, completely failing to notice that the man was no longer listening, staring after the departing apprentices with a worried frown. 'Well, I'll show them!' Ormus continued, working himself up into a frenzy. 'I won't have it! I'll make them listen. I'll hold the entire Lords Chambers to ransom if I have to! I will not be ignored!'

Gerald ignored him, taking a ponderous step towards the end of the street where the sound of laughter had now changed to something else. Ormus opened his mouth to continue his tirade, then shut it again as the sound of running feet filtered its way through his rage filled mind.

Then somebody screamed.

'What by Melethin...' he grumbled, following his friend's gaze to the end of the street. The apprentices had reappeared, joined by several other people, all of whom were running towards them with the pale, determined faces of people who want, above all other things, to not be where they currently are. Ormus caught the gaze of the large apprentice. He was looking suddenly extremely sober.

'Run!' the man shouted. 'Run for your lives! It's the Lord of Misrule!'

As if to punctuate this statement from the far end of the street, an almighty bellow rose above the pattering of the rain and the splashing of running feet.

'ZIGELDER IS OUR SAVIOUR!'

A solitary figure appeared, silhouetted against the driving rain. There was something wrong with the shape. Ormus quickly realised why when the form separated into two as a larger man held out the limp body of a second in one arm, before tossing it aside where it landed with a sad splash, unmoving.

Gerald swore an oath.

Ormus strained his eyes to see, then gave an enraged cry and stepped forward as he recognised the ugly wooden mask covering the figure's face. 'It's him! It's the swine who tried to kill me! Guards! Guards!'

Gerald grabbed him by the shoulder, pulling him back.

'There are no guards here, you daft sod. Get back in the Eyes. We can bar the doors.'

Ormus goggled at him. 'Run away?' he hissed.

'Bloody right!' Gerald dragged him towards the open doorway where Quimby had appeared and was staring at the approaching killer, his mouth a wide O of surprise. Gerald continued, 'What are you planning to do? Fall over on him?'

'I beat the blaggard once! Besides, he's a ruddy wizard. A door won't stop him!' Ormus cried, struggling against the larger man's grip.

'And neither will you!' The door'll slow him down and we can escape out the back,' Gerald persisted, refusing to relinquish his grip.

'Wait!' Ormus shouted, gripping the door frame with numb, wet fingers as Gerald tried to shove him through it. 'Something's not right.' He had been watching their approaching adversary with a fierceness born of hatred, but even through the red mist of his anger he could tell something was amiss. The figure was still advancing up the street, driving a small crowd of terrified people before it.

'What's he doing?' Ormus asked himself out loud. Gerald paused his tugging to look, and Quimby leaned out into the street to do likewise. Closer now, they could clearly make out the Lord of Misrule costume. The black and grey cowl of rags was slick with rain, the green man's face carved into the mask ran with little rivulets of water. But the man moved strangely.

'Why's he doing this?' Ormus asked.

"Cos he's a raving nutter, that's why!' Quimby spluttered.

'No,' Ormus said impatiently. 'I mean, this doesn't fit his previous behavior. He kills by stealth. That's his strength. He strikes out of nowhere, then disappears before anyone can catch him. But this...this is like he's—'

'On the bloody rampage!' Gerald finished for him.

As they watched, an unlucky straggler came into the man's reach and was plucked from the street, then thrown with a rage filled roar through a nearby window.

'Did you see that?' Ormus hissed.

'Of course we ruddy saw that! He just threw that poor bugger like a straw dolly! Now come on, inside!' Gerald hissed back, resuming his tugging.

'Not that, not that. His mouth. Did you see? I'd swear it...'

'It what?' Quinby asked, a slight tremor in his voice.

But the former duke did not have to answer. The man was by this point only twenty feet away and when he let out another ear-splitting roar, all three of them clearly saw the wooden face wrench open at the sound. The wood cracked and splintered as the mouth moved like it was alive, forming and reforming before the roar ended and the mask became smooth once more.

Gerald let out a long line of swearwords. 'Melethin's craggy trunk! He's not human!' he spluttered. 'Why didn't you tell us the bugger wasn't human?!'

'He was! At least...I *thought* he was.'

'Clearly you were wrong!'

Gerald finally succeeded in prying the duke-no-more from the doorframe and tossed him through the doorway with a grunt. Ormus landed on the terrified Quimby and they stumbled backwards into the pub, gripping each other for support. Gerald turned back to the street. 'In here!' he cried. 'For Melethin's sake, if you want to bloody live get your arses in here!' He then stepped back sharply, leaving Ormus and Quimby struggling to clear the doorway as a stream of terrified people poured into the pub. When the last was through, there were about a dozen in all, Gerald slammed the door closed, swiftly turning the large key which Ormus had left in the lock.

'ZIGEEEEEELDER!!!'

The enraged cry from outside was barely muffled by the walls of the pub or the pounding of the rain on the tiled roof.

'Balderdash?'

As if in answer the question rolled over the whimpering huddle of dripping people by the door. Ormus slipped on the now slick tiled floor, righted himself and hobbled over to where Terrance was still sitting in his chair by the window.

'Spot of bother, old chap,' he breathed at the man, grabbing the handles to his chair. 'Time we were going!'

Gerald meanwhile was berating the petrified people he'd saved from the street. 'Acorns and roots, don't just bloody stand there! Out the back! No not that way you fool, *this* way! Come on everyone, follow me!'

He'd not herded them far, however, before the room was filled with the sound of tortured wood, then filled with the wood itself as the door exploded inwards. As the debris settled their pursuer was revealed, letting loose yet another echoing roar that bounced around Ormus's head making him wince. Panic ensued. Terrified people scattered and slid on the tiled floor, pushing each other out of the way and bowling over tables and chairs in their desperate attempts to get away. Gerald guided them best he could, calling for people to follow as he disappeared into the back of the building towards the rear exit. The Lord of Misrule thrashed around in the wreckage like a wounded animal. Ormus made to follow those fleeing, but as he heaved Terrance's chair out from the table and through the upturned furniture he caught sight of a boy who seemed to be tangled up in a fallen chair and was sat on the floor, completely frozen in fear. Ormus cursed as their attacker moved closer.

'Quimby!' he cried as he gave Terrance an almighty shove which sent his chair careering across the room to where Quimby was hovering fretfully.

'Baaaaalderdaaaash!'

Quimby intercepted the chair with a grunt.

'Get him out! I'll get the boy!' Ormus shouted. Quimby didn't need asking twice, bouncing the chair off the walls in his haste to comply.

The Lord of Misrule had now spotted the child and was advancing towards him with heavy, ponderous footsteps that seemed to shake the very building. Was it Ormus's imagination, or had he grown? He seemed more beast than man now, growling as he bore down on his prey.

'Run boy!' Ormus screamed and with a surge of strength he didn't know he had launched his stick at the beast. He felt his bad shoulder wrench as the stick sailed through the air and… stuck. It didn't so much hit their attacker as plunge through it, sticking through the things arm like a huge crossbow bolt. The beast paused to stare at it, then did something that made the former Duke's heart freeze.

It's arm fell off.

It hit the floor with a squelch, dissolving into a heap of black goo, before squiggling across the floor and being reabsorbed by the thing's foot.

The boy on the floor pissed himself and began to cry, which as far as Ormus was concerned was a perfectly reasonable response. The beast leaned over the child and paused, as if considering. Ormus, throwing all caution to the wind, grabbed the nearest chair, tore across the intervening space and brought it down on the things head with all that remained of his strength. This time the projectile simply passed straight through the thing's body with a sickening sound like sucking mud, clattering away harmlessly. Ormus himself collapsed helplessly on the floor, his energy spent. He could just reach the boy, however, and with a desperate lunge he grabbed the child's leg. The boy shuddered and whatever spell keeping him frozen broke at the duke-no-more's touch. He turned and locked his petrified eyes with Ormus.

'Go!' Ormus urged, and finally the child complied, scrabbling to his feet and scurrying away before the thing, that was looking less and less human, never mind like the Lord of Misrule, could react.

Left alone Ormus rolled onto his back, spent, and waited, helplessly. In front of him the beast was withering and shaking, it's shape bulging and sinking like the surface of a boiling stew, until eventually it stilled, solidifying once more into a shape very much like the familiar figure of the Lord of Misrule. But at this close distance Ormus could see clearly how it was all fake. The cowl wasn't worn, it's rags simply appeared to protrude directly out of the things skin. And the wooden mask wasn't a mask at all. It was a face.

'What *are* you?' Ormus breathed.

The beast leant over him, resting it's hands either side of his helpless body, bringing its face, the wooden mockery of a Green man's, to within inches of Ormus's own. The wood splintered as the mouth opened and a long tongue emerged, flicking over the duke-no-more's face like a snake tasting the air.

But just when the former duke thought his time was up, a shudder ran through the beast and it stiffened, looking up at something Ormus couldn't see. Then without further warning it stood, lumbered into a run, and without so much as raising a hand to protect its face it smashed through the nearest wall with a deafening crash and disappeared. Ormus twisted his head to look at the hole it left behind, bits of plaster and wooden boarding still tumbling to the floor.

'Bugger me!' he said, then passed out.

3.

'*D*ooooooooom!*' the hedgewitch cried.

Master Lettuce collapsed, folding down onto the stone floor with a little sigh. Beatrice had to skip to one side to avoid being brought down with him. The hedgewitch stepped into the light produced by the rat's torches. She was skeletal thin, all sharp angles, her green dress hanging off her like a threadbare rag left on the washboard.

'Ooooh, did you see his face?' she cackled, her gaunt features crinkling into a grin. Her teeth were a dentist's nightmare. 'I thought he was going to piss himself he was so scared!'

Beatrice looked down at the unconscious Lettuce, then back up to the grinning crone. 'That wasn't very nice,' she said simply.

The witch's grin faded slightly, and she regarded Beatrice with her green eyes appraisingly. 'No, little girl, I suppose it wasn't at that. But I get few enough laughs in my life, and that man's been on the edge of nervous collapse for the last thirty minutes. He's probably better off. I hope you won't begrudge me my little joke.'

The captain stepped in front of Beatrice protectively. 'You've been watching us?' he growled.

The hedgewitch shrugged. 'You make an interesting bunch,' she admitted. 'And I'm sick of talking to these rats.'

'Oi!'

'Oh shush, Boss! You're as sick of me as I am of you.'

The head rat sniffed. "Snot my fault all you wanna talk about is nonsense,' he said. 'I'm very good at conversation. Famed for it, I is. There goes Boss, they say, very witty rat.'

The hedgewitch ignored him, turning her attention back to the group of humans. 'I'm Madame Reedswail. A pleasure to meet you.'

Gloamblight stood forward eagerly, unable to keep the urgency out of his voice. 'We understand you know something about the new star? Please, what is it?'

Madame Reedswail narrowed her eyes at him, the line of her mouth sharpening. She pointed at him with a long, crooked finger. 'I'm not sure I should discuss such things with the likes of you. There is something decidedly unsettling about you, lad. Your auras pulsating like a glowworm in heat. What are you?'

Gloamblight's face stiffened, but the spark of anticipation didn't quite leave his dark eyes. 'I'm a wizard, Madame. Now if you—'

'No, you ain't,' Madame Reedswail cut him off. 'I know Wizards. Pompous fools most of 'em, with that fancy charter of theirs. But safe. Stable. Most of 'em, anyhow. But you... magic's pouring into you like I ain't never seen. You're like a plughole.'

Gloamblight scowled. Captain Snekchesser slapped a fist into his open palm with triumph. 'I knew it!' he hissed. 'I knew there was something not right about you. All those Talents. It's not normal. What is he, then?'

This last he directed at the hedgewitch, who shrugged her bony shoulders. 'Ain't seen nothing like him before. Maybe he was a wizard, once, but then something happened to him. Maybe he never was.' She peered closer at Gloamblight, looking through him like she could read his inner workings. 'Bits of him look normal. It's like someone reached inside...tweaked a few things.'

Gloamblight glowered back at her. 'If you've *quite* finished, Madame? What I may or may not be is neither here nor there. There are more pressing concerns. Like the star and the monster.'

'What do you know about the monster?' the witch said

sharply.

A satisfied expression passed across Gloamblight's face. 'So there *is* a monster, then. Now we're getting somewhere.'

'I'd say there's a bloody monster!'

'You've seen it?' Gloamblight asked eagerly.

'No,' Madame Reedswail admitted. 'But it ate my colleague... most of her, anyway.'

'If you didn't see, how do you know it was the work of a monster?'

'Because it would have taken more than a bloody bear to finish off old Madame Bitterwhack, that's why!' the witch snapped. 'And you should've seen the mess it left behind. No animal did that. Anyway, I'm a hedgewitch. We can see traces of magic, as I'm sure you know, and this thing...well let's just say its auras even more unstable than yours.'

'Where is it?' Gloamblight asked.

'Nowhere near here, I hope!' Madame Reedswail exclaimed, glancing over her shoulder into the shadows, like she expected the thing to be lurking there.

'You haven't been tracking it?' Gloamblight sounded disappointed.

'Tracking it? What would I do if I caught it? Smack it's bum-bum and send it to bed with no supper? I just told you it *ate* my colleague. You think I want to go the same way? No. I needed more information.'

'So you came here.' Gloamblight nodded understanding.

'Right. We've got long memories, us hedgewitches, but they do have their limits. We knew the star had appeared before, we just didn't know what that *meant*.'

'But, begging your pardon, Miss Witch, how did you know there was a link between the star and this monster?'

It was Oatey who spoke. He had been lurking behind Beatrice since the arrival of the rats, but seemed to finally have plucked up enough courage to join the conversation. He looked at the hedgewitch like he wasn't sure if she was about to give him a sweetbread, tear his head off, or sprout wings out of her back and fly away. To Beatrice's mild surprise, the old woman smiled at him kindly.

'And what's your name, pumpkin?' she said.

'Oatey, miss.'

Madame Reedswail nodded in approval. 'Good name that. Solid. Filling. It'll keep you going a name like that will. Well Oatey, if there's one thing I don't believe in its consequences... no hang on, not them. The other thingies...coincidences! I don't believe in coincidences. And a big scary monster turning up just as a mysterious new star appears in the sky? Well, if they're not connected, I said, I'll kiss a moglin on the...well, no matter, because luckily I was right.'

'So there *is* information about the star here? I knew it!' Beatrice cried excitedly. 'You see, captain? It was worth the trip!'

Snekchesser looked unimpressed. 'We'll see about that,' he said grumpily. 'What I'm more interested in right now is our friend, the non-wizard, here.' The guard folded his arms and looked at Gloamblight expectantly.

Gloamblight made a sound of repressed exasperation, pinching the bridge of his nose. 'For Melethin's sake, captain! What will it take for you to trust me? We do not have time for these constant bouts of questioning. The information we require is here. We must find it at once!'

Captain Snekchesser didn't move. 'I'm not going any further until we get some answers,' he persisted.

Gloamblight glared at him coldly, and in the flickering light of the rats' torches, Beatrice could have sworn she saw an entirely different spark of green light flare into life deep in the man's eyes.

'Fine,' he said levelly, his voice as tight as a bowstring. With very deliberate movements, he unbuckled the belt holding his right arm to his side by the wrist. 'If you can't let it go, I'll show you, shall I? In this confined space. Underground. I'll show you what I am. What happened to me. What I can do. Will that make you happy?' The first belt hit the stone floor with a clatter far louder than it had any right to be. All eyes in the room swiveled to follow it. Gloamblight started on the second, never once taking his eyes off the captain. 'Will that you make you happy, Snekchesser?' he continued. 'To see magic? Real magic. *Wild* magic. The sort of power that keeps me in constant pain. It's like a fire, Snekchesser. It's like a fire in my blood that takes every ounce of my control to stop from spilling out and igniting the very air! But if it'll satisfy your *curiosity*,' he spat the word, 'then I'll unleash it right here and now. I'll let it free. Oh, how it *longs* to be free, captain!' The second belt hit the floor. But Beatrice didn't see it. She was too busy staring at the man's right arm. Wreathed in a growing white steam, the arm strained to be free. It pulled away from Gloamblight's body like it was desperate to escape from him, pulling at the final belt around his shoulder and thrashing at the wax seal that held its hand at the wrist. From the steaming container strapped to the man's thigh issued the unmistakable sound of liquid boiling furiously. Sweat ran down Gloamblight's face, tendons stood out from his neck like ropes. His fingers shaking now, he started on the final belt.

'That's quite enough o' that, cloud-grazer! You stop that right now or, so-help-me, I'll shove this sword somewhere that's head-height for me and extremely unpleasant for you!'

Suddenly the world was full of rat. Boss and his fellows had rushed into the group, brandishing their little swords, waving torches under noses and chittering angrily. Beatrice raised her hands and tried to stay very still as one jabbed his flame at her face threateningly.

'I think you should stop now, Gloamblight. Please,' she said, carefully.

The wizard's eyes gleamed with rage and madness. His black hair clung to his slick forehead in straggly lumps. 'But the captain want's to see!' he hissed. The wax seal around his wrist began to melt, little drops of wax congealing on the stone at his feet.

'I think Captain Snekchesser has seen enough, haven't you,

captain?'

Snekchesser had his hand on the pommel of his sword and was eyeing the wizard in alarm. 'Yes,' he said slowly. 'I've definitely seen enough, thank you.'

'Oh, but I haven't even shown you anything yet!' Gloamblight cried. He was shaking now and his fingers fumbled over the final buckle. There was the sudden smokey smell of singed fabric and the right arm of his coat burst into a fierce green flame.

Gloamblight screamed.

Boss drew back his blade.

But before he could strike, Madame Reedswail stepped smartly forward. With one cupped hand raised to Gloamblight's face, she took a deep breath and blew a light purple powder into the wizard's sweat soaked face. The effect was almost immediate. Gloamblight staggered, his rolling eyes disappearing into the back of his head, then he fell unconscious to the floor with a thud. There were a frantic few moments while those closest scrabbled to put out the green flames before they spread to the clothing of Master Lettuce, who was still out cold, just a few inches away. In the end, the captain had to use his own coat to smother the fire. Then they all stood back, looking at the now still Gloamblight. The offending arm had stopped struggling, the bubbling sound was silenced, and the steam was already reduced to a tiny trickle. The arm of his coat was completely burnt away, the flesh underneath a vivid, scorched pink.

'Well, you lot ain't dull, are ya?' Boss said, sheathing his sword. He motioned to the other rats, and they backed off.

'By Melethin!' Snekchesser breathed. 'We've been walking around with a bloody time bomb!'

'Is...is he alright? You didn't hurt him, did you?' Beatrice stammered. It had been a shock to see the calm, controlled mask of the wizard slip so quickly.

Madame Reedswail smiled at her kindly. 'He will be fine, child. He's just unconscious. Perhaps a little sleep will do him good.'

'I don't think forty winks is going to cure whatever's wrong with that man,' Snekchesser said with heat. 'It's lucky he didn't kill us all! I knew he couldn't be trusted.'

'And yet you did,' the hedgewitch pointed out. 'You arrived here together.' She bent over the recumbent form of the wizard with interest.

'Circumstances left us little choice,' Snekchesser replied defensively. 'What exactly is he then, do you think?'

The hedgewitch looked thoughtful. 'I don't know,' she admitted. 'Something new. Oh, what's this?' Something on the man's burnt arm caught her attention and she knelt down to inspect it. 'There's…there are words here. Old scar tissue.' Then she sucked in air through her ruined teeth in a little hiss. 'It can't be!' she whispered.

'What? What is it?' Beatrice said, making to join her at Gloamblight's side. She was halted, however, by the immoveable arm of Captain Snekchsser, so had to make do with peering down with squinted eyes. Boss bought his torch nearer to help.

In its yellow-orange light, Beatrice could just make out what the hedgewitch was talking about. There were indeed words written on the exposed flesh. Each letter was a raised bump of scar tissue, still plainly visible through the fresh burn, like they had been carved into the flesh some time ago.

'It's a poem!' Beatrice said in surprise.

'A poem?' Oatey gaped, also trying to skip around the captain's outstretched arms, without success. 'What's he doing with a poem written on his arm? What's it say?'

Madame Reedswail seemed deep in thought, so Beatrice squinted hard and read aloud.

> 'This is he with the fire of green,
> The choice must be his, truth unseen.
> When new star lights the town of mud,
> And monsters rage and rivers flood.'

There was silence when she'd finished as those assembled took it in. It was broken by Boss, who scratched a large ear vigorously and said 'Funny sort of poem, that. I'd have gone for a short limerick. There was a young maiden so pretty—'

'It's not a poem,' Madame Reedswail cut him off. Her voice was awed. 'It's a prophecy.'

'It never is?' Oatey said excitedly. 'A real one?'

Captain Snekchesser scoffed. 'A prophecy?'

'You don't believe in prophecy, captain?' Madame Reedswail asked.

The captain shrugged. 'I can't say I've ever given it much thought. But I fail to see why you should read a few rhyming couplets carved into the arm of a madman and assume its something significant.'

'Fair point that,' Boss piped up. He was cleaning under his claws with his sword, an operation that could easily end in severed fingers in Beatrice's opinion. 'I know blokes who 'ave all sorts tattooed on their arms. Usually when drunk. Most of it's nonsense.'

Madame Reedswail tutted in annoyance. 'This is not nonsense. I know because I've seen it before, parts of it at least, in this very archive.' She stood up, cleared her throat and began reciting in her reedy, scratchy voice.

> He who burns with a fire of green,
> Will appear when sky-fire is seen,
> He with a heart of good or ill,
> Is set by fate to save or kill.
>
> He whose past remains a mystery,
> Will act for man or act for tree,
> His choice will shape the world to come,
> One path to take, one path to shun.
>
> The first tree will act for vengeance,
> Blind to the world's inheritance,

> For when the great beast threat returns,
> In human hands the choice will burn.
>
> Monsters above, monster below,
> Which one will win, we cannot know,
> With just one man the choice must rest,
> To be consumed or pass the test.
>
> Kill must he, in order to save,
> Beneath the new stars fiery gaze,
> One must die for others to live,
> A choice to make, future to give.
>
> When rivers burst the time is set,
> To the town of mud he must get,
> To do the deed he must be,
> Ready to court catastrophe.
>
> Garesilin's true nature revealed,
> Across this worlds great battlefield,
> Will knowing the truth set us all free,
> Or only death be truths true fee?

Her words echoed around the underground chamber. When she had finished, the hedgewitch lapsed back into a thoughtful silence.

'Where did you read *that*?' Oatey asked, clearly impressed.

'In a book of our oldest memories,' Madame Reedswail replied, staring into space. 'Hedgewitch memories, that is.'

'Well, it's all very pretty I'm sure, but I don't know how it helps us?' Snekchesser growled.

'Both rhymes mention a man with green fire,' Beatrice said, thinking hard. 'And a choice he has to make. Then there's the new star, a town of mud, monsters and floods.'

'Well we've just seen the green fire!' Oatey said excitedly. 'Does that mean Gloamblight is this bloke they're talking about?'

Madame Reedswail pointed a crooked finger at him. 'My

thoughts exactly, my boy.'

'But, what does that *mean*?' Beatrice asked quickly.

'That is what must be riddled out,' the hedgewitch answered. 'I'm afraid our prophecies have never been big on clear instructions. It's not an easy thing, reading the future. Whoever made this one will have only seen fragments, discerned the shadow of meaning. But…I think at least one thing is clear.'

'What's that?' Beatrice asked.

'Whoever this man is who *'burns with a green fire'*, it would appear that he has to kill someone, or indeed *something*, and he has to do it when the *'new star'* appears. Let's think about what we already know. We know there is a new star. We know there is a monster. We know Gloamblight here burns with a green flame, and has phrases from the prophecy etched into his arm. It would seem to me that -'

'That I'm supposed to kill the monster,' Gloamblight said, sitting up with a groan.

There was the sound of a dozen tiny swords being drawn at once.

'It's alright, I'm ok now,' Gloamblight said, raising his good hand placatingly.

'I'm not entirely sure we can take your word for that,' Captain snekchesser said, brandishing his own sword and edging Beatrice further behind him.

'It's true then?' Madame Reedswail said eagerly, ignoring them both. 'You are the man the prophecy speaks of? Incidentally, I gave you a large enough dose to knock a gwalmok out for a week. You have a strong constitution, it would seem.'

'You tell me,' Gloamblight said, pointing to his bunt arm. Even as they watched the flesh was mending. Within seconds it had completely healed. The captain swore.

'That is quite remarkable,' Madame Reedswail said, eyebrows raised.

'The one benefit of my condition,' Gloamblight explained.

'And that condition being?' the witch prompted.

Gloamblight sighed heavily, making no attempt to stand. 'Right now you know about as much as I do. Probably more,' he said. 'That is the first time I have heard that prophecy. That there is a link to the marks on my arm seems evident. But I cannot be sure, as I did not write them. Or perhaps I did, I don't know.'

'Your gonna need to start making more sense than that,' the captain said gruffly.

Gloamblight sighed again, pushing his wet hair up off his face with his good hand. 'I shall try to explain,' he offered, getting to his feet. Swords bristled, but no one moved to stop him. Standing now, and brushing himself down, the wizard continued. 'I woke up, three months ago, in the very depths of the Blackwood, naked, alone, and with absolutely no memory of anything before that point. I didn't even remember my name, which incidentally is not Gloamblight. I picked that later. I awoke with those words etched into my arm and…and the Blackwood on fire all around me. My own work, I would later surmise. My arm has been in this state from the moment I awoke. It is…difficult to control. You earlier described me as a plughole, Madame Reedswail. That is quite an accurate description. Magic flows into me freely and I have no way to stop it. The human body can only hold so much it would seem, until…well it has to find an escape.'

'You have no idea what happened to you?' Beatrice asked in awe when the wizard paused and no one else spoke.

Gloamblight looked at her for some time before replying. When he did, he did so slowly, as if choosing each word with great care. 'I believe…that I am the man mentioned in this prophecy. That I have some terrible choice to make. Beyond that I cannot be sure.'

Captain Snekchesser grunted. 'This all seems like a lot of self important twaddle!' he said. You think you're the chosen one, do you? Sent among us to do…well to do Melethin knows what?'

'Oh, I'm sure that Melethin does know, captain.'
'Oh? And why's that?'
'Because of the one memory I *do* have. I believe I met him.'

CHAPTER TWELVE: LOSING CONTROL

1.

'You think you've met Melethin?'
'Yes. Believe me, captain, I know how that sounds,' said Gloamblight.

'Do you? See, I don't think you do know how that sounds,' Captain Snekchesser replied, fingering his sword uneasily. 'Because if you did, you wouldn't have said it.'

'I'm trying for honesty here, captain.'

'But...but you can't of!' Beatrice said, her mind whirling. 'I mean, Melethin, he's...he...well he's not actually *real*, is he?'

'Of course he's real!' Madame Reedswail snapped.

'You've met him too, have you?' Snekchesser grumbled.

'Don't be facetious, captain,' the hedgewitch said. 'Of course I haven't met him. But I've seen his work.'

'I mean, not real in the sense that he's not actually a walking, talking tree. More of a...a concept,' Beatrice tried again.

'Well, I don't know about no concepts,' said Madame Reedswail. 'but he predates the Book of Oak's interpretation, if that's what you mean.'

Boss, the rat, was jumping up and down impatiently. 'Never mind about interpretations! I want to hear how the crazy wizard thinks he met the god of the Blackwood!'

All eyes turned back to Gloamblight, who scowled a little.

'I'm not crazy,' he said.

'No, no. Sane as a box of frogs, I'm sure. Get on with it!' the rat insisted.

'Well, I had this dream—' Gloamblight began.

Boss stopped his jumping. 'A dream?' he said. 'A dream! Is

that it? I had a sodding dream myself last night. I met an unusually attractive and friendly doe, but that doesn't mean it actually happened.'

Gloamblight glowered down at him. 'Why are you still here?' he said.

'We're always here,' the rat replied cheerfully. 'You're never more than six feet from a rat!'

'Most of them aren't as chatty.'

'Ain't you lucky you got me then? Carry on.'

The wizard pinched the bridge of his nose. 'As I was saying, I had a dream. It was right before I woke up for the first time, with the Blackwood on fire around me. In the dream, I sensed this voice...this presence.'

'What did it look like?' Oatey asked eagerly. 'Was it, like, this huge, ancient tree? Or, or was it more like—'

'I don't know what it looked like!' Gloamblight snapped. 'Like I said, it was a presence...like a feeling. Like...like old soil, wet bark and fresh leaves. It felt like the forest. It spoke to me, only not with words. I just knew what it was saying to me. It said I had been chosen. That I had been given a chance...and that I shouldn't mess it up.'

'That's nice and cryptic,' Boss said. 'You sure you didn't just have a concussion or something?'

'Forget it!' the wizard said. 'I'm done with the show and tell.' He pushed his way through them, headed for the stairs.

'Where are you going?' Beatrice asked.

'Upton-Myzzle,' Gloamblight called over his shoulder as he climbed. 'Follow or don't, it really makes no difference to me. I have all the information I need.'

'Wait!' the captain called. 'You can't just go running off. You insisted we come here. Are you really leaving without even looking at the records for yourself?'

The wizard turned at the top of the stairs. 'Look, I needed confirmation of my path and I have it.'

'A few lines of poetry? That's what you're basing this on? So what are you going to do when you get to town, exactly?'

Gloamblight glowered. 'Make a choice!' he snapped, then stalked out of view.

'Great!' Snekchesser said, finally sheathing his sword.

'We should follow him, captain,' Beatrice said.

'Why? Because he's the chosen one? Give me a break. We don't even know if this whole thing is going down in Upton-Myzzle. That's assuming the whole thing is real and I'm less than convinced of that.'

'C'mon captain, you heard the prophecy; *A town of mud.* That's got to be talking about Upton-Myzzle!'

'Well, maybe,' Snekchesser admitted. 'But he don't know that, does he? He's never even been to Upton-Myzzle! And what about all this flood business?'

'Didn't you see the river Myzzle before we left? It was already on the verge of breaking its banks.'

The captain eyed her grumpily. Beatrice noticed that a thick bristle had appeared on his chin and there were large dark smudges beneath his eyes. He was probably tired, she thought. That's what happened to old people. Her father always seemed to be tired. Personally, she had never felt more awake in her entire life. Things were happening! Exciting things! She wasn't entirely clear on exactly what those things were, but they were happening regardless, and she was a part of them. She glanced over at Oatey. All signs of her friends' earlier trepidation at being in the Blackwood were gone. The boy was grinning from ear to ear, busily prodding a rat, who stood next to him, in an investigative sort of way. The rat seemed more astonished than angry, and when Beatrice caught Oatey's eye his grin widened even further.'Talking rats!' he mouthed at her, giving her the thumbs up. Beatrice beamed back. She was feeling rather smug. She'd done it. She set out to reach the old Upton-Myzzle archive to learn more about the star, and that is exactly what she'd done. She couldn't wait to see her father's face when she delivered the news.

She felt a slight pang of guilt at the thought of her father. Had they been missed yet? How long had they been in the woods for now? She was losing track. Hopefully, he wasn't too worried. Then she remembered Rupert, the little robin, and the message they'd sent. Presumably, her father would know all about it by now. He'd understand, she reassured herself, when he realised the importance of what she had uncovered.

Captain Snekchesser was still glaring at her, but appeared to come to a decision. 'Well, I guess we have no choice,' he said. 'Gloamblight seems to know which way is home, so crazy or not, we need to follow the amnesiac wizard with the bomb lashed to his torso.' He shook his head as if he couldn't believe what he was saying. 'If I ever get you home, your father is going to kill me.'

'Oh, I shouldn't think so, captain. The duke's a reasonable man,' Madame Reedswail chimed in mildly.

A dark look crossed the captain's face 'How'd you know the duke's her father?' he said, edging ever s slightly between the witch and Beatrice.

Madame Reedswail rolled her eyes 'Just because I'm a hedgewitch doesn't mean I live in on , my dear,' she said. 'Everyone in Upton-Myzzle knows young Beatrice here. She is the heir to the duchy, after all.'

'Ooooh, is she?' said Boss, squinting at the girl with renewed interest. 'Didn't know I was in the presence of royalty. Charmed, I'm sure!' he said with a snicker, taking a bow theatrically. 'Does that mean you're rich?' he asked after a moment's thought.

'Not as much as you'd think, I'm afraid,' Beatrice replied, ignoring the captain, who had begun to growl threateningly.

The rat looked disappointed, but brightened up almost immediately. 'Oh well, we'd better be off, ay? Before ol' green flames up there disappears or blows himself up or something.'

'We?' Captain Snekchesser said with a raised eyebrow.

'Oh certainly,' said the rat, giving a roguish smile. He gave a signal with his hand and the other rats scurried to form a neat line behind him. They stared at the captain expectantly. 'You lot 'ave been more entertainment in the last 'arf hour than we've 'ad down 'ere fer years!' Boss explained. 'I'm kinda excited to see how it's all gonna turn out.'

Snekchesser glowered. 'I'm glad we amuse,' he said stonily.

Boss beamed at them. 'Well, come on then! Let's go save the world!'

2.

Punduckslew stared at the limp, soggy form of the late Toflo Higginbottom and wondered where it had all gone wrong. Why had a baker's apprentice, barely old enough to be wearing long trousers, murdered his master and then gone on to commit the largest act of indiscriminate murder in the duchy for decades? He raised a clay pipe to his lips, sheltering the bowl from the persistent rain with one hand, then ignited the tobacco with a practiced flick of a finger from the other. It was second nature to him now, he mused as he took a deep pull on the pipe and leant back against the sodden wall of the alley. But it had taken ages to learn how to do it. Not to mention an awful lot of broken pipes. And he'd had training. The Wizards Charter found him young. It hadn't been that hard, of course. People tend to sit up and take notice when you accidentally blow up the family privy. But what would it have been like for him, if the Charter had never come? He mused on this for a few seconds, pulling on his pipe, its smoke mingling with the persistent rain, before coming to the inevitable conclusion. Most likely, he'd be dead. He thought about what Corporal Tritewine had said to him when they'd visited that infernal institute of hers. How the charter couldn't even explain how magic worked. The bloody cheek of the woman. It still rankled. Mostly, Punduckslew allowed himself to admit, because it wasn't entirely untrue. Magic was not some plaything. It was powerful. Unpredictable, even to those with years of training.

But Toflo had survived the discovery of his Talent,

even mastered its use. Without the Charter. Which in Punduckslew's considered opinion meant one of two things; he was either very, very lucky, or he'd had help.

It was an unsettling thought.

Then again, he could be wrong. The wizard's thoughts strayed to the duke, and his little...problem. Punduckslew had heard about split personalities before. He had a distant cousin who worked at the much-maligned Upton-Myzzle hospital. He liked to brag about cases Punduckslew felt sure the odious little man should have kept between himself and his patients. It wasn't a common condition, from what he understood. But the duke's case seemed different. There was magic at play there, Punduckslew was sure of it. The implications of which he couldn't begin to fathom. It would mean that, at the very least, the Wizards Charter had let a second emerging Talent slip through their fingers. One belonging to the future—now current—ruler of the state, no less! It was a miracle the man had kept it secret this long.

He'd have to break his suspicions to the duke, eventually.

He should tell the Charter, too. He'd taken an oath. If he was right and the duke really did have a Talent of some kind, it was Punduckslew's obligation, as a member of the charter, to turn the man in. He didn't like to think what Grand Wizard Pike would do with such information. It would most likely spell the end of Wigbert Stonemorton's rule.

Of course, that might be academic, given the way things were going.

The wizard sighed, sending a puff of smoke out into the street above the body at his feet. At the news of the Lord of Misrule's death, yet another emergency session of the Lords Chambers had been called. The duke was there now, no doubt struggling to make himself heard over the torrent of abuse that Sir Sweetspire was undoubtedly aiming in his direction. Punduckslew was, among other things, a practical man. He knew what the duke was, and it was not a political animal. But he was a basically good man, and to the wizard that counted for a lot in a ruler. He was trying. The man had potential. Punduckslew just hoped the duke could hold on long enough to fulfill it.

The wizard was brought out of his reverie by the approach of Corporal Tritewine.

'When are your men going to move this body?' he asked the corporal. 'If it's all the same to you, I'd like to get out of this blasted rain before my backside gets permanent water damage.'

'Something's happening,' Tritewine said, ignoring the question. She looked worried. 'I'm getting reports of...well to be honest, I'm not sure what.'

Punduckslew sighed. 'Well, can you narrow it down some?'

'Something is moving through the streets, attacking people.'

'... Something?'

'The reports are...well, I think we should go see for ourselves.'

'We're not talking about a person here, are we?'

'I think perhaps not,' said the corporal.

'Are we, perhaps, talking about something that could say, do *that* to a man?' Punduckslew looked down meaningfully at the ragged body.

'I think perhaps we might, yes,' said Tritewine.

'By Melethin,' the wizard sighed. 'As if things weren't bad enough already!' He removed the pipe from his mouth and knocked out its contents against the sodden wall before stowing it in his coat. 'Well, come on then, let's go see what disaster has befallen us now!'

He splashed after the corporal at a trot. They moved through the thin, twisting alleys of the Thickets, stopping only once to collect a small contingent of miserable-looking guards.

'Any more news?' Tritewine asked a pot-bellied man with large grey mutton chops.

'Yes, ma'am. Billy the grocer came through, ma'am. Running like the clappers he was. Wouldn't stop. He was white as a sheet, he was, ma'am. Never seen Billy so scared, ma'am.'

Ma'am, Punduckslew thought. She's a corporal, and yet even seasoned guards are treating her like she's in charge.

'Well, what did he say, man?' Corporal Tritewine said.

The guard looked awkward. 'Well...well he said it was the Lord of Misrule, ma'am.'

'The so-called Lord of Misrule is dead, private,' said Tritewine, squeezing herself through a small gap between two buildings. Punduckslew followed, his belly scraping against the wet, grimy wall before he emerged into another, wider street. Something had clearly happened here. A smashed wooden door was hanging off its hinges. A barrow full of turnips was lying on its side, abandoned. The vegetables were spread across the mucky street, some of them smashed into the grime, trodden on by running feet. He hurried to catch up to the others.

'I'm just saying what Billy said, ma'am,' the guard with the mutton chops was wailing. 'He said it was him alright. Had the mask and everything. Said he saw him toss a man through a window like he was a feather, ma'am.'

Further discussion was curtailed by a scream, followed by a crash that rang out from the next street along.

'Weapons out, I think, corporal,' Punduckslew said, wheezing slightly. The guards readied a variety of swords and blunderbuss. Punduckslew tried not to notice the rust and rotten wood. The group advanced, more cautiously now. There were further sounds of commotion, louder than before. Something smashed. There was the splash of running feet. The group rounded the corner and...

An enormous figure filled the street. Twice the size of a normal man, it stood, sniffing the air like a dog. The rain hit it, bouncing off, streaming down its black cowl of tattered scraps, steam rising from its massive shoulders. Around it was a scene of destruction. A man lay unconscious, or worse, at its feet. A modest shopfront to its right had been completely smashed in. Glass was everywhere and several people cowered inside the ruins. Corporal Tritewine swore, losing her composure for the first time in the short while Punduckslew had known the woman.

'What is that?'

'Magic!' said Punduckslew. 'I can smell it. Whatever the thing is, it was born of magic.' It was true. The wizard could practically feel the stuff coming off the thing in waves.

'Is that…normal?' the corporal asked, fingering her battered sword nervously.

'That would depend on your definition of normal,' Punduckslew replied. 'It happens, certainly. From time to time. There are things in the Blackwood that…well let us just say you wouldn't want to meet them on a dark night. Or a sunny day, come to that.'

'Ok. But why does it look…like that?'

Punduckslew didn't reply. Truthfully, he had no idea. Monsters created by magic were usually very unstable. Most lasted no longer than a few minutes before the magic ripped them apart. He himself had only ever seen one before, on a trip into the Blackwood many years ago. That one had far more of an emphasis on teeth and tentacles. It hadn't looked human. And it certainly hadn't looked like a near exact replica of a festival mascot, recently used as a disguise by a mass-murdering religious fanatic. It was all wrong.

Regardless, there the thing was. It was bending over now, sifting through the rubble like it was searching for something. It picked out something large and raised it to its head to inspect.

'Is that…is that a bookcase?' Punduckslew asked aloud.

It was. The remains of one, at least. It even had a few books still on the remaining shelf. The creature looked at it critically, then…ate it. The whole thing. The mouth in its wooden-looking face just sort of grew to accept it, and down it went.

'By Melethin! Is *that* normal?' Tritewine asked weakly.

The creature made a face like it didn't like the taste. Then it threw back its head and let out a roar. Punduckslew's heart lurched at the sound and behind him, the guard with the mutton chops let out a high-pitched scream. The beast's head whipped round at the noise and the empty sockets in its wooden face centered in on the group like eyes.

Tritewine swore again.

The thing lurched forward towards them. By instinct, Punduckslew's arm came up in front of him and a second later there was a wet-sounding bang as the monster's head exploded. The rest of the body slumped forward, falling face first...well, neck first into the mud of the street.

For a moment, the only sound was that of the hammering rain.

'Well,' said Tritewine at last. 'That was easy.'

But she spoke too soon.

The body lurched. Then it sat up. Then slowly, but with a horrible sense of inevitability, a head reappeared, bubbling up out of the tattered neck like tar. At first, it didn't seem to know what shape to be. It flicked through almost a dozen forms, resting briefly on the likeness of an old woman, before changing once more until the unmistakable face of Toflo Higginbottom was staring back at them. Then, as they watched, creeping forward from behind the ears, the wooden mask reappeared. It flowed forward to cover the face until the rictus grin of a green man was once more all that could be seen. Then the mouth fractured and split, the wood cracking open until there was a gaping maw. The thing roared in rage.

'I think,' said Punduckslew. 'That we should probably run.'

They ran.

3.

Rain hammered against the roof of the Lords Chambers. It made such a din that the occupants had to raise their voices to be heard above it. Luckily, everyone was shouting anyway.

'Your prime suspect is dead!' Sir Sweetspire called to the duke from the far end of the Toads Tonge. 'Yet the murders and mayhem continue.' The man's voice was deadly serious, but Wigbert could see the barely controlled glee in his opponent's face. 'Clearly, you have once again failed to do what this great duchy requires of you!'

Things were not going well.

The news of Toflo Higginbottom's death had leaked even before Wigbert had a chance to get his own head around it. To make matters worse, once the timelines had been worked out, it became clear he had died *before* some of the other latest victims. This obviously put the duke's theory that Higginbottom was the man behind the Lord of Misrule's mask under some scrutiny. The Coins were loving it.

'Tell me,' Sweetspire exclaimed as he strutted up and down the stone platform, chest thrust forward as the many eyes of the lords and ladies above followed his every movement. 'When will we have the courage to say *enough is enough*? When will we stop letting the Stonemorton family stagger this once great nation from one disaster to another? How many more people have to die while our noble leaders shutter themselves up in their stone fortress, oblivious or uncaring to the plight of the common man? Killers...no, *terrorists* stalk our streets and the duke does nothing! Well, I say that *now* is the time! *Now is the time to take charge of our own destiny! We must finally free ourselves of the Stonemorton yoke, rise up in the name of justice and form a people's republic!'

There were whoops and cheers from the galleries above as a swell of excited conversation broke out amongst the gathered nobles. Wigbert watched them nervously. He was losing control. What was worse, he couldn't even entirely blame them.

Sweetspire is twisting events to his advantage. Don't let him, old boy, Wolfe warned.

But he's not entirely wrong, is he? Wigbert thought back at him. I have allowed many people to die on my watch.

When a tsunami destroys a village, is the fisherman to blame?

What? What does that even mean? Am I the fisherman in that scenario? No, don't bother telling me. I don't have time for riddles!

Wolfe was silent for a moment, and Wigbert returned his attention back to the chambers. Sweetspire was whipping the crowd up into even more of a frenzy.

Why haven't you told anyone about the monster? Wolfe asked at length.

I...I don't know, Wigbert thought. What if it's all a bunch of nonsense? I don't know if I can trust the word of this Gloamblight. I've never even met him! Can you imagine what Sweetspire would do if I started shouting about monsters and it turned out to be completely untrue? Especially after I've spent the last few days convincing everyone that the star is a comet!

Something killed all those people, Wolfe pointed out.

Wigbert thought hard. What was the right thing to do? He couldn't see the path forward anymore. All his focus had been on catching the Lord of Misrule. He'd thought if he could just do that...well then everything else would sort itself out. But now the man was dead. And Toflo Higginbottom *was* the man, he was sure of it. Even now. There was something else going on, but he couldn't bring himself to believe that the star, the comet, had somehow brought a monster to his door. He didn't know what to do.

Luckily for him, the decision was taken out of his hands when the doors to the Lords Chambers burst open and two men came charging into the room.

'What is the meaning of this?' Sir Sweetspire demanded in the ringing silence that followed. Surely that's *my* line, Wigbert thought bitterly.

'MONSTER! Monster in Upton-Myzzle!' one of the men shouted.

The words echoed around the chambers and mingled with the collective gasp of surprise from the galleries. The duke peered down at the newcomers in shock. His heart sank. It was Sir Gerald Frostweight who had spoken, former member of the Lords Chambers, and his father's closest confidant. The second man was Wigbert's father himself. The old man looked pale. He was bleeding from multiple cuts to his face and was leaning heavily on his stick and his friend.

'Ormus Stonemorton, this is an outrage!' Sir Sweetspire thundered. His face had turned a florid red, and he pointed at the two men with a finger that shook with rage. 'You were expelled from these chambers and bid never to return! To do so is the grossest breach of this venerable institution. I insist you remove yourselves at once!'

'Oh shut up, boy!' Wigbert's father wheezed. His voice was weak and Wigbert heard dozens of creaking chairs as the people above leaned forward in their seats to hear. Sir Sweetspire's mouth flapped in astonishment. The duke-no-more didn't wait for the man to recover, calling out to the galleries above in a thin, reedy voice. 'Upton-Myzzle is under attack. The alarm must be sounded! A defense must be organised!'

'From a monster?' Sweetspire sneered, recovering himself. 'How convenient. It just snuck past the Watch, did it? I hardly think—'

But what he hardly thought would remain a mystery, because at that moment, the doors of the chambers burst open once more and Sir Quinby Corbett ran in, pushing Sir Terrance Bashford ahead of him in his wheeled chair.

'It's getting worse out there!' he cried, then stopped abruptly as he saw how many faces were staring down at him. 'Oh, hello...full house, is it?'

'This really is intolerable!' Sweetspire said, but he was smirking once more. Wigbert could see why. The quartet of old men hardly made for an impressive display. 'First, we are led to believe a dead baker's apprentice is the Lord of Misrule,' Sweetspire continued, 'and now the Stonemortons break the laws of this institution to tell us that a *monster* is terrorising the town.' He gave a humourless chuckle and turned to the men and woman above, raising his arms in mock supplication. 'Is there no depths of desperation they will not sink to in order to cling to power?'

This gained him a smattering of laughter and Wigbert watched, feeling utterly helpless, as his father glowered up at the man.

'You would do well to listen, boy!' he shouted up, taking a faltering step forward. He looked exhausted, but he held himself upright proudly. Unfortunately, at that moment, Sir Bashford cleared his throat noisily and shouted, 'Undercarriage!'

The word bounced its way around the chambers and Sir Sweetspire began to laugh, genuinely this time. 'Guards! Someone roll that cretin out of here!'

The duke's father turned red with rage, but it was Gerald Frostweight who advanced angrily toward the man. '*Show some respect!*' he thundered. 'Sir Bashford is a decorated veteran. A hero of the Goblin Siege who has given this nation better service than the likes of *you* could ever achieve! By Melethin, I will not stand by and see him insulted!'

Sweetspire looked unimpressed. He continued to smirk down at the men until a cry from the galleries above made his expression falter.

'That's right! Sir Bashford deserves better than that. Great man!'

Wigbert couldn't see who it was that had spoken, but he did see a second man rise from his seat and cry 'Here here!', then a woman stand and shout 'Disgraceful!'

A susurration of indignation ran through the galleries, and Sir Sweetspire looked uncertain for the first time. He had overplayed his hand.

This is your chance to take back control of proceedings, Wolfe prodded. Wigbert stepped forward and cleared his throat. 'I think perhaps we had better adjourn until we can properly—' he began, but his opponent cut across him angrily.

'No! I will not have the due process of this assembly derailed by another desperate Stonemorton attempt to—'

But Sir Sweetspire was interrupted in turn as a distant, but unmistakable, bellow of inhuman rage drifted into the chambers via the still partially open door, echoing softly around the high-ceilinged room. It was followed by the sound of splintering wood and the rumble of collapsing plaster.

'You were saying?' Ormus Stonemorton said, almost sweetly.

What followed can most succinctly be described as an undignified scramble for the exits. Feet thudded. Shoulders were squeezed. Waistcoat buttons popped and skirts were unceremoniously dirtied by boots. Liberal application of elbows were applied as the great and the good of Upton-Myzzle battled each other to be the first down the narrow staircases that led from the galleries to the ground floor.

'Wait! That could have been anything!' Sir Sweetspire cried desperately. 'Do not be fooled! We must take a vote to—'

But the chambers were no longer listening. As people flowed past and out of the doors, Wigbert quietly climbed down from the stone platform and made his way over to his father and his friends.

'What's going on, father?' he asked.

The old man regarded him stonily. 'Oh, want to speak to me

now, do you?'

Sir Frostweight cleared his throat noisily and gave the duke-no-more a pointed look. Wigbert's father sighed, but his face softened a little and he began to explain. As he unfolded his story, the group made their way through the throng and out of the building, pausing under the eaves of the roof next to the huge oak leaf door, out of the torrential rain. The square was once again the scene of chaos. Roads and central grass alike were now covered in a churning layer of water that danced and spat as the rain came down. The ruins of the Church of the First Tree stood out like an ugly scar to their left, its remains still strewn across the space in substantial chunks of splintered, blackened wood. The platform from Longest Night had still not been removed, but had collapsed into just another pile of timber.

The lords and ladies of Upton-Myzzle emptied themselves from the Chambers and milled around like clucking hens. But otherwise, the streets seemed oddly empty. Of a monster, there was no sign.

By the time his father had finished recounting his tale of the monster's attack, Wigbert's mind was reeling.

'It was dressed as the Lord of Misrule?' he asked.

'Had the mask and everything,' his father confirmed with a nod that made him wince and rub the back of his neck with a grimace.

'But I found the mask with Toflo Higginbottom's' body. There's only one.'

His father just shrugged, but Sir Frostweight spoke up. 'This one was more like a copy...a facsimile. It wasn't...I don't think it was really wood. Or even really a mask. It was like the thing had just used it as a face.'

'It wasn't the same man that attacked me in the castle,' Wigbert's father confirmed. 'That was definitely a human.'

'It was Higginbottom, I'm sure of it,' Wigbert said. 'But then...I don't understand what's happening. Did...did you ever hear of wizards from outside Upton-Myzzle?'

His father looked at him sharply. 'What do you mean?'

Wigbert explained about Beatrice's disappearance and the letters he'd received that morning. He dug out the second letter, the one warning about monsters, and handed it to his father.

'You're telling me you had warning of this thing and you did nothing, boy?' his father asked.

'And I suppose you'd have shouted it from the rooftops, would you, father?' Wigbert replied. 'There's nothing mystical about the new star. It's a comet. There's data to prove it. There's certainly no data to suggest that it's somehow linked to some creature wearing the Lord of Misrule's face!'

'You and that bloody Institute of Propositional Logic!' his father spat. 'There is more to life than what you can measure with a set of scales, boy! And what about my granddaughter? You're quite happy to have her running about the forest in the company of this supposed wizard, are you?'

'Of course not! But in case you hadn't noticed, father, there's quite a lot going on. Besides, captain Snekchesser is with her.'

One of his father's eyebrows quirked upwards. 'And that's good, is it? Some commoner.'

'Don't start with that again!' Wigbert snapped.

'Perhaps we should focus on finding the monster? Wherever it's got to,' Sir Corbett suggested.

'I think we're about to find out,' Wigbert said with a sigh. Across the square, Punduckslew had just appeared. He was hurrying towards them, Corporal Tritewine and a few of the Castle Guard trailing behind. All looked extremely concerned.

4.

Seabass Street was, as ever, a hive of activity. But the artery of Upton-Myzzle had been clogged. Wagons queued back down the long street in both directions. The air was filled with not just rain but an equally fierce downpour of curses and obscenities as frustrated drivers and traders sat atop their soaking wagons, forced to a standstill. The only thing moving with any urgency was the torrent of thick muddy water that ran down the gently sloping street towards the river. Unspeakable things swirled and bobbed in its flow, visible one minute, then thankfully swept away the next. They were all drawn inexorably towards the Myzzle, which churned and frothed alarmingly, rising ever closer to the top of the river walls, which seemed increasingly insufficient to constrain it.

The cause of the traffic jam was a large knot of people gathered roughly halfway up the street between the river and the castle. In the centre of the gathering was a large, dark pile, spread across the centre of the street like a poorly placed delivery of firewood. But the pile, which was being added to all the time by the gathered crowd, was not wood.

It was books.

Or rather, many copies of one particular book.

The man in the wide-brimmed hat lurked in the shadows of a shopfront and observed proceedings with a professional interest. Things were going wonderfully. They must have gathered nearly every copy of the Book of Oak within the town's limits. Some willingly, others not so much. But enough of the public seemed sufficiently terrified to think burning a gigantic pile of books to appease Zigelder was worth a shot. Many disagreed violently, of course, hence the current commotion. Sir Sweetspire would be pleased.

Not that it had been easy. The man was increasingly finding that organising the varyingly hate-filled and scatterbrained members of the Church of the Cracked Acorn into doing as he wished was about as simple as herding moglins. The contempt he felt for the whole ridiculous lot of them had grown to almost unbearable proportions. But it would soon be over. Sir Sweetspire was even now seizing power from the inept Wigbert Stonemorton. Once he had, the church members would be dealt with quickly and thoroughly. There could be no loose ends. The man watched the black-robed church members as they moved amongst the shouting crowd and imagined that blissful moment when he could end his association with them for good. He fingered a knife at his waist in anticipation. The idiot Krikwell had already met his end at its wicked blade. The others would follow soon enough.

He reflected upon the stroke of luck that had been the death of Toflo Higginbottom. He had no idea how it had happened, no doubt the unstable zealot had run afoul of some lowlife or other. It seemed magical Talent was no substitute for brains and training, after all. However it happened, the timing could not have been better. Not to mention it saved him the particularly tiresome job of tracking the idiot down and silencing him himself. He had to admit the scale of destruction the fool had wrought surprised even him. Still, things worked out very neatly indeed. His primary concern now was how to set alight a pile of books in this accursed rain.

As the man pondered this problem from his hiding place, an unfamiliar noise rose above the splashing, cursing, and gwalmok grunts that filled the street. It was a distant roar, like that of some enraged animal, and it drifted over the many rooftops like a foghorn. The bustle and chaos in the street stilled for a moment as all eyes turned toward the unexplained sound, but it was completely forgotten seconds later when a greengrocer's gwalmok stood on a butchers foot and the litany of anguished screams and graphic insults that followed broke the spell. The man in the wide-brimmed hat reached up and adjusted it over his face, shrugged his shoulders, then slipped away to see if he could acquire some lamp oil.

5.

'There's good news and there's bad news, you grace,' said Punduckslew as he came puffing to a halt in front of the duke. 'The good news is, I've solved the mystery of who killed the Lord of Misrule and those other people.'

'The bad news is, it was a monster which has taken his face,' Wigbert finished for him. 'I know. Where is it now?'

The wizard was taken aback for a moment, but he recovered himself quickly. 'It's moving through the Thickets like a bull… well, like a bull moving through the Thickets, frankly.'

'You've seen it?'

'Yes. It shrugged off my Talent like it was a fly swat.'

Corporal Tritewine stepped forward. She looked pale. 'It's moving fast, headed north.'

'Where's it going?' Wigbert asked.

'Can't say for sure. But—'

'But that brings us to our next problem,' Punduckslew cut in. 'We've had reports of a large crowd gathered on Seabass Street. The Church of the Cracked Acorn, your grace. They've finally resurfaced.'

The duke ran a hand across his face. 'Of course they have. What's going on?'

'It seems they're burning books, your grace. At least they intend to.' The wizard shot Wigberts' father an uncomfortable look. 'I'm afraid they've got their hands on rather a large number of copies of The Book of Oak, your grace.'

'WHAT?' Wigberts' father roared, standing up straight.

'That's an outrage! Sacrilege! They must be stopped at once! If you know all this, Mr Wizard, then why, by Melethin's craggy trunk, are you not there right now blowing the buggers to smithereens? That's what we pay you for, isn't it?'

Punduckslew looked affronted. 'I'm paid to protect the duke. Not police the streets!'

'You, then!' the duke-no-more rounded on the corporal. 'Why are you not, at this very minute, shoving your blunderbuss up one of the seditious bastards jacksies and pulling the bloody trigger!'

Tritewine looked wretched.

'Where are the rest of your men?' Wigbert asked.

'*My* men?' The corporal asked, pointedly. 'I have them tracking the monster, your grace. In truth, that's about the only useful thing we have the numbers to do. There're hundreds of people gathered on Seabass Street. As you know, we've been attempting to break up fights all day, but we just don't have the force to counter something like this. The Watch —'

'Are probably only making matters worse, if I know Watch Commander Posternos,' Wigbert finished for her.

'Possibly. But the fact remains, they are now the only force left in Upton-Myzzle large enough to deal with issues of this scale.'

It will be a bally bloodbath, old boy, Wolfe said in Wigberts head. *If the monster doesn't attack, that pompous buffoon of a watch commander will!*

Wigbert knew he was right. But what could he do about it? With a handful of men, and his credibility crumbling by the second, he was lucky he still had even the slightest shred of power left. Sweetspire would take it all, given half the chance, and if the odious man forced through a final vote, he could do it within the hour. Wigbert could see him now. He had left the Chambers and was working the crowd of confused, flustered lords and ladies like a proud cockerel. He had already rounded up quite a few and was ushering them back inside. His eyes met the dukes from across the square and they blazed in triumphant defiance.

'Well, whatever we do, we had better do it quickly,' Wigbert said. 'Oh, and Tritewine?'

'Yes, your grace?'

'You've just been promoted to captain. Congratulations.'

6.

The separate crowds, groups, and gatherings of Upton-Myzzle's populace had funneled their way through the soaking, stinking town to Seabass Street, and finally, after days of threatening, coalesced into a mob.

Human intelligence is an interesting thing. As a singular, the human mind is capable of truly astounding cognitive processes, feats unparalleled in all of nature. It is possible for one human brain to push forward the species' understanding of the very fabric of reality itself, carving hitherto unthought-of ideas into the mass of human understanding with the fierceness of its intellect. But start adding more brains to the mix and the net effect is a steady decline in cognitive function. The more you add, the harder thought becomes, until it is almost impossible to achieve even the most rudimentary of tasks.

Anyone who has ever sat on a committee will know this is true.

But it is worse even than this. Once the collective minds reach a large enough volume, the thought patterns begin to shift, warped out of shape by the sheer overwhelming presence of other minds. The individual is silenced, absorbed by the Mob. The Mob brain is dull. Its thought processes run like driverless wagons; in straight lines, at a steady but increasing speed. Once it's in motion, it is very hard to stop. It will smash through fences and people alike. But it's when it meets real resistance that the Mob mind becomes truly dangerous. Imagine that wagon hitting a thought that doesn't mesh, like a brick wall. It's as deadly to the passengers as it is to the nearby pedestrians. This is the mind of the Mob. This goes some way to explaining why, when Wigbert entered Seabass Street at a run, almost every head turned instinctively to face him. The angry shouts and oaths, the excited conversations and clatter of various waving farm implements—all of this focused on the duke like an arrowhead. An angry hum rose from the steaming masses.

'Er...what's all this then?' the duke stammered.

Wigbert stared into the teeming, rain-soaked street, and it was the Mob that stared back. He was immediately struck by two things; The first was the notion that perhaps running headlong into a gathering of people who most likely hated him had not been the smartest idea. The second was a sharp stone, flung by a particularly swift-handed member of the crowd and which served only to enhance the first thing.

'*Ere, it's the duke!*' someone shouted.

'*Oppressor!*' screamed another.

'*Emperor of lies!*' cried a third person, which Wigbert thought was a bit much. He felt the presence of Punduckslew and the Castle Guard behind him, which is the only reason he didn't turn around and run right back the way he'd come.

'People of Upton-Myzzle, listen to me!' Wigbert shouted as loud as he could muster. 'You are all in great danger!'

Nothing happened,

'*He wants to date a stranger?*' Wigbert heard someone to his left shout to their neighbor over the hubbub and the hammering of the rain. '*Whatever for?*'

'*Dunno,*' cried his companion. '*They do say it's lonely at the top.*'

'*Well yes, but it hardly seems a pressing matter.*'

'*He said we're all in great danger, you blithering idiots!*' said a third voice.

'*He's changed his tune!*' came the outraged reply. '*Given up on all that* 'It's just a comet' *rubbish, has he?*'

'*I don't know, do I?*'

'*Typical politician!*'

'*Shhh! He's going to say something else.*'

The duke turned to the wizard at his side. 'This is hopeless. They can't even hear me!'

Punduckslew's eyes narrowed. 'I've got an idea, your grace. Permission to get a bit...destructive.'

'Just try not to hurt anyone.'

The wizard rolled up his sleeves and began scanning the street. His eyes alighted upon a large wagon piled high with wooden barrels. It sat in the centre of the street, marooned in the sea of people. The gwalmok between its shafts seemed perfectly content with the current state of affairs, busy as it was munching its way through a pile of cabbages in the back of the wagon in front.

'Everybody follow me!' Punduckslew said and set off through the press of shouting, jostling people towards it. With a glance back at the freshly minted Captain Tritewine, who simply shrugged, Wigbert obeyed.

It wasn't long before they met their first resistance. A large man wearing a blacksmith's apron and a deep scowl stood in Punduckslew's path and refused to be moved.

'Move aside there!' Punduckslew snapped at the man.

The man hefted a large hammer into the palm of his hand. 'Why should I?' he rumbled in a deep bass.

What happened next happened very fast. There was a flash of movement from the wizard's hand, and then the head of the blacksmith's hammer exploded in a flash of heat and a shower of molten metal. The man stared at the smoldering handle for a moment before hastily dropping it to the ground.

'Because next time, that will be your head,' Punduckslew said, smiling sweetly and waving the man to one side with an impatient gesture. Silently, the man obeyed, and after that, their progress was much quicker. A path opened up before the wizard like...well, like a crowd of terrified people before the angry finger of a powerful wizard. When they reached the wagon with the barrels, its driver held his palms up.

'I don't want no trouble.'

'What a coincidence, neither do I,' Punduckslew replied. 'We just want to borrow your wagon.' He pointed unnecessarily and the driver's objection died in his throat at the sight of the wizard's sturdy finger. He slumped hopelessly. 'Just, please try not to damage anything,' he said.

'Can't promise that, I'm afraid,' Punduckslew said, heaving himself up on the cart with a grunt. 'But I would like to purchase one barrel of your finest...what's in the barrels, anyway?'

'It's moglin mash, sir, but I—'

'Perfect. Just send the bill to the Castle, will you? Up you come, your grace.' The wizard elbowed the flustered driver to one side, then reached down and grabbed Wigbert's hand, hauling him up beside him. 'Captain, surround the wagon, if you would be so good. Except that bit,' he pointed to the street directly behind the wagon, a space currently occupied by a group of suddenly nervous faces. Tritewine did as she was bidden, his men forcing their way in a ring around the wagon, whilst Punduckslew clambered up the pile of barrels until he was standing at the very top. He looked down at the faces below.

'I will say this only once!' he bellowed. '*Get out of the bloody way!*' He then rested one mud-caked boot against an outermost barrel, paused just long enough for the more quick-thinking mob members to scurry desperately out of the way, and then pushed off hard with his foot.

The barrel toppled. The people ran.

It hit the road with a splash of brown filth, bounced slightly, and then exploded.

The sound hit Wigbert like a slap over the ears. A fireball illuminated the falling rain for a moment before a litter of charred wood and melted metal bands hit the—now thankfully empty—area of the street where the wizard had pointed just moments before. The smell of fermented apples hung in the air. Wigbert found himself looking at the wagon's gwalmok. He had expected the beast to bolt, but it merely looked over its shoulder in a brief, disinterested way before returning to its impromptu lunch. The rest of the Mob, however, had fallen silent. Wigbert looked out at a sea of angry, upturned faces. From this height, he could clearly make out the intended bonfire. It was an impressive pile of books. Black-clad figures surrounded it protectively. He could feel them watching him, even over the white-hot focus of the Mob between them. In the silence, a peal of thunder, with a particularly good sense of dramatic timing, rolled.

'Now would be a good time to say something clever,' Punduckslew prompted under his breath. Wigbert glanced at him in alarm. The man was soaked through to his skin. The red of his coat had turned almost black. Water ran freely down his lined face and formed little rivulets that dripped from his sagging beard. The duke reached up and pushed his own sopping hair out of his eyes. I must look like a drowned rat, he thought. Hardly an impressive figure.

It's all about confidence, Wiggy old boy, Wolfe thought back at him. *About how you portray yourself.*

Oh really? Why didn't you say so before? I've had all this confidence here just lying around, but never knew what to do with it. I'll just use that, shall I?

Just trying to help, said Wolfe. *I could always—*

Don't you dare! Wigbert thought. I can do this.

'People of Upton-Myzzle!' he cried, in what he hoped was a carrying voice. 'You are not safe here. Please disperse in a calm and orderly fashion.'

Silence. Then somebody laughed.

Oh yes, that'll have put the fear of the daemon into them, Wolfe said. *I'd follow up with a strongly worded letter if I was you, just to really make sure.*

Well, what would you say then? Wigbert thought.

Wolfe told him.

Alright, Wigbert thought to himself this time. I guess it's worth a shot. He cleared his throat.

'Subjects of the Duchy of Blackwood!' he thundered. 'Your commander calls to you! Listen not to the poisoned tongues of those who would do our great nation harm. Believe not the false promises and honeyed words of those who would take power for themselves. I, the third of my name, the twenty-ninth of my station, stand before you, humbled. My family may not have always ruled fairly. There have been dark days. But I am here to tell you this; *We are still here!*'

Wigbert paused for breath. No one moved.

Don't bally well stop now! Wolfe said. Wigbert took another deep breath and continued.

'For one thousand years, the Stonemorton family has guided you. And yes, there have been mistakes along the way. Injustices. But we are still here. Upton-Myzzle is still here. The kingdom has crumbled, and the Blackwood has risen against us, but still, we prevail. For together, we are strong! I know that many of you are angry. I know that many things in our great town could be run more smoothly. More fairly. Well, I am here to tell you that as your leader, I am listening! I know there is much to fix. But fix it I will! With your help. That is my promise to you.'

Wigbert paused again. The only sound was the hammering of the rain. He had them. For the first time in his life, he had them. They were listening. Actually listening to what he was saying. He carried on before the spell was broken.

'We have seen troubled times these last few days. A killer has stalked our streets. But whatever you may think you know, whatever you may have heard, now know this: *The Lord of Misrule is dead!*'

There were murmurs at this. At slight shifting pattern in the sea of upturned faces. Wigbert pressed on. 'But the threat to our town has not ended!' he cried. 'A new killer approaches. A monster from the Blackwood itself is upon us. It has killed already. It will kill again unless we stop it. I will not lie to you. No one yet understands this beast. Why it is here. What it wants. How to stop it. But I believe in this town! I believe in its people. And I know together we will stop this monstrosity.'

The buzz of conversation was growing. The spell was breaking. He didn't have much time.

'I ask of you now; let us put aside our differences! There will be time enough to discuss the future of our great nation. But right now is the time for us to band together. So, in the name of Upton-Myzzle. In the name of the great Duchy of Blackwood and our glorious future. I ask this now of you; Go home. Disperse. Take your loved ones to where it is safe, lock the doors and allow us to deal with the threat that has already breached our walls.'

As the duke's words echoed away, Punduckslew whistled softly under his breath behind him. 'Where in Melethin did that come from?'

Wigbert coughed self-consciously. 'You wouldn't like the answer.'

The wizard's eyebrows knotted slightly, but he said nothing. Instead, they watched the crowd, which was a hubbub of animated conversation once again. At first, not very much happened, then, slowly, and to Wigbert's utter astonishment, the edges of the Mob began to fray outwards as people drifted away.

'Did...did it actually work?' he said.

'It might have,' Punduckslew said. 'But we have another problem. Look.'

Wigbert looked to where the wizard was pointing and noticed for the first time that the Watch was in attendance. He could see Watch Commander Posternos, his face puce, shouting orders to his men who were hurriedly fanning out around the slowly departing crowd, attempting to hem them back in.

'What, by Melethin's craggy trunk, does he think he's doing?' Wigbert said.

'I don't know, but we need to find out.'

'We'll never get over there before a riot breaks out!' Indeed, Wigbert could already see several citizens remonstrating angrily with the Watch as they tried to pass. Then, before he really knew what he was doing, his mouth opened again. *'Watch Commander Posternos!'* he cried with as much volume as he could muster. *'In the name of Castle Blackwood, let the people pass!'*

His words rang out across the street and Wigbert saw the people still. He heard the voices fall quiet. It was like the entire city was holding its breath, waiting to see what happened next. But even from this distance, he saw Posternos turn to face him, smiling nastily.

'But I do not answer to the Castle, your grace,' he cried. 'And I certainly do not answer to *you*. It is the Lords Chambers who decide what happens on these streets. They appointed the Watch to protect them and, by extension, myself. These are *my* streets, your grace. And *I* will decide who goes where. I will not have unlawful gatherings go unpunished. And as for you… even now, the Chambers are voting to strip you of what little power you retain. You use pretty words, your grace. But the time of Stonemorton tyranny is at its end.'

At this, the Mob erupted into a roar. People surged in all directions. Some, it seemed, were still trying to leave, but the watchmen shoved them back viciously, so that many fell, to then be trampled by those behind. Others crowded angrily around the wagon where Wigbert stood, shouting and shaking their fists. Yet more advanced towards the makeshift bonfire, where black-robed figures were once again swarming over it like ants. Fights were breaking out between those trying to add to the pile of books and others who appeared to be attempting to dismantle it.

It was chaos, and all the while yet more watchmen funneled into the street. Wigbert looked down at his own meagre force of Castle Guards with growing despair. He turned to Punduckslew helplessly. 'What is wrong with that man? He's going to create a bloodbath!'

'I could take his head off from here, you grace. Just give the word,' the wizard growled, leveling his finger in the Watch

Commander's direction.

'No!' Wigbert said. 'You'll create a panic, for sure.'

'I hate to break it to you, your grace, but I rather think that ship has sailed! What about the bonfire? I could blow that up?'

'And destroy the very books we're trying to save?'

'*Are we* trying to save them?'

'Yes! Popular or not, the Church of the First Tree is still, at this moment in time, our state religion. I will not allow a bunch of zealots to attack it any further, not if I can stop it! And besides, the monster...'

'What about it?'

'I don't think it's coming here for the people,' Wigbert said, the idea coalescing in his brain, even as he said it.

'Oh no? Then what's it bloody coming here for? The shopping?' Punduckslew snapped.

'The books!' Wigbert said. 'I think it's coming here for the books. Think about it. What do all of its victims have in common?'

The wizard looked bewildered. 'They're dead?' he said.

'They were all carrying books!' Wigbert said excitedly. 'Or at least writing of some kind. Gloamblight mentioned a hedgewitch writing in her diary and a guard reading a novel. Then we have the poor scribe we found. He must have been carrying writing of some kind. I think that's what's attracting it. That's why it stopped short of killing my father and disappeared. It sensed these books.'

'Okay...' Punduckslew said slowly. 'But what about Toflo? Why did it kill him, and why has it now taken his face?'

Wigbert thought hard. There had to be a connection. 'The wanted posters!' he cried. 'We put them up all over town. They must have somehow led the monster right to him.

'If...if that were true, then where is it? Shouldn't it be here by now?' Punduckslew indicated the pile of books with a sweep of his arm.

'I...I don't know,' Wigbert admitted. 'Maybe it's waiting for something?'

'Well, if you're right, surely we want the books destroyed!'

'I don't...I don't know,' Wigbert said, thinking hard. '

His train of thought was interrupted by a huge cry from the churning crowd and a burst of yellow light. Someone had lit the bonfire. A plume of flickering yellow flame spread greedily across the books. Too greedily.

'Someone's added something to that!' Punduckslew cried. 'There's no way books should catch light that fast. I'm surprised they're burning at all in this rain!'

He was right. Wigbert watched in horrified fascination as the flames raced across their fuel with frightening speed. The Cracked Acorn members retreated in panic, some hurling themselves into the crowd to escape the fire. One man was not quick enough. His black robe burst into flames and he fell, screaming, from the top of the bonfire to the street below. People threw themselves out of his path, but when he hit the ground yet more flames erupted all around him, dancing on the surface of the water that covered the street, spreading ever outwards into the crowd in trails of searing light.

'*Oil*!' Punduckslew roared. 'It's seeped into the rainwater!'

Screams filled the air. The people stampeded away from the fire like frightened animals, rippling out across the street until the swell reached the wagon where Wigbert and Punduckslew stood. It shook under the pressure of advancing bodies, and the two men fell to their knees as the barrels swayed violently. Punduckslew was almost cast into the throng, but Wigbert grabbed the wizard by his thick red coat, hoisting him back to safety in the nick of time. Tritewine and her guards battled in vain against the unstoppable tide of bodies. The gwalmok finally lost its cool, squealing into the air with a mixture of shock and rage, rearing up on its hind legs, then crashing down again on those unfortunate enough to be beneath.

There was an answering roar from the other side of the street. It rose above the noise and chaos, rumbling through the saturated air like nothing Wigbert had ever heard before. Then he watched, helplessly, as something that looked very much like the Lord of Misrule, swollen now to the size of three men, its face a mass of angry, splintered wood, cannoned out of a side street and crashed into the terrified crowd. The screams of the people reached an all-new volume of terror. They smashed into one another with the force of an unstoppable tide, trapped between the fire and the beast.

'*Oh shit!*' Wigbert cried before the gwalmok finally bolted and he was thrown from his perch headlong into the crush.

CHAPTER THIRTEEN: THE GOLDEN BEAR

1.

Wigbert could no longer tell what was happening. He'd landed on top of the churning crowd and been carried for some way by sheer momentum until eventually slipping down through a crack in the press of bodies. Fortunately, he went legs first, so that his feet touched down on the waterlogged ground and not his head. *Un*fortunately, they rested there only long enough to feel the icy chill of the water soak into them before they were lifted once more with a squelch, as Wigbert was forced along in the crush. The hot thunk of the bodies caught in the duke's throat as the crowd moved this way and that, forcing the air from his lungs. Arms pressed to his sides, feet dangling uselessly six inches from the ground, Wigbert gasped for breath and fought with all his might to free himself.

The noise was incredible.

Everyone around him was yelling or gasping for help. He could hear the crackle of the fire. See it as an orange glow somewhere off to his left. The monster roared again, but Wigbert couldn't tell from which direction. Mud splashed up from stamping, struggling feet as the downpour of rain continued to fall on the heads of the people. Despite this, the duke's vision swam.

Then, momentary relief.

The bodies parted. Wigbert felt his feet touch the floor and stumbled to his knees in shock. He threw out a hand, and it sank into the water with a splash. Mud sucked at it greedily. In terror of being stuck, and then enveloped again, Wigbert pulled himself free of the mud with an effort that left his legs shaking. He gasped in air in great rasping mouthfuls, looking around wildly to get his bearings.

He had been pushed to the very edge of the bonfire. Charred books lay at his feet, but the flames were already subsiding, simply unable to compete with the deluge from above. Wigbert skirted around the smouldering pile as best he could, aiming for the edge of the street. Of the black-robed Church of the Cracked Acorn, there was no sign. He was pushed into the ashes and half burned books on more than one occasion and was forced to hop, stumble and jump his way through the heat to the next area of relative safety.

What had become of Punduckslew, Tritewine, and the rest of the Guard? He looked for them, but it was hopeless. He needed height.

He finally reached the edge of the street, only just managing to avoid being sucked into the stream of terrified people breaking free of the main crowd and stampeding away down a side street.

The trampled body of a Watchman lay half submerged in the water.

Wigbert flattened himself against the wall and edged along it towards a doorway. He lost track of exactly where on Seabass Street he was. Then the smashed window of a familiar bakery came into view. Tanco often purchased delicate sweetmeats from the shop, but the usual sumptuous display was now a ruined mess full of mud and glass. The shop itself was empty, apart from the red-faced proprietor, who was leaning desperately against the door, and his terrified wife and child, who were cowering behind the counter, heads just visible as they peered out at the madness threatening to force its way into their domain. People were already climbing through the broken window in their desperation to escape the street, and the baker was howling at them to get out.

Wigbert followed them through just as the groaning door was forced inwards and the screaming baker was swept aside as people poured into the shop. Unable to help, but feeling wretched, Wigbert made for the doorway at the rear of the premises and thumped up the stairs to the living quarters. He had to find the front facing room. There was a small balcony that looked out onto the street, which would afford him a better view to figure out what was happening. After a false start into a broom closet, he found the right room; a sort of parlour. Dodging through the tangle of wooden-footed chairs and tables full of tasteless ornaments, Wigbert threw open the doors to the balcony and stumbled back outside. Now above the chaos of pressing, thrashing bodies, he could see clearly.

A large number of people were still caught between the remains of the bonfire and the monster, which appeared to be trying furiously to force its way through them to reach the pile of books. Some people were escaping down the two side streets between the threats, but they were little more than thin alleyways, and it was a trickle compared to the mass still stuck in the main street. The monster once more roared its frustration as the press of people was too thick for even it to move through with ease. It was making progress, though. Those people unfortunate enough to find themselves in front of the thing were swept aside, back into the crush, or, worse yet, plucked from their feet in its hideously swollen hands and flung unceremoniously through the air. The duke could see no sign of the Watch, but after some scanning, he found a small huddled group of the Castle Blackwood Guard. Tritewine and Punduckslew were among their number and Wigbert watched helplessly as they fought desperately to stay together and make their way towards the monster. But it was a hopeless task, and they were pushed in the opposite direction just as often as they made progress.

What do I do? Wigbert thought. What do I do? I have to go help them!

Go back down there and you'll be just as stuck as them, Wolfe warned. *We need a bally plan!*

'Well, you're the action hero. I'm open to suggestions!'

Wigbert said out loud. He could already hear the tread of other people on the stairs, no doubt as the shop below filled up and people were forced higher to escape.

Then the crowd outside reached a tipping point. The roaring, thrashing monster had forced its way so far into the heart of the mass of people that suddenly there were those at the sides who found themselves no longer trapped. Realising this, they ran for freedom, and pretty soon, the entire crowd was streaming away from the beast down the sides of the street. The rumble of running footsteps became almost deafening as hundreds of people fled downhill towards the river, water spraying up from their feet into the air. The patch of street below the duke emptied until just a handful remained, either too dazed or injured to get away. Several bodies lay in the brown water; those who had been unable to escape the crush of people and had suffocated or been trampled. Wigbert felt sick.

Then a stream of people emptied out of the bakery door just beneath his feet, disappearing down the street at full speed. Other buildings emptied too, those inside seeing their chance for escape.

Wigbert looked out and saw that Punduckslew and the others had remained behind and were now advancing slowly on the enraged monster who, even as Wigbert watched, launched itself into the smoking pile of books and landed among them with a crash. The duke turned his back on the scene and thundered back across the room, stopping only briefly to untangle himself from a particularly tricky footstool, before careering back down the stairs. He caught sight of the baker and his family, thankfully unharmed, huddled in the centre of their ruined shop as he dashed past and back out onto the street.

'Your grace!'

The shout rang out and Punduckslew broke away from the group of guards, running towards Wigbert. He was covered in filth and one arm of his dress coat was completely torn away.

It made Wigbert look down at his own soaking clothes and realise that he, too, was now mostly brown with mud.

'Thank Melethin!' the wizard said as he came splashing up to the duke. 'We feared…well, it's good to see you in one piece.'

'What do we do, Punduckslew? How do we stop this thing?'

'I don't know,' Punduckslew said, shaking his head. 'I could try blowing it up again, but last time it only pissed it off! What…what's it doing?'

'It's eating the books,' Wigbert said, watching as the thing clawed out two huge handfuls of the smouldering, blackened Book of Oaks and shoved them into its splintered mouth. There was already a significant dent in the pile.

'You were right then. It *is* attracted by the books. But why?'

'You're the wizard. Isn't this your area of expertise?'

Punduckslew shook his head. 'I've never seen anything like it. It's…it's almost like the thing is feeding off them—'

The monster cut him off, roaring again, throwing its swollen head back and projecting the noise into the blackened sky. Something was happening to it. It began to shake, parts of its body swelling outwards, distorting and reshaping as the beast rose, expanding outwards as it increased in size at a terrifying speed. In seconds it was the height of four men, then five, six, seven… They watched in horror as it roared at the sky once more, throwing its arms outwards, arms that withered and changed. They grew thicker, stronger, sprouting a thick brown fur that faded to a golden colour before their eyes. The monster unfolded and before them was no longer the Lord of Misrule, but a gigantic bear. A golden bear the size of a building.

Captain Tritewine splashed over to where Wigbert and Punduckslew stood, rooted to the spot in awe.

'What's happening?' she yelled above the noise.

'I've no bloody idea!' Punduckslew shouted back.

'The Book of Oak,' Wigbert said, only just loud enough for the others to hear. 'It's eaten The Book of Oak and turned into a giant golden bear.'

'Yes, we can see that, but why?' Punduckslew said.

'Don't you see?' Wigbert tore his face away from the monstrosity before him and looked at the other two with round eyes. 'It's Melethin. The bloody thing's turned into the Grandfather Oak! Melethin turned into a giant golden bear to fight Garselin, remember?'

They gaped at him. Then at the bear.

'Because...because of the books?' Captain Tritewine asked in a terrified hush.

'It must be! It makes perfect sense!' said Wigbert, ignoring a spluttering protest from Punduckslew and ploughing on at a gabble as the idea solidified in his head. 'Look, don't you see? It must have eaten the posters of Toflo Higginbottom. That led it right to the man. Then, when he killed him, it...it *became* him. It became the Lord of Misrule. Now it's eaten a book all about Melethin, and hey presto!'

'Then it's just getting more and more powerful!' said Tritewine. 'It's basically a *god* now! How are we supposed to stop a god?'

As if to emphasise her point, the monster chose this moment to move. It turned on all fours in a great, ponderous arc, its furry behind swinging around until it met with the nearest building, a watchmaker, which crumbled beneath the mammoth buttocks touch as if it was made of kindling.

'It's too big. It's going to destroy the whole town!' Punduckslew cried, hoisting back his remaining sleeve and raising his hands towards the beast. 'I have to try to take it out.'

Wigbert grabbed his arm. 'No! You'll just make it mad. There's a better way,' he said, thinking furiously.

'What better way?' the wizard cried as a second building collapsed. The bear had tried to use it to pull itself to its hind legs, but the weight had been too much for the timber construction.

'We have to get it to change form,' Wigbert said. 'We need to make it eat something else. Something that will weaken it.'

And then Wigbert saw the solution.

Now, wait just a bally minute! Wolfe spluttered from the

darkness in the duke's head.

No choice, Wigbert thought back. Sorry!

'I've got an idea,' he said to the others. 'Follow me!'

2.

Beatrice stumbled on a protruding root and had to grab hold of Captain Snekchesser's arm to stop herself from falling. The captain slowed, helping her to regain her footing. A fat raindrop fell from the thick forest canopy above and splashed across the man's grim face. He wiped it away with an irritated movement, before calling forward, sotto voce, to where the wizard Gloamblight was already beginning to disappear between the trees.

'We need to slow down! The children can't keep this pace up and I'd rather not run face first into another pack of gwyf because we weren't taking the proper precautions.'

'We must press on, captain. Time is running out!' came the shouted reply. Snekchesser winced as the wizard's words seemed to echo through the trees, excessively loud.

'That fool's going to get us killed,' he said to no one in particular.

'At least we're finally heading out of this miserable forest,' said Master Lettuce, coming puffing up behind them with Oatey and Madame Reedswail in tow. The master looked even paler and wan than usual. The Blackwood didn't seem to agree with him, Beatrice decided.

Snekchesser grunted, scratching his stubbly chin. 'So says the madman. But how does he even know we're running out of time?'

'I think he's awakened, captain,' said Madame Reedswail. Snekchesser made an extremely skeptical face. The hedgewitch sighed and added, 'He's in tune with his destiny now. He feels the urgency of his calling.'

'Codswallop,' the captain said.

'Well, if we're going to continue following him, we had better not tarry,' said Lettuce. Indeed, Gloamblight was already a receding shadow in the perpetual gloom beneath the forest canopy. The captain's face showed the agony of indecision, but he quickly relented.

'Come on then. But keep your eyes and ears open, all of you,' he warned, breaking back into a trot. As Beatrice made to follow, she gave a start as a bush to her right rustled ominously. She sighed with relief as a flash of grey fur and a long pink tail passed her. It was just one of the rats. Boss and his men had never been far from the group. But they mostly travelled through the undergrowth and lower branches, only occasionally visible as they dashed from bush to bush or leapt between branches. Beatrice was impressed by their agility, and couldn't help wishing she could move the same way. But she had to settle for thudding down one foot in front of the other, most of her energy taken up just by trying to avoid falling flat on her face on the uneven ground.

She'd lost track of how long they'd been traveling. The everlasting twilight of the Blackwood made it very hard to tell what time of day it was. On the one hand, it felt like only a few minutes since they had left the ruined archive, but her feet ached like they had been moving for hours. She felt the hedgewitch fall into step beside her.

'Doing all right, young un?' the strange woman asked.

'*I'm* fine,' Beatrice hadn't meant for the words to come out quite like that. But the truth was, she'd been surprised by the frail-looking witch's ability to keep up with the rest of them. The woman chuckled, her papery face wrinkling into a thousand smile lines as she trotted along with apparent ease.

'We're tougher than we look, my girl, us hedgewitches. Of course, I reckon you know a thing or two about being tougher than you look, aye?'

Beatrice said nothing, but a small glow of pride filled her

chest. She *was* tough.

'Yes indeed,' the witch continued. 'Very impressive.'

'Do you mean because I've survived the Blackwood?' Beatrice asked.

'Partly that,' Madame Reedswail said, pursing her lips. 'But mostly the other stuff.'

'What other stuff?'

The woman chuckled again. 'Look around you, my girl. It's not any child who could bring together this motley crew for a common purpose. That takes influence, that does. You'd make a good hedgewitch, I reckon. Shame about all that duchess business, really. Still, I'm sure you'll do some good.'

'You really think I'd make a good hedgewitch?' Beatrice wasn't so sure she'd done all that much. She had convinced Oatey to come along, but he usually did whatever she said anyway, so she wasn't sure that counted. As for the others, well, she hadn't really convinced any of them to do anything. It was all just the way things had gone.

Madame Reedswail gave her a knowing smile. 'Oh yes,' she said. 'I see it behind your eyes. More in that head of yours than the sawdust you get in most of your family. No offense meant, of course. Your father seems bright enough,' she admitted. 'But he's still a man.' She said it with a dismissive wave of her thin wrist, as if it was a sort of handicap.

Beatrice felt another burst of pride. A hedgewitch? Her? She didn't really know much about them. They'd always been around on the outskirts. But they didn't get involved in politics like the Wizards Charter did.

'Can a man not be a hedgewitch?' she asked.

'Oh, there have been a few, but they're operating at a sort of natural disadvantage,' the witch said with a sparkle in her eye so that Beatrice wasn't sure if she was being serious or not.

Their conversation was interrupted by Boss, who dropped out of the trees above them, landing softly on his four pink paws and scampering along beside them.

'You don't want to listen to this old goat,' he said. 'Some

males is very smart. Handsome and brave too!' He grinned at her, flashing his large yellow teeth.

Madame Reedswail gave a bark of laughter. 'It's easy to be brave when your fleas have a larger combined brain power than you do!' she said. The rat stuck a long red tongue out at her before scampering off ahead.

'Will you keep it down? This isn't some family picnic!' Captain Snekchesser hissed across at them. The hedgewitch made a face at Beatrice, who had to stifle a laugh.

'Quite right, captain, we're so lucky you're here,' Reedswail said. 'But it appears we are stopping again.' She pointed ahead to where Gloamblight had indeed come to a standstill. He seemed to be talking to something cupped in his hands.

'If he's talking to a bloody mole or something, I swear to Melethin...' the captain grumbled.

But it wasn't a mole.

'Rupert has returned with word from the town,' Gloamblight explained when the others caught up. 'I was right. We must hurry!'

'What's happening? Is that a note from the duke?' said the captain, ignoring the proud robin who had hopped up to Gloamblight's shoulder and puffed out his feathers, instead reaching for the loosely rolled scroll in the wizard's hand.

'It is,' Gloamblight confirmed, allowing him to take it, then fishing half a broken biscuit out of a coat pocket, crumbling a small section onto his shoulder. Rupert chirped in gratitude and set to pecking his little head at the crumbs enthusiastically. 'But it is already somewhat outdated, I'm afraid. Rupert says things have moved quickly in Upton-Myzzle since he left this morning.'

Captain Snekchesser scanned the note quickly, a frown creasing his already lined face. 'How does he know that if he left this morning? No, forget I asked that... it's a bloody robin. It can't know anything!'

Rupert stopped his pecking, just long enough to chirp angrily at the man, his beak full of biscuit.

'Birds talk, just as humans do,' Gloamblight said, in the way of explanation. He didn't bother to expand. 'He's had word that a great crowd has gathered. Quite the hubbub, it seems.' Here the wizard looked more uncertain. 'There's something to do with a seabass?' he added.

'Seabass Street?' Snekchesser asked. 'If a crowd was gathering, it might well do it there.'

The wizard shrugged. 'Perhaps,' he said. 'But come. Rupert says we are close to the edge of the forest now and our path is clear. We must hurry!'

'The bird told you that too, did it?' Snekchesser said, giving Rupert a suspicious look. The robin ignored him.

'The monster has made itself known,' Gloamblight called over his shoulder, already moving away. 'And it would seem your duke is in grave danger.'

Beatrice's mouth went dry. 'What? What do you mean? What's happening?' she demanded, breaking into a run after the wizard. She felt the others follow.

'I'm afraid that is all Rupert was able to ascertain. He had word from a pair of passing wood pigeons, but…well they are not the smartest of birds,' said the wizard as Beatrice raced to his side, matching the man's pace, her little legs moving twice as fast as his long ones. He looked down at her, and seeing her expression, his own softened. 'I am sorry, child, that is all I know. But that is why we must hurry!'

Beatrice's mind reeled. Her father was in danger? What had happened? Suddenly, the reality of the situation hit home to her. If this was all real…if the things she had discovered were true…well, then this wasn't some grand adventure. This was a genuine threat, and her father was right in the firing line. Her hopeless, befuddled father, with his kind eyes, perpetually bemused expression and utterly distracted brain.

She had to hurry.

She increased her speed, pulling in front of the wizard and ignoring the shouts of caution from the captain behind. Rupert took off from his master's shoulder, swooping down low through the air, showing the way between the massive trees all around. Beatrice focused in on his tiny form, willed her feet between the rocks and roots, and sped on into the gloom.

3.

In the dukes' walled garden, all was quiet. The only sound was the steady patter of the rain on the earth and the few remaining tougher winter leaves. A rhubarb leaf rustled. A solitary moglin broke the cover of vegetation and made a mad dash across a patch of open ground, holding a brown and wrinkled leaf above its head as a makeshift umbrella. It reached the relative shelter of the apple tree trunk and flattened itself against the bark, looking up into the bare branches. There was still an apple or two hanging on up there, but it was after a different prey. A few branches up sat a fairy. It dangled its tiny legs in the air, looking down at the moglin and fluttering its eyes coquettishly. The moglin needed no second bidding and was already shimmying its way up the trunk with commendable speed when the garden door swung open, hitting the stone wall with a bang. The fairy was gone in an instant, leaving the disappointed moglin to shake its tiny purple fist in impotent rage at the colossal figures who came stamping into the peaceful scene, before disappearing itself.

'Your grace, why are we here?' said Punduckslew, wringing out his beard. 'Unless you're hiding a secret weapon in the potting shed I don't know about, I really don't—'

'Actually, that's exactly where it's hidden,' said the duke.

'What!'

'Relax. It's not really a weapon. Well, not usually. But it might just work in this case,' said Wigbert.

'Whatever it is, if we don't get to it soon, that bloody bear will have flattened half of Upton-Myzzle,' Captain Tritewine warned. 'There isn't much the Guard can do!'

'This way,' Wigbert led the other two through the regimented rows of plants to the potting shed, wrenching open the wooden door that had swollen in the rain and ushering them inside. Punduckslew stamped his feet on the earthen floor and tried to shake out his sodden coat. 'We need a bloody good fire!' he moaned.

'My thoughts exactly!' Wigbert said.

'Eh?'

We need to make another bonfire,' Wigbert explained. 'We need to burn something else to attract the monster.'

'Here?' the wizard said, looking around at the tools and jars of moglin mash doubtfully.

'That would draw it away from the more populated areas of the town,' Tritewine said. 'But what have we got that would attract it? Unless you've got a gigantic pile of books lying around...'

'I've got exactly that!' Wigbert said, unlocking the door at the back of the room with a key from around his neck and pushing it open. It swung backwards with a satisfying creak, and the guard and wizard peered into the darkness within. Before them lay a large stack of wooden crates.

'That's not...Wolfe?' Punduckslew said, catching up at last. 'Bloody hell, there are hundreds of them!'

'The pre-orders were quite substantial,' Wigbert admitted with an embarrassed flush.

'I don't understand. What's in the boxes?' Tritewine said.

'Books! *His* book!' Punduckslew explained, pointing to the duke.

'What? *The new Wolfe Starlingcloud novel*?' Captain Tritewine said excitedly. She dashed forward into the room and grabbed a book from the top of an open container, goggling at it. 'This is it! This is actually it! I can't believe it!' She looked up at the duke in amazement. 'All this time I've been working for the author who created Wolfe Starlingcloud! No wonder you had to keep it such a secret.' Then her face fell. '*But we can't burn these!*' she cried. 'This is the next Wolfe Starlingcloud! We can't *burn* the next Wolfe Starlingcloud! It's…it's sacrilege!'

'More sacrilegious than burning The Book of Oak?' said Wigbert.

'Two wrongs don't make a right!' Tritewine said. 'Er…your grace,' she added guiltily.

'I'm afraid we don't have a choice,' Wigbert said.

'Hang on a minute though, can we actually do this?' Punduckslew said, staring at the crates of books with a thoughtful expression.

'What do you mean?' Wigbert asked.

'Well, when you first told me about all this, it got me thinking. And suddenly the Castle Blackwood finances made a lot more sense! I might not be privy to the inner workings of the Castle's bank balance—old Dribbets keeps far too tight a hand on the purse strings for that—but I certainly wasn't the only one who'd questioned just how the castle was surviving. The outgoings just seemed to far exceed anything coming in. But when I learnt about your forays into literature…your grace, I'm pretty sure the sales of these books are the only thing keeping the Castle afloat! Can we afford to burn them?'

Wigbert grimaced. 'It'll be a hit, I don't deny that. But we have little of a choice. Unless anyone has a better idea?'

'But how is it going to work, exactly?' Tritewine asked, unable to tear her eyes away from the cover of the book in her hands, which featured a very gung-ho-looking Wolfe, swinging from a chandelier and seeming very smug about it. 'So we lure the thing here, it eats all these books…won't that just strengthen it?'

Wigbert had been thinking about this. 'We know when it ate The Book of Oak, it turned into a facsimile of that book's main focus, Melethin. Before that, we know it looked and acted like the Lord of Misrule. We saw Toflo Higginbottom's body. It's pretty safe to assume we are correct in thinking the monster killed him, too.'

'Yes, but why?' Punduckslew said. 'If it gains powers from

books...from *words*, then why kill a man?'

'I have a theory about that too,' Wigbert said. 'It's attracted by words, right? Well, we put wanted posters up all over town! We practically invited it in. So just maybe, it fed off all those words about Toflo Higginbottom and *that's* what made it turn into him, not killing the man himself.'

'Okay...' Tritewine said, finally laying the book back down. Her forehead creased in thought. 'But still...why kill the man, then?'

'Well, I guess once he'd taken the Lord of Misrules form, then...then the real one was a threat!'

Punduckslew stroked his sopping beard. 'That makes a certain sort of sense, I suppose,' he admitted. 'When we first saw the beast, and I tried attacking, it reformed momentarily with an old woman's face. Another victim, perhaps?'

'Sounds likely. The hedgewitch, If I'm right about all this,' Wigbert agreed.

'But where did the thing come from in the first place? It's all very...odd,' said Tritewine.

'Believe me, there are things in the depths of the Blackwood that make this look tame. Never underestimate the power of magic!' the wizard said with a humourless laugh. 'But we can worry about its origins when it's dead! Getting back to this plan of yours, your grace, won't we just be feeding it more?'

'Yes, but think about *what* we'd be feeding it. My silly little novel. The things just consumed hundreds of copies of a book containing religious ideas that go back centuries. It's basically just become a god! Now think what happens if we feed it *my* book.'

'It'll...it'll become *Wolfe*!' the captain said.

'Exactly! And as much as I designed Wolfe to be the perfect swashbuckling adventure hero, I'd rather fight him than a god.'

Hang on a bally minute! Wolfe suddenly chimed in from the darkness in Wigberts's head. *That's your plan? You want to turn the monster into a doppelgänger of me? Unacceptable old boy! I'll not have that dastardly knave going about eating people with my face!*

Look, I'm sorry, Wigbert thought back. But it's the only plan we've got.

But I've got a reputation to uphold! Wolfe whined. *What will people think? I'm supposed to be a bloody hero!*

Wigbert did his best to block the man out. 'Look,' he said out loud. 'We don't have a lot of time to discuss this. As we speak, that bloody thing is probably destroying half the city. So, unless either of you has a genuine reason we can't do this, we need to act now. At the very least, we can draw the thing away from the rest of the population.'

Punduckslew sighed. 'I guess it's worth a try,' he said with a shrug. Captain Tritewine simply nodded, but she shot a regretful look at the stack of crates.

'Then it's decided,' Wigbert said. 'The next issue is figuring out how we do it.'

Punduckslew walked over to the workbench that held the duke's bottles of Moglin Mash. He interlaced his fingers and pushed his arms out in front of him, cracking his knuckles loudly. 'You just leave the *how* to me,' he said.

4.

The man in the wide-brimmed hat was feeling deeply uneasy. To say that things had not gone quite according to plan was an understatement. But then how could he have predicted *that*, he reasoned with himself? Sir Sweetspire had said nothing about bloody great monsters! Perhaps it was not of his masters doing? Either way, the man felt exposed. He was uncomfortably wet and getting wetter with every passing second. Being uncomfortable was not a familiar feeling. He planned so fastidiously exactly to avoid this sort of thing. But he'd been forced to flee, just like everyone else. Caught in the scrum with the mindless peons, running for cover. He'd escaped the square and found a quiet corner to regroup. It had quickly become apparent to him the course of action he must take. Things truly were chaos now. There were people and confusion on every street. The inhuman rage of the creature could be heard ringing out across the city, as could the damage it was wreaking. Rumbling of collapsing buildings was an almost constant backdrop. The man had kept his distance at first. But it was at this point in an operation you had to be extra careful not to make a mistake. To that end, he had decided to act now, reentering the fray without his master's permission. Time was of the essence.

He lowered the black-robed body carefully to the mud-splattered ground, removing his knife and wiping it fastidiously on the unfortunates clothes. He stowed it out of sight and slipped away, round a corner, through a small alley and out onto another completely different street. Here he trotted along, doing his best to blend in with the rest of the frightened masses as they ran this way and that in their panic.

But he wasn't panicking.

He was hunting.

The Church of the Cracked Acorn had served their purpose. Now they were just loose ends. He'd always planned to kill them, eventually. The way he saw it, he was just taking advantage of the current situation. Who would notice a few more bodies in all this? Of course, someone might figure out foul play eventually, but by then, any ties to him would be long gone. And that was the whole point, of course. There could be no ties to him or Sir Sweetspire. And that monster appearing like that...well it was the sort of shock that set tongues wagging. That couldn't be allowed to happen. So best to silence the lot of them now, while the opportunity presented itself.

He jogged through several streets, working his way in a large arc across the central part of town, careful to keep the monster at a reasonable distance as it continued its apparently mindless destruction, the man's eyes scanning the fleeing populace. After about ten minutes, he found his next target. A fat man in an oversized brown frock coat. It was a poor disguise. The man could see the hem of the fat fool's black cloak clearly beneath. Even if he couldn't, he would have recognised that pathetic waddle anywhere; The Pig. The man allowed himself a small smile beneath the shadow of his hat. He would enjoy this one.

He followed the fat man at a safe distance, making sure not to be seen, as the fleeing Cracked Acorn member worked his way across the town and away from the scenes of destruction. He wasn't heading home. The fool must have secured himself some sort of bolt hole. Clever. Cleverer than the man in the wide-brimmed hat would have given the chubby fool credit for. Just as well he'd found him now. It would have taken up valuable time ferreting him out later.

As The Pig turned a corner which led to a quieter part of town, the man allowed himself to get closer. He could hear the fat man's wheezing as he struggled along, great hammy thighs rubbing together in his haste. The man pulled the brim of his hat down lower against the rain, his lip curling at the disgust he felt for his prey. Truly, such a pathetic specimen would not be missed. He was practically doing a public service.

He was only a few steps behind the man now, his tread light, lost amongst the rain and The Pig's own labored breath. When the last potential witness turned down a side street and left the two of them alone, the man in the wide-brimmed hat wasted no time in taking his chance. He leapt forward, blade appearing in his hand in one fluid motion, knee hitting The Pig in his flabby back, bringing him down to the street face first, his attacker kneeling on top of him, knife darting to his neck in a quick flash. There had been no time for a scream. The man allowed himself just a second to relish the sound of The Pig's final, gurgling breath. Then he sprang to his feet and moved away, stowing his blade once more and removing himself from the scene of the crime without a backward look. There was no need. He was good enough to know when his knife hit its mark.

As he put distance between himself and the latest body, he ran through his mental checklist. Including the ones caught in the fire and the following stampede at the monster's appearance, he could now account for all but one of the church members. The Bird. He wasn't surprised. If any of the sorry bunch could have been said to possess even slightly more brains than the ridiculous livestock they were, then it was The Bird. But it wouldn't be enough to save her from him.

He continued his search, doing his best to ignore the incessant rain that had now thoroughly saturated every fibre of his clothing. He was more than usually glad of his hat. Reaching the Myzzle—now a brown churning mass of angry water, mere inches from breaking its banks—he headed back towards the centre of town. He hoped the bitch wasn't going to make things difficult for him. He was getting cold. But if he knew the woman, and she really hadn't been that hard to figure out, then she would not have fled too far from the action. It would not have occurred to her that a member of the truly faithful such as herself was in any real danger. This unwavering belief, coupled with an instinct to stick her abnormally large nose into other people's business, would no doubt have kept her near to the body of the remaining crowd. Indeed, it took another twenty minutes in the accursed rain, but he eventually found her, just a single street away from where a large group of particularly stupid individuals had raised weapons against the monster. It seemed the Watch Commander was leading them, spouting some nonsense about civic duty and the glory of battle. The man in the wide-brimmed hat ignored his pompous braying, focusing instead on his final prey and the unfortunate situation she seemed to have got herself into.

'I really must protest at this detestable treatment!' The Bird was saying. She was up against a wall, held firmly by two nervous-looking members of the Castle Guard. Two old men stood before her. One now spoke.

'Protest all you want, my dear, but don't think I don't know a filthy heretic when I see one!'

The man in the wide-brimmed hat squinted his eyes, trying to make out the man's face through the rain. Then they widened in the shock of recognition. The man that had spoken was none other than the duke-no-more himself, Ormus Stonemorton. His companion was another old disgraced politician…Sir Gerald something. What were they doing here?

The Bird was spluttering with rage. 'Heretic? Heretic! I'm no heretic!'

'So you deny being a member of the group styling themselves The Church of the Cracked Acorn?' Stonemorton said, eyeing her with undisguised contempt.

'I've no idea what you're talking about…your grace,' The Bird replied, endeavoring to look down her nose at him, but eventually erring on the side of deference instead.

'Liar!' Stonemorton pounced, waving a frail-looking finger under the woman's prodigious nose. 'I know that getup you're wearing. You think I'm stupid? We've practically caught you red-handed!'

Indeed, the woman was still clad in the Church's signature robes, not even a covering coat as an attempted disguise. The duke-no-more continued to rail at her. 'I'll teach you and your band of terrorists to destroy my church! I want names! Places! You can start with the whereabouts of that snake, Angston Krickwell!'

'Never heard of him,' the woman said.

The man in the wide-brimmed hat rolled his eyes. It had been a stupid thing to say. Upton-Myzzle was not that large a place. Everybody would have heard of Krickwell, even if in passing. She'd as good as admitted their association. Apparently Ormus Stonemorton felt the same because he grinned evilly, rapping his cane on the ground in triumph.

'I can read you like a book, you miserable traitor.'

The man in the wide-brimmed hat leant forward as far as he dared, straining his ears to hear, as the duke-no-more's companion, Gerald, took the old man to one side and muttered into his ear.

'We should get her back to the castle. We'll get more answers out of her there.'

'Technically, I don't have the authority,' Stonemorton admitted in little more than a whisper. 'But you're right. We'll do it in the name of my son.'

'Then let us do it now,' the man Gerald replied, shooting a concerned look toward the militia steadily being worked up into a frenzy not far away. 'It's not safe on the streets.'

'What about the monster?' Stonemorton said.

'Let someone else deal with it. Better yet, let that idiot Posternos get himself killed trying. What would you do about it, anyway? Throw your walking stick at it? We were lucky to survive that first encounter. Let's not push our luck further. We should join Quimby and Terrance at the castle while we still can.'

'This is *my* town, Gerald. I can't just sit back and let it be destroyed!'

'Ormus!' the man Gerald snapped, grabbing the former duke by the shoulders. 'You have to stop! You can hardly stand for Melethin's sake. We must return to the castle. Take this bloody woman if you want, but this adventure ends here!'

The man watched from his hiding place as the duke-no-more stared back defiantly at his friend, but then sagged, suddenly appearing spent.

'Very well,' he muttered.

It suddenly occurred to the man in the wide-brimmed hat he had been granted a rare opportunity. Here was the former duke, more or less alone, exposed and clearly vulnerable. There would be no better chance to correct the mistake of that fool Higginbottom. He could put the old goat down once and for all. He considered his chances. There were five people in the street, not including himself. The Bird, the two Castle Guards, the man Gerald, and Stonemorton himself. None alone would pose much of a challenge, but the man knew he was tired. The wet had penetrated his body with a chill and his reflexes would be dampened.

But he still liked his chances.

It was too good an opportunity to miss. He felt sure Sir Sweetspire would agree. One less Stonemorton getting in the way would be a big help to their eventual goal.

But he had to act fast. The rumble and crash of falling buildings were getting closer. An animal noise filled the rain-soaked air. The monster was headed this way. The noise of the mob just a street away was also increasing. No doubt Posternos meant to intercept the beast. He couldn't afford to lose his targets in the resulting chaos.

He edged closer, formulating his plan of attack as he went. The two older men were now in close consultation with the two guards. All five targets were in close proximity. He would have to hit them hard and fast. He couldn't afford a scene.

He was just a few feet away now, crouched low behind a handy barrel. He slipped a small throwing knife into each hand, picked his first targets, then waited, ready to spring, until his oblivious quarry arranged themselves into the ideal shot.

His moment came. He sprung.

Leaping out from behind the barrel, he let the knives fly. The first to fall was The Bird, a spray of blood erupting from her neck. Almost simultaneously, the second knife buried itself in the chest of a guard. He went down too, slumping to the soaking floor, still clutching the arm of his falling prisoner. The second guard, also still holding his charge, was pulled off balance and went sprawling face-first in the mud. Before he could rise, his attacker was on him. He buried his long knife in the struggling man's back and that was all it took to silence victim number three. The two remaining men had barely moved. They stared at the scene before them in total shock and the man in the wide-brimmed hat almost laughed at how easy it would be to finish them. The man Gerald opened his mouth to shout but choked on the noise as a fist was rammed into his throat, then staggered backwards as another smashed him in the face. He hit the far wall and slid from his feet. The man in the wide-brimmed hat allowed himself a moment for breath, calmly returning to the face-down guard and pulling his knife free. Then he focused on his one target that remained standing.

Ormus Stonemorton opened and closed his mouth like a guppy. He raised his stick in defense, but a vicious foot lashed out and the thing was snapped in two with a loud crack, the force sending the ancient statesman flying backwards and landing on his rump in the filth. He struggled to rise but fell back with a splash, unable to get his arms to take his weight.

The man in the wide-brimmed hat smiled. But he resisted the urge to taunt. Do the job. That's what mattered. He stepped towards his prey but was hit with a wall of sound. Suddenly, the street was full of flying debris. The man in the wide-brimmed hat was knocked from his feet and hit the wall with his shoulder, the hat flying from his head. One of the houses had been obliterated. The man watched as what remained of its shell collapsed in on itself in a cloud of dust. In its place stood a giant, golden bear. The monster.

The man struggled to his feet, clutching his aching shoulder and mouthing a curse. The thing had its gargantuan back to them. It had backed into the building, barely noticing. Cries and shouts could be heard from the neighbouring street, the freshly formed militia no doubt, and the creature let out a roar of rage, falling forward onto its front paws. It disappeared momentarily from view, but the battle cries became screams of terror as it fell on its would-be attackers.

The man tore his attention away. He had to find his quarry. The street was now awash with bits of the former building. Was Stonemorton beneath it? Or had he scurried away? The other man, Gerald, was out cold, sprawled close to where the man had dropped him, blood oozing from a nasty gash to the head.

The sound of running feet told the man he was no longer alone. He scrabbled for his hat in the rubble, slamming it back in place just as half a dozen people rounded the corner at a run. Their faces were terrified. At the head of the pack was Watch Commander Posternos himself, face even redder than usual, arms and legs pumping like pistons. There was another almighty boom as the corner house behind the fleeing group exploded to be replaced by thirty feet of angry bear. Its monstrous claws scrabbled through the ruins as it lurched after them.

Reluctantly, the man in the wide-brimmed hat saw that his time was up. He'd just have to hope the duke-no-more was dead. He took to his heels for the second time that day, joining the fleeing group in their desperate scramble through the debris-strew street. There was an anguished scream as the bear caught up with a straggler and the man's body was sent sailing through the air to smash into a large chunk of what had, until recently, been part of a wall, just to the left of the man in the wide-brimmed hat's head. He staggered sideways and collided with the puce-faced Watch Commander, who shoved him away desperately. Regaining their footing, the pair sped on, side by side as a second man was thrown through the air over their heads to be impaled on an exposed beam with a noise best not described. The ground shook with the weight of the beast behind them. The man in the wide-brimmed hat felt an unfamiliar panic. He needed to find a way off this street! Was that hot breath on the back of his neck or just his imagination?

He reached into his coat for his final throwing knife and thrust it almost blindly at the man to his side. There was a cry of pain as the blade connected and the Watch Commander dropped back from view. The man didn't dare look back, but leapt over a broken wooden beam, landing with a splash and forcing his legs to move faster.

Up ahead. A side street.

The man in the wide-brimmed hat raced towards his salvation. He just needed a place to hide. Some small space to slip away where the monster wouldn't notice. There were fresh screams behind but he didn't look around. He practically threw himself around the corner, scanned the street with practiced eyes, and slid into the barest of alleyways between two houses. It was dark down here. His heaving chest pressed against one wet wall, his sweat-soaked back against another. He stared at the grey plaster, wide-eyed, as he heard the thundering paws approach the corner...then pass right on.

The man closed his eyes in relief, allowing his body to sag against the alley walls. If he'd believed in anything very much, he might have given a prayer of thanks.

There was a shuffle of feet. The man's body re-tensed.

He opened his eyes to find the bloodied face of Ormus Stonemorton mere inches from his own, wedged into the alley behind him.

'Fancy meeting you here,' the duke-no-more growled, then plunged a blade into the man's unprotected neck.

5.

In the Castle Blackwood gatehouse infirmary, there was a lull in activity. Many of the staff had run to the battlements, keen to get a good view of the chaos unfolding in the town below. There's nothing more interesting than chaos. From a distance, mind.

So it was that when Mr Tanco Dribbets opened his eyes, he did so to an almost empty room. If you didn't count the bed-bound invalids, of course, and people usually don't. He stared at the stone roof for several seconds while his brain, which for some reason ached like the billy-o, did a little action replay in his head. When it eventually caught up, the man sat bolt upright in his camp bed and said, 'The bastard! The mad bloody bastard!'

There was silence, broken only by a weak groan from somewhere in a far corner. Then someone said 'Ah, Mr Dribbets, you're up. Jolly good.'

'He blew us up! The bloody mad bastard blew us up!' Tanco said, not quite ready to relinquish his theme just yet. 'With gunpowder!'

'Yes, I'm afraid so. A bit of a mess. You seem to be recovering nicely though, so there's that, I suppose.'

Tanco moved his head and wished he hadn't. The bibliothecary, Mr Bombroffe, was sitting next to him with a book in his lap. 'How do you feel?' the man asked.

'Very alive.'

'That's good.'

'Is it? It hurts.'

'Ah,' Mr Bombroffe said, closing the book with a snap and a little puff of dust. 'Never a truer word spoken.'

Tanco swallowed. His throat felt like the inside of a very dry joint of beef. 'I think I'll leave off the philosophy for the time being, if it's all the same to you,' he croaked. He tried to massage his throat but found that someone had tied invisible weights to his arms while he was sleeping. Mr Bombroffe held a glass of water to his lips and Tanco sipped at it tentatively.

'That's it, easy does it,' the old bibliothecary said.

They sat in silence for several minutes while Tanco recovered himself. Details were slowly filtering back in.

'How many died?' he asked at last.

'Everyone, I'm afraid to say. Except for yourself, of course, but that was touch and go.'

'Shit.'

'Indeed.'

'What about...?'

'The Lord of Misrule? Also dead, but not in the explosion. Later, by...other means.'

'Well, that's something.'

A very loud rumble in the distance drifted in through the window.

'What was that?' Tanco asked.

'Ah. Well, that might take a bit of explaining. You might prefer to—'

'Just tell me.'

Mr Bombroffe told him.

Tanco got out of bed on the third try.

'Where's the duke?' he said.

'You really ought to—'

'*Where!*'

'I believe he said something about luring the thing into the walled garden.'

Tanco stumbled to the nearest window with a view to the north. Outside, the rain fell like it had a grudge against the ground. He could just make out a small trail of smoke coming from inside the garden walls. He looked down towards the town and saw...

'Get me some bloody crutches right now!'

CHAPTER FOURTEEN: LIGHTNING, FIRE, AND STONE

1.

Wigbert watched as his potting shed burned.

'Was this really necessary?' he asked again, as another jar of moglin mash exploded with a violent pop, sending out a spray of white sparks from the orange inferno. He'd been sure to evacuate any remaining moglins before letting Punduckslew do his thing. He didn't need any more innocent deaths on his conscience.

'Quickest way I'm afraid, your grace,' the wizard replied, standing beside him, sucking on his clay pipe.

'Will it work, do you think?' said Captain Tritewine, rain streaming down her worried face.

'If it doesn't, I just burnt up two-thirds of the castle's yearly income for no reason,' the duke said.

'Right. Positive thoughts then.'

'I suppose so. Then again, if it *does* work, thirty feet of angry bear will soon be smashing through the garden wall, so...'

'There's not exactly an upside to this, is there?'

'No.'

What he really wanted right now, Wigbert thought, was a nice lie down somewhere quiet. And dry. He was starting to forget what being dry felt like.

Now is no time for a nap! Wolfe snapped at him. The figment of the duke's imagination had been sulking for several minutes. It was an odd sensation. Wigbert could feel the man's ire like a black cloud in his subconscious.

I don't know what you're so upset about, he thought back at the man. It's my hard work going up in flames.

Yes, but it's my life, isn't it!

I can't have this argument with you again, Wigbert thought, smothering a sigh.

You don't care, do you? You created me, but you don't care.

Of course I care! Wigbert thought, simultaneously wondering if that was true. The man wasn't real after all. Not *really* real.

See! I knew it! Came Wolfe's outraged response.

Wigbert winced. Stop doing that, he thought. It was intolerable, having someone else know your every thought.

Well, it's not my fault, is it? You created me. Do you think I like being stuck in here?

Wigbert realised he'd never really thought about it that way.

No, I know! Only ever thinking about yourself. Not a thought for old Wolfe.

'Oh, do shut up!' Wigbert said.

The wizard and the captain looked at him in surprise.

'No one said a word,' Tritewine said, looking concerned.

Punduckslew arched a bushy eyebrow.

The duke shifted uncomfortably. 'What? Oh. Well, what I meant to say is, what do we do now? How are we going to beat the damn thing when it gets here?'

'An excellent question!' called out a voice.

They turned to find Mr Dribbets hobbling towards them through the garden gate. He was still wearing a nightgown from the infirmary under his dress coat and had a large swathe of bandages wrapped around his head. He swung forward unsteadily on two wooden crutches. Mr Bombroffe scurried along beside him, arm out to catch him if he fell.

'Tanco!' Wigbert darted forward to help his friend, afraid that if he stumbled, both men would end up in the mud. The ancient bibliothecary was hardly a steady pair of hands. 'What are you doing out of bed?' he chastised. 'Not that I'm not relieved to see you awake!'

'I've slept long enough, it seems. Stop fussing!' the man replied, shooing the duke and the bibliothecary away impatiently. 'Mr Bombroffe has been filling me in. Any longer asleep and I might have awoken to no Upton-Myzzle at all!'

'You have missed quite a bit,' Punduckslew said, ambling over to them, Captain Tritewine in tow. 'How's the head?'

'Like an egg that's been run over by a cart,' Tanco grimaced. 'But never mind me. What exactly are you planning on doing about the bloody great bear that's approaching the castle?'

'It's coming, then? We've drawn it away from the town?' Wigbert asked, looking out the gateway as if expecting to see the monstrous form of the beast. Silly. If it was here already, they'd have heard it a mile off.

'Oh, it's coming all right. Last I saw, it was halfway up the hill sniffing the air like a bloody bloodhound. The men on the ramparts were frankly pissing themselves!'

'They mustn't engage it. They'll only get themselves killed!'

'I've given orders for all guards to hold back. Strictly observation, no engagement. The men we left in town will follow it here at a safe distance,' Tritewine said.

'Good, good,' said Tanco, nodding. 'And what, pray tell, were you planning on doing when the sodding great thing gets here? I will not be the Castle Blackwood steward who allows the bloody castle to be destroyed on my watch!'

'Um, technically, the castle is my responsibility. I am the duke,' said Wigbert.

'Wrong, your grace. Whilst I'm delighted to see you've finally accepted your position, your responsibility lies with the Duchy of Blackwood. The castle is mine, and I will not let that damn bear flatten it, so I hope you have a jolly good plan!'

'Err…'

'That response has me overflowing with confidence.'

'No offense, old chap, but we're not dealing with a simple situation here. There are powerful magical forces at play,' Punduckslew said, looking aggrieved. 'You can't just come hopping down here having slept through the whole thing and bully us for not having it all straightened out.'

Mr Dribbets shot him a withering look.

'The trouble with you wizards,' he said. 'Is that you think anyone not in the Magical Charter is an idiot.'

Punduckslew appeared to consider this. 'To be honest, I think most people in the charter are an acorn or two short of a bushel as well,' he said.

Tanco ignored him. 'I assume your plan is to feed it your latest books in the hope of it changing from its current Melethin form into something a little more...manageable?' he said to Wigbert, who nodded, feeling a little like a naughty apprentice. 'Good,' Tanco continued. 'That seems a logical plan. The question remains; how do we tackle the beast after that? Magic has proven ineffective?'

'My Talent has, certainly,' Punduckslew said.

'And the rest of the charter? How have they fared?'

'Um...'

'Where *is* the rest of the charter? Isn't it exactly events like this we keep you people around for?'

Punduckslew bridled. 'The Wizards Charter is a private, civilian organisation, Mr Dribbets, as you well know.'

'Still, a bit of a poor show, don't you think? A magical monster on the loose and the Talented are all cowering behind their window shutters?'

'Perhaps,' the wizard conceded, tight-lipped. 'Regardless, I know of no Talent held by any member that would prove effective if my own did not.'

'Then we shall have to rely on more traditional arms,' Tanco replied.

Captain Tritewine stepped forward. 'I'm afraid to say, sir, that the Castle Guard armory is rather low at present.'

'How low?'

'I could probably get you a rusty bayonet.'

Tanco sighed. 'Bloody budget cuts will be the death of us!'

'Fortunately, I have something else in mind,' Tritewine said.

'You've got an idea?' Wigbert asked, perking up.

'I do. Do you remember the electrostatic generator?'

'That Lord Nugent contraption you have in your office at the institute? I thought you said the thing was a deathtrap?'

'Well yes, exactly.'

'Oh. Right. Is that a good idea, do you think?'

The woman shrugged. 'Probably not, but I can't think of another. Can you?'

'What exactly is this electrostatic generator?' Punduckslew asked suspiciously.

'It's a weapon…well, maybe a weapon.'

'Will it take down the monster?' Tanco asked.

'Err, I once saw it destroy a medium-sized siege engine,' Tritewine said, looking nervous.

Wigbert gaped at her. 'You never told me that!'

She gave an apologetic shrug. 'As I recall, the wizard interrupted us. I haven't thought about it again until now.'

Punduckslew glared at her. '*The wizard* would like to know who this Lord Nugent is.'

'He's a long-dead natural philosopher,' Wigbert supplied.

'Good grief…we really are doomed!'

'Enough,' Tanco snapped. 'Where is this thing?'

'That's the problem,' Captain Tritewine said, looking wretched. It's still at the institute.'

Wigbert groaned. 'And the monster is between us and there.'

'I can help with that!' Tanco said brightly. 'Follow me, captain, and we shall retrieve this electrostatic generator of yours.'

'How are you going to—' Wigbert started, but his steward cut him off.

'Never mind that. There's no time to explain now. We must go.' He grabbed Captain Tritewine by the shoulder and began hobbling away, dragging her with him. 'Come, my dear. You men hold the fort till we return!'

'Oh great, we'll just stand here and wait like a couple of lemons then, shall we?' Punduckslew said, frowning fiercely.

'Err, permission to vacate the field, your grace. I'm afraid I'd not be much use in a fight these days,' said Mr Bombroffe, looking over his shoulder with some concern. The first sounds of a disturbance were drifting over from the gatehouse.

'Of course Mr Bombroffe!' Wigbert said. 'This is no place for a scholar. Get yourself to safety immediately.' The old bibliothecary hurried away, and the duke turned to the wizard. 'We should probably get out of the line of fire too, don't you think? Not much we can do against the thing for the time being.'

There was the sound of smashing timber.

'There go the front gates,' Punduckslew said. 'Come on, let's hide behind the apple tree. We'll be able to see it approach from there.'

As they crouched in the wet grass, peering out around the wide trunk towards the garden wall, Punduckslew cleared his throat awkwardly.

'Your grace, there is something I have been meaning to talk to you about ...'

'Can it not wait, man? This hardly seems the time.'

'Well, I have been waiting, your grace. Only the right moment never seems to present itself. It's about this voice of yours.'

'Punduckslew I really don't want to—'

'We have to discuss it sooner or later. And seeing as there's a fairly good chance at least one of us is about to be eaten by a giant bear...'

'Oh, all right! Say what you have to say.'

What's the matter? Not embarrassed of me, are you? Wolfe said sulkily.

'Shut up!'

Punduckslew bridled. 'Well, which is it, you grace? Say what I have to say, or shut up?'

'No, not you!'

'Oh. Right, I see,' said the wizard, cottoning on. 'Well, I've been thinking about it, and the more I do, the more certain I am.'

'If you're about to say that the Duchy of Blackwood shouldn't be run by someone so clearly losing their mind then—'

'That's just it, your grace. I don't believe this is…some sort of mental illness. It's worse than that.'

'Worse?'

'Yes.'

'Worse than me going insane.'

'Possibly. Depending on your perspective.'

'Well…Aren't you a little ray of sunshine? And this couldn't have waited till after our confrontation with a sixty-foot tree god?'

'Like I said, your grace…'

'We might get eaten, yes, yes. Well, the way you tell it, that might be for the best!'

'Don't be silly, your grace.'

'Well, I mean…'

'Look, what I'm trying to say is that I believe this issue you've been having may…may be magical in nature.'

Wigbert turned to stare at him. 'Are you saying…' he said slowly.

The wizard nodded. 'Yes, your grace. I believe it may be a Talent of some kind.'

Wigbert gaped at him. 'But…but…that would make me…'

'A wizard, your grace. A rogue wizard, technically.'

Wigbert thought about this. 'Shit,' he said at length.

'Quite, your grace.'

'But, I mean, I can't be. Can I?'

'If you'd asked me a week ago, your grace, I would have laughed at the idea. But now…well it seems there is much I do not understand.'

'A Talent,' Wigbert repeated, his mind racing. He could feel Wolfe getting excited in his head. 'But…what kind exactly?'

'That's an excellent question. Each is different, as you know. We would have to do some tests.'

'We can't tell people!' Wigbert hissed.

'By Melethin no!' Punduckslew agreed. 'Tell people the duke is a rogue magic user? The town would rip itself apart. No. We'll have to keep it a secret, but in order to do that, we really need to understand exactly what is happening to you a little better. We can't afford for you to make any more...slips.'

What does this mean? Wolfe asked. Wigbert could practically feel him jumping up and down with excitement. *Does it mean I'm a bally wizard too? That'd be a turn up for the books, ay? Wolfe Starlingcloud, adventurer, man at arms, wizard extraordinaire!*

I don't know, do I? Wigbert thought back at the man.

Further conversation was curtailed by a great roar from the approaching beast.

Punduckslew shifted his position, swapping knees. 'We had better talk more about this later,' he said.

'Oh, *now* you want to concentrate on the task at hand! You can't just drop a clunker like that and expect-'

'Your grace.'

Wigbert sighed. 'Yes, yes. Alright.' He returned his focus to the growing noises coming from the other side of the garden wall. The monster was close now. It had to be inside the castle walls. There was a crash and the sound of falling stone. Wigbert winced. He hoped the bloody thing wasn't causing too much damage.

What if it is? We can just zap it with our mighty magical powers! said Wolfe, clearly getting overexcited.

It doesn't exactly work like that, does it, Wigbert thought. Do try to calm down.

Who knows how it works, old boy? That's the whole point! The world's our, wossname...shellfish of some sort.

Let's just try and concentrate on not getting eaten for now, shall we? Wigbert thought back. He felt he could hear the beast's approach now. Practically feel it through the earth. A rhythmic thud of gigantic paws.

'This had better bloody work,' he said out loud. 'I hope Tanco has found a way through.'

'Tanco knows what he's doing, your grace,' Punduckslew replied soothingly.

'Yes, but I don't, that's what concerns me.'

'Look, worst case scenario we'll be dealing with something

man-shaped again, right? That's got to be a win.'

'Has it? Have you read my book? Wolfe's a bloody monster!'

How dare you, Sir!

'I thought he was the hero?'

'Well yes, he is. But he still spends half his time chopping people up with swords. I made him the perfect fighting machine. Do you fancy fighting that?'

'This was your idea.'

'Yes, well as we've already established, I don't know what I'm bloody doing!' Wigbert was beginning to feel a little hysterical.

Don't worry old bean, said Wolfe, whose mood seemed to have improved drastically. *If the curr turns into me I shall know all his moves! We'll soon have the buggers head off his shoulders.*

But surely he'll know all your moves too! Wigbert thought.

Yes, but I'll have the advantage.

How so?

I've been me for longer!

Wigbert didn't feel much comfort. He might have a tactical fighting genius in his head, but he himself had never so much as scratched an enemies cheek with a blade. His father had tried, of course, when Wigbert had been a boy. Fencing lessons. Archery. Hunting. But they'd eventually both agreed it was a waste of everyone's time. Wigbert sucked in a deep breath of the damp air and held it.

And then the monster appeared.

It roved into view heading their way, head and shoulders far above the not-insignificant height of the garden wall. It sniffed the air greedily, huge golden-haired muzzle dripping with the rain. Acorns and roots, Wigbert thought, those teeth are the size of my arm.

Then it walked through the garden wall like it was a piece of wet paper.

The duke watched the stone topple miserably. A patch of winter brassicas disappeared under a paw the size of a wagon. His garden. His beautiful garden.

The beast spotted the burning potting shed and made for it

with all speed, bounding through the vegetation on all fours, flinging up loose soil, roots and entire plants as its gargantuan claws sank into the wet ground.

Wigbert let out a stifled moan of remorse.

The bear reached the shed and knocked aside what remained of the burning shell with one swipe of its massive golden paw. Burning debris was strewn across the disturbed soil, exposing the flaming crates of books inside. Without a second thought, the thing threw itself upon them. It buried its great muzzle into the fire, ripping open a crate with its mighty jaw, smouldering books cascading out. Then it began to eat, completely unconcerned by the heat of the fire. Flames licked its huge form with no effect. Smoke was sucked up into the monstrous nostrils, just to be blown back out in billowing jets.

'It's working!' Punduckslew muttered. 'How many does it have to eat, do you think?'

'How should I know?' Wigbert murmured back. 'Let's just hope Tanco and the good captain get back before its finished eating!'

The two men watched from their hiding place, moisture soaking into their knees, rain dripping from the branches above their heads, as the bear started on its second box. Then it's third. And fourth.

It's loving them, Wigbert thought.

Of course it is! Wolfe said. *That's quality literature that is. Very lifelike characters.*

Wigbert ignored him. Where was Tanco? He caught sight of a cluster of Castle Guards lurking by the fallen wall, keeping well back. But reinforcements were useless unless they found some way of tackling the beast. They were running out of time.

2.

The trees were restless here. They thrashed their branches in the pouring rain, reaching out towards the ruins, the swollen river Myzzle and the town beyond. Their roots bulged under the sodden earth so that it seemed to move and shift before Beatrice's eyes.

'Is this normal?' she asked, breath ragged in her throat.

She stood next to Oatey, the two of them huddled under Master Lettuce's coat, which he had insisted on removing and holding out above their heads when the group had stopped. The trees were thinner here towards the edge of the forest, so more rain penetrated the canopy. They'd approached the town from a different direction than the one she and Oatey had originally fled. They'd avoided the advancing trees that time, but now they found themselves right amongst them. Beatrice had never seen them act like this.

'Normal? My dear girl, if this was the speed with which the trees normally moved Upton-Myzzle would have been swallowed by the Blackwood decades ago,' Madame Reedswail announced with a frown. 'Something must have riled them.' Indeed, Beatrice could see that the hedgewitch was right. Even as she watched, the trees were pulling themselves forward towards the town. A particularly aggressive Black Oak was swelling in size by the second, its branches and roots moving it across the earth with shocking speed. In its path, little seedlings punched through the soft earth, reaching for the stormy sky above. The air was full of the groans of flexing wood.

'Where are the Watch?' Captain Snekchesser asked the group at large. 'Why is no one fighting back?'

He was right, Beatrice realised. The familiar thud of axes and buzz of saws was missing. The Watch had abandoned their posts. Beatrice couldn't remember a time that had ever happened before. She looked out to where Castle Blackwood crouched on the horizon, above the cluster of roofs and chimneys. Was her father there? Was he safe?

'How do we get through?' she asked, eager to be back on the move.

'Carefully,' Captain Snekchesser replied, looking tense. 'I don't think the trees will attack us directly, but we can't be sure. I've never seen them act like this.'

'It's the monster,' Gloamblight announced. 'They can sense it. It must have passed through this way.' The wizard was looking more alarming than ever. His pale brow glistened with more than just the rain and he almost seemed to vibrate with repressed energy, like he might explode at any minute. Beatrice could see the tendons straining in the man's neck again, and a thick trail of steam rose from his tethered hand.

'Should we really be bringing him into Upton-Myzzle?' Oatey whispered into her ear, obviously noticing what she had.

'According to the prophecy, it'll mean disaster if we don't!' she whispered back.

'But what if we're wrong about that?' Oatey looked worried. 'My family lives on this side of the river. What if I'm helping to bring the danger directly to them?'

Beatrice reached out and squeezed the boy's damp arm. 'We're right about this, Oatey. I know we are. We have to believe in everything we've seen. I think there's a reason we bumped into Gloamblight that first night in the forest. I think we were supposed to find him. To lead him here.'

'But we've been following him!'

'Well, yes...but, oh don't you feel it, Oatey? We're part of history. I'm sure of it!'

Further conversation was interrupted by Master Lettuce,

who bent his head down towards theirs and murmured, 'Whatever we're walking into, you two, I want you to promise me one thing; You see danger, you run in the opposite direction. The captain and I are here to protect you, but we can only do so much.'

'But—' Beatrice began, but the master shook his head, cutting her off.

'No 'buts' this time, my lady. This is serious. If all the prophecy and monster stuff is even remotely true…well, I would never forgive myself if I let something happen to the two of you. So promise me!'

Beatrice stared into the man's watery eyes, as serious as she had ever seen them.

'I promise,' she said reluctantly.

The master's thin lips formed a smile. 'Thank you.'

The patter of tiny paws announced the arrival of Boss and his men. The rats appeared out of the undergrowth one by one, several shimmying down the trunks of the more stationary trees.

'Sumthin's going on out there!' Boss announced, waving his tiny sword towards the river as he landed on the ground amongst them. 'Sumthin big.'

'Elaborate,' Captain Snekchesser barked, glaring out across the town as if he could just squint his eyes hard enough he might see into the future.

Boss twitched his long nose. 'Sumthin' *really* big.'

'Helpful,' the captain grunted.

'Look, if you want to scamper up a tree and look for yourself, then be my guest!' Boss said, unconcerned. 'We're rats, not eagles. Our eyes only see so far.'

The captain scowled but did not respond. A rumble drifted out across the river from the town beyond.

'It is time!'

The words came from Gloamblight, who sprung forward like a pouncing fox. He nipped between the waving branches of a beech and a hazel, dodging a slithering root that threatened to tangle his feet, jumping onto its exposed arch and launching himself from it further into the mass of moving limbs.

'Wait!' Snekchesser cried, too late. 'Acorns and roots, let's go. Everybody stay together!'

Needing no second bidding, Beatrice threw herself forward towards home.

3.

Tanco peered ahead into the gloom of the stone-walled passage. It was damp down here and his torch gutted and fluttered, making the shadows dance. He stubbed his toe on something and stumbled, almost dropping his crutch, cursing.

Captain Tritewine hurried to his aid. 'Are you sure you should be out of bed, sir?'

'No,' said Tanco, letting the woman help him to his feet. 'But there's more at stake than my convalescence.'

They pressed on, the sound of their footsteps echoing back at them. The air smelt of mushrooms.

'Exactly where do these tunnels lead?' the captain asked, shuddering as a drop of water fell from the low ceiling onto her exposed head.

'A back alley just off Seabass Street, I believe.' Tanco had never actually needed to explore this particular tunnel before. It was one of an entire system of subterranean walkways that radiated out from the castle like the warrens of a very confused colony of giant rabbits. They weren't so much secret, as forgotten. Tanco had always made a point of keeping track of the ones he could. This one was marked on several of the castle maps, going back a couple of hundred years. He just hoped it was still intact.

They hurried on. Or shuffled on, in Tanco's case, grimacing against the sore in his armpit already developing where it rested on his crutch.

'So, congratulations are in order, I suppose,' he said, as much to distract himself from the pain as anything else.

'Sorry?'

'Your promotion to captain.'

'Ah. Yes...thank you.'

'I'm sure you and Captain Snekchesser will have the rest of the Castle Guard whipped into shape in no time...with my help, of course.'

'Of course, sir. Thank you, sir.'

'Acorns and roots, call me Tanco, girl.'

'Yes, sir...er, I mean Tanco.'

Tanco grinned into the darkness. This was entirely too much fun. 'Tell me about this Lord Nugent. I've heard the name, of course. Something to do with you lot, wasn't he? The Institute, I mean, not the Castle Guard.'

'He was,' the woman said, sounding surprised. 'Not many people know that.'

'I've always enjoyed a bit of history,' he replied in way of explanation. 'In fact, it might interest you to know that Nugent's name comes up in the Castle records a number of times.'

'Really?' Tritewine said, sounding very interested indeed.

'Oh yes, he seems to have been involved in various projects for the duchy at one time or another. I'll have to show you the documents sometime.'

'I...I would like that very much.'

It was then that Tanco's torchlight hit something solid and wooden in their path. On closer inspection, it turned out to be a door. When Tanco pressed his ear to it, he could hear sounds of life on the other side.

With a look to Captain Tritewine to be ready, he grasped the metal handle, pressed his shoulder against the wood, and pushed. The door slid open with surprising ease and he half stepped, half fell out into a deserted alley. Rain was still falling and the sound of a fair bit of panic and excitement drifted into the alley from the main street just a few steps away. The captain followed him out and quickly shut the door to the passageway behind her.

'Right, let's find this machine of yours!'

4.

The giant bear had now eaten seven crates of books.

'How much longer, do you think?' Punduckslew hissed into the duke's ear. His breath smelt of stale tobacco.

'I've no idea. Funnily enough, I've never tried this before,' Wigbert whispered back. 'But if it doesn't change soon, we're buggered. That's the last crate of books.'

'Maybe it's not going to work?'

It has to work, Wigbert thought. Because if it doesn't, I don't know what to do.

We could always charge the bally thing, Wolfe offered. *Take it by surprise while its back is turned. Not very sporting, but then it has eaten people, so I suppose the gloves have rather come off!*

Is that the best you can offer? Just rush blindly at it and hope for the best? I thought you were supposed to be a tactical genius, Wigbert thought bitterly.

I'm what you made me! Wolfe shot back. *If you think that's lacking, then maybe you need to take a long hard look at yourself, boyo.*

Wigbert stifled a sigh. Look, can we not, ok? He thought.

'You're muttering to yourself again,' Punduckslew whispered, poking the duke in the side with a muddy finger.

'Wolfe thinks we should rush the monster,' Wigbert explained.

The wizard scratched his sopping beard. 'Well, I hate to agree with a figment of another man's imagination, but he might be right. If we've got this wrong, and nothing's going to happen, then attacking now might be the best chance we have.'

Wigbert didn't reply. There had to be another option!

A movement over by the collapsed wall caught his attention and, with great relief, he saw Tanco had reappeared and was silently waving a crutch at them.

He waved back. 'Thank Melethin, they're back.'

'Yes, but what with?' Punduckslew asked.

It was a good question. Tritewine appeared to be fiddling with something on the ground, but from this distance, Wigbert couldn't make out what. When the captain stood up, she appeared to be holding some sort of long wooden stick with brass globular nobs all along its length.

'What the devil is that?' Punduckslew hissed. 'It looks like a fancy walking stick.'

Wigbert squinted. He could just make out what looked like a metal box or chest, which he thought he remembered last seeing in the institute's attic. It had a long brass handle coming out of the top, a bit like the handle of a garden fork, and strands of wire or rope connected it to the stick the captain was holding.

The two men watched as Tritewine handed the stick, carefully like it might explode at any moment, to Tanco, who took it hurriedly and said something they couldn't hear to the captain. She replied, and he shot her a confused look. Then Tritewine mimed something, bending down at the knees and quickly rising again, like she was pressing something down into the earth repeatedly.

'What by Melethin's craggy trunk are they playing at over there?' Punduckslew hissed.

The duke's attention was drawn back to the golden bear, who seemed to have finished the final crate of books and was now using its monstrous paws to sift through the potting shed's remains for anything it had missed.

Then, finally, it happened.

A juddering convulsion swept through the beast. It threw back its mighty jaw and howled, and then the change gripped it. It shrank in size, receding towards the ground as its shape withered and shook.

Wigbert's heart leapt. It was working!

The bear's powerful muzzle melted back into its skull to become a nose. Paws lengthened and thinned to become hands. The bulk of the creature receded.

Now! Wolfe cried. *Hit it now, while it's still changing!*

Wigbert didn't need to be told twice.

'Do it!' he cried over to the group by the wall as he leapt out from behind the tree. 'Hit it now!'

Tanco, wobbling only slightly, sprang forward, crutches forgotten, with the brass gilded stick in his hands. 'Pump!' he bellowed over his shoulder, and Captain Tritewine obeyed. She grabbed the strange brass handle sticking out of the box on the floor and pushed it down with all her might. The shaft disappeared into the box with a strange rumbling, fizzing sound, and soon the captain was rising to her feet to repeat the process once more. Up, down, up, down, up, down. She bobbed back and forth with increasing speed, and all the while a whizzing, crackling sound built in the strange contraption at her feet.

It drew the attention of the creature, who noticed them at last. With a mouth half full of bear teeth and half full of human, it screamed at them in fury. Wigbert felt the sound loosen his bowels, and he raced towards Tanco and the others, determined to intercept the monster before it reached them.

'Get back!' Tanco shouted, waving him away urgently. The stick in his hand was vibrating now, and he was struggling to hold it.

Wigbert hesitated, then was knocked, sprawling into the mud as Punduckslew came barreling into him from behind.

The creature, now a nightmarish mix of animal and human, held together by something unspeakable, was pulling itself towards them, its limbs kicking and flailing as they tried to decide what shape to be. Tanco aimed the stick as best he could and pressed a button on the shaft with an audible click.

Nothing happened.

'Shit!' Tanco said. 'I think—'

But before he could finish the sentence, the beast shot out a hideously elongated arm and he was knocked to the side; the weapon skittering harmlessly into a patch of Wigbert's special dandelions, which shook tiny, leafy fists at him in silent rage.

'No!' Wigbert shouted, struggling to his feet from under the wizard's considerable bulk. Captain Tritewine faltered in her pumping. Wigbert hurried toward his fallen steward, but the man was already sitting up.

'Don't stop!' Tanco cried to the captain, who resumed her pumping immediately. The stick began to shake and bounce on the ground, now emitting a high-pitched whine that hit Wigbert right between the ears.

'The stick! Pick up the stick!' Tanco yelled, gesticulating wildly from his seated position. Wigbert changed course, skidding on the wet ground, and headed for the bucking object. Clumsily, he grabbed at the thing but missed. It leapt up into his face with a painful crunch before his flailing hands eventually found purchase on the slick wood. It was like trying to hold on to an angry snake. Or so he imagined, not being in the habit of doing any such thing. The noise was getting louder. The monster bore down on Wigbert with a bellow of rage louder than all that had come before.

'The button! Press the button!' Tanco screamed.

Wigbert battled with the stick until it was vaguely facing the monster, who was now mere inches away. Its face was now human. And horribly familiar.

By Melethin, is my nose really *that big?* said Wolfe.

Then Wigbert pressed the button.

Power surged through the strange contraption and Wigbert felt his grip tighten involuntarily. Something brilliant white and searing with heat erupted from the end of the stick, arcing through the air in a jagged stream and burying itself in the monster. Every cell in Wigberts' body felt like it was vibrating. Dark shadows crept around the edges of his eyes.

Lightning, he thought. The damn thing's actually conjured lightning.

The monster thrashed and screamed, then seemed to bunch up on itself into a ball, before bursting forth at the duke in a flood of darkness that enveloped him.

5.

Ormus Stonemorton was helping Gerald limp towards the shattered gatehouse gates when he saw the brilliant white flash.

'Acorn's and roots, what now?' he said, shifting his friend's weight with a grunt. Everything hurt. Everything. He was pretty sure the only thing keeping him upright was adrenaline. He didn't want to think about it wearing off. Getting back to the castle had taken so long they'd completely lost track of where the monster had got to, but the state of the gatehouse rather answered that question. He had dragged them directly back into its path.

'Looked like a lightning strike,' Gerald muttered. He was in a bad way, blood seeping from a nasty gash across his forehead.

Ormus looked up at the black clouds suspiciously, rain hammering his face. 'Didn't hear any thunder though.'

A bent figure was hobbling down from the gatehouse to meet them. Ormus squinted through the rain. It was the bibliothecary, Mr Bombroffe.

'Your grace—' the old man began, then faltered when he got close enough to see the state they were in. 'My word, are you alright?'

'Peachy,' Ormus growled. 'What's going on?'

'It's the monster, your grace.'

'I can see that you old fool, mostly because of the monster-sized hole in my gates! How did it get in? The Guard—'

'Oh, the Guard were stood down, your grace. Sir Corbett and Sir Bashford are inside. Are you sure I can't get someone to—'

'What?' Ormus roared, making Gerald flinch and hold his head. 'On whose orders? What lily-livered idiot let—'

'Your son, the duke, your grace,' Mr Bombroffe interrupted in turn. 'It's a trap, I believe. In the walled garden.'

Ormus mouthed soundlessly at the Bibliothecary for a moment. 'What's he planning on doing? Digging a big pit and hoping it falls in?' he said at last.

'No, I don't believe so, your grace.'

Ormus ran a bloodied hand across his dirty face. 'By Melethin's craggy trunk, will this day never end?'

Gerald was looking over his shoulder, back down the hill towards the town. 'Someone's coming,' he said.

Ormus turned to look. There was indeed a ragtag-looking group hurrying in their direction.

The bibliothecary rubbed a sleeve across his rain-splattered glasses. 'Is…is that man *steaming*?' he asked.

But Ormus's attention was taken up by the pack of what appeared to be giant rats.

'What now?' he sighed.

6.

Wigbert opened his eyes to see an impossibly handsome face staring down at him. It had the sort of jaw you could cut steel with and thick brown hair that fell across its smooth forehead in ridiculously perfect curls. It was a face he had only ever seen in his imagination. He cursed, flinching away, but the figure held out its arms and said, 'It's alright, old fruit, it's me. The real me, mind.'

Wigbert stared. Before him stood Wolfe Starlingcloud. Just as he had always imagined him, right down to the waxed mustache and bulging biceps. He was wearing some kind of improbable leather britches with every sign of complete comfort and looking down at the duke with some concern.

'What's happening?' Wigbert said, struggling to his feet.

'Bally good question, old boy,' said Wolfe, straightening up.

'How are you here?' Wigbert tried again.

His creation scratched his smoothly shaven chin. 'I've always been here,' he said. 'The question is; What are *you* doing here?'

Wigbert gave him a perplexed look. Then looked about himself for the first time. All was in darkness. Complete black. He could see nothing but Wolfe and himself. 'Where…' he began.

'We're inside your head, old bean,' Wolfe said with a shrug. 'Don't ask me how. You just sort of appeared. Gave me the willies, to be honest.'

Wigbert gave this due consideration. 'It's a bit empty, isn't it?'

'No comment.'

The duke screwed up his eyes and stared at the back of his eyelids. There was little discernible difference. 'But...how can I be standing in my own head?' he asked.

Wolfe grinned a dazzling grin and shrugged, making an impressive collection of muscles move beneath his shirt. 'Buggered if I know. Some sort of magic, I reckon. Don't bother with the stuff myself. I find a blade is more direct.' He unsheathed a rapier thin sword hanging from his belt and danced it through the empty air. Wigbert watched him, mesmerized. It was just like he'd always imagined it. The man moved with a fluidness someone of his size had no business possessing. He was like a cat, only one of those big ones, the wild ones that sometimes came out of the Blackwood. The type that hunted cattle.

A roar of rage rang out from the darkness.

'Oh, and I think that monsters here too,' Wolfe said, performing an expert parry in mid-air.

'*What*? You didn't think to mention that first?' Wigbert spluttered.

'Would it have made a difference?' Wolfe said calmly, not missing a beat of his maneuvers.

'Would you stop that?' Wigbert snapped.

His creation ignored him, continuing to leap and prance, the tip of his blade swishing through the empty space like an angry wasp. 'Not much else to do in here, old chap. Till now, of course. By Melethin I've been dying for a good fight! I'll cut that beastie down to size, just you watch, Wiggy old chap.'

'You can't have a fight in here!' Wigbert said.

'Why not?'

'It's my brain!' he spluttered. 'You...you might damage something,' he finished lamely.

Another roar echoed out of the darkness. It seemed closer this time, although it was hard to tell.

'You might have to explain that to the monster,' Wolfe said, pirouetting.

Wigbert looked over his shoulder into the inky blackness. 'Did it do this, do you think?'

Wolfe finally ceased his acrobatics and came to stand by the duke's side. He wasn't even out of breath. 'Could be,' he said. 'Or it could have been that lightning stick thingy. That was marvelous, by the way. Bloody good show!'

Something else occurred to Wigbert. 'How did you see that?' he asked. 'Physically, I mean. It's all black here now.'

Wolfe put his head on one side. 'Never really thought about it,' he admitted. 'Can't see anything now, though. Maybe that's because you're in here.'

Wigbert groaned. 'This place makes no sense at all.

'Don't look at me,' Wolfe said cheerfully. 'I just live here.'

Maybe I'm unconscious, Wigbert thought. Maybe this is just a dream. Or maybe I'm dead.

Wolfe continued to beam at him and Wigbert realised something. 'You didn't hear that, did you?'

'Hear what, sport?'

'My thoughts! You can't hear my thoughts anymore!'

The man appeared to consider this. 'Well,' he said after some time. 'I don't know about that, Wiggy old boy. If we're both in your head, then surely all of this is your thoughts.'

'But…but, then how can I still be having more thoughts? Separate thoughts you can't hear? Is it my subconscious? Or like second thoughts?' Wigbert asked, wringing his hands.

Wolfe clapped him on the shoulder, almost sending him sprawling. 'Best not to think too hard about it, old bean. Believe me.'

As he said it, a shape loomed out of the darkness.

It was human-shaped.

In fact, it was Wolfe shaped.

The monster's mouth opened, and it was Wolfe's voice that spoke.

'Only one!'

The real Wolfe, if such a thing existed at all, regarded it with disgust. 'Bally unsettling, that!' he exclaimed. 'Take my face off, you filthy knave!'

The creature hissed. 'Only one!' it repeated, advancing towards Wolfe.

'I think it wants to kill you,' offered Wigbert.

Wolfe redrew his sword with a smile. 'I'd like to see it bally try.'

'Can't kill a figment,' the quasi-Wolfe hissed and began circling them like a predator, looking for an opening.

'What's it mean by that?' Wolfe said, looking uneasy for the first time.

'You're asking me?'

'This is your head, old boy!'

'Well, I didn't invite it in!'

'Did!' the monster hissed. 'Gave me food. Gave me form. Form from your head. Now I make solid. Solid so I can *kill*. Only one! ONE!'

The creature leapt and Wigbert passed out for the second time.

7.

Tanco Dribbets was not a man given to fits of hysteria. He considered them luxuries of the under prepared. There was little he was not prepared to face armed with a good, solid clipboard and a freshly cut quill. That and his tokens of course. The wooden trinkets that hung from his frame in their dozens were all the protection he needed from the more supernatural elements of life in the Duchy of Blackwood. That's probably why he screamed and grabbed at them with such force when the lightning machine went off, the monster leapt at the duke, and then appeared to disappear inside him. Several cords gave way under his frantic administrations, and the severed amulets fell to the ground, forgotten as the Castle Blackwood steward struggled to his feet and limped over to where Wigbert lay, unmoving.

'What happened?' cried Captain Tritewine, running up behind him. 'Where did it go?'

'Wigbert?' Tanco shook the duke's shoulders urgently. 'Wigbert, my boy?' Nothing happened. The duke lay pale and unresponsive.

A shadow fell across them. Tanco looked up to see Punduckslew, his face furious.

'What was that?' the wizard demanded. 'By Melethin's craggy trunk, what have you done to him?'

'Me?' said Tanco, shocked.

'If you've bloody killed him, I'll...' Punduckslew said, elbowing Tanco out of the way and leaving the threat unfinished.

'You'll what?' Tanco said, squaring up to the man, hands shaking. 'You think Wigbert Stonemorton means more to you than he does to me? I practically raised the boy!'

The wizard glowered back at him. 'It's my duty to protect him!'

'And he means more to Upton-Myzzle than to either of you stupid old men!' Captain Tritewine said angrily, bending down to the duke's prostrate form and feeling for a pulse in his neck. 'So stop arguing and bloody bring him back!'

The wizard and the steward looked suitably chastised.

'Is he ok?' Tanco asked, still clutching at the talismans around his neck.

'There's a pulse, but it's weak,' the captain confirmed.

'What exactly happened? The machine it—' Tanco began.

'Didn't do this,' Tritewine said. 'I'm sure of it.'

'How can you possibly know that?' Punduckslew said, his face red. 'That wasn't magic. That was…something else.'

'That was natural philosophy,' Tritewine said with a hint of smugness. 'Electrostatic generation. But I don't believe that is what caused the duke harm. There are no burns on him. No physical signs of injury. We all saw what happened, the monster it…it went inside him!'

'Well, how do we bloody get it out?'

'Surely that's your department, wizard?' she said.

'Unless you want me to blow him up, there's nothing I can do about it. That's not how—'

'Not how magic works. You've said.'

'Wait! Something's happening!' Tanco said, jumping back from the duke's body, which began to twitch and convulse.

What happened next would keep Tanco awake at night for years to come. The duke's mouth opened, and from it issued forth something extremely large and solid. Too large. At great speed. It knocked the steward off his feet once more and landed on top of him. It was person-shaped.

'*Get it off! Get it off!*' Tanco cried, pushing the heavy lump away. It groaned. Tanco looked up to see a second high-velocity object vomit forth from the duke's mouth, sliding across the ruined garden and landing in a swarming, pulsating black mass at the foot of the apple tree.

The figure who had landed on Tanco opened its eyes and sat up.

'Terribly sorry, old chap. I hope I didn't break anything,' it said.

8.

And then Wigbert opened his eyes. He was back in the garden. It was still raining. He lay on the sodden ground, shivering uncontrollably.

'Whazerfigz?' he said.

'Melethin's craggy trunk! Are you alright, your grace?' Punduckslew leant over him, momentarily blocking out the persistent rain. The wizard's eyebrows were so far up his forehead they were threatening to creep around the back of his head.

'What happened?' Wigbert managed, sitting up and smacking his lips. His mouth tasted like he'd been eating compost.

'We were rather hoping you could help us there,' Punduckslew said.

The duke got unsteadily to his feet, still shivering. He felt, if it were possible, even more drenched than he had before. Muddy water ran in a steady stream from his ruined coat. The white of his hose has long since turned muddy brown. Above him, thunder rolled. He looked around. His eyes were drawn immediately to a figure in leather britches and a dazzlingly white linen shirt, undone to halfway down the chest.

'Oh shit,' Wigbert said.

'Wotcha, Wiggy old boy!' said Wolfe, giving him a cheery wave. 'This is a turn-up for the books, aye?'

Wigbert just stared. The man standing in front of him, the very real, solid-looking man, was Wolfe Starlingcloud. Every detail was right, from the perfect teeth to the broad chest and impossibly styled hair. While everyone else looked muddy and sodden, he looked merely slightly damp. The water beaded off him like a duck's feathers. He seemed too bright, somehow, for the real world. Too perfect. Everyone was staring at him. Wigbert too. It was somehow hard to look away, and yet it hurt a little, like staring directly at the sun. Wigbert watched as his creation beamed back at the stunned faces.

'Brilliant!' Wolfe said, stamping his leather boots up and down in the mud with every sign of enjoyment. 'Bloody brilliant!' He turned to Tanco, who was standing next to him, gaping. 'I say, Tanco old fruit. Is it always this wet?'

'W...what?' Tanco said.

'Not that I'm complaining!' Wolfe continued with a huge grin. 'It's bloody good to be here, whatever the weather! I'm famished. What time's lunch?'

'Who...?' Tanco managed, finally tearing his round eyes away from the apparition in front of him and shooting Wigbert a questioning look.

'Um...everybody, may I introduce Mr Wolfe Starlingcloud,' Wigbert muttered. What else could he say? Little point in denying it at this stage.

'*The* Wolfe Starlingcloud?' Tanco said weakly.

'Err, yes'

'But that, um, not wanting to be rude, sir, but that's impossible,' Tanco said, turning and addressing Wolfe himself, who laughed and slapped the man heartily on the back, making him stumble.

'Impossible's my middle name!' he said, flashing more white teeth.

'Is it?' said Tanco desperately.

Wolfe looked momentarily confused. 'Actually, I'm not sure. Wiggy old boy, do I have a middle name?'

Wigbert shook his head dumbly.

'Ah, well, there you are then. May as well make it official. I'm Wolfe Impossible Starlingcloud. A pleasure to meet you in person!' He grabbed Tanco's unresisting hand and shook it with such vigor the man winced. 'Whoops. Sorry old chap. Forgot about the bounce on the bonce. Nasty business. Glad to see you up and about!'

'Th...thank you,' Tanco said weakly.

Frowning, Punduckslew took a step towards the beaming Wolfe and raised a hand uncertainly. 'Er...should I blow it up?' he asked the duke.

'Now, now, no need for violence, my fine friend!' Wolfe said cheerfully, before Wigbert could respond. 'Besides,' and at this point, he moved through the space between himself and the astonished wizard in less than the blink of an eye. He wrapped his arm around Punduckslew's shoulders and patted him on the stomach. 'I'd have you skewered like a suckling pig before the magic left your finger. Not that I would ever do such a thing to the great Punduckslew! Impressive beard, by the way. I've always thought so.'

Punduckslew had frozen. His eyes followed Wolfe's hand in horrid fascination as it continued to pat his round belly.

'It's ok. He's on our side,' Wigbert said at last, desperately hoping it was true. He turned to find Captain Tritewine at his side. The woman lay a hand gently on his shoulder.

'Are you ok?' she asked, looking at Wigbert with deep concern.

Wigbert gave her the best smile he could manage. 'I seem to be in one piece,' he said. Then his eyes were drawn back to Wolfe, who had now left Punduckslew's side and was shadowboxing good-naturedly with one of the dumbfounded guards. 'Or possibly two,' he finished.

A wet, squelching sound drew all eyes to the base of the apple tree. The monster, momentarily forgotten at Wolfe's dramatic appearance, was a roiling pile of black muck. It formed and reformed, one minute one shape, the next another. As they watched, it slowly took the form of a man, striding towards them on unsteady legs.

'Only one!' it hissed from a face that solidified back into a mirror image of Wolfe's.

The real Wolfe grinned wickedly. 'Ah, woken up at last, have you, you blaggard? Let's finish this!'

'Finisssssssssssh!' the thing hissed, an arm appearing from out of the mess, already complete with the twin of Wolfe's rapier thin sword. Wolfe drew his own in one fluid motion and sprang at the advancing beast. It surged forward to meet him and the clash of steel rang out like a bell.

Afterwards, it was hard for those who witnessed the fight to say who had moved quicker; Wolfe Starlingcloud or his doppelgänger. Both flew through the air with seemingly impossible speed. Their blades cut silver arcs through the pouring rain, which almost seemed to linger in the air, their creators already having moved on, dancing around each other and across the upturned ground, never staying motionless for a second. Wigbert tried to follow them, but his eyes were blurred from the rain and their incredible speed made his head spin.

'This is futile!' Punduckslew cried out to him over the sound of the two blades clashing against each other yet again. 'He won't kill that thing with a sword. I blew its bloody head off and it just grew a new one!'

Wigbert feared he was right, for although Wolfe continued to fight with apparently unending enthusiasm and stamina, something was happening to the beast he confronted. His mirror image was growing, swelling out and up, slowly becoming twice his size, then three times. Now when it struck, the force of the blow sent the real Wolfe reeling, scrabbling in the dirt to regain his footing.

'He's going to get himself killed!' Wigbert said.

'Is he? Asked Tanco. '*Can* he? I don't understand what magic is going on here, but Wolfe Starlingcloud is no more human than that thing he's fighting. How can he be?'

'Let's not wait to find out. We have to find a way to help him!' said Tritewine.

'How?' said Punduckslew. 'I don't know about you, but I don't think my swordplay is quite up to par. I could try using magic, but I'd be just as likely to hit Wolfe as...well the other Wolfe.'

'There has to be something we can do!' Wigbert cried, as a powerful sword thrust from the monster sent Wolfe skidding across the ground several feet. It bellowed in rage and leapt after its prey, coming down with a crash exactly on the patch of earth where Wolfe had been a second before. But he was now several feet away, breathing hard, but otherwise unharmed.

'FATHER!'

The shout came from behind them and Wigbert turned with his heart in his throat to see his daughter standing in the rubble. '*Beatrice!*' Relief flooded through his body at the sight of her, instantly turning to icy dread. 'No!' he screamed. 'You can't be here!'

9.

Beatrice ignored her father, watching as the two figures in the ruined garden clashed again. The smaller man was thrown backwards this time, landing on his back with a sickening jolt. The larger of the otherwise identical pair tilted back its oversized head and bellowed into the dark sky.

'Is…is that it, do you think? The monster?'

'It had better be,' Oatey said at her side. 'I think Gloamblight's about to lose it!'

Beatrice could see the boy was right. Gloamblight looked paler than ever and was panting heavily. A mess of tendons and veins stood out on the right side of his neck and his whole body was shaking and contorting as his arm fought to be free of its binding. He fumbled desperately with the buckles.

'Oh no you don't!' Captain Snekchesser said, advancing on the wizard. 'We don't know what's going on yet. I won't let you unleash whatever crazy—' He lay a restraining arm on the wizard and was immediately sent spinning through the air in a searing flash of green light.

'Captain!' Beatrice screamed, running to the fallen man's side. He was dazed but alive, the palm of his hand badly burnt.

'Get away, all of you!' Gloamblight cried. 'This is happening. *Now!*' A violent spasm ran through his frame and he cried out in pain as his arm finally tore free, snapping the three belts like blades of grass. A brass buckle shot through the air and buried itself into the ground inches from her father's feet, and he jumped back with a curse. The flask around Gloamblight's hand had been wrenched free from his thigh and now exploded in a spray of foul-smelling liquid.

'GET AWAY!' Gloamblight bellowed again, then screamed as his hand blossomed into flames of green, the flames rapidly chasing up his arm.

'Green flame!' Madame Reedswail cried. 'Green flame! The prophecies are true. He is the one!'

'Beatrice, what is happening?' her father shouted.

'Everyone, do as he says!' Beatrice shouted as she helped the captain to his feet. 'Get back! Father, you have to get everyone clear!'

'Do it! Snekchesser cried. 'Get as far away as possible. *Run you idiots!*'

The spell broke, and the crowd scattered. Master Lettuce grabbed Oatey and cleared the fallen wall in a single bound. The rats scattered like cockroaches. With Madame Reedswail's help, Beatrice heaved the still stunned and stumbling captain away as fast as her legs would carry her. She looked back over her shoulder just in time to see Gloamblight yanked forward by the power in his arm, feet dragging uselessly through the rubble as it pulled him onwards towards its target. Her father stumbled backwards out of his path and fell. She swore, uncoupling herself from the captain, then turned and dashed back towards the fallen garden wall.

'Stop!' she heard Snekchesser cry, but she raced on towards her fallen father and the battle that was still going on between the two identical men. By the time she reached her father's side, Mr Dribbets was already there, looking pale and wearing a large swathe of bandages around his round head. She had no time to question this, however, because just a few steps away, Punduckslew was raising a pointed finger at the still advancing Gloamblight and squinting his aim.

'*Uncle Ducky, no!*' she screamed, and the man faltered, turning to them in surprise.

'Beatrice, what's happening?' she felt her fathers's desperate hands close around her shoulders and forced herself to look into his eyes.

'He mustn't, father. Gloamblight is the only one who can destroy the monster!'

She saw the confusion on her father's face. She held her breath for the eternity it seemed to take before that confusion turned to decision.

'Stand down, Punduckslew!' he bellowed, struggling back to his feet. 'Everyone, do as Beatrice says. Get as far away as you can. Wolfe! Wolfe, if you can hear me, get away!'

Without stopping to question who Wolfe was, Beatrice tugged at her father's arm, pulling him away from the figure of Gloamblight, whose entire arm was now ablaze with the strange green flame.

Beatrice started as a man appeared at her side as if he'd fallen out of the sky. It was the smaller of the two combatants. Up close, there was something vaguely familiar about him. He winked at her and before Beatrice could so much as react, had scooped her up into his well-muscled arms.

'Off we go, Bea old girl!' he said with a blinding grin, then shot them forward with the speed of a fox. It was all Beatrice could do to hold on. She looked back over the man's shoulder to see her father and the others fleeing in their wake. Behind them was the now glowing figure of Gloamblight and the monster, which screamed in rage, a sound like no other Beatrice had ever heard. It rent the rain-filled sky like a thunderclap as the beast leapt at its opponent. A stream of green fire shot forth from Gloamblight's burning hand, hitting the creature in mid air. There was a flash so bright Beatrice had to close her eyes tight, then felt herself falling to the ground as a shockwave of hot air blew past, knocking the man who held her from his feet.

10.

The destruction of the Beast from the Blackwood, as it would later become known, was seen as a blinding flash of green light by those gathered, staring open-mouthed, on the castle's battlements. Among them were Ormus Stonemorton, Mr Bombroffe the bibliothecary, Gerald, Quimby and Terrance. The latter had been heaved up the stone steps in his wicker chair with not inconsiderable effort and was in fact not staring with his mouth open, but humming amiably to himself and looking at nothing in particular at all.

'Balderdash,' he said softly and chuckled.

The beast's destruction was heard, if not seen, by the squabbling members of the Lords Chambers, who stopped their arguing just long enough to hear the sound reverberate around the ancient joists of that most venerable institution. Sir Sweetspire heard it from where he stood, alone, on the Toad's Tongue. He glowered at the ceiling for a moment before calling for order.

The noise was also heard by Ged, and indeed by Gladdis, as she pulled the night soil man's wagon through the ruins of Seabass Street. The gwalmok swished her curly tail just once and farted. A noise like that of a bugle someone had sat on. Ged, sitting directly behind the expulsion of fetid-smelling air, barely noticed it. 'Nothing to worry about, huh?' he said, and the wagon rumbled on.

Finally, the sound was heard by the many Upton-Myzzle townspeople who had fled to the opposite side of the Myzzle. Trapped between the threat of the beast and the restless

Blackwood behind, they stood, shivering in the pouring rain, on the banks of the raging river, waiting for a sign it might be safe to return. They remarked afterwards how very strange it had been that, just as the thunderclap of the beast's destruction rang out, the river finally burst its banks.

CHAPTER FIFTEEN: CLEAR SKIES

1.

When the next dawn broke over Upton-Myzzle it did so in a clear sky. Light the colour of weak ale fell on the beleaguered town, picking out the shells of ruined buildings, shining off the mirrored surface of a network of rivers and streams that had once been streets. The Myzzle was a wide brown streak through the landscape. Castle Blackwood stood proud of the floodwaters, solid and dark on its little hill. A toad at the water's edge. The town's populace squirmed like tadpoles through the flooded streets, some wading, holding goods and rescued belongings above their heads, others punting through the new waterways in a myriad of improvised watercraft. People shouted jolly greetings to each other.

'Wet enough for you, Bill?'
'Nothing like a bit of drizzle!'
'This is a turn up for the books!'
'Worse than the great flood of fifty-six!'
'It never is!'
'Your Madge and the kids alright?'
'Nothing a good airing can't fix!'

This is called Community Spirit and is a temporary side effect of any widely shared disaster. It will ebb with the waters, disappearing by the time the Myzzle has regained its regular flow.

But for now, the people smiled and waved. They laughed, safe in the knowledge that, for now, danger had passed them by. Relief brought on a public spirit not seen for a generation.

Neighbours who had never spoken a word before chatted amiably over fences. Bitter rivals called a truce for the day. Those occupants of houses that had been destroyed or affected worst by the subsequent flooding found themselves accepting offers of blankets, food and other such useful items, from people who would happily have watched them starve just a few days before. In the castle's great hall, the duke sat in front of a bowl of cold porridge. In his hands was the morning edition of the Upton-Myzzle Gazette. He cleared his throat and read the news sheet aloud.

Grizzly attack on Upton-Myzzle!

Fifty-foot bear defeated by Wolfe Starlingcloud! The author's true identity revealed!

A fearsome beast of gigantic proportions wreaked havoc in Upton-Myzzle yesterday, flattening several buildings, killing twelve and injuring many others. The creature, thought to have emerged from the Blackwood in the last few days, took several forms during its rampage, including that of the so-called Lord of Misrule killer who has been stalking our streets unchecked since Longest Night. It is thought the monster was responsible for the supposed death of prime Lord of Misrule suspect, Toflo Higginbottom, as reported by the Gazette just yesterday.

The recent unrest in the town, caused by the destruction of The Church of the First Tree on Tuesday afternoon, came to a head yesterday when hundreds attended an illegal book burning in Seabass Street. The monster, its exact origins unknown, is thought to have been attracted by the vast crowds and attacked those gathered, spreading panic and chaos despite the duke's ineffectual appeals for calm. It then stunned onlookers by transforming into a fifty-foot bear and proceeded to destroy many of the shops and businesses already suffering from a fall in profits due to the stalled Longest Night celebrations.

But the biggest shock was yet to come for the terrified crowds. The monster turned its destructive attention to Castle Blackwood itself, only to be destroyed in a spectacular confrontation by none other than the swashbuckling adventurer Wolfe Starlingcloud. Wolfe, made famous by the bestselling book by Sir Rumbould Theaksteak, was thought by many to be simply a work of fiction. But he revealed his existence in true spectacular form as he fought the monster with his bare hands during their epic confrontation within the castle grounds. Questions now abound about this dashing hero's rise to fame and the exact nature of his relationship with author Theaksteak.

But the surprises didn't stop there! In a shocking revelation, the Gazette can exclusively report that Theaksteak was revealed yesterday to be a pen name for none other than Wigbert Stonemorton, the Duke of Blackwood himself! The Gazette has reached out to the castle for comment, and we will keep you all updated on this exciting story as it develops.

In related news, serious questions are now being asked about the Lords Chambers-backed City Watch and its leader Watch Commander Posternos, who has not been seen since the disturbance in Seabass Street yesterday afternoon...'

Wigbert stopped reading and looked up at Tanco, who was sitting across from him at the great hall table, sipping a cup of spice and prodding his head bandages gingerly.

'Well, the cat's out of the bag now and no mistake. At least they got some of the details almost right, I suppose,' he said.

Tanco nodded, then winced. 'Indeed, your grace. And actually, early reports seem rather more positive than we'd feared. I took the liberty of increasing the guard at the gate until we can see to the repairs. I hope you don't mind, and they've already had to turn several excited fans away.'

'You're kidding?'

'Not at all, your grace. In fact, the news seems to have rather increased your popularity. It hasn't hurt that The Gazette is citing our new friend Wolfe as the one who defeated the monster. It seems his popularity is rubbing off on you by association. There has been another surge of preorders for your second book. Quite a considerable one.'

'But we haven't got any books left!'

'Oh, don't worry too much about that. I'm going to go into town and have a word in the ear of our friendly printers this afternoon. With these numbers and publicity, I feel sure we'll be able to come to some arrangement. I might even take Wolfe with me!'

Wigbert frowned. The freshly minted Mr Starlingcloud was currently practicing his swordplay in the outer ward. He'd been drawing quite a crowd when Wigbert had left him. The man was already more popular with the servants than he was. He couldn't help feeling slightly uncomfortable about the whole thing. Not that word seemed to have got out about exactly where Wolfe had come from, thank Melethin. But it was a strange feeling, having the voice in your head suddenly be walking about, flirting with the servants and flashing his perfect grin around like it was a dentist's convention. And Wigbert still didn't understand exactly what Wolfe was. Human? Some sort of magical apparition? He'd had both Punduckslew and Captain Tritewine examine the man, but it hadn't been much help. The wizard had simply prodded him with a stubby finger and announced he seemed human enough. Ambrosia had been a bit more precise about it, but had basically reached the same conclusion. Wolfe graciously agreed to stick around until they could figure it out. Not that he exactly had anywhere to go.

'There is the Sir Sweetspire matter to discuss, your grace,' Tanco said.

Wigbert grimaced. 'Yes, I imagine there is. I suppose he got his vote to go through?'

'Actually, no. It seems once word of the monster truly got out yesterday many of the lords and ladies…how to put it politely? Well, they ran, your grace.'

'Ran?'

'Yes. Many of them have estates out in the farmlands, of course. It seems they all suddenly remembered pressing engagements that would see them out of the city with as much speed as their gwalmok could muster.'

'So where does that leave us?'

'Well, technically, there is nothing to stop Sir Sweetspire from tabling his vote of no confidence again, but I rather suspect he won't,' Tanco said with a small smile.

'Why ever not? He's closer than his family has been to stealing power for decades.'

'Yes, but he still needs public opinion to be on his side.'

'And it's not?'

'Not so much. Right now one thing is ringing out loud and clear in the mind of Upton-Myzzle. Whilst the Lords Chambers fled, and the Watch collapsed, it was yourself who helped to defeat the monster—with Mr Starlingcloud's help, of course—and it's the Castle Guard who's been helping with the cleanup. Congratulations, your grace. You're more popular right now than you've ever been.'

Wigbert shook his head. It was baffling. If the people knew what had really happened, he doubted they'd be so calm. The hard truth was, he had no clear idea how exactly the monster had been defeated. Beatrice had tried to explain it all to him, but, frankly, it all rather sounded like a lot of gibberish. Prophecy…He wasn't sure he believed in prophecy.

'Is Beatrice up yet?' he asked.

'I believe she is in the infirmary, your grace.'

'I see.'

They had put the strange wizard Gloamblight in the infirmary. They hadn't been sure what else to do with him.

'Your father is still abed, I believe. I'm sure he would appreciate a visit before you go,' Tanco said, not meeting the duke's eyes.

'Are you?' Wigbert said before he could stop himself. 'Acorns and roots, he must be in a bad way! I don't think I can remember a day where he didn't rise with the dawn. I suppose I'll check in on him, too.'

Truthfully, he wasn't at all sure what sort of reception he'd receive.

2.

The duke-no-more was indeed in a bad way. Even he had to admit that. Ormus lay in his bed, bolstered by about a dozen pillows and staring sullenly out at the blue sky, visible through the window on the far wall of his chambers. Everything hurt. Everything hurt, and he was exhausted. He didn't think he'd ever felt so tired in his life.

You're a silly, stubborn old man, Ormus Stonemorton, he said to himself. He'd refused to stop. To listen. He'd kept going because he was terrified of what would happen if he didn't. But then a giant monster had attacked his town. It had attacked and there had been absolutely nothing he could do about it. He hadn't known what to do. But someone else had.

There was a knock at his chamber door, and his son slipped into the room.

'Good morning, father.'

Ormus grunted a response. Then there was an awkward little silence as each man tried to think of something appropriate to say.

'I hope you're not feeling too bad?' Wigbert enquired eventually, studying the bed's tapestry hangings intently.

Ormus didn't reply, but took the opportunity to look properly at his son's face. He's older than he was, he decided. There were new lines there. 'It's been a long few days,' he said eventually.

Wigbert smiled a tight little smile. 'That's one way of putting it.'

Another silence.

Wigbert walked over to the window and looked out. Ormus followed him with his eyes. He's moving differently too, he thought.

'I never had a chance to say, but I'm sorry about your church, father,' Wigbert said, not turning around. 'I know how much it meant to you.'

'Just a building,' Ormus grunted. 'Buildings can be rebuilt.'

'Of course. I'll be contacting the families of those killed in the explosion. Sending our sympathies, seeing if there's anything the Castle can do, that sort of thing. I wondered if maybe you'd want to add something?'

'I'll jot something down and have it sent to you this afternoon.'

'Great. There's still a lot of cleanup to do, of course. It's going slower without the Watch's help. But perhaps there might be something salvageable from the ruins.'

Ormus stared at the back of his son's head. 'Perhaps,' he said. 'But perhaps it's best if there's not.'

Wigbert finally turned to face him with a look of surprise.

'Perhaps it's best,' Ormus continued slowly. 'If whatever you choose to rebuild there is something totally new. A break from the past.'

'Father I—' Wigbert began, but Ormus spoke over him.

'Shut up and listen, will you?' he said. 'It has to be new because it has to come from *you*. The Church of the First Tree was the greatest achievement of my reign. But it was a failure. People never really accepted it. Just like people never really accepted me. Oh, they feared me! Some of them, at least. But never accepted. I fought my whole life to hold on to the powers still left to our family. I fought so much that I forgot what those powers were really for. But I see that there is another way now. It's the people that will decide the future of Upton-Myzzle, boy. Not me, not the Lords Chambers, not even you. I thought I had to keep fighting. I thought I had to fight to keep the Stonemorton legacy alive. I thought I had to fight because you wouldn't. I tried to mould you into me, but I see now that you were right all along. The Duchy of Blackwood doesn't need another me. It needs you.'

His son's mouth had fallen open.'Father, I nearly lost power to Sir Sweetspire just yesterday!'

Ormus glowered at him. 'I know. You're a bloody idiot and a terrible politician!'

He smoothed out the wrinkles of his bed linen, not meeting Wigbert's eyes. 'But maybe an idiot is what we need right now. You have something I never had. Empathy. A discourse with the people. It might be through these bloody ridiculous books,' he picked up a copy of Wolfe Starlingcloud from his bedside, 'but that's a start. That's something to build on.'

Wigbert looked guilty. 'About the books, I never meant to—'

'Yes, you did, boy! You knew exactly what you were doing. And you did the whole thing behind my back, and do you know what's even worse? I had no idea. None.'

'I'm sorry.'

Ormus slapped a hand down on the fabric he had just smoothed. 'Don't be! That's my whole point. I'm old. Older than I realised. This isn't my world anymore, boy. My way didn't work. Nor did my fathers, or his, come to that. So I might not understand it, but, just maybe, your way can. Maybe you're the type of duke the Blackwood needs.'

There was silence for a few moments, each man lost in his own thoughts.

'Things are changing out there, boy. I can feel it in my bones. Monsters. Rogue wizards. I don't know what it all means, but challenges are coming.'

'But father, I don't know what I'm doing!' Wigbert cried, rushing forward to lean on the end of the bed. 'Don't you understand that? I tried. I really did. I thought if I could solve the murders, or stop the monster, then maybe I'd get the people to trust in me. But *I* didn't do either of those things! I failed!'

'And yet the killer is dead, and the monster destroyed,' Ormus said, laying back and folding his arms across his chest.

Wigbert looked pained. 'But I didn't do it! Nothing I did

mattered at all. It's all just…just coincidence!'

'It did matter,' Ormus said, more softly than before. 'It mattered a great deal. Who you are matters. I didn't see it before, but now I understand. You say you nearly lost power yesterday. But do you understand why you didn't?'

'The lord and ladies, they—'

'No!' Ormus said, picking up the book again and rapping it sharply on the bedsheets. 'It's got nothing to do with them. It's about what the people *saw*, and what they saw was a duke willing to face down a monster. They see you now. And that's an opportunity.'

Wigbert stared at him. Ormus could feel his son's eyes searching his face. He coughed and looked away. 'Now bugger off!' he said. 'I'm tired.'

Wigbert straightened up. 'Do you need anything?'

'I'm fine! You're as bad as that bloody steward! Always fussing. Anyway, Gerald and the others are coming over later. I want a proper look at that infernal chair of Terrance's, see if I can't get one made for myself. I don't see why I should be made to walk everywhere, a man of my age!'

'As you wish.'

Wigbert made to leave, but as he slipped out the door, Ormus called him back. 'One more thing,' he said. 'Keep a bloody good eye on that granddaughter of mine! She's smarter than either of us!'

3.

'You're an idiot!' Oatey said.

'I am not!' Beatrice snapped.

'You are if you think your father is going to let you just go swanning off again,' said Oatey, unabashed. 'My parents went ballistic when I got home. Well, mum did, not sure dad even noticed I was gone. Anyway, my point is I practically had to beg before they let me out of the house again and I'm not going to be the next duchess. There's no way the duke is letting you out of his sight anytime soon.'

'I don't see him here, do you?' Beatrice looked around the crowded infirmary theatrically.

'I meant figuratively,' Oatey said, rolling his eyes. 'Anyway, why do you think they're here?' He pointed to the doorway where two large guards stood, watching their every move.

Beatrice pouted. 'Well, I didn't mean we should go *right away*. But after a while, once Gloamblight is feeling better.'

The wizard lay in the bed around which they sat. His right arm was stretched out at right angles to his body, resting on a little table to which it was also tightly secured with rope. Captain Snekchesser had ordered the table to be nailed to the floor, just in case. The arm was also thickly slathered in a greasy substance that smelt strongly of herbs and something else that made Beatrice's eyes water if she got too close. To cool the burns, Mr Dribbets had said. Beatrice tried to explain about the wizard's extraordinary healing powers, but the steward had insisted.

Gloamblight had not regained consciousness since he'd

killed the monster. The power released by his own arm had been too much for him, it seemed. Rupert had not left the man's side. The little robin was currently sitting on the wizard's forehead and twittered angrily if anyone got too close.

'You really think he's going to want to go back into the Blackwood?' Oatey asked. 'He's only just made it to Upton-Myzzle.'

Beatrice nodded enthusiastically. 'He'll need more answers and I don't think he'll find them here.'

'But he killed the monster. It's over, isn't it?'

'I doubt it. Do you remember what the prophecy said? He had to make a choice.'

'Right. And he chose to kill the monster,' Oatey said, picking at a scab on his arm. A tree scratch, no doubt.

'Yes, but that can't be an end to it. There'll be consequences. You just wait and see if there aren't!' said Beatrice with a grin. 'There's more to all this and I intend to find out what. There's still so much we don't understand. What the monster was? Why it came? What happened to Gloamblight to make him this way, and why did it have to be him to kill the monster? We've barely scratched the surface!'

'And you think we can find those things out by going back into the Blackwood?' Oatey asked.

'It makes sense, don't you think? That's where the monster came from. It's where Gloamblight woke up after losing his memory. I reckon this is all bigger than we think. Don't forget about the green men we saw.'

'What about them?'

'They had to be meeting for a reason! Maybe they know something about what's going on that we don't. I wish Madame Reedswail was here.'

The hedgewitch had disappeared shortly after Gloamblight's confrontation with the monster. She hadn't given a reason, just said she'd be back soon. But she hadn't returned and Beatrice burned with unanswered questions.

Oatey shrugged. 'Well, whatever. Your father's never gonna

let you go, anyway.'

Beatrice set her face. 'I'd like to see him stop me!'

But truthfully, she had little desire to pull the wool over her father's eyes a second time. She would have to speak to him. He seemed...different since they'd got back. They'd sat up late into the night talking in her room. He'd wanted to know everything that had happened to her in the Blackwood and had listened with rapt attention. He hadn't even told her off for running away. Just said he loved her. But he had doubled her guard. If she'd thought it had been awkward before, it was nothing compared to now. The guards followed her every move. If she did end up having to sneak away again, it would be much harder than before. She'd need help.

'Have you seen the rats?' she asked Oatey, who was now playing with a bandage, wrapping and unwrapping his arm with the soft white fabric.

'I heard they bought a house in the Thickets this morning,' he said.

'*What?*'

'That's what I heard. Just marched right up and paid in full.'

'What with?' Beatrice asked incredulously.

'A bunch of king's favours, apparently. The whole town's talkin' 'bout it. There ain't been that many of the old coins seen in decades, or so my dad says.'

'Where did a group of rats get that kind of money?' Beatrice asked, amazed.

Oatey shrugged. 'No idea. I'd pay good money myself to see their neighbor's face though...well, I would, if I had any.'

At that moment, Captain Snekchesser entered the infirmary. He was looking much smarter than Beatrice was used to. He'd changed his uniform for a fresh one at last, with shiny pips denoting his new rank. He'd shaved, and it appeared he'd even attempted to comb his thick mass of hair. It hadn't been a particularly successful attempt, but he'd hidden the worst of it by stuffing it into a new tricorn hat. He didn't look comfortable.

He exchanged a few words with the guards by the door, then glared over in Beatrice's and Oatey's direction.

'Uh oh, busted,' Oatey said with a smirk as the captain made his way towards them. Beatrice schooled her expression into one of polite innocence.

'I thought I told you two to stay away from the infirmary?' Snekchesser said with a glower. The expression made his hat slip slightly further up his forehead and more of his black hair sprang free.

'Did you?' Beatrice said. 'I don't remember that.'

The captain pinched the bridge of his nose with his stubby thumb and finger. 'You know, it wouldn't hurt either of our reputations, my lady, if you at least pretended to listen to me.'

'I'm sure you're very highly respected already, captain.'

'Yeah. Right. Don't think I don't know what you're thinking. It may surprise you both to learn that I was not born yesterday and let me tell you right now that you can forget all about it!'

'I don't know what you mean, captain,' Beatrice said sweetly.

Captain Snekchesser grunted in clear disbelief, but turned his attention to the unconscious Gloamblight. 'Since you've completely ignored my instructions and have clearly been here some time, you'll be able to tell me if there's been any change in our magical friend here?'

'No. Nothing,' Beatrice said. 'So, are the restraints really necessary?'

Snekchesser gave a humorless bark of laughter. 'I wouldn't remove that rope for all the spice in the Blackwood!'

'But do you think it'll help?' Oatey said. 'I mean, if Gloamblight goes off the deep end again, is that little bit of rope actually going to stop him?'

The captain regarded him stonily. 'Don't you have a home to go to?' he asked.

'He's keeping me company,' Beatrice pointed out.

'Well, *you* have a lesson to get to, my lady. And the book repository is one place Master Crabblebottom here cannot follow you.'

'Is it that time already?' Beatrice cried, jumping to her feet.

'It's gone that time. Off you go!' Captain Snekchesser said.

With a quick wave to Oatey, Beatrice tore out of the infirmary. She didn't want to keep the elderly Mr Bombroffe waiting any longer than she already had. She was feeling guilty enough about disappearing before their first lesson. She didn't want to miss another.

She ran down the stone steps and out of the gatehouse into the outer ward where she ground to a halt, all urgency forgotten at the sight of Wolfe Starlingcloud, who was somersaulting through the air like an acrobat to whoops and cheers from a crowd of onlookers. He landed with perfect precision and took a bow, catching sight of Beatrice and winking. Beatrice waved back, hesitantly, then hurried on. She hadn't worked out quite how to feel about the appearance of her fictional hero. There was definitely something fishy going on and her father's explanation had been decidedly lacking.

When Beatrice arrived at the book repository, she found that Mr Bombroffe had dozed off behind his desk. She cleared her throat noisily, then, when this didn't work, shook him gently by the arm. The bibliothecary woke with a little start and blinked at her through his spectacles.

'You're late, my lady,' he said, but there was a smile in his eyes.

'I'm sorry, Mr Bombroffe. I lost track of time,' Beatrice said with a grimace.

'Then perhaps the first thing I should teach you is time management,' the man replied with a wry grin. 'Then again, with all your adventures, maybe you should be teaching me now? Is it true you saw a passage of green men?'

By the time Beatrice had finished talking, the sun was already on its downward path. The old Bibliothecary had listened patiently, asking the occasional question but remaining mostly silent. When Beatrice's words eventually ran out, he scratched his chin thoughtfully and spoke in his dry, gentle voice. 'Quite the tale, my lady. This Gloamblight sounds like a curious character indeed. The question is, what do you believe?'

Beatrice considered. 'That there is much going on that we do not understand. But I feel the answers are out there.' She waved her hand in the general direction of the Blackwood.

The old man nodded slowly. 'And what about the Melethin question? If I remember correctly, we spoke on that subject before your departure. Do you feel differently now you have returned?'

'Yes,' Beatrice said, then 'No. I'm not sure. I feel...I feel like I've discovered so much, but that I don't know anything new. I just feel...different. Like I've changed somehow. Does that make sense?'

'Perfect sense, my dear. For whenever we go on a journey, be it physical or otherwise, we are never the same people when we return. That's why I love books!' he affectionately patted a pile of dusty tomes stacked on his crowded desk. 'Whenever I read one, I become a different person.'

'A better one?' Beatrice asked.

'Ah well, that would depend entirely on the book,' he replied with a wink.

EPILOGUE

Darkness fell and a sky full of stars hung over Upton-Myzzle for the first time in days. Among them was the new star, still hanging in the sky, fat and brilliantly white. In the uppermost rooms of the Institute of Propositional Logic, among the piles of paper and the heaps of miscellaneous equipment, Captain Ambrosia Tritewine adjusted her telescope. She wanted to take some measurements while the skies were clear and she could still get a good view. Who knew when she'd have another chance to study a comet like this? It had been a busy couple of days and all her experiments were sorely behind. She put her eye to the telescope, then jotted down some measurements on a scrap of paper. She did some quick mental arithmetic, then frowned, muttering under her breath as she scribbled out what she'd just written. She'd be there all night if she kept making mistakes. She repeated her measurements, her frown growing deeper when she got the same results. She tried again. Then once more.

Ten minutes later she arrived at the Castle Blackwood great hall stairs, chest heaving and sweating profusely having run all the way, stopping only momentarily to argue with two very confused guards at the gate-less gatehouse arch. She practically bumped into Mr Dribbets, who had been consulting with the duke, and he dropped the scrolls he held in shock. They bounced off down the steps and the man sighed.

'Really Captain, *do* watch where you're going. I say…are you alright? You've gone all red.'

'Is he in there?' she gasped between breaths.

'The duke? He's having his dinner, yes. Whatever is the matter?'

But Ambrosia didn't stop to explain. She pushed past the astonished steward and burst into the great hall to find a merry fire blazing in the fireplace. The duke himself was sitting alone at the long table, his dinner in front of him. His fork paused with what looked like a sprout halfway to his lips.

'Captain Tigervine...I mean, Ambrosia!' he spluttered. 'What a pleasant surprise...er...I've had a fire lit. But you can see that, of course. A little treat, I thought, after the week we've all had! Um...would you like something to eat? I'm sure Tanco could—'

'The star!' she gasped.

Wigbert's eyebrows rose. 'Um...yes, it's still there, I believe. Luckily, most of the townsfolk seem to have got used to it by now. I was worried we'd have more unrest when the clear skies made it visible again, but I suppose everyone has enough to deal with, what with the flood and the rebuild. Perhaps-'

'I've done the maths, your grace, and it doesn't add up at all!'

'Ah, well, it rarely does for me if I'm honest,' Wigbert said sympathetically. 'A drink maybe? There's still some—'

'Shut up and listen!' Ambrosia cried.

The sprout paused once more on the way to duke's mouth. 'I'm sorry?'

'I mean, I'm very sorry, your grace, but you have to listen to me,' Ambrosia wheezed. Little stars were bursting in front of her eyes. 'The star, your grace, it's changed direction.'

'I see...' Wigbert said slowly. 'And that's...bad?'

'Yes!'

'Um...why?'

'Comets don't do that.'

'So, you're saying...'

She took a deep breath, marshaling her agitation. 'Your grace, I was *wrong. It's not a comet!*'

The sprout fell from the duke's fork and bounced off the table with a sad little splat.

'Oh,' he said with considerable feeling. 'Oh, *Bugger.*'

THE END

WANT MORE?

Try My Cosy Fantasy Series:

Trussel and Gout: Paranormal Investigations

Sign up to my newsletter and get the free prequel novella!

Www.maknightswrites.co.uk

ABOUT THE AUTHOR

M.a.knights

Hello. I'm M.A.Knights, an English writer who's just moved back home after living in the glorious countryside of wild west Wales for nearly fifteen years. There the rugged cliffs, rolling hills and ever-changing sea inspired the worlds of my creation. After achieving a BSc in Countryside Conservation and an MSc in Geographic Information and Climate Change, I realised I am, in fact, not a scientist at all. It's the what-do-you-call-it? … memory! Not what it used to be, don't you know? And what with all those numbers and things … dreadful! Simply dreadful. So I've left the data crunching to those cleverer than I and instead have returned to the fantastical imaginings of my youth. I hope one day to lose myself in a world of my own creation.

Printed in Great Britain
by Amazon